A Sinner Glimpses Paradise
a novel by Shea Kelly

Dedicated to the memory of Carlos "Los Dollaz" Fitzpatrick-Fowlkes.
Only the good die young. I miss you bruh bruh.
Also dedicated to my family, friends, teachers, and everyone else who has nurtured, inspired, and guided me over the years.
And to my fellow "professionals" at Renato's for the laughter and teamwork. "I will see you in hell," and the list goes on.
And especially to my grandfather, Pa Pa, for introducing me to the art of storytelling.

Prologue: An Introduction to Hell

Satan likes to think he runs a tight ship down there, or up there, or over there, wherever *there* is. The screams and moans of his adherents - Hellions as they're officially known - suggest he certainly does, and the austere disposition and fastidiousness of his minions, the Dark Army, suggest the same. The Devil's Midas touch is reflected in every detail of his kingdom. His duties are not limited to those of a managerial nature: he is the curator, the architect, the interior designer, the cleric, the scribe, the historian, the judge, and the jury. Since Satan has his hand in just about every aspect of Hell's operation, the appearance, procedures, and customs of the domain bend to his will, and there have been several great revivals.

In order to understand Hell and its history, it's imperative to know "the underworld" is a misnomer. Hell exists in its own dimension, not in some dark, fiery recess of the Earth's core. Therefore, everything about time and space as humans understand it must be ignored to usefully contemplate Hell. Helltime is completely unrelated to mortal time. There is no formula to translate one to the other. Helltime is not linear, and it's not measurable. It's completely relative to the Hellion who is experiencing it. A Hellion might remember how mortal time is measured, but having no clocks or a Sun to reference, what is one day in mortal time could feel like one thousand years or four seconds, or both, in Helltime, and the Hellion would have no way of knowing the difference. Any effort to quantify Helltime would be pointless anyway, seeing as it's eternal. Imagine Helltime as mortal time during an intense LSD trip, only the trip is never-ending, and given the set and setting, the amount of time passed is of little concern.

For most of its existence, Hell looked like it does in its classical depictions. It was a gloomy, rocky, subterranean abyss (though not within Earth), and did, in fact, consist of seven circles corresponding to each of the deadly sins: wrath, greed, sloth, pride, lust, envy, and gluttony. However, after Dante Alighieri's *The Divine Comedy* was published in 1472, mortal time, Satan felt this motif had become oversaturated and clichéd. Art had begun to mimic the afterlife a little too closely for a little too long. It was time for a reboot, thus The Great Third Renovation.

The Devil, after closely studying his pupils for a long time, came to reject the Christian notion that there are degrees of sin, and decided to abandon the descending chambers of the classical era. He retained the seven circles, but opted for a horizontal scheme to reflect his newfound belief in the parity of sin. Inspired by one of his favorite symbols of the macabre, the spider, and hoping to assuage the nagging input of one of his minotaurs, Satan redesigned Hell to resemble a labyrinthine spider web. The center, or hub, contains the cafeteria, school, and Satan's office, and is surrounded by a succession of circles, seven of which are dedicated to the mortal sins, while the countless others have auxiliary purposes which Satan can manipulate to his liking. In the space between the spirals there are numerous landscapes. Many of these can be found on Earth, but most are environments from other, much harsher planets or are conjured from the Devil's imagination. The circles are connected by a dense maze of radial corridors, which meander through the scenery bounded by the spirals. From a distance, out in the void of its dimension, Hell looks like a spiral galaxy. A close look at its structure and an astronomer might call it The Silky Way.

Hellions in good standing can roam The Great Third Renovation as they please. Satan wanted to see how Hellions would act given the ability to choose a form of suffering and switch to another whenever the mood strikes: damnation with free will. He figured he would give them this underhanded privilege to reinforce the idea, originating in Hell's design, that all sins are equal.

The average atmospheric forque level in The Silky Way is 45 (a forque being a unit Satan concocted to quantify pain, scaled 0-100, and atmospheric forques being pain induced by the atmosphere alone). Every imaginable point measures 39-50 forques. The base corporal forque level, maintained by the burlap sacks Hellions are clothed in, is 24 (corporal forques being pain induced by physical torture). The corporal forques being experienced by a Hellion at any given moment are 24-50 forques, and the average, like the atmospheric forques, is 45. Therefore, Hell yields an average of 90 total forques, and at any given moment a Hellion is experiencing a minimum of 63 and *the* maximum of 100 forques.

The first circle in this incarnation of Hell, that closest to the hub, is committed to wrath. Every occupant is fitted with a collar that emits a painful electric shock - 18-22 forques depending on how the Devil has set it at the time - whenever the Hellion uses profanity or speaks contemptuously. This form of negative reinforcement has a predictable outcome: a curious snowball effect. The instinctive reaction of the recipient of the shock is to utter a curse, precipitating another shock, followed by another curse, and so forth. Consequently, the circle of wrath features a perpetual cacophony of zaps and slurs.

Satan finds this highly amusing.

For the most wrathful offenders, murderers and gangster rappers and such, there is a twelve-screen cinema designated for their displeasure, inspired by one of The Dark Lord's favorite movies, *A Clockwork Orange*. The theater never closes, and Hellions arrive in droves to watch the gruesome entertainment, despite their foreknowledge of the harrowing cinematic experience. Upon entering the theater, a goblin usher hands the patron a pair of 3D glasses with *blinkless technology*™, one of Satan's many patents. The moviegoer then picks the feature of his choice, blockbusters like *Necromancers vs. Werewolves*, *Vacation in the Carnivorous Forest*, and *Splatter, Volume II*. An usher escorts them to a seat fitted with leather bracelets to hold the wrists and ankles in place, and a vise-like steel headset to immobilize the neck and head. The usher then checks the functionality of the 3D glasses, for the *blinkless technology*™ can be temperamental, and barring any issues the Hellion is cleared to enjoy the show.

The cinema is frequently the scene of convulsions and nervous breakdowns, yet Hell remains filled with cinephiles.

Between the circle of wrath and the next circle, that of greed, is the first of Hell's inclement natural environments. It's a vast desert with hulking dunes and not a single oasis. The average temperature is 120° Fahrenheit and the wind, though usually calm or nonexistent, can reach gusts of 80 mph, stirring up behemoth sandstorms that blind, choke, and scald any unlucky Hellion in their path. In the aftermath of these storms, thousands of grains of sand end up lodged in the Hellion's burlap clothes, causing terrible irritation.

The desert's premiere feature is its pyramids, which appear in sets of three identical to those at Giza. Their number is potentially infinite, because once a set is completed construction on another begins, and normally many are being worked on simultaneously, as many as the available manpower can accommodate. Satan likes disciplining unruly Hellions by sentencing them to pyramid labor, and the rest of the workforce comes from desert wanderers who stumble upon a construction site and decide to stay for the camaraderie.

Hell's next spiral, the circle of greed, is appropriately minimalist, so far as the Hellions are concerned. "Want not and waste not" is its theme. Occupants of this circle are constrained to concrete barrens strewn with weeds. There are penitentiary-grade fences with razor wire bounding the wasteland, and on the other side Satan's minions can be seen living the high life. The gentlemen minions wear three-piece Italian suits and drive Italian sports cars. The lady minions tote Louis Vuitton bags and parade around in horse-drawn carriages. They all have yacht parties on the lakes of fire, drink 25-year triple malt scotch, and retire at night to magnificent châteaus. All the while the Hellions watch through the impregnable fences in their meager burlap sacks. The Hellions are constantly teased by the minions' litter which gets blown over the fences or washes up on the nearby banks of the lakes and rivers: receipts from exclusive boutiques, leather couches, scraps of cardboard boxes, bamboo ceiling fans, bubble wrap, fountain pens, half-burnt $100 bills, and plasma TVs. It's forbidden to touch any of the litter. This mandate is enforced by Hellbirds: fire-breathing phoenixes who survey the barrens from the sky and flame-broil any transgressors.

On the perimeter of the circle of greed is another Earthly environment, a primeval habitat teeming with lifeforms that, according to science, were never mankind's contemporaries. Scripture would argue otherwise, and Satan, having no interest in the truth, or the politics of science versus scripture, simply wanted to experiment. Thus, *Tyrannosaurus rex* chasing the terrified, damned souls of *Homo sapiens* across a Cretaceous landscape. When entering Hell's Lost World, Hellions are provided with a fist-sized stone and a stick. Some of them attempt to create fire, an ironic endeavor, and others opt to whittle miniature spears, which prove inadequate as dissuasive devices when combating the Cretaceous predators, but come in handy as disciplinary tools for the domestication of the herbivores. Many Hellions have successfully converted ceratopsians into pack animals. Just as many have predictably been skewered in the process. Volcanic eruptions are the preeminent cause of misery in Hell's Lost World. Satan has programmed the volcanoes to erupt at regular enough intervals for lava flows to cover much of the land, minimizing contact between bands of caveman Hellions, and thereby reducing the transference of knowledge and culture. The ubiquitous magma, crisscrossing the scenery, also causes a familiar dilemma for the inhabitants: a choice between wading through a lava flow to elude a pursuing therapod, or offering themselves up for dinner to avoid the agony of the escape route. Hellions generally prefer becoming fecal matter to the third-degree burns, citing a perceived obligation to contribute to the energy cycle rather than perpetuate their carbon footprint.

They're martyrs in a way. It's a wonder none of them are in Heaven.

The Great Third Renovation's circle of sloth is a site of feverish activity. Upon entering this spiral, Hellions are fitted with a device that measures their heart rate. After a two-minute transitional period, the device emits a low-voltage shock whenever the Hellion's heart rate falls below 140% of its resting rate. The shock continues uninterrupted until the Hellion's heart rate returns to the threshold. Hellions in the circle of sloth are continuously moving to keep their heart rates elevated, however, their options are limited to two tedious activities: running on a treadmill or mowing an endless uphill lawn. The Hellions have created various ways to break the monotony of these activities, such as pushing the lawnmower at a slight lateral angle to reduce resistance, or in the case of the men, choosing a treadmill behind a woman with an agreeable buttocks and enjoying the view. Unfortunately, Satan eventually picked up on these tactics, and employed minotaurs carrying whips to lash any violators. Hellions have henceforth been calculating in weighing the opportunity cost of engaging in these distractions. Most of the time they daydream, only to have their fantasies rudely interrupted by the bone-rattling electrical current of the heart rate monitor.

Outside the circle of sloth is an environment Satan designed to simulate Mars. In designing this environment, Satan had some logistical considerations. Now, obviously mortal humans cannot survive in Mars' conditions, but the souls of the damned can persevere under any circumstances. Meanwhile, the flesh they inhabit can be damaged or destroyed. When destruction occurs, their souls wander about until Satan has the opportunity to issue a "corporeal regeneration." Souls don't have as acute a sense of pain as bodies do, so Satan attends to disembodied souls as quickly as his schedule allows him. If Hellions were to enter the Mars landscape in their standard-issue burlap sacks, their flesh would be destroyed in a matter of minutes. Satan would be faced with a surplus of disembodied souls floating about his incarnation of the Red Planet, experiencing relatively little pain. This is bad for business. To combat this issue, Satan designed a suit, similar to astronaut suits, which allows Hellions to "survive" indefinitely, while also facing considerable pain. The suits are sufficient enough to allow the Hellions to endure, yet insufficient enough to expose them to trace amounts of Mars' atmosphere with agonizing results. Hellions ordinarily don't find the gorgeous view outside their spacesuits worth the gaseous smothering taking place inside. They'd rather take their chances elsewhere.

In Hell, space is more a last resort than the final frontier.

After the Mars environment is the circle of pride. Since Hellions guilty of pride spent most of their mortal lives building themselves up, and oftentimes bringing others down, the purpose of the circle of pride is to break their spirits – to cut them down to size. Inhabitants of this spiral are forced to practice acts of humbleness. The most common act of humbleness is to work at a simulated fast-food restaurant called Hellburgers®. At Hellburgers®, Satan's minions are the managers and do nothing but bark orders at the Hellions, who do all of the work. The Hellions must abide by four policies, lest they be whipped or doused by hot cooking oil by their manager. First, they must address their superiors and the customers, a finicky bunch composed of ghouls, demons, and hydras, as "sir" or "ma'am." Second, they must conclude any requests from their co-workers with "please" and "thank you," to which the second party must respond "you're welcome." Third, they must greet the customers with a friendly smile. Fourth, and most important, while on their break they must repeat the mantra, "Pride cometh before the fall, I am the humblest of them all," or alternatively, the Hellburgers® slogan, "Can't get enough of that mmm, mmm stuff."

The size of the workforce at Hellburgers® rises and falls with the popularity of the company slogan, and the current one is all the rave.

The circle of pride is succeeded by an unforgiving arctic landscape. This land of ice and snow has an average temperature of 3° F, and winds averaging 34 mph, yielding an average windchill of -8°. Hellions venturing into this winter not-so-wonderful-land adopt the penguin strategy and huddle together by the thousands. Unlike the penguins, whose adult members rotate positions in the cluster to equitably distribute exposure, thus promoting the survival of as many individuals as possible, the Hellions jostle for position in the center of the bunch. Ironically, this uncooperative approach is equally effective as the penguins' cooperative scheme. While some infant and elderly penguins perish during the harsh Antarctic winters, about the same proportion of scrawny Hellions, unable to buttress themselves amongst the tonnage of heftier bodies in the interior of the huddle, freeze to death on the outside looking in. Satan issues a "corporeal regeneration" for these fallen souls, and oftentimes the survivors cannibalize the corpses.

Another case of Hellion martyrdom.

Beyond the frozen tundra lies the circle of lust, where Hellions are deprived of their senses and forbidden contact with the opposite sex. Upon entering this spiral, Hellions are fitted with blindfolds, earplugs, nose clips, and oven mitts. Their exposed skin is sprayed with Numbify™, an aerosol Satan created which induces total, permanent numbness, unless treated with the antidote, SensoRize™, an ointment that's like methamphetamine[3]. Hellions were once given a swab of SensoRize™ when exiting the circle of lust, however, many of them weren't using the ointment to treat themselves, choosing instead to use it as an item of trade with Hellions looking for a good high. Nowadays, Satan's minions apply the ointment to departing Hellions, and usually do so in cruel ways, such as forcing the Hellion to ingest it, or putting it on the end of a whip and lashing the Hellion. The irony, of course, is that these acts of cruelty inflict no pain, as the Hellions remain numb for about a minute until the SensoRize™ kicks in.

Every once in a while, Satan decides to spice things up in the circle of lust by disabling the barriers between the men and women. Occasionally, a wandering male will haphazardly bump into a female, the two will recognize the contours of the stranger's body as that of the opposite sex, and despite knowing no pleasure will be had, a pitiful, disoriented attempt at coitus will ensue. Satan finds these desperate encounters hilarious, and they keep Hellions coming back to the circle of lust in hope of experiencing the slightest hint of pleasure, but that pleasure will forever remain out of reach.

Numbify™ is infallible.

The circle of lust is circumscribed by an equatorial rainforest. Hell's Amazonia is unbearably humid and infested with large, aggressive mosquitoes the Devil genetically engineered. Innumerable howler monkeys also call the rainforest home. They too were genetically engineered by The Dark Lord to be as bothersome to the Hellions as possible. Their howls are cacophonous, and they frequently join together to do renditions of traditional gospel songs and African-American spirituals. Their favorite is "Swing Low Sweet Chariot." Hell's Amazonia also has a lot of leeches. Satan didn't bother to alter them, figuring leeches are horrible enough as God made them. Most Hellions avoid the water. A cool dip to escape the mugginess isn't worth the price of admission. Another nefarious creature abiding in the thick jungle is the poison dart frog. While some of these colorful amphibians excrete potentially deadly toxins, others have toxins with hallucinogenic properties. Hellions spend most of their time in the rainforest searching for frogs to lick. They call it Amazonian roulette. The smarter Hellions observe the others and catalog the different frogs and the symptoms induced by their toxins. However, like always, Satan keeps tabs on these things and mixes the frogs up. It would make sense for Satan to make all the frogs identical in appearance to eliminate the Hellions' strategies, but he tried that once and realized it made the rainforest drab.

Vanity is his greatest indulgence.

Subsequent to Hell's Amazonia is the circle of envy, which is essentially the inverse of the circle of greed. The Hellions have everything, and Satan's minions have nothing. A constant war of attrition is waged between the two factions. The Hellions, unwilling to abandon their grandiose lifestyle, defend their cities from relentless hordes of minions, who, when victorious, simply dispose of the spoils in the nearest lake of fire. When the Hellions aren't warding off swarms of demons and specters, they're protecting their possessions from covetous peers, or seeking the next thing needed to elevate their status. Only a smidgen of their time is spent enjoying their affluence, let alone the little things in the afterlife, and this usually comes at the expense of losing something dear to them: someone hosts a wine and cheese party, two drunken attendees have a disagreement on the compatibility of a pinot noir and brie pairing, punches are exchanged, and the host wakes up to find his wine cellar has been stripped bare and the vineyard has been burnt to cinders.

"Was it the Dark Army or my own kind who did this?" he'll ask himself.

Meanwhile, if the minions aren't looting and pillaging on another estate, they're out in the barrens reciting tales about the last haul and plotting their next go-round, and the Hellions are too preoccupied with sustaining the high life to notice it's all a farce. The only things the minions haven't incinerated over the years is a harp, an accordion, and a baby grand piano.

The Hellions' only true enemy is themselves.

After the circle of envy is an environment composed of a vast ocean dotted with tiny desert islands. Each island is unique, featuring its own flora and fauna which the islanders use for sustenance. Some have coconut trees and crabs, and others have palms and turtles. Some have little more than fescue and ants. The smallest islands are only a thousand square feet, while the biggest are three or four square miles. Sometimes the distance between two islands is merely a few hundred yards, and sometimes that distance is a few thousand miles. Hellions lucky enough to happen upon the largest islands make a decent existence for themselves. Their island communes are not much different than a Caribbean fishing village. The biggest daily concern for such Hellion islanders is getting wet sand in their burlap clothes. Contrarily, many Hellions end up on the tiniest islands alone, without so much as a volleyball for company, or perhaps worse, with people they don't trust. Whether a Hellion's island adventure ends up mimicking *Gilligan's Island*, *Castaway*, or *Lord of the Flies*, if Satan senses too much fun is being had, he fervently spoils the party with a hurricane, tsunami, plague, or minion armada. The minion armada is the worst possible outcome for the Hellion islanders, who would much rather drown or catch a nasty tropical disease than be forced into slavery aboard one of the Dark Army's pirate ships. Once captured, mutiny becomes their only hope, and there's only been one successful mutiny in Hell's infinite history. Speculation about the fate of that ship, *The Santeria*, and its crew of nineteen courageous Hellions has become a staple of Hellion folklore.

Only the mutineers and the Devil know the real story.

The outermost spiral, and the last stop on our tour of The Great Third Renovation, is the circle of gluttony. In this circle the Hellions are only allowed to eat raw vegetables, which grow in abundance in an unending lattice of impeccably curated gardens. Satan's minions who tend these gardens don't use fertilizers or pesticides, and so the vegetables grown in the circle of gluttony taste the way nature intended them to: earthy and bland. In order to create a supportive environment to further promote a healthy lifestyle, Satan inundated the circle of gluttony with massive billboards featuring runway models and world-class athletes pitching various motivational slogans, such as "Lumps are for chumps," "Famishing, vanishing, you look so ravishing!" and "Beauty is in the bones." There are also scales everywhere, and the occupants of the circle of gluttony are subjected to random weigh-ins. The Devil and his minions keep a record of each occupant's weight, and if that weight is exceeded during a weigh-in, the Hellion receives one hundred lashes for every extra pound. Eating disorders are therefore common, especially among the Americans, whose mortal lives conditioned them to such cultural pressures anyway.

Hollywood in Hell.

Chapter 1

Inside a dilapidated barn in the boonies of America there is a clandestine gathering. It's a meeting of nefarious minds, something that should never take place before the eyes of God. About fifty men and women stand in roughly a circle on the barn's dirt and hay floor. Speckles of dry blood are strewn about the blades of hay - human blood - for the barn hasn't been used to raise animals in quite some time. Everybody in attendance at this barn rendezvous is wearing a gray, hooded cloak with an emblem of a black squirrel on the right breast. The one exception is a man in a white cloak who also dons the black squirrel emblem, only it's on his left breast. These mysterious gatherers hold candles to supplement the natural light provided by the full moon, a faint glimmer which strains through the partly ajar barn doors. In a trance-like state, eyes closed and heads down, they hum a tune approaching that of a classical symphony.

The Spooky Barn Cult Orchestra's "Symphony No. 666," most likely.

After the conclusion of the hummed magnum opus, the man in the white cloak steps out of the circle. He reaches inside his cloak and removes a Bible, which he proceeds to cradle in his forearm, tight against his bicep and the crook of his elbow, much like a running back would carry a football. The Bible-totting gentleman paces slowly around the inside of the circle, clockwise, for nearly a full revolution, then makes a right turn toward the middle of the barn floor, where lies a foreboding assemblage: a bed of burning coals in the shape of a crucifix, approximately twelve feet in length and six feet across the arms. When the man's deliberate gait brings him to the edge of the coals, he slips off his modest footwear, a pair of brown leather sandals, and pauses meditatively for a few seconds. The white-cloaked man lifts his bare left foot a few inches off the ground, moves it forward with a short protraction of the knee, and allows it to hover above the flaming coals by a mere centimeter or two. He then presses on one of the hot coals with his big toe, lifts his heel, and smudges the coal with a swift back-and-forth motion, like he's stamping out a cigarette butt. With the smoldering flesh on the bottom of his big toe producing an unwelcoming odor, the man returns his left foot to the sanctuary of the dirt and hay floor, and repeats the masochistic act with his right foot. He slides back into his sandals and addresses his audience.

"Welcome, Brave Minions, to The Sacred Barn."

"Ahoy, Virtuous Leader," the Brave Minions zealously reply, "widdy wee, widdy wah, widdy wallacka-zallacka zoo!" They conclude this nonsensical salutation with an equally nonsensical dance, actually more of a spasm, in which they rapidly shake their arms at their sides and roll their heads in a sweeping, circular motion. Their torsos and legs remain static during this routine, which finishes after about twenty seconds with a salute to their leader and a cross blessing - Father, Son, and the Holy Ghost - both performed with the right hand.

"Widdy woo, widdy wish-wish-wish-wish, loyal companions," Virtuous Leader exclaims. "Now, let's discuss business," he bellows, pounding on his Bible to rouse anticipation from his followers, who now stand at attention with flawless posture. "Over the last Harvest period, our collective has made tremendous strides. We have inducted two new members, one in our Middle East chapter, and another in our Canadian chapter. As you all well know, induction does not come easy in this thing of ours, and two fresh soldiers in one Harvest period is reason for optimism."

Virtuous Leader goes on to describe several of the organization's recent accomplishments. Violence is the prevailing theme. Corruption is a close second. Sexual deviance is a not-too-distant third. While highlighting these various deeds, Virtuous Leader paces around the edge of the scorching coal-cross in the same deliberate gait used in his circumscription of the Brave Minions, all the while pounding on his Bible to demonstrate the importance of each fact and deed. He serenades his onlookers for quite some time in this manner, listing facts and deeds, deeds and facts, while pacing and pounding, pounding and pacing. The Virtuous Leader's techniques approximate that of a televangelist. He is a consummate inspirational orator, compelling and authoritative.

The Brave Minions are mesmerized by the performance, especially the women. One of them, a pretty, buxom 20-something with jet black hair, ogles the white-cloaked gallivant with amorous eyes. Her schoolgirl crush is evident, though it goes unnoticed by the rest of the circle; no one takes their eyes off Virtuous Leader when he unravels a sermon. Each time Virtuous Leader reaches the foot edge of the cross, which brings him within three feet of the young lady, who must have deliberately positioned herself at that spot in the circle, twelve-o'-clock or six, depending on how the head and foot of the cross are interpreted, she lifts her left hand, presumably to reach out and touch the object of her affection, but stops this seemingly unconscious gesture with her hand at waist level. This subtle measure of insanity also goes unnoticed by the other Brave Minions.

Virtuous Leader is indeed fully aware of it. He has been indulging in pleasures of the
flesh with the girl for almost two months. She initiated the affair on the night of the cult's annual Summer Solstice Gala. Virtuous Leader was leaving the amphitheater where the event takes place every year and she caught up to him in the parking lot. Due to his status and a vow of celibacy which he

thought was necessitated by that status, Virtuous Leader was initially impervious to her advances. His restraint didn't last long. In ten minutes, she was despoiling him in the back seat of his car. Virtuous Leader fell hard for her, but his feelings were brought on almost entirely by a dumbfounded thankfulness for being introduced to ecstasy he had sworn to abandon for a lifetime. His gratitude eventually faded and their roles reversed. She is now infatuated and developing a sense of entitlement.

The speech reaches its crescendo when Virtuous Leader recalls the organization's crowning achievement, its most elaborate and glorious annual deed, "The New Year's Operation." His listeners, coaxed by their leader's shift into a celebratory mood, betray their earnest demeanor. Some of them glance at each other knowingly. The secret girlfriend offers an impish smile. Virtuous Leader proceeds with the news.

"For those of you fortunate enough to have participated in The New Year's Operation, I will take the liberty of speaking on your behalf in declaring it a tremendous achievement. You helped make it happen, you witnessed the end product, and you have reviewed the final report. I thank you a dozen for your service. For those of you who weren't selected for the mission, it is my pleasure to inform you that this past New Year's Operation, statistically, was our most successful to date."

"Widdy wee, widdy wah, widdy wallacka-zallacka zoo!" the Brave Minions chant. They embellish the motto with its complementary dance.

"Widdy woo, widdy wish-wish-wish-wish, indeed," Virtuous Leader answers, before continuing. "Conceptually, I believe it is only exceeded by the NYO of 1989. Some of you were around in '89 and can appreciate the reverence I have for the abstract genius of "Yellow Droppings." Well, we came close this time around. Non-participants in this year's triumph need not be discouraged, there's always next year. Start brainstorming now."

Virtuous Leader walks from the position where his exultation has landed him, about midpoint on the cross's left arm, to the foot of the cross. He pauses for a moment, wiggling the Bible in his forearm to reassert his grip, and turns to face the twelve-o'-clock or six-o'-clock point on the circle at the opposite end. The Brave Minion presiding over that spot locks eyes with Virtuous Leader, whose demeanor has resumed its pre-NYO announcement seriousness, crosses himself – Father, Son, and the Holy Ghost – and salutes his white-cloaked chief. Virtuous Leader returns the gesture with a hearty nod of his head.

"Brave Minions, it is time to proceed with the finale of tonight's meeting," Virtuous Leader says, raising his Bible and holding it at arm's length, pointed at the Brave Minion facing him. "Let us induct new blood. Aspiring cohort, you may enter our domain." Virtuous Leader slightly tilts the Bible skyward with his wrist, as if flipping a light switch.

The gray-cloak standing opposite Virtuous Leader takes one step forward, then one to his right. A man in a plain black cloak appears through the void and stands at the edge of the circle's interior. The gray-cloak, having granted the stranger passage, returns to his place, brandishes a salt shaker from inside his cloak, and sprinkles a generous portion of its contents onto each shoulder of the initiate now standing in front of him. The black-cloak stands at attention as Virtuous Leader looks him over, eyes pierced and brow knitted.

"Aspiring cohort, remove your cloak," Virtuous Leader demands. The initiate abides, leaving him completely bare excepting his sandals. "You come before us blind, poor, pitiful, wretched, and naked. You are a sinner, but are willing to give up your dastardly ways and sacrifice yourself to this thing of ours, are you not?"

"I am willing, Virtuous Leader," the blind, poor, pitiful, wretched nude proclaims.

"Very well. You must now endure the initiation gauntlet in order to prove your dedication and worthiness. You will begin by removing your footwear and standing at the edge of your end of the crucifix. I will list your sins and deviances, one by one, and following each one you will pronounce, 'Mighty Lord, I repent for my aberration, forgive me.' If your repentance is sincere and satisfactory, I will say, 'Absolved,' and you will take one step forward on the coals. Between steps you must keep both feet on the coals, side by side. This process will continue until you reach me on the other side. Is this understood?"

"Yes, Virtuous Leader."

"Good. If you succeed, we will advance to the second phase, in which you will repeat the process across the arms of the crucifix, while I read you our oath. After I recite each promise and duty, you will say, 'Yes, Virtuous Leader, I swear to fulfill this purpose lest I burn for all eternity.' If your pledge is to my liking, I will say, 'Hear, hear,' knock on my Bible twice, and you will take one step forward. Need I explain further?"

"No, Virtuous Leader."

"Excellent. If you complete the second phase, we will conclude with the third and final phase, which I will explain at that juncture." The cult hopeful nods pensively. "Shall we begin the festivities, aspiring cohort?"

"Yes, Virtuous Leader."

"Remove your footwear and take your place."

The naked initiate does as he is told. He is shivering a little. It's a chilly, mid-November night in the boonies, but his shakes will subside soon enough and be replaced by an entirely different homeostatic reaction. As he stands at the head of the sizzling coal-cross, glancing alternately between Virtuous Leader and the hellish path between them, reservations pick at his conscience.

'It's too late now,' he relents.

"Aspiring cohort, you have a proclivity for taking the Lord's name in vain. These heathenish utterances have taken place on innumerable occasions, some, admittedly, as recently as yesterday," Virtuous Leader announces. He appears to be referencing some loose-leaf notes in his Bible.

"Mighty Lord, I repent for my aberration, forgive me," the initiate declares. Virtuous Leader senses contrition in his voice.

"Absolved."

The cult hopeful begins to step forward with his left foot, then balks, staggered by the intensity of the heat as his toes approach within six inches of the coals. His left foot retreats to the side of its counterpart and the refuge of the barn floor. He inhales generously, shakes his arms at his sides, rolls his shoulders, and exhales slowly. 'This is no time for pussyfooting, pun intended,' he tells himself, and coyly peeks at Virtuous Leader, who is thumbing through his Bible, seemingly indifferent to the delay. The first step requires some moxie, and Virtuous Leader has come to expect delays.

"Think of it like a frigid lake. It's better to jump in and get it over with then to shimmy in by fractions," Virtuous Leader muses, barely looking up from his Bible.

With that advice in mind, the initiate inhales generously, shakes his arms at his sides, rolls his shoulders, exhales slowly, then quickly steps onto the simmering coals, left foot followed by the right. The contact between skin and charcoal produces a low 'hsssssssss,' and after about three seconds, when the initiate's adrenaline and stoicism is conquered by the inferno dancing about the soles of his feet, he screeches in pain.

"Eyyyaaaaaaaaaaaaaaaaaaahhh."

"Aspiring cohort, as a young boy you were quite the kleptomaniac. In school, you would habitually steal milk boxes from the cafeteria even though your parents gave you enough money for an adequate meal. You also stole magazines from the school library. One of your hobbies, 'collecting chromies,' entailed pilfering chrome or steel tire valve caps from neighborhood cars. The moral precariousness of youth is no excuse for these crimes."

"Mighty Lord, I repent for my aberration, forgive me," shouts the wannabe. The words forcefully race out of his mouth, spurred by the heat nipping at his feet and ankles and the urgency to move forward. He shifts his weight from one leg to the other. Virtuous Leader analyzes his body language for an instant.

"Absolved."

The nude initiate steps forward. As he settles his feet together, he refrains from yelping, but cannot prevent a customary grimace. He begins to swivel his jaw and roll his eyebrows, thinking maybe the secret to relieving the pain lies somewhere within the contorted musculature of his face.

"Aspiring cohort, you have engaged in many sexual acts throughout your life which are not sanctioned by God. Considering the private nature of the matter, I will spare you the embarrassment of mentioning any specifics. You are, unequivocally, a sexual deviant, and we'll leave it at that."

"Mighty Lord, I repent for my aberration, forgive me."

The initiate isn't sincere about this one. Some of the instances Virtuous Leader was referring to flash into his mind, and he doesn't regret or wish to be forgiven for any of them. No man or woman should be judged in their pursuit of carnal knowledge. It was worth it, he supposes, even if it means remaining stationary and suffering a bit longer than expected. Virtuous Leader detects his lack of remorse, sighs, and moves on.

"Aspiring cohort, you are a self-described gambling man. You have spent many weekends in Las Vegas on the craps and black jack tables, accumulating a net loss in the tens of thousands. Conversely, you have come up a big winner in the sports books, though you once put up your house as collateral in a Super Bowl pool. For better or worse, you won that bet, but no amount of money can recoup the bereavement cast upon your family because of your toxic habit."

"Mighty Lord, I repent for my aberration, forgive me," the cult hopeful pleads, truly sorry for his gambling and its negative impact on his home life. The shame and secrecy, the late bills and missed car payments, the impulse buys when he was going good, the visits from bookies, the intervention, the divorce, and the limited visitation rights. Compared to the mental anguish caused by all of that, the physical pain he is now experiencing is relatively bearable.

"Absolved."

Gambling man moves one step closer to salvation, happy to have moved past the hurdle posed by the sexual lewdness charges.

"Aspiring cohort, you have imbibed spirits in an abusive manner at an alarming rate. Fortunately, you have been on the wagon for over a year now, but that does not mean you are exempt from your days as a drunkard."

"Might Lord, I repent for my aberration, forgive me," exclaims the initiate, meaning it, if only for his liver's sake.

"Absolved," says Virtuous Leader. His pledge moves one step closer.

"Aspiring cohort, you once refused free tickets to game seven of the 2001 World Series, featuring your favorite team, the New York Yankees, because the game was being played in Arizona, and quote, 'Arizona is for peasants.'"

"It *is*."

"I beg your pardon?"

"Arizona *is* for peasants. Haven't you been?"

"Aspiring cohort, you seem to be missing the point. This is about pride," Virtuous Leader asserts, camouflaging his annoyance with a smile. *If only this fool knew what happened to the last pledge who went off script, and each one before him.*

"Mighty Lord, I repent for my aberration, forgive me."

Virtuous Leader shakes his head and signals with his index and middle finger to the gray-cloak opposite him. The initiate, fear-stricken and regretting his sassiness, turns 180 degrees to see the gray-cloak pull the handle on a steel chain fastened to one of the barn's support beams. He hears a metallic squeak just below his feet, the coal-cross drops from underneath him, and he plummets into darkness.

Minutes later, after regaining consciousness, the blind, poor, pitiful, wretched, and naked man, lying at the bottom of a human furnace on a pile of charred bones, looks up through the thick soot at a dull, cross-shaped portal of light and hears, "Widdy wee, widdy wah, widdy wallacka-zallacka zoo!"

Chapter 2

When Hubert Raymer arrived in Hell, Satan's ship set sail for uncharted territory. The afterlife was ordinary for Hubert for a long, long time. He accepted damnation for what it was, and like every other halfway competent Hellion, his first priority was to keep as low a profile as possible. That's how you get by in the Devil's lair. Hubert's best friend and mentor, James, taught him that the moment they met.

Hellion Survival Rule #1: Don't draw attention to yourself.

Hubert was in no position to question James, a tenured and reputable Hellion, and so that's how it went until Hubert began to have strange inklings about his mortal life, mostly in the form of déjà vu. At first, he ignored these feelings, reminding himself that Hellions are incapable of remembering their mortal life and he was no different.

Yet here he sits in the cafeteria, picking a dead fly out of his ham and cheese sandwich and dissecting the most recent moment of insight into his life on Earth. Hubert is an unassuming white man in his fifties. People used to tell him he was handsome, except his wife, who found him ordinary looking. Not dull or homely, just ordinary. Hubert always believed whatever handsome qualities he has are offset by a few aesthetic idiosyncrasies. For one, he has an unusual case of male pattern baldness that originates on the crown of his head and has spread slowly outward, like an exaggerated cowlick. The rest of his scalp is generously covered in wavy, black hair with traces of gray. Taken as a whole, his hair resembles a hurricane when viewed from satellite, the exaggerated cowlick serving as the eye of the storm. It's quite the natural disaster, Hubert Raymer's hair.

The second unusual aspect of Hubert's appearance is his eyebrows. No, he does not have a unibrow. In fact, from certain angles or a considerable distance, Hubert Raymer appears to have only a left eyebrow. His right brow is almost completely white while the left remains black with spattered gray. The whitening process began in his mid-thirties, and seeing that his wife was continually reminding him of how ordinary looking he was, Hubert decided against hair dye because he thought the ebony and ivory contrast made him look distinguished. Of course, his wife would go on believing he was ordinary looking, with or without the illusion of having one eyebrow.

Hubert raises his ebony eyebrow as he lifts the dead fly, pinched between his right index finger and thumb, a few inches in front of his nose for inspection. It's a big fellow, big enough to see its proboscis, as many of Hell's flies are. Good source of protein. Hubert peers from side to side to check for witnesses, and finding none, he shrugs his shoulders and devours the winged morsel. Not bad. A little acrid, but not bad. What this place really needs, Hubert observes, is one of those chocolate fountains. Just about any vermin that regularly finds its way into Hell's fare would border on delicious if it were chocolate-covered. Of course, Hubert knows amenities such as a chocolate fountain are outside Hell's realm of possibilities, and he quickly dismisses the subject, returning to his analysis of the most recent epiphany.

It was a black cat. Such a stereotypical motif associated with déjà vu that Hubert ignored it as it passed him in one of the radial corridors traversing the desert environment. He figured it wandered in from one of the pyramid sites; cats are just as common to Hell's imitation of Ancient Egypt as they are to the real thing. After his initial disregard for the rogue feline, Hubert was overcome by an irrefutable familiarity with the critter. It was the look in its eyes. A look that had Hubert convinced the cat pitied him and would be kind enough to put him out of his misery, if only it were possible. Hubert, feeling an obligation to investigate this issue on behalf of his conscience, doubled back and caught up to the cat. His interrogation was fruitless. Nevertheless, he knew he knew the cat, or the soul of the person inhabiting its body, from some time and place in his mortal life. But he couldn't recall the details.

Right when Hubert thinks he's on the verge of a breakthrough – something about tourists – his introspection is disrupted by a customary nudge on the shoulder and an accompanying chuckle.

"Heh-heh-heh, what's happenin' partna?" James asks in his Midwest twang. "Any non-traditional fixings in that ham and cheese today?"

"Housefly. Big one too, and tastier than most," Hubert tells him. He takes the first bite out of his sandwich.

"Shoot, I wish I had the kinda luck you have with them flies. I'm always gettin' them puny suckers. Ain't got no meat on 'em, lookin' like they ain't found a turd to slurp on in weeks."

"Well, you just ruined it for me. Now all I can think of is how much fecal matter *my* flies have consumed to attain their portly figure." Hubert gives James his finest shit-eating grin, swallows the first bite, and takes a second.

"Now you got me workin' up an appetite, talkin' bout doo-doo with a mouthful of sandwich. I'll be back." James heads toward the kitchen, pauses after three steps, and turns to Hubert. "By the way, Huey, you still got pieces of fly wing stuck in ya teeth." James mimics his old pal's shit-eating grin while swiveling his right index finger in front of his mouth like a toothbrush. He continues to the kitchen and merges with the seemingly endless lunch line, eventually disappearing into the fray.

Hubert dreads the time he spends alone at the cafeteria table while James goes to get a meal. It doesn't bother him to arrive alone, because that he does by choice. It's not solidarity he fears, but abandonment. Although his loyal friend has never given him reason to anticipate such an event, Hubert has always feared that one day James will merge into the lunch line and never return. Then what? In need of a friend, would he scour the cafeteria looking for some befuddled rookie to take under his wing the way James did with him when they met? Forget about it. He'd rather be forever lonesome than have to assume the burden of an apprentice as ignorant and hopeless as his former self. Companionship or not.

James was a saint for that.

Hubert fretfully twiddles his thumbs and surveys the vicinity before him. Bunch of freaks in these parts, he thinks, realizing, of course, the absurdity of his observation. Freakishness is a universal Hellion attribute; however, Hubert finds the denizens of this section of the cafeteria to be particularly abnormal. There are two teenage boys playing marbles with eyeballs. They appear to be Hellion eyeballs, which makes Hubert wonder where the boys got them. Eyeballs from any number of animals could easily be obtained in Hell, but eyeballs from a Hellion would be considerably difficult to procure. Life in Hell is the opposite of life on Earth in many ways, especially where the five senses are concerned. The fewer senses you have in Hell, the better. Satan would never allow a Hellion to wander around without eyeballs. Hubert decides there must be some sort of eyeball racket. A black market for eyeballs. Perhaps the two teenage boys are running it, swiftly plucking the eyeballs out of exhausted Hellion bodies before they're issued a "corporeal regeneration." After all, Satan wouldn't expect such a dangerous and innovative scheme to be the brainchild of, well, children.

Before Hubert moves on to analyze the next freaks in his realm, a trio of heavily tattooed yodelers, he sees James approaching from a few tables away. He breathes a sigh of relief and takes another bite out of his sandwich. James reaches their table, sets his tray down across from Hubert, and sits. There are only french fries on the tray, and the smell reminds Hubert the frying oil is allegedly 50% vegetable oil and 50% Hellion sweat. He toothlessly grins at the prospect.

"Plate full of fries for lunch. Healthy and salubrious choice," Hubert sarcastically remarks. He grins again and takes the last bite of his sandwich.

"Man, that deli line is ridiculous. I wasn't gonna wait all day for a ham and cheese sandwich like you do, even if it came with the biggest, tastiest housefly this place ever saw. What you smilin' at, Huey?"

"Oh, just something I saw when you were gone. How are the fries?"

"Not bad," James responds, picking up a few fries and shoveling them into his mouth. "Could use some more seasoning."

"Say, doesn't it kind of smell like the treadmill lot in the circle of sloth?"

James narrows his eyes at Hubert and slows the pace of his chewing.

"I know what yer gettin' at, but you can put it outta ya mind. That's all nonsense some of the old-timers made up when they were bored." James picks up the largest fry left on his plate and holds it at eye level. "*But*, sometimes I wish it were true. Like I said, these things could use some more seasoning." He smiles, looks at the fry for another moment, then devours it.

"You never know. This place is full of surprises," Hubert contends, thinking back to some notable rumors that turned out to be true: the lake of absinthe, the Elvis Presley

Pyramid, the underwater city, Monster's Island, the radioactive clam chowder, and, lest he forget, Satan's affair with a transvestite hydra. "I mean, nobody believed Satan was getting freaky with that she-boy hydra...but then the video surfaced. And the radioactive clam chowder...nearly one quarter of all Hellions got cancer, and then Gerald Bachmann found the uranium bars in the kitchen. I guarantee there's a connection between the soup and Monster's Island...that's what we'll discover next."

"I didn't forget none of that, Huey. Remember, *I* been here long before *you*. Ain't nothin' new to me when some crazy stuff turns out true. What you seen in ya modest time here is just a little taste of what I seen rise to the surface. But, just because the faculty has a tendency to mess with the food don't mean I'm eatin' sweaty fries." James munches on a few more fries. "They ain't salty enough to be sweaty fries. Here, have some before they run out." He nudges the plate toward Hubert.

"Hmm, no thanks buddy. I like my fries cooked in peanut oil."

"Don't be preposterous, yer in Hell, what difference does it make what kinda oil it is?"

"Well, it makes a difference when it's not any kind of oil."

"Suit yaself," James says, pulling the plate back. He goes to work on the remaining fries and leaves one on the plate. He looks down at the fry, parts his lips, then looks up at Hubert, who looks down at the fry, raises his dark eyebrow, then looks up at his friend.

"Screw you, James." Hubert snatches the lone fry off the plate and sweeps it into his mouth. He chews it voraciously.

"50% vegetable oil and 50% Hellion sweat, is that what they tell you?"

"Yeah." Hubert narrows his eyes at James and his chewing practically comes to a stop.

"Well, let me assure you that's another false rumor." Hubert relaxes and resumes chewing at a moderate rate. "It's actually 40% oil and 60% sweat." James breaks out laughing and his guffaw draws the attention of several neighbors. Hubert spits out what little remains of the fry onto the plate and tosses the sweaty fries saucer at James like a frisbee. He fails to hit his target.

"*Aaaaccckkkkkk!* Damn you, James!"

Hubert tries to rid himself of the taste by licking the collar of his burlap top and spitting onto the floor. The two-point resolution isn't particularly effective, and it attracts an even wider assembly than James' maniacal laughter. Hubert notices he's made himself a topic of interest and abandons his spasmodic undertaking. His cheeks redden in embarrassment.

Hellion Survival Rule #1: Don't draw attention to yourself.

James doesn't stop laughing though, and despite being acutely aware of their growing patronage, slaps his knees in triumph. Hubert scowls, imploring him to stop making a scene. The motion goes unheeded, however, as James interprets it as another reaction to succumbing to the genius of his practical joke. Hubert leans over the table.

"Rule number one," he whispers to his tormentor.

"I'm sorry, I'm so caught up in my revelry I seem to have forgotten the rules. Remind me, which is number one? Somethin' to do with table manners, right?" James riffs. He downgrades his derision to a mild chuckle to appease Hubert, who is now fuming.

"Alright, buster. Have it your way. If you don't want to abide by your own rules, be my guest." Hubert settles back into his seat and crosses his arms. "It's a slippery slope though, old buddy."

"Slippery as the sweat off them fries, jack." James resumes his boisterous cackle. Hubert rolls his eyes and resigns to being temporary fodder for the peanut gallery. He'll run out of gas soon enough, he thinks. Either that or some diversion will draw them away.

Gaaaaaaaccckkkkk-aack-aack!

Much to Hubert's elation, a diversion – in the form of a Hellion two tables away choking on a habanero pepper – immediately presents itself. Every Hellion within earshot of the man's gurgles and gasps intently watches his struggle, depriving James of an audience. James eventually takes the cue from Hubert, and joins him in gawking at the asphyxiated man. One of the man's tablemates attempts to dislodge the pepper by administering karate chops to the man's stomach and sides. After half a dozen thwacks, the would-be rescuer takes a step back and delivers a side kick to the man's sternum, knocking him to the ground. The kick doesn't achieve its desired effect, at least not for the choking man, and it becomes apparent to the spectators the kung fu master is more a sadist than a good samaritan. Hubert and James look at each other and shake their heads.

"Does anyone know the Heimlich?" shouts a concerned woman.

Hubert nudges James on the shoulder. James ignores him and continues watching the habanero Hellion, who is wriggling along the ground on his stomach. This unorthodox method for clearing the trachea mesmerizes James. Hubert prods his friend a second time. He realizes James has drifted into a trance and wrests him vigorously with both hands.

"Alright, Huey. I thought someone else woulda volunteered by now. Rule number one, remember?" James responds without taking his eyes off the writhing stranger. "Hang back, I guess I oughta take care of this real quick. Keep outta sight if things go awry." James gets out of his seat and coolly strolls over to the fellow. The judoka is still lingering at the prone man's side. James looks down at the choking man, hands on hips, and then turns to the brute.

"Pardon me, sensei, you mind if I apply my technique? I'm a second-degree black belt in Nochoka, ever hearda it?" James wryly asks.

"No. I doubt you're as proficient in your technique as I am in mine," replies the sensei.

"I disagree. Allow me to demonstrate." James gestures at the choking man while turning his palms up.

"Go ahead."

"Hey, buddy. I'm gonna get you up and clear that pepper outta ya," James informs the pitiful, slithering mass on the floor. No response.

James straddles his fallen patient, grabs him by the wrists, and with great effort, for the man is barely conscious, lifts his deadweight body to a semi-erect standing position. The man is sweating profusely and it immediately begins seeping into James' burlap clothes. Naturally, James thinks of the treadmill lot in the circle of sloth and his beloved sweaty fries. He looks in Hubert's direction and smiles, but there's too much commotion going on between their respective perspectives for Hubert to notice. James sees Hubert is more interested in the frenzied onlookers than in his impending heroism, and turns his attention back to the latter. He grapples the man around the chest and clasps his hands in a ball atop the man's solar plexus.

"OK, jack! I'm gonna pump that sucker right outta ya. On three, ready!? One, two, three!" James squeezes hard and jerks the man backwards and off his feet, using his own body as a fulcrum. Not your typical Heimlich. The habanero doesn't exit the man's throat, but he shows signs of invigoration. James returns him to the floor, and the choking man gyrates his hands, beseeching James to repeat his extreme Heimlich. James obliges, and a small fragment of pepper pops out of the man's mouth, followed by a stream of saliva. A pocket of oxygen spells the man's lungs from the upper limits of their anaerobic capacity, but his airway remains partially obstructed by the rest of the pepper. The man waves his hands.

"A-gck-ain, a-gck-ain," he gurgles.

"OK, this is the one, jack! One, two, three!" James thrusts his hands into the man's chest and pries him back and up. The offending chunk of habanero launches through the air in a parabolic arch. It lands at the karate man's feet. The choking man drops to his knees and catches his breath in abrupt, syncopated huffs. James beams, but instead of inspiring adulation, his moment of glory rouses jeers from a disapproving crowd.

"Booooo! Hisssss!" the Hellions shriek. They throw plates, trays, and half-eaten fruits at James. The kung fu master picks up the expelled pepper and heaves it at the formerly-choking man. James covers his head with a tray and zigs and zags his way back to Hubert.

SCRAAAAAAAAAWWW! A Hellbird signals the end of lunch. The Hellions must report to their various "afternoon" activities.

"Saved by the bell, old pal. You had a riot brewing there," Hubert tells James as he emerges from the dissipating raucous.

"Nothing I can't handle, young grasshopper. Catch you later." The sage and his precocious understudy perform their secret handshake and part ways.

Chapter 3

After bidding farewell to his mentor, Hubert
indignantly stares at the nearest exit and the throng of
Hellions jostling through the obsidian archway. Obsidian is
Satan's favorite building material, despite, but perhaps
precisely because of, its lack of tensile strength. Hellions are
often injured, either buried or impaled, by collapsing
obsidian structures. The volcanic glass has great decorative
properties, however, as Hubert has noted time and again.
While staring at the exit and noting its great decorative
properties, Hubert is stirred into motion by the incessant
screeching of the Hellbird, whose alarm will not cease until
the cafeteria is cleared of Hellions, and he begrudgingly joins
the undulating mass. It's time to attend Bible study.

"Monday" is what Hubert Raymer has determined to
label the days on which he must go to school for Bible study,
and this afternoon he has a virulent case of the Monday
blues. He attempts to alleviate his grumpiness with
existential musings: Why must they call it "afternoon
activities" when "afternoon" has no bearing here? What
lessons can the damned possibly glean from Bible study? Are
we supposed to retroactively become wholesome and then be
considered postmortem candidates for admittance to Heaven?
Doesn't Satan realize this place would be better off, to *his*
end, without the signs?

Inflammable and flammable are synonymous. That's
valuable information in Hell.

Hubert passes through the obsidian archway and out
into the main corridor of the hub. He stops in the middle of
the cavernous limestone hallway, puts his hands on his hips,
and looks up. Gargantuan stalactites are barely perceptible
way up in the blackness. Hubert has yet to decide whether
they are artificial or not, and this particular examination

doesn't improve either argument. It's too dark up there to know with certainty. In his daze, Hubert's mind abandons stalactites and Hell's sign ordeal and bounces back to the real issue, Bible study; specifically, how to delay arriving at Bible study. Hubert has many proven and preferred procrastination rituals and he mulls over which is most fitting for this occasion. The one that makes an immediate beeline to the front of his mental Rolodex, for it's the one most intimately related to recent events, is also conveniently Hubert's most proven and most preferred: sightseeing at the treadmill lot in the circle of sloth. It will take a while to get there and then to school, and Hubert hates upsetting his teacher, but the tongue lashing for excessive tardiness, and the probable whip lashing to go with it, is never enough to keep Hubert from his sweaty spandex haven.

He heads down the hub to his right and walks for a few hundred yards, dipping and dodging one Hellion after another as they scamper past in the opposite, perpendicular, and oblique directions, whilst trying to maintain the frantic pace of the corresponding traffic to avoid being elbowed headlong into the stampede. He arrives at the doorway of the desired corridor nearly out of breath from the brief but laborious commute. This part of the hub is only scantily populated and Hubert decides to sit down to catch his breath. He plops himself down against the wall adjoining the doorway, but the sight of a large, green ogre patrolling the hub several doorways away jolts Hubert to his feet. There's no sense spelling my aching bones only to have them bruised and splintered by the mace of that ugly monstrosity, Hubert thinks, while brushing the dirt off his rear. He turns and enters the doorway, leaving the hubbub of the hub for the relative placidity of his favorite radial corridor.

For the majority of his brisk walk, Hubert seldom encounters another Hellion. That begins to change when he gets within range of the circle of sloth, whose proximity is marked by the strength of the odor permeating from Hubert's beloved treadmill lot. Once Hubert hits that scent trail, a hypnotic effect takes place, and he unconsciously begins walking faster. He is seduced by the smell and appears to euphorically glide toward its source, like Pepé Le Pew to Penelope Pussycat.

A flicker of light appears up ahead and a low rumbling of voices. As Hubert glides around the gradual bend of the corridor he comes into view of the gateway to the circle of sloth. Two demon guards with torches stand at attention on each side of the gateway. They each have a bottle of vodka attached to the utility belts on their hips. Hubert is reminded of how the guards use the vodka to spew flames from their torches at any Hellion who reappears from the circle of sloth in unsatisfactory physical condition. The group of toned fitness enthusiasts conversing in front of the entrance are surely not candidates for the makeshift flamethrower treatment. Hubert, however, certainly is, although that was never the case until the recent development of a doughy stomach.

Upon thinking of his unflattering tummy, the tractor beam effect pulls Hubert right into the crowd of fitness enthusiasts and he bumps into a female bodybuilder-type, which jolts him out of his reverie.

"Watch where you're going, shrimp," the hulking woman sneers in a suspiciously husky voice, likely altered by steroids.

"I'm, I'm very sorry miss. I must have been lost in thought," Hubert replies in a barely audible, neutral tone.

"You don't sound very sorry, pipsqueak. Am I going to have to make you sorry?"

"No, that won't be necessary. Say, what do you do to work your lats? You have a wonderfully developed back, and

I'm beginning to lose that mesomorphic V-shape that men so desire." Hubert makes a V motion with his hands as if tracing the woman's contours.

"Is that supposed to be funny? Are you suggesting I look like a man?" The woman's face twitches as she glares down at Hubert.

"Well, do I really have to? That's not a bad thing, you know. I think people who defy gender expectations are brave and commendable beings." Hubert pauses, noticing the woman's Adam's apple. He smiles devilishly. "What kind of exercises did you do to get that Adam's apple, though?"

"Enoughhhhhh!" the woman loudly demands. She crouches into a tense and animalistic stance. Her feet are wider than shoulder-width, and her arms are held out from her sides. The veins are popping out of her neck. She takes one step closer to Hubert, who retreats in kind. The woman's chest heaves, her eyes bulge out, she grunts, and with a piercing scream, she lunges at Hubert. Hubert attempts to dodge his hulking assailant, but she is too large and too quick for his comparatively languid movement, and she clotheslines him with a forearm to the chest. The vicious blow sends Hubert head over heels, and he crashes, tumbles, and rolls, coming to a stop several feet from where he initially stood. Before he can steady the whirlwind of blurry images in his eyes, the bodybuilder woman is on him, pinning him to the ground. She slugs him in the jaw with a right hook. The other fitness fanatics gather around in a circle and instigate.

"The jokes on you now, funny man," the woman seethes.

"Hey, baby cakes. I always dreaded being the victim of domestic violence, but this is kind of a turn on," Hubert mumbles through swollen lips. "Let me guess though, I'm nothing special to you. I bet there's a long list of former hubbies you've beat up before me."

"You got that right, honey." She hits him again, this time in the temple. Hubert's eyes roll back and his jaw slackens. "You're not the first, and you certainly aren't special." She delivers another punch to the mouth.

"Is that all you've got? You hit like a girl."

"Ooooooh!" taunt the spectators, egging on their workout pal.

The commotion of the crowd and the mismatched scuffle catches the attention of the guards, who march over to the frenzied circle and push aside two of the Hellions, creating a domino effect. Hubert and his attacker look up to see the entire circle fall one person after the other as the guards approach them.

Hellion Survival Rule #1: Don't draw attention to yourself.

"Stop this nonsense at once, heathens!" one of the demons commands.

The 'roid raging woman, perhaps feeling Hubert is owed at least one more concussive blow, strikes him in the side of the head with a left elbow. Down goes the champ.

"Back away from that man, lady, or there will be consequences," the other demon warns.   Bodybuilder woman doesn't comply. Both demon guards reach for their handles of vodka. Bodybuilder woman springs to her feet. The demon guards take a swig of vodka and swirl it in their mouths. Bodybuilder woman kicks Hubert in the side, and he is jolted into a semi-conscious state just in time to hear the wails of his nemesis and detect the pungent odor of burning Hellion flesh.

When Hubert fully regains consciousness the only remnant of the madness of his encounter with the berserk woman is the faint smell of a barbeque pit mixed in with the permanence of Hellion sweat. The corridor is empty save for the two demon guards, who have returned to their stations. Hubert stands and hears the guards chuckle as he wipes the grime off his legs and arms, and shakes out his burlap sack. He manages an obsequious smile and approaches the entrance. No amount of humiliation will keep me from my sweet destination, Hubert tells himself, and he politely addresses the guards.

"Good day, sirs."

"Nice defense you put up, fiend," remarks one demon, winking at his partner.

"It was certainly bolstered by your torches, gentlemen. Thanks for bailing me out," Hubert says with a slight bow.

"Do not thank us, sinner. We're not here to help you, we're merely doing our job. It coincidentally worked out in your favor this time. That giant wretch put such a beating on you that we should be thanking *her*. Unfortunately, she is now in need of a 'corporeal regeneration,' and then she will be sent to the circle of wrath for anger management," the second demon sternly comments.

"That's a shame. I wonder if her regenerated body will be as sinewy and awe-inspiring as the original? I guess she deserves that little bit of consolation. Anyway, may I proceed? After taking that walloping it's become obvious now more than ever that I need to improve and maintain my physical conditioning."

"Access granted, imp."

The second guard reaches into a pouch on his utility belt and removes one of the heart rate monitors. It's basically an oversized watch, but instead of having a band, it has small metallic teeth around the underside. The demon presses the device against Hubert's neck, directly over the jugular vein, and rubs his thumb on the watch face. After a few seconds, the device emits a low beep, and the metallic teeth imbed themselves into Hubert's skin, fastening the monitor firmly to his neck. Hubert grimaces and briefly massages the area around the gadget.

"Much obliged. Good day, fine sirs," Hubert says. He pushes open the wide, heavy oak double doors of the entryway, which have images of Hellions engaging in various laborious endeavors carved into the panels. At the top of the doors is the Latin phrase, "labor omnia vincit," or "hard work conquers all." Hubert mulls over the words as the doors close behind him.

The vestibule of the circle of sloth oddly resembles that of a museum. It has marble floors and towering granite pillars. In a sardonic effort to discourage a sedentary lifestyle, Satan has on display a re-creation of a primitive scene in which an early hominid hunting party is abandoning their pursuit of a wounded mastodon to rescue their fat companion, who is being dragged away by a pack of wild dogs. Along the walls are paintings of kinetic scenes in sporting events and portraits of rugged, anonymous outdoorsmen, one of whom bears an uncanny resemblance to Theodore Roosevelt. In the middle of the entry hall stands a replica of Myron's *Discobolus*.

Hubert wastes no time elevating his heart rate, choosing to sprint across the capacious vestibule, pausing only briefly to admire the archaeological exhibit while running in place. On the far side, he approaches two familiar marble staircases, atop of which are obsidian archways, each with an inscription. The left reads, "Push," while the right reads, "Run." Hubert, without breaking stride, continues his sprint up the right staircase and through the archway, where he is again struck by Hellion body odor as an infinite grid of treadmills opens up before him. The vulcanized rubber which covers the entirety of the chasm, at least as far as Hubert can tell, adds an element of chemical flavor to the salty musk stimulating Hubert's nostrils. It's like a pheromone to Hubert, who again becomes entranced and alternatively sprints and jogs to the nearest available treadmill, propelled by the will of the sweat fumes.

Unfortunately, the Hellion directly in front of Hubert at the first open station is not who he was hoping to be the mantelpiece of his backdrop. A man with a solid body is one thing; at least Hubert can imagine himself morphing into the man's superior figure as he exercises. However, a man whose puffy love handles comically bounce up and down underneath his burlap sack as he jogs is almost insufferable, not to mention uninspiring.

Fortunately, Hubert's disconsolation with the pudgy schmuck to his front is mitigated by the luscious lady jogging at his left side. Yowzer, this isn't so bad after all, our hero assures himself. In a typically macho effort to strut his stuff, quite literally, Hubert turns up the speed on the treadmill. He sucks his stomach in and puffs out his chest, and focuses on keeping his running form as sprightly and efficient as possible.

Peacocking.

Once he finds his stride he begins taking surreptitious glances at the object of his affection every minute or so. Hubert is infatuated by the woman's flowing brown hair and stellar, undulating assets, and his spying activity gets increasingly bolder as he scans the woman from head to toe, each peek slightly longer than the one before it.

After indulging himself for a substantial chunk of time in this covert surveillance, Hubert realizes he would like the woman to take notice of his admiration for her, even if she's appalled by the realization she's being ogled. He begins coupling his occasional ganders with erratic arm movements, as if he's loosening up his joints. This produces no effect and the foxy lady continues on her steadfast course, eyes fixed straight ahead. She sure is zoned in, I bet she could spend eternity on that treadmill, Hubert silently opines, what a machine! The acme of human perambulation!

By now it's apparent to Hubert he will have to try something drastic and possibly harmful to his health. He will have to go verbal. There are restrictions against talking in the treadmill lot, which Satan drafted to prevent Hellions from being distracted from the task at hand. The circle of sloth is for working, not socializing. Hubert, looking down at the treadmill's control panel, thinks back to his mortal life and how it would drive him nuts when he would go to the gym and find the usual suspects chit-chatting and milling about the free weights area. It would be awfully contradictory to betray his mores because of some bodacious Hellion. Then again, hypocrisy must be paltry compared to whatever he did to wind up here.

Hubert, intent on attempting verbal engagement with the vixen, decreases the speed on the treadmill in order to bring his breathing down to a level that won't be an impediment to his vocal control. Almost nothing is more embarrassing than trying to flirt with a gorgeous woman between frantic gasps for breath. When Hubert reaches a manageable breathing level, he rehearses an opening line in his head, and confidently addresses his hopeful companion.

"You have impeccable running form," he says, as if he's an expert on the matter. "Were you a track athlete in the time before?"

The woman, pretending not to hear for a moment to heighten the stakes, turns to Hubert and begins to offer a response. Before the first word fully forms on her pouting lips, her feet fly out from underneath her, her head whiplashes into the control panel, then she faceplants on the treadmill belt, and is violently swept off the end of the machine. An aghast Hubert turns off his treadmill, steps down to the floor, and rushes to the woman's side.

"Holy heck, are you OK?" Hubert asks, standing over the woman, who lies face down on the vulcanized rubber, writhing in pain and cursing under her breath. She tries to roll onto her back, but in the process her right hand gets snagged by the treadmill belt, pulling her right arm into the undercarriage of the treadmill up to the elbow. She screams and kicks her legs back and forth, trying to free herself. A demon guard, dressed in pink and black 80s-style spandex, hears the woman's panic, and begins walking toward her and Hubert from his position about fifteen treadmills away.

Hellion Survival Rule #1: Don't draw attention to yourself.

"Sorry, miss. I gotta go. Hope you feel better," Hubert lamely consoles. He pats her on one of her flailing thighs, and begins a quick jog to the vestibule.

"Screw you, creep!" he hears the poor woman cry as he departs. A few seconds pass and Hubert hears the woman's screams amplify in between the crack of the guard's whip. He resists the temptation to look back, and takes solace in the thought that the woman's heart rate is bound to stay above the threshold under such circumstances. What a dreadful sequence of events, Hubert laments, but it would certainly be worse if her punishment were exacerbated by shocks from the monitor.

Hubert, impelled by the horror behind him, makes great time covering the expanse of the treadmill lot, then runs straight through the vestibule to the exit. He stops in front of the mammoth oak double doors. Unlike the entry side, the exit side of the doors are unadorned, which Hubert finds enticing for its simplicity and purity. He examines the knots, patterns, and imperfections of the wood, and runs his fingers down the grain. To his surprise, the wood is bizarrely cool to the touch. A draft from the vestibule, perhaps. Hubert lays the side of his face against the doors and relishes the alien coolness, which spreads through his head, neck, and shoulders. I could spend the rest of damnation up against these oak doors and be perfectly content, Hubert dreams. After a brief respite, Hubert realizes his heart rate is getting perilously close to the limit, and sighing, he reluctantly pushes open the doors.

"Welcome back, Cassius," one of the demon guards chides. Hubert ascertains that this guard must be here for the comic relief of the other, the one who fit him with the heart rate device. A good cop, bad cop arrangement.

"Glad to be, although I thoroughly enjoyed myself in there. I must have run ten miles. I feel like a million bucks," Hubert cheerily replies, although his solemn expression upon recalling the lovely lady's not-so-lovely screams belies his tone.

"No one cares what you feel like, Hellion scum," bellows the serious guard while removing the gadget from Hubert's neck.

"Alright then, well I guess I'll be seeing you fellows around the bend," Hubert says, departing.

"Hold on a minute, fiend." The serious minion approaches a frozen Hubert, who, knowing the drill, tightens up his abdominal muscles and straightens his back. The demon stands before Hubert and scrutinizes his midsection with narrowed eyes. "Hmm, you must have sweated off a substantial amount of heft. Very well, carry on, sinner."

Hubert turns away and power walks down the corridor, maintaining the feigned posture, until the two guards are out of sight. Then he exhales, lets his stomach hang, returns his shoulders to a partially slumped position, and eases his pace to a leisurely stroll. At this rate, Hubert deduces, I will get to Bible study toward the end of the class period. It takes him seemingly forever to meander back to the hub, where he walks down the main corridor, past the obsidian archway where he exited the mess hall, and into the first radial corridor that follows.

The corridor is bathed in yellow ambient lighting. School bus yellow. Hubert marches through the tunnel, passing many doors, some of which are virtually identical to the oak double doors of the circle of sloth, minus the bas-relief illustrations. A few have inscriptions, such as "Members Only," "None Shall Pass, But All Shall Enter," and "Herein Lies Thy Score." Hubert passes a metal door on his right with a white sign with red lettering that reads, "Dangerous Chemical and Biological Materials: Authorized Hellions and Minions Only." The next door on his left is an ordinary single wooden door with a battered door knob. A dry erase board hanging from a nail in the middle of the door has a note on it, ostensibly written by one of the minion teachers, though whether it's one of Hubert's teachers is unclear. It says, "Assignments that do not adhere to EDLA (Eternal Damnation Language Association) format will now receive zeros." What a tyrannical policy, Hubert observes. He opens the door, prepared to accept whatever punishment is about to come his way.

Low gasps and whispers fill the classroom as Hubert steps in, trying to avoid eye contact with the professor, a minotaur who stands at the chalkboard, temporarily ignoring Hubert's presence as he continues jotting in yellow chalk. The minotaur professor, Mr. Gramble, proceeds with his notations until Hubert, conscious of his intrusive advance, slyly but noticeably slinks into a seat in the back of the room. Professor Gramble steps back from the chalkboard, and contemplatively rubs his chin with his right index finger and thumb. He turns to face his students and flashes a disapproving look at Hubert, not much of a repercussion for excessive truancy. Hubert knows the stare is only a preface, a cruel teaser, and he anxiously wriggles around in his chair. Hellion Survival Rule #1: Don't draw attention to yourself. So much for all that.

"So there you have it, diabolical pupils, the ethics of good and evil as seen in Genesis," Mr. Gramble says to the class. "Adam and Eve were created as good and innocent creatures, but Eve's disobedience to God, original sin, and the knowledge man gained from that selfish and treacherous act, brings into question the true nature of your kind: is man inherently good or evil?" The professor looks around the classroom. "Based on my experience, with the caveat that it's highly imbalanced, I humbly opine that your kind is inherently evil. Anyone feel differently?"

The Hellions, including Hubert, are still and silent. Mr. Gramble stands before them with his hands held together on the small of his back. He taps his right foot on the floor at an even pace, as if the rhythmic beat will coax a response from someone in the room. Eventually it does. An elderly female Hellion in the front row raises her hand and offers her take on the topic.

"I'm not sure whether man is inherently good or evil, but I certainly don't believe Eve's tasting of the fruit from the Tree of Knowledge of Good and Evil is an evil act. Shouldn't man know about the nature of our existence? I mean, if we're created in God's image, and God knows about these things, then shouldn't he have welcomed Adam and Eve to taste of the fruit? It doesn't seem fair that he punished them for it," the wise senior theorizes.

"Yeah, it's not right," chirps a sympathizer in the bunch. Several others nod their heads in agreement. Hubert is not one of them.

"Fair? Right? Apparently, my heathen pupils, you haven't been reading the Old Testament too closely. Fire and brimstone, remember. "For I, the Lord your God, am a jealous and vengeful God." Adam and Eve were given everything they needed to live in leisure and contentment. God only demanded one thing of them, and Eve was unable to honor that simple rule. They had all the blessings the Creator could bestow upon them, yet wanted more, and God punished them principally for their *ungratefulness*, not just their disobedience."

The students are unable to concoct a rebuttal. Mr. Gramble, with a self-satisfied grin, saunters over to his desk in the front corner of the room. He removes something from one of the drawers, shielding it from the view of his students, and returns to the center of the room with the object hidden behind his back. Nervous looks are exchanged between the Hellions, whose lack of X-ray vision doesn't prevent them from knowing with absolute certainty what Professor Gramble has removed from his desk, and is now mockingly hiding behind his back.

"Is there anyone who would like me to reiterate what was just said?" inquires the professor. The students shake their heads, 'No,' in unison. "I want to be sure it's clear to each of you before I move on." Mr. Gramble looks determinedly at Hubert, who is adamantly shaking his head. "Mr. Raymer, is that a 'No, you would not like me to reiterate,' or a 'No, it's not clear to me'?" Hubert, caught off guard by his professor's furtive, potent line of attack, breaks into a sweaty panic.

In Hell, all panics are of the sweaty variety.

Hubert curses himself in low tones for the tenacity and duration of his head shake, and entreatingly looks around at his classmates, none of whom express an interest in aiding him.

"Crabs in a bucket," Hubert mutters.

"Come again, Mr. Raymer," says Mr. Gramble.

"I, uh, I said I meant 'No, you don't need to reiterate.' Sorry about the ambiguity.'" Hubert wipes the sweat off his forehead with the back of his hand. "So everything is clear to you then, correct?" Hubert nods his head, 'Yes.' "Yes, you say. Well, Mr. Raymer, I'm not sure it's sunk in quite yet. Come down here, pronto." The professor points at the floor directly in front of him.

Hubert is overcome with fear. He tries to get out of his chair, but his knees are weak and he falters. He sits back in his chair, shaking from head to toe like someone with a nasty case of the flu. Professor Gramble gives him an aggravated goggle, which intensifies his incapacitated state. A second attempt to stand is equally pathetic, but Hubert manages to stay on his feet by leaning onto his desktop. He senses that Mr. Gramble, now engaged in his signature toe tap, is growing impatient.

"One moment, sir, my legs seem to have fallen asleep from sitting for too long."

"Sitting for too long, ha! That's a good one, Mr. Raymer. I wonder how your fellow pupils must be feeling? Anybody else had their legs fall asleep?" Hubert's classmates are unresponsive. "That's odd, I'm surprised your entire bodies haven't fallen asleep. Unlike Mr. Raymer, the rest of you have been here the entire class period!" The professor takes a step toward Hubert and again points at the floor. "Mr. Raymer, get your sorry hide up here this instant. You don't want me to come back there." Hubert knows he's doomed, and relegating himself to another public chastisement, walks to the front of the classroom to face his sadistic pedagogue. He is greeted with a pompous smirk.

"As I said before, unholy pupils, God provided Adam and Eve with everything your kind could possibly want or need. He only demanded one thing in return, and Eve found it too difficult to respect that conditionality." Mr. Gramble pauses to monitor the room and make sure everyone is attentive. He holds up an index finger to emphasize the rest of his dissertation. "God blessed Adam and Eve with a satisfactory existence, an Eden free of worry and toil, but it wasn't enough to contain the selfish inclinations of man. Adam and Eve betrayed God's trust, and were rightfully punished for their ungratefulness and disobedience." The professor unveils the bullwhip from behind his back, holds it up for a count of two, and then unravels it with a lateral flicking motion, like casting a fishing pole. "In this classroom, like in the Garden of Eden, I, like the Creator, have one simple rule, which you, like Adam and Eve, must abide by. That rule is *arrive on time*. Most of you faithfully abide by this rule. A few of you break it from time to time. But only one of you, Mr. Raymer here, consistently breaks the rule. Mr. Raymer's chronic truancy suggests he doesn't appreciate the educational opportunities I offer here, and for that he must be punished."

The minotaur professor lashes Hubert's sorry hide until the pain renders him unconscious.

Chapter 4

Hubert sits in the back row of a small class of about twenty college students. *Philosophy of Race and Gender*, a title he couldn't forget in one thousand lifetimes. The professor, a lipstick lesbian, is leaning against the lectern listening to a student's response to a query. Ms. Hollis, was it? That Hubert should also remember for one thousand lifetimes. A vivacious blonde in her early-thirties with stunning, makeup-free facial features: immaculate skin, a delicate, slightly dimpled chin, voluptuous, expressive lips, high, full cheekbones, and effulgent eyelashes and eyebrows that accentuate her icy blue eyes. The paradox is her angelic face plays second fiddle to an even more sublime figure. If she hadn't already found her calling in education, Hubert thought she could easily have been a supermodel. She certainly dresses and walks like one. Ordinarily, this sexpot of a professor would be a distraction for Hubert, but as fate would have it, his future wife is also in the room, and, though objectively speaking he's utterly wrong, Hubert thinks she's the most beautiful woman in the room, if not on the entire campus. And unlike Ms. Hollis, she likes men, which means Hubert can daydream about wedding bells and making little Huberts and Hubertettes with the eventual Mrs. Hubert Raymer.

Philosophy of Race and Gender takes place in the fall semester (of Hubert's junior year), and it's now the Monday before Thanksgiving break. Hubert's hypothetical girlfriend, as per usual, wows her classmates and Ms. Hollis with illuminating assertions. This girl is too good to be true, Hubert thinks. After class, he finally speaks to his crush for the first time.

"Excuse me, Janice. Hi, I'm Hubert," he says awkwardly, intimidated by her beauty. Instead of offering his hand to shake, Hubert presents a goofy half-wave. Janice giggles.

"I'm aware, Hubert. Nice to meet you."

"You too. I felt compelled to tell you I'm really impressed by some of the things you've said in this class, especially today about the unforeseen negative consequences of the women's rights movement. I never much considered those things."

"Well, thanks for the praise, Hubert. Don't give me too much credit, though. My mom was heavily involved in the movement, so many of my ideas about gender are derived from her. I wish I could say they're entirely self-generated. Hope you're not disappointed."

"No, no, of course not. No idea is original, right? I mean, your mom likely borrowed some of the ideas of your grandmother and so on. One generation of astute feminists begetting another. You can call me Huey by the way, please."

"OK, Huey. I don't exactly consider myself a feminist, though. You can call me a humanist."

"Alright, astute humanist then."

For the first time, Hubert notices Janice's rich amber eyes. They're not only beautiful, but have a wise, discerning quality. Hubert temporarily forgets about their conversation and gets lost in Janice's eyes, contemplating what universal truths must be hidden in those amber pools of rods and cones. The two stand in silence, blinking at each other. Hubert begins to slowly rock forward and back. Janice puts her right hand on his left shoulder to steady him.

"Earth to Huey, come in." She snaps her fingers and Hubert returns from the outer limits.

"Sorry, I was thinking about something. You have beautiful eyes, by the way." Janice bashfully turns her head a few degrees. An admission of genuine flattery.

"Thanks, Huey. I have to give partial credit to my mom for that, too." Hubert smiles.

"So...where is your next class? Perhaps I could walk you there and pick your brain some more. I'm sure you're an expert on other things besides feminist theory."

"I'm going to Tarble Hall."

"Well, I'm going to the library, which isn't exactly in that direction, but I don't mind taking the circuitous route. What do you say?"

"You can accompany me, but only if you tell me what you were thinking about when you went narcoleptic on me."

"Agreed."

The two walk and Hubert discloses the contents of his daydream. He blushes a little over some of the details. Janice laughs at said details and assures him that his secrets are safe with her. Before they arrive at Tarble Hall, Hubert asks Janice her opinion on a current event. Turns out she's an expert on foreign policy as well. Hubert is beyond smitten. It appears on this afternoon that Cupid has expended his entire quiver on Hubert Raymer. A few arrows seem to have gone astray and struck Janice as well.

Collateral damage.

The lovebirds head their separate ways, but not before they agree to meet for coffee the following morning. Coffee leads to the movies; the movies lead to candlelit dinner; candlelit dinner leads to another candlelit dinner; another candlelit dinner involves a few glasses of wine; and a few glasses of wine leads to a consummation of Hubert and Janice's budding love. They are inseparable for the rest of college. Their friends make jokes about their latent co-dependence, but Hubert and Janice are impervious to the barbs. They embrace the nickname "Raystler," an anagram of their last names. On graduation day, Hubert and Janice receive class rings, each with "Raystler" etched onto the inside of the hoop. They also introduce one another to their families for the first time. It goes delightfully well. Hubert has never been happier in his life, while Janice, a bright ray of sunshine by default, is a few shades brighter. After commencement week, they move into a small one-bedroom apartment. Lucy, a gregarious and mannerly black Labrador from the adoption center, adds levity and supplemental companionship to their lives.

Their wedding day on a comfortably warm June day in Janice's hometown. The ceremony takes place in the Unitarian church her family has attended since her childhood. It's the first time Hubert has been in a church, although it doesn't resemble a place of worship so much as a community center with pews. But isn't that what a church should be? Hubert wonders as Janice, gorgeous as ever in a modest wedding dress, walks down the aisle in her father's arm. The father of the bride gives Hubert a ratifying nod when he relinquishes his precious baby girl. Hubert's spirits are lifted by the signification and a giddy smile emblazons his face while he and Janice exchange vows. The same smile continually reappears throughout the ensuing reception, where the newlyweds dance the night away to familiar 70s hits: the Bee Gees' "Stayin' Alive," Parliament's "Give Up the Funk (Tear the Roof Off the Sucker)," James Brown's "Get Up Offa That Thing," and KC and the Sunshine Band's "Get Down Tonight."

Ice clinks against cocktail glasses and the ocean breeze whisks through majestic palm trees. Hubert and Janice sit on a beach towel on the beige sand of a remote Central American fishing village, toasting to a wonderful future together. At the suggestion of a vagabond, surfer bum friend, the couple chose to honeymoon somewhere unique and virgin, far from the resort crowds and all-inclusive tackiness that have come to characterize tropical couple's retreats.

Their bohemian friend proves a sagacious travel agent; the getaway is precisely what Hubert and Janice are looking for, though they didn't know it beforehand. The selling point was the village is within driving distance of two major Mesoamerican archaeological sites, but the honeymooners are so enamored with the village – its people, food, drinks, street boutiques, gringo backpackers – they never discuss a day trip to the ancient ruins. Instead, they spend each day of the week immersing themselves in the lifestyles of the villagers. They go fishing on Saturday, play stickball on the beach on Sunday, ride mules to the local aquifer on Monday, make beaded jewelry on Tuesday, surf on Wednesday, cook sea bass and plantains on Thursday, and drink mescal and the local beer on Friday. More accurately, they drink mescal and the local beer every day, but on Friday drinking is the day's main event, not a complementary activity. On the flight home, in the detached, frivolous mood that accompanies many hangovers, Hubert looks at his bride, peacefully asleep at his side, places his hand over hers, and thinks the world is his oyster shell.

The revelation is short lived. In the near future, Hubert finds himself sitting bedside in a hospital room. Janice lies in the bed, sickly and pregnant, losing the battle against a rare tropical virus she contracted on their honeymoon. Childbirth proves too much of a shock to Janice's immune system, and she gives life to a healthy son at the cost of her own. Hubert tries to make sense of the tragic irony.

The Lord giveth and the Lord taketh.

Chapter 5

A palpitation of awestruck gasps spreads through the classroom and Hubert starts out of his sleepy vision, surprised to find himself back in his seat, a development he attributes to sleep walking or to Professor Gramble putting him there so he could resume lecturing. Minotaur professors don't like to share the stage. Hubert rubs the cloudiness from his eyes, and wondering what all the fuss is about, directs his sight to the object of his classmates' excitement. Now that's something you don't see every day, Hubert notes, contributing a curious grunt of his own to the chorus of pneumatic sounds. A black squirrel, frantic and engulfed in flames, jumps about near the doorway. Its movements remind Hubert of a rodeo bronco, except the poor squirrel's bucks only seem to embolden the pest on its back.

Professor Gramble, who stands in the corner by his desk clutching a broom to his chest, rolling his head and shoulders around as if trying to burrow into the wall, at last feels an obligation to take control of the situation. He vacates his hideout and stalks across the front of the room toward the squirrel, broom raised in striking position. With the target a broom's length away, the minotaur takes a lethal swing, but the squirrel, apparently cognizant of its new threat despite the extant viability of the old one, leaps out of the way. Another swing and another miss. The squirrel bounds across the classroom as Mr. Gramble gives chase. Another swing and another miss. The professor roars in frustration. Some of the Hellions' gasps seamlessly switch to chuckles. The squirrel concludes its zig-zagging escape with a leap onto Professor Gramble's desk, where it continues its frenzied springing. Papers and books are scattered onto the floor, and the ones remaining atop the desk are set ablaze. The minotaur is further distraught by the loss of his various documents. "Mindless cretin, look what you've done!" the professor yells. The squirrel pauses and looks at Mr. Gramble with a curious expression. From his vantage point, Hubert swears there's contrition in the squirrel's beady eyes, but before he can confirm his suspicion the squirrel is batted senseless by an overhand swing from the minotaur's broom. The blow, much to the minotaur's dismay, extinguishes the fire. Even worse, it doesn't kill or mortally wound the bushy-tailed bugger, which drunkenly stumbles around the surface of the desk, attempting to regain its senses. The minotaur snaps the broom over his thigh, tosses the pieces aside, and with a new strategy in mind, lunges at the rodent, only to grab and bite at phantom traces and slide off the far end of the desk. The students erupt in laughter as their professor thuds to the floor.

The black squirrel peers over the edge of the table at his befuddled adversary, then hops to the floor and races into the aggregation of student desks, passing underneath jittery Hellion feet and weaving around chair legs. A light billow of smoke trails from its tail and the room starts to smell like singed fur. Mr. Gramble gets to his feet, removes the whip from his desk drawer, and charges into the middle aisle of the student desks, where he begins lashing at the squirrel and shuffling up and down the aisle in accordance with the squirrel's unpredictable movements. The Hellions' laughter becomes successively louder after each miss, and they begin cheering and clapping for the squirrel.

"Quiet, worthless scullions!" the minotaur angrily insists.

He hits one of his pupils at random with the next lash and the implied threat of another partially restores order. Professor Gramble resumes attempting to exterminate the squirrel, but after a minute or two of continuous whipping his shoulder and elbow burn to the point of failure. He tries to switch hands, but his non-dominant arm produces awkward and inaccurate lashes, so he decides to sit down and rest on one of the student's desktops until the lactic acid subsides. The furry adventurer realizes it's safe for the moment and stops running wild. It walks to the front of the classroom, stands upright on its hind legs, and sniffs the air. Its beady eyes dart from one spot to another, searching the room for signs of danger. None are present and the squirrel, with an incredulous eye on the temporarily dormant minotaur, jumps onto one of the desks in the front row. The occupant of the desk laughs nervously and reaches out to pet the squirrel, which ducks away from the Hellion's touch and leaps to an adjacent desk, where the tentative exchange is repeated. The squirrel continues its jaunt from desk to desk and eventually finds itself in a stare down with Hubert Raymer.

Hubert lowers his head to match his eye level with the squirrel's and refuses to break eye contact. The bold critter doesn't budge and after a prolonged visual investigation, Hubert has the same conviction about the black squirrel as he did about the black cat he encountered near the desert environment: the squirrel is a relic from his mortal life. He senses something hauntingly familiar in the black squirrel's eyes, something valiant but menacing, noble but unsettling. Alright buddy, you win, Hubert thinks, and breaks eye contact. As his eyes recalibrate, Professor Gramble raises his whip in the unfocused background. While Hubert and the squirrel were preoccupied, Mr. Gramble took the opportunity to sneak into a favorable striking position approximately seven feet behind the squirrel. Hubert tries to shoo the squirrel away, flailing at it to warn it of the impending danger, but it's too late.

Thwack (crunch)!

The minotaur connects with a thunderous blast, snapping the black squirrel's spine and producing a variety of horrified reactions from the students. One student runs out of the room, another claps his hands to his cheeks and shrieks, evoking the fellow from Edvard Munch's *The Scream*, a third vomits, and a fourth weeps and yells, "Innocence lost!" Hubert sits motionless in his seat. He has resumed staring into the squirrel's eyes, thinking if he maintains eye contact long enough, perhaps for eternity, the squirrel's soul will be resurrected. The squirrel lies paralyzed and involuntarily twitching on his desk, still looking at Hubert as the life slowly drains from its eyes. Hubert slams his fists on the desk and shoots a deathly glare at Professor Gramble.

"You coward, you monster, you killed him," Hubert growls. He pushes away from his desk and storms toward the professor.

"Crying over spilled milk, huh, Hellion fool?" Mr. Gramble replies with a hearty, insidious laugh.

"I knew him, damn you! He had the answers, but you slaughtered him like he was one of you – common cattle!"

Hubert throws a flurry of punches into the minotaur's gut, but the impacts do nothing other than break the continuity of the minotaur's laughter. Professor Gramble walks over to his desk with Hubert in tow, still futilely punching, and reaches into the chair alcove. Every Hellion in the class knows what this means: the dishonorable dismissal button. In a matter of seconds, a trio of demon guards busts into the classroom. This outfit carries a billy club on their utility belts instead of a bottle of vodka. Hubert snatches a three-hole puncher from Professor Gramble's desk, and the demons draw their billy clubs.

"Stand back, pigs! I'm not wrapped too tight," Hubert warns. He assumes a fencer's stance to keep the demons at bay.

"Uh-oh, watch out boys, he looks like a trained swordsman," the largest demon sarcastically remarks. The two smaller demons fan out to take Hubert's flanks, while the largest one remains directly in front of Hubert and takes a small step forward. Sensing a coordinated bull rush, Hubert clambers onto Mr. Gramble's desk to gain the higher ground. He kicks the ashes and remnant desktop miscellanea at the demons, who clear the detritus from the air with their free hands and parry the solid projectiles with their clubs.

"Are you going to subdue him or am I going to have to do it myself?" Professor Gramble shouts at the demons. "He's damaging my pedagogical tools and desecrating the remains of my books and lesson plans."

"You heard the professor, boys, let's get 'em," the largest demon orders, and they attack.

Hubert, in his best imitation of the black squirrel, hurtles over the swinging club of the first minion, then leaps off the desk in time to avoid being tackled by the second. He runs into the nearest aisle of student desks, hoping to use his fellow students as cover and a means of distraction, but after a few strides a whirring billy club strikes him in the back of the head, knocking him to the floor in a daze.

"Hurts, don't it? Blah-ha-ha."

A wincing Hubert gazes up at the largest demon, who guffaws once more, reaches down to pick up his club, and teasingly taps Hubert in the ribs with it.

"Good try, fiend, but your luck's run out. Time to go to the big house. Boys, cuff 'em."

Chapter 6

Hubert lies on the concrete floor of a jail cell, recovering from the effects of a heavy sedative. There are low voices in the air, seemingly in every direction. Too tired to stand, Hubert sits up on his elbows and checks to see if his house is in order. His wrists are sore and have deep imprints in the skin where the handcuffs had been. It feels as if his back has been rubbed raw by friction from his burlap sack. His ankles are red and irritated, and the skin is hot to the touch. And, of course, there is a knot on the back of his head. The source of the other afflictions may be lost to sedation, but that one he can be sure about. Hubert knows that regardless of the causes of his ailments, there must have been a struggle, which there was; he was unwilling to go peacefully, and after being lugged under the armpits halfway to the jail, kicking and flailing, his captors sprayed him with Numbify™, shot a powerful tranquilizer dart into his neck, and dragged him by the ankles the rest of the way. It is probably better they knocked Hubert out, considering how embarrassed he would have been being dragged by the ankles through the main hub. Hubert shivers at the idea, thinks "thank goodness," and massages the lump on his head.

The throbbing in his skull subsides following a few minutes of massaging, and with a clear head, Hubert's interest is piqued by the whispers. He crawls to the front of the jail cell, takes hold of two of the cool steel bars – which pleasantly reminds him of the door in the circle of sloth – and pokes his head in the space between to get an optimal view of the surroundings. His cell appears to be near the end of a concrete hallway, occasionally lit by torches hanging from the wall on the opposite side. There is empty darkness to the right, a dead end Hubert presumes, and a long row of steel bars to the left. Hubert can only identify three distinct cells, judging by the keyhole panels, before the line of metal becomes too muddled by his low viewing angle to make out farther cells. The adjacent cell has "GLUTTONY" engraved into the center of the top frame and painted in white letters. Hubert deduces, based on Satan's predictable design tendencies, there are seven cells, one for each of the deadly sins. Hubert wonders which one he's in. It must be "WRATH" after lashing out at Professor Gramble, he decides. He lies on his back to try to get a look at the engraving on his cell, but cannot achieve a wide enough viewing angle to make out the letters.

"Miscellaneous," a voice chimes from somewhere in the jail cell. Hubert is frightened half to death and scrambles to his feet. He tries to make out figures in the darkness. How big can one jail cell possibly be? he wonders.

"This is the eighth cell, it's designated for miscellaneous offenders" says another voice, this time a woman's.

The man and the woman appear from the shadows and greet Hubert with demure smiles. The man is in his late-60s, Caucasian, with grayish-whitish hair and a ruddy, angular face. He stands about six-foot-three and wears bifocals, which rest precariously about two-thirds of the way down the bridge of his narrow nose. Hubert finds this trait rather ridiculous, but concedes that the man must have been quite regal in the time of his mortal life, likely the late-eighteenth century. The woman is decidedly 21st century. She is in her early-40s, Caucasian, with mid-length blonde hair. Her facial features are ordinary, but she has electrifying green eyes that stand out even in the gloom of the jail cell. She is tall and slender, and moves with the cosmopolitan purpose of 21st century movers and shakers. Hubert finds her a little intimidating, perhaps a former stateswoman.

They continue out of the shadows and reach out to shake hands. Hubert, in accordance with the rules of chivalrous conduct, or maybe just what he imagines to be proper form, takes the woman's hand first.

"Hello, I'm Claudia," she says, in what Hubert now recognizes as a British accent.

"I'm Hubert, good to meet you, gov'ness," Hubert cheekily responds. His attempt at humor is met with a stern look.

"An American, I see. Let me guess, Generation X, Northeastern origins, either in real estate or finance." She crosses her arms.

"Actually, I don't really remember. But as far as stereotypes go, you could do a lot worse, my lady. Baby Boomer, Californian, either in herbal remedies or a drum circle." The ice remains unbroken.

"I'm Lawrence, by the way," the man interjects, trying to ease the tension. He extends his hand to Hubert. "Lawrence Rutledge, esquire."

"Nice to meet you, Lawrence Rutledge. I'm Hubert Raymer, licensed realtor."

"What miscellaneous offense are you in here for, Hubert?" asks Lawrence with genuine interest.

"Base foolishness, no doubt," Claudia flatly suggests.

"That could be it. But I think it was more unruliness that did me in. I yelled at my Bible study professor and punched him in the stomach several times," explains Hubert. "Professor Gramble, if you know him." He looks to Lawrence and Claudia, expecting the name to ring a bell.

"No. Never heard that name," says Lawrence.

"The name is familiar, but I've never met him. I have Ms. Dubock for Bible study," Claudia adds.

"Shucks, oh well. So, what are you guys here for?"

"We removed our burlap clothes and went streaking through the main hub," says Claudia with a hint of pride.

"I guess it doesn't exactly fall under 'lust,' so here we are," Lawrence observes, shrugging his shoulders. "But enough about that. Back to your situation. How did that come about? I'd love to hear the details."

"Let's see, it began with deciding to delay my arrival at class..."

Hubert goes on to tell the events leading up to his arrest. He tells them about the confrontation with the bodybuilder woman, which very well could have caused his first arrest of the day. He wistfully describes the woman on the treadmill next to him and her awful accident. He tries to articulate the euphoric feel of the exit side of the circle of sloth's door. He summarizes the Adam and Eve discussion and how Professor Gramble used him as an example. He recalls the faint-inducing pain of the whipping and what he remembers of his dream, or perhaps hallucination. He solemnly explains the appearance, triumph, and execution of the black squirrel. Lastly, he reenacts his assault of Professor Gramble and his attempt to duplicate the squirrel's evasive brilliance, which was also neutralized, in his case by a hurling billy club. Claudia and Lawrence are left wide-eyed and open-mouthed by the account.

"My God, that's one heck of a day," exclaims Lawrence.

"I've had worse," says Hubert.

"Worse? I don't doubt it, but that was a dreadful trip. Professor Gramble must be a real curmudgeon," Claudia asserts.

"Yeah, but I should know better. Play with fire and you get burnt." They all laugh at the circumstantial literalness of the figure of speech.

"Couldn't say it any better, Hubert. We know the rules and therefore deserve the consequences of breaking them," says Lawrence.

"It's odd, though, recently I've been feeling that I *don't* deserve them, because I'm picking up the vibe that I shouldn't be here in the first place," Hubert confesses.

Lawrence and Claudia laugh.

"You mean in Hell?" Claudia asks.

"Yes."

"Honey, that's what everyone says. You must still be in the first stage. How long do you think you've been here?"

"Not positive, but does anyone know? I'm certain it's not long in the grand scheme. What do you mean 'the first stage'?"

"The five stages of grief. You're still in denial."

"Which means you haven't been here nearly as long as we have. We've fully accepted our bid," states Lawrence.

"Sure have," Claudia iterates. "In a way, we accepted that bid long before we arrived here, what with the lives we chose."

"And what lives were those?" Hubert inquires.

"Well, I was a bit of a hedonist," Claudia admits, "I grew up in Birmingham, England and started running with the fast crowd at an early age. By the time I was fourteen I was already a heroin junkie and a sex addict." She pauses and gazes at the floor, which resembles a quilt of dusty footprints. She tries to make sense of the pattern, hoping the footprints will guide her explanation of the footprints of her life. "I spent most of my time on the streets scoring drugs, sometimes turning a trick or two to do so, and the rest of my time I spent at the night clubs. School was an afterthought and eventually I got expelled. That was the last straw for my father.

"You see, my father was a highly successful industrialist. He owned and managed most of the factories in Birmingham, and a few in London as well. He was self-made and placed a lot of value on hard work and education. Naturally, he was distraught about the path I was on, but since he worked so much he only knew the half of it. My mother died when I was six, and I bribed the nannies my father hired over the years to keep him in the dark. I basically raised myself.

"Anyway, like I said the expulsion was the tipping point. It really opened my father's eyes to how wild and irresponsible I had become. He used his connections in London to get me into a prestigious all-girls boarding school. What good that did! It just made me more rebellious, and London was a proving ground for juvenile delinquency. Since there were no boys at the school, I would sneak off the school grounds at night to hit London's club scene. The London clubs were where I was introduced to ecstasy. They also had the best cocaine you could find in all of Europe probably. I became sensually familiar with the biggest dealers to help support my habit. At one point I was dating one of the club owners. He thought I was twenty-two.

"So, that was my life for the last two years of high school: ecstasy, cocaine, clubbing, and de facto prostitution. Somehow I managed to graduate; I think my father pulled a few strings. He really loved me and wanted the best for me, but he was completely out of touch. My graduation present was a Bentley. What I needed was a swift kick in the butt and a reduced allowance. Instead, I got quite the opposite." She pauses again and retraces the dusty footprints. Her bottom lip quivers for a barely perceptible instant, then she steadies it with a firm, toothless bite.

"Claudia, you OK?" asks Hubert, concerned.

"Yes, sorry. Where was I?"

"The allowance, dear," Lawrence gently reminds her. "Right. Not long after graduation my father died. I was an only child. So instead of a swift kick in the butt and a reduced allowance, I inherited his entire estate. In his will, I was designated the owner, President, and CEO of his industrial empire. He stated his wish for me to continue his life's work. How was I expected to do that!? I hadn't worked a day in my life. On top of that, I hadn't any business sense or interpersonal skills. But I decided to give it a shot anyhow. It was the least I could do on behalf of my father.

"My tenure as boss didn't last long. I basically ran everything through my father's partner and things turned out OK. We actually increased revenues for the first quarter of that year. I even managed to stay clean and sober for a few months. However, after about six months running the business the party life beckoned me. The temptation was too strong, so I decided to resign and declare my father's partner President and CEO. Like I said, he was making all the decisions anyway, and he was my father's most trusted friend. I sold a portion of my stock in the company to him; enough for his holding to be worthy of his position, but also for me to remain majority owner." Claudia pauses a third time to examine the dusty footprints. This time the footprints inspire her words.

"Then it was off to the races for me. I was only twenty, and although I began the fast life at fourteen, relatively speaking I had barely gotten my feet wet. I sold the family house in Birmingham and bought a large flat in London, the West End. In a few years I had ascended the ranks of the London social scene and became known as what we 21st century folks call a 'socialite,' which means I was famous for the sake of being wealthy, visible, and well, famous. I woke up many a morning to find myself on the cover of the tabloids. If I didn't remember the night before myself, oftentimes I could rely on the tabloids to remember for me. That attention, in some sick way, helped fill the void of my childhood, but it didn't stop me from going down the destructive path I was on, it only fed the monster.

"At thirty I met my eventual husband at a benefit some friends and I arranged for our charity organization, Hope for Endangered Species. I did try to do some good with my money and influence, although obviously not enough to keep me out of *here*." She laughs and shakes her head. "He was an actor, my husband. He started in the English theatre, then moved into film, and eventually broke into Hollywood. What a sweetheart. He came from a good family, he was selfless, unaffected by his fame – at least as unaffected as a Hollywood actor can be – and he was a true humanist, as well as an animal lover. He deserved someone better than me, but he was also a drug and sex addict, and our mutual sickness sparked and preserved our romance.

"We had a daughter when I was thirty-four. Ophelia was her name, after the character in *Hamlet*. She brought a sense of meaningfulness to my life. I was clean and sober during the pregnancy and remained so for another eleven months after Ophelia was born. I remember thinking I was in it for good, that the storm had passed permanently. My husband had at least one foot on the wagon for all that time, too. Then we were at a friend's Christmas party and they had some really good blow. Ophelia was staying overnight at my in-laws', so we figured what the heck. That first line was divine. It knocked me far off the wagon, and the wagon disappeared over the horizon.

"After that fateful Christmas party, I returned to my hedonistic ways with more maniacal zeal than I ever had before. My husband continually tried to get me to go to rehab, but I had no interest in addressing my problem. Then he offered an ultimatum: either I get clean or he files for divorce and custody of Ophelia. I was too blitzed to realize he was serious, and I was too self-deluded to think the courts would ever take my daughter from me. Of course, I was wrong about both. I told the judge that despite my personal issues I was still a good mother. At the time I think I believed it, but now I know it was a lie." Claudia's bottom lip quivers again. A thick tear runs from her left eye down the length of her face. She wipes it with the back of her hand.

"That is the only thing I truly regret. Not being there for my daughter. Letting her down. Not only was I denied partial custody, but I was denied visitation rights until I received clearance from an assigned psychiatrist along with a clean urine sample. What little light there was at the end of the tunnel was stamped out. I felt I had no reason to live, and ironically, my chemical dependencies were what kept me alive. The constant state of numbness and apathy shielded me from thoughts of suicide.

"But eventually the drugs ended up killing me when I passed out while driving. One night I left one of the clubs I frequented. I must have done two grams of cocaine that night and had eight or nine gin and tonics. The valet tried to prevent me from driving, but I gave him a fifty pound note to look the other way. I started the car up, the newest edition of the same model Bentley my father had bought me for high school graduation, and lit a spliff I had waiting in the glove box. That was part of my driving-while-intoxicated routine. It helped balance me out, or at least that was the idea. The last I remember was turning onto the Southwark Bridge." She's silent. Hubert waits a second to make sure the story is finished before he speaks.

"Wow. Life in the fast lane," he comments.

"It sure was. If I had ever taken the time to slow down I may have actually appreciated what I had. The only thing I was ever grateful for was my daughter, and even that I screwed up."

"We all make mistakes, dear," observes Lawrence. "Heaven knows I've made my share. And Hell knows even better." He laughs at his joke.

"Indulge us, Lawrence. I'm sure Claudia has heard your story many times, but perhaps it will lift her spirits after recalling her own shortcomings," says Hubert.

"Believe me, Hubert, it does."

"Please, call me Huey."

"Very well. Where do I begin..."

Lawrence proceeds to shock Hubert with his macabre life story. He was a slave owner in colonial America. The tidewater area of Virginia, just north of the mouth of the Potomac River, to be exact. His family had owned the plantation for three generations and he was the fourth. Their staple crop was tobacco, but they also grew cotton, raised cattle for leather, and operated a sawmill. The Rutledge plantation was one of the most profitable plantations in the land. Rutledge tobacco was famous for its rich, full flavor and dark, billowy smoke, and was a favorite among people of influence, except other tobacco growers, of course.

Lawrence was a person of influence himself, and became known throughout the Western world for single-handedly quelling the Northern Virginia Slave Rebellion of 1772. One of Lawrence's passions aside from his plantation duties was trapping. He had over six hundred leghold-style traps of various sizes, some for bear, some for foxes, some for beaver, set up over a one hundred square-mile swath of land around his plantation, on both sides of the Potomac River. Of the 216 escaped slaves, 183 were caught in Lawrence's traps. The agonized screams of the incapacitated struck such fear into the other runaways that they either fled the scene and returned to their masters or stood motionless until the search teams found them. The other slave owners were grateful to Lawrence for his contribution to the search effort, and were happy to have their chattel back, broken legs and all. 'An injured slave is more profitable than a lost slave', they told an apologetic Lawrence.

Slave owner maxims.

Lawrence met his maker in the Revolutionary War. He was not a combatant. While watching The Battle of the Chesapeake from the western shore of the bay, he and his horse, Excelsior, were struck by an errant cannonball. As per the conditions of his will, his entire estate was handed down to his two sons; one of whom was the result of his affair with one of his slaves. Today the Rutledges are much darker in complexion than they were in Lawrence's time, and Rutledge Tobacco Company is a multi-billion-dollar enterprise. Lawrence thinks it's a redemptive legacy, but realizes it's also precisely the kind of story Satan cherishes in Hellions.

"I think it *is* a story of redemption, Lawrence," submits Hubert. "Just one that fit the times. You can't help the circumstances you were born into. Everyone is a product of their environment."

"That is true, Huey. But I lived in a perpetual state of moral conflict. I knew slavery was wrong, despite the justifications wealthy white men invented to serve their own ends, and I should have cut ties while I was young and idealistic," Lawrence contends, musingly.

"Like you said, we all make mistakes. And I agree with Huey. What you did in your will was courageous and progressive. A merciful slave owner you were, and I'm sure your descendants are thankful," Claudia assures him.

"They may be. If only the Rutledge name was known for something other than tobacco. My family name is synonymous with suffering and death. Of course, back in the day we didn't know all the horrible things about smoking that modern medicine has uncovered," Lawrence observes.

"Again, those were different times. Hindsight is twenty-twenty, no use sweating over it now," says Hubert. Lawrence and Claudia laugh at the pun while dabbing their glistening foreheads.

"So Huey, tell us more about these strange vibes you mentioned," Claudia urges, "perhaps there's some weight to your theory of being wrongfully accused."

"Hmm...like I said I don't remember much about my mortal life. The only knowledge I have comes from dreams and dejá vu, so it's not entirely reliable. I don't want to bore you with the dreams, they're kind of personal anyway, but the dejá vu has some real substance to it I think. Each instance is one piece of the puzzle, and if I'm lucky and they keep occurring, then eventually I'll have the complete picture."

"OK, and what pieces do you have so far?" Claudia asks.

"Well, not too long ago there was a black cat. It looked at me funny, like it knew me from the life before and pitied me." Hubert is interrupted by a synchronized burst of laughter.

"Maybe you were a witch," suggests Lawrence.

"A black cat? Come on, Huey, what a cliché," Claudia adds.

"I know, I know. But then there was the black squirrel I've told you about. We shared a moment. I was staring into his eyes and there was a vast world of knowledge in there. Answers to the mysteries of my mortal life. But Professor Gramble killed him before I could delve into the information."

"Sorry, Huey, but this sounds like a bunch of crock," Lawrence declares.

"Now hold on a minute, Lawrence. Maybe there's some validity to what Huey is saying. They could be messengers. Angels in disguise sent by God to offer guidance," Claudia counters.

"Well, I think they're relics from the life before. But angels, yeah, I guess that's possible too," Hubert submits.

"Angels? Relics? Dejá vu? I can't believe I'm hearing this nonsense," exclaims Lawrence, throwing his hands in the air to embellish his consternation.

"Lawrence, honey, look around you. Is anything really beyond belief?" Claudia questions, rhetorically. Lawrence opens his mouth to retort, wavers, and remains silent. "Exactly, I think we need to hear Huey out." She turns to Hubert. "We should meet on the outside, Huey. Where do you sit in the cafeteria? We would love to hear more about this, and about you in general."

"Let's see...do you know where the biker gangs sit, by the Grecian pillar?" replies Hubert.

"Yes."

"I sit eight tables from there, directly back from the kitchen. You'll see an older black man with me, James Jenkins, he's a long-time resident and trusted friend. You'll like him."

"Look forward to it."

"As do I," Lawrence confirms.

Their pleasantries are cut short by the arrival of a tentacled, kraken-like creature and a Helldog. Lawrence and Claudia, seemingly by rote, move away from the door and back into the shadows. Hubert follows them. The tentacled creature takes a ring of keys from its utility belt, sifts through the collection, and inserts the "Miscellaneous" one into the lock pad. The heavy steel door creaks open, and the Helldog rushes in, followed by its tentacled master, who restrains the overzealous mutt with a telepathic leash.

"Hubert Raymer. Which one of you fiends is Hubert Raymer? Step forward," requests the tentacled creature in an executive tone. Hubert retreats a little farther toward the back of the cell before his friends urge him to cooperate with an affirmative nod.

"I'm Hubert Raymer," Hubert announces, stepping out of the shadows.

The Helldog gnashes and growls at him, but is held firmly in place by the mental grip of its master. This kraken figure better not have a lapse in concentration, Hubert thinks, his well-being at the mercy of a magical, pseudo-scientific, and thus fallible concept. Many times Hubert has theorized the minion/Helldog telepathic bond is a hoax; a feigned display used to inspire reverence for Satan's mastery in dumbstruck Hellions.

Satan the great charlatan.

"Come with me, Hubert Raymer," says the tentacled creature. Hubert shillyshallies, still not trusting the Helldog and its mode of control. "Carry on, if you go peacefully there will be no need for the hound."

Hubert gives in and leaves the cell, bidding Lawrence and Claudia farewell with a suppressed wave. He is ushered down the long line of jail cells by the tentacled creature and its Helldog. The forlorn faces of Hellion convicts protrude from each cell as Hubert and his marshals pass by. Some beckon to the kraken; others snicker and jeer at Hubert. They eventually reach the end of the hallway, which is partitioned by a large, windowless, riveted steel door. The tentacled creature brushes Hubert aside and sifts through the key ring. Hubert subtly rolls his eyes, unable to understand why the dullard must do this. *Have the key ready when you reach the door!* The tentacled blockhead produces the right key, inserts it, turns it clockwise, and pulls the massive door open with a trace of effort. Hubert goes through first, at the minion's request, and is met by an ovular lobby with several small rooms and offices occupying the circumference. It isn't any more inviting than the cell block. Everything is uniformly concrete and steel, even the scant furnishings. The one point of accent is the fountain that stands in the middle of the room, which spouts lava from the mouth of a sculpture of Lucifer. Hubert is taken aback by the thing, mostly because it is made from a mysterious blue mineral that can withstand the magma.

"That one, over there," the tentacled creature says in monotone, pointing across the lobby at an office door. They walk toward the office and Hubert stops midway to admire the fountain.

"Stop your rubbernecking, sinner. Carry on," the minion demands in a raised, but still moderate voice. He makes a vaguely threatening face at Hubert, and then looks at the Helldog, intimating that he will sick the hound on Hubert if he doesn't get moving.

Hubert continues walking to the specified office, and when he gets close enough he can read "Sentence Processing" on the half-open door. The tentacled creature pushes the door back into the rubber door stopper and he and Hubert enter. The Helldog is left outside.

"Name please," the Hellion secretary asks without looking up from her daytimer and logbook. So this is where the sycophants end up for duty call, Hubert tells himself.

"Hubert Raymer, ma'am."

"Raymer, Hubert. Let's see..." the lackey flips through the logbook to "R" and runs down the page with her finger.

Outside, the Helldog wanders over to the fountain and laps up mouthfuls of lava. Hubert sees this out of the corner of his eye, and leans to the side to get a better view through the opening of the door.

"Hey! Pay attention, wretch!" the kraken shouts, finally losing his modicum of calmness. Hubert shudders in response to the uncharacteristic outburst and returns his attention to the secretary. She finds his listing at last.

"Raymer, Hubert. OK, Mr. Raymer, for the offense of assaulting a member of Satan's faculty, first degree, and verbal insubordination, second degree, your penalty is two hundred hours of manual labor at a pyramid site in the desert."

"Is that fair? I've never been through this before," Hubert rebuts, but before the secretary can say anything he is whisked away by the tentacled creature.

Justice in Hell: no Miranda rights, no due process, no trial, *no mercy.*

Chapter 7

Hubert is being led out into the desert on a carriage drawn by two pale horses and driven by another tentacled, kraken-like creature. It is furiously hot and bright, and the conditions are made worse than they have to be by the carriage not having a cover. Hubert squints and shields his eyes with his hands. There is nothing on the horizon but sand. Occasionally a gust of wind emerges, flinging sand into Hubert's eyes and mouth. He curses the elements, and the two pale horses bray and rear up in response.

After traveling many miles over the course of many days, the pyramid site finally appears over the horizon. Hubert rejoices, despite the hard work that lies ahead. He will be grateful just for getting off the carriage and away from the horses' shrill braying. When they reach the outskirts of the construction zone, Hubert realizes the project is being directed by outer space aliens. Maybe all those wild 'ancient astronaut' theories are right, after all, Hubert considers. The tentacled creature stops the carriage, and an alien foreman with a clipboard greets them. Hubert identifies the alien foreman as a Grey – a small, grey-skinned humanoid with a large head and large, almond-shaped black eyes – the type made famous for allegedly crash landing at Roswell. The Grey and the kraken converse in a bizarre language that sounds like pig Latin. Hubert eavesdrops, but cannot make sense of any of it. He wonders why they don't communicate via telepathy; surely the aliens are advanced enough, so why the goofy dialect? They wrap up the conversation and the Grey approaches Hubert.

"Welcome to site 558D, earthling. You're going to be a chiseler, come with me," the alien says in an unfitting deep baritone.

Hubert enthusiastically hops off the carriage, and says goodbye to the tentacled creature and the pale horses with a disingenuous smile. The foreman leads him through the construction zone. There are several ten-foot-high mixing barrels producing mortar. The finished mortar runs down a long metal chute, and a number of Hellions bearing wheelbarrows scurry back and forth from the mortar chutes to the base of the pyramid. Hubert passes by a few large holes in the ground with Hellions still digging at the bottom, heaving clumps of sandy dirt into the sunlight. Another contingent with wheelbarrows loads from the pile of displaced sediment, and runs their wheelbarrows across the work zone, disappearing behind a corner of the pyramid. At the base of the pyramid there is an array of pulleys and derricks set up to move the huge stone blocks into place. Hubert tries to watch a group of Hellions in the process of the lofty undertaking, but the Grey hurries him on.

"You needn't bother yourself with that. You'll be spending the entirety of your sentence here as a chiseler."

Hubert grunts in disappointment and follows the alien around the corner of the pyramid. Upon turning the corner, he hears a loud snap and a piercing scream, and decides he is thankful the foreman whisked him away from the magnificent, but hazardous production. They walk another fifty yards or so away from the second edge of the pyramid and stop at a pile of rectangular slate tablets.

"This is your work station, earthling Hubert. For ten hours a day over the next twenty days you will be chiseling hieroglyphs into these slate tablets," the alien proclaims.

"But I have no experience as a chiseler," Hubert protests. "I'm far from being a handyman."

"Not a problem. All it requires is a steady hand and close adherence to these instructions." The Grey hands Hubert a thin booklet, and he begins browsing the pages.

"What if I botch something? Some of these look complicated."

"I'm confident you won't, otherwise I wouldn't have selected you for this job. But be sure that you don't, because that slate comes from a long way away, and if you waste any it will be your responsibility to trek to the source and get more. Let that be an added incentive."

"*Added* incentive? What were the others?"

"Why, to finish your assignment and get out of this torrid desert, of course. You earthlings, I'll never understand why you put up with such environments. One day my people will have to return to your dimension and precipitate the development of terraforming." The foreman turns and begins to walk away, but stops and raises a hand in recollection of something. "I almost forgot, your chisel and hammer, earthling Hubert." He takes the tools from his work belt and tosses them simultaneously to Hubert, who drops the instructions to free up his hands, and catches the tools with uncharacteristic competence. "See, off to a good start already. Good luck."

Hubert looks at the pile of tablets, then at the chisel and hammer in his hands. He reaches down for the instructions and a question occurs to him.

"Mr. Foreman, hold on a minute..." but when Hubert looks up the alien is gone. Hadn't it only been a few seconds? – teleportation – Hubert reasons.

He returns his attention to the instructions. There are at least three hundred different hieroglyphs, and the booklet doesn't specify which ones Hubert, specifically, should make. He guesses they're ordered sequentially by importance, and turns to the first page. The first hieroglyph listed isn't too complex: a scarab beetle, a rectangle, and a few curvy lines. Hubert grabs the tablet on the top of the pile, puts its bottom end into the sand, and leans it upright against the rest. He then kneels in front of the canvas, places the instruction booklet at his side, and juggles the chisel and hammer in his hands, getting a bearing for their weight and feel. He raises the chisel to the rock with his left hand, and is about to strike his first cut into the surface with the hammer, when it occurs to him he should make a few practice lines on the back. No one will notice, he hopes, and if they do they will understand his desire to fine-tune his craft. He flips the slate to the other side, glances at the instructions, and jabs out a rough impression of the beetle. Leaning back, he nods in approval of his work, then turns the slate back over, prepared to create a masterpiece.

The first piece goes well for Hubert Raymer, Hell's newly-commissioned hieroglyph draftsman. The beetle's back, right leg is a tad longer than the back, left leg, and there is a nick near the bottom edge of the panel where Hubert had dropped the chisel, but other than those two minor errors, the hieroglyph is an exact copy of the one in the instructions.

Hubert proceeds to the next picture in the booklet, which is a little more involved than the first: a papyrus leaf, a goddess figure, two vertical lines, and one curved line that resembles a shepherd's crook. He contemplates what the images mean, wishing the instructions included an explanation of each hieroglyph, or at least a deciphering key. After a couple minutes of deliberation, he decides their meanings are not important; he's here to chisel ancient nonsense into rocks, no questions asked, and that's what he's going to do. But, Hubert can't ignore the familiar feeling that the hieroglyphs are relevant to his mortal life. He suppresses the intimation, crediting it to the desert heat, and moves forward with his work.

By the time dusk creeps in on site 558D, Hubert has produced three six-foot high stacks of completed tablets. The alien foreman appears, and Hubert, chiseling away like a man possessed, sees him in his periphery, but doesn't look up. He is almost done his 100th hieroglyph of the day – an eye of Horus, three reeves, an eagle, and two "T" lines – and he wants to avoid distraction.

"My, my, that's a prolific assemblage you have there, earthling Hubert. And all in your first day's work, I'm impressed. You can relent now, the ten hours is up," the Grey comments. Hubert punches the final touches into the slate before responding.

"I appreciate the praise, Mr. Foreman," Hubert begins to ask what the hieroglyphs mean, but remembers his compromise, and changes course, "so what do I do now? I mean, until my next shift starts?"

"You're free to do as you please. Just make sure you report for duty at 0900 hours tomorrow. I advise you don't roam too far, it gets pretty cold out here at night."

"I wasn't planning on going anywhere anyway, but thanks for the warning."

"You're welcome, earthling. I'll check in on you tomorrow, have a good night."

"You too, Mr. Foreman."

Hubert watches the alien depart, hoping to catch him teleporting, but the Grey walks away in a pedestrian fashion, passing behind the pyramid and out of sight. He must only do it when he knows no one is watching, Hubert concludes, disappointed.

As the final aperture of daylight shrinks into darkness, Hubert lies on his back and looks up at the night sky. He has never seen the sky so black and the stars so crisp in relief, at least not to his knowledge. It doesn't look real. For a long, contemplative moment, Hubert absorbs the unreal beauty, tracing constellations and scanning for meteor showers, until a thought occurs to him that spoils the fun. It doesn't look real because it isn't real; it's an optical illusion; another one of

Satan's tricks; a cheap distraction to try to make you forget where you are, what you've done to get here, and the eternity you have to spend thinking about it. This realization makes it difficult for Hubert to sleep, and the disturbance is compacted by the frigid nighttime air. He stirs and shivers until dawn.

At 0900 a horn signals the commencement of the daytime shift. Hubert doesn't see the alien foreman, but begins his work anyhow. It isn't beyond the realm of possibility that the Grey is omnipotent, or omnipresent, or omniscient, or all three, and Hubert doesn't want to get caught slacking off on the job. Hubert eases into the first tablet, his nerves racked by the fretfulness of the night, but by the third tablet he gains the proficient rhythm and pace of the second leg of the previous workday. When the alien checks on him at the end of his shift, the stacks of finished hieroglyphs are slightly higher than the first ones. The foreman duly praises the yield.

Day 3: After sleeping significantly better than the night before, an energized Hubert almost matches the combined total from the first two days: six six-foot high stacks. The Grey inspects the stones and shakes his head in astonishment.

"You're a natural, earthling Hubert. Keep it up and you might set a record," the alien posits.

Day 7: Hubert continues at the breakneck rate his foreman has come to expect from him. A camel gets spooked by something and runs rampant through the construction zone, breaking several pieces of equipment and injuring Hellions in the process. Hubert sees his first meteor shower right after sundown.

Day 13: A solitary vulture circles above site 558D. Hubert is beginning to notice a repetitive motif in the hieroglyphs. The acquaintanceship of the first day returns, and this time he cannot subdue it.

Day 16: The original vulture is joined by several others. They pluck at the dead bodies of Hellions who have been defeated by heat exhaustion and dehydration. Hubert fears he is not far off from that misfortune, and in his near-delirium chisels one misshapen icon after another into the slates. In the mid-afternoon, he stands up to stretch his limbs, topples over, and takes the day's stacks of completed hieroglyphs with him. A handful of the tablets crack, and Hubert passes out next to the rubble. At dusk, the alien foreman performs his routine check, and seeing his prized pony passed out beside a smorgasbord of damaged and bungled hieroglyphs, covers his mouth in bemusement, and then covers Hubert in a blanket to let him sleep off the fatigue.

In the morning, Hubert wakes up to the 0900 horn, and at first cannot remember his surroundings. He looks at the partially-built pyramid and spattering of contraptions and feels displaced, as if Satan had suddenly dropped him there for kicks. However, his memory is immediately restored when he rolls over into the stone wreckage. His heart sinks, his stomach dances nauseously, and his throat lumps up. He wants to cry out to relieve the tension, but he knows it would be considered uncouth by anyone who happened to hear. Instead, he pounds his fists into the sand and releases a series of intense, salivary grunts. During the tantrum, Hubert sees the Grey approaching, stands, and tries to assume a semblance of composure.

"Mr. Foreman, I can't explain it. Vultures overhead, scarab beetles and squiggly lines, the heat! I'm really sorry," Hubert exclaims, fighting back tears.

"It's OK, earthling Hubert. It happens to the best laborers all the time. Unfortunately, you're going to have to replace those tablets," the alien affirms with palpable regret. "But look how much I've done! And I still have four shifts left. I can still set the record, even after this setback." "I'm sorry, the rules are the rules. If I had the authority to amend them, I would. Until then, you must hike to the slate quarry and gather replacements. Here is a map to guide you." The Grey holds out the map. Hubert takes it and his hand falls forcefully to his side, like the map was made of lead. "I suggest you make haste. Again, I'm sorry things are the way they are." The alien foreman puts a consolatory hand on Hubert's shoulder, sighs, and walks away. "Darned Luciferian bureaucracy," he grumbles on his way to an adjacent work station. He doesn't intend for Hubert to hear this, but Hubert does. If there is any hope in Hell, and any chance of attaining a non-Hellion ally, it's with that (space) man there, Hubert thinks.

Hubert opens the map, pinpoints his destination, and starts walking north. The sand makes it a laborious affair. In less than ten minutes, Hubert's calves and ankles ache, and his chest heaves with short, heavy pants. He looks back to whence he came, expecting to have put some distance between himself and the work camp, but he can clearly see the pyramid and derricks, and can even make out moving Hellion silhouettes. This makes Hubert apprehensive, not because he has gained so little ground, but because the others can still see *him*. In order to rectify the problem, he runs up and down the next three dunes, stumbling and rolling down a portion of each descent. Completely spent, he crawls to the top of the fourth dune and rechecks the view. The pyramid remains, foreshortened by the newly added yardage, but no Hellions are distinguishable. 'That's better,' Hubert says to himself, awash with relief. He struts down the backside of the dune, whistling as he goes.

For the rest of the day, Hubert trudges on at a decent pace, stopping occasionally to look back at his progress. At some point in the late-afternoon, 1600 by Hubert's estimate, the pyramid is no longer visible on the horizon. Hubert considers this a major achievement, and opens the map to approximate his position. He believes he has covered about one-third of the eleven-mile trip. Seven and a third to go, Hubert thinks. Then, of course, the long journey back. Hubert fantasizes about a taxi waiting for him at the quarry.

Satan & Minions Cab Co.: Serving the Hellion Community Since the Beginning of Time.

When night sets in Hubert decides to rest. As much as he would like to keep going, the inherent dangers of traveling in darkness are best worth avoiding. He could easily stumble upon a scorpion or viper, and a sting or bite would be the first thing to inform him of the fact. Plus, at night the most reliable navigation tool is the stars, and Hubert's knowledge of the stars isn't thorough enough to ensure he won't get lost. He can find the North Star, but if he happens to lose it, then what? All the other stars and constellations he's familiar with are significant only as far as their names and their beauty. Best to hunker down until the old home star rises. Hubert tucks the map into his burlap clothes, wriggles his bare arms and legs into the sand, and drifts away to dreamland.

He sleeps better than he ever has since coming to the desert, even better than the time he passed out. His slumber lasts well past sunrise, when he is at last disturbed by the brightness of mid-morning. Hubert yawns, shimmies his arms and legs free from the sand, gets to his knees, then to his feet, and removes the map from inside his coveralls. He runs his index finger along the worn paper, calibrating and envisioning the route. After doing this several times, he looks up from the map, and by judging the sun's height above the horizon, determines the departure time for the second leg of his expedition is 0930.

By day's end Hubert has yet to arrive at the slate quarry. Frustrated, he carries on past sundown, determined to reach his target before midnight, thus preventing his travel time from trickling over into a third day. Much to his dismay, it trickles well into a third day, and by dawn Hubert still hasn't made it to the quarry. He obsessively examines the map every five minutes or so, and by noon he's convinced the alien foreman gave him a faulty map. Perhaps the slate quarry doesn't exist at all, Hubert considers with dread. Perhaps this is a drill to test his commitment, or rather a sick practical joke to test his psychological reserve. Whatever the case, Hubert is sullen and marches on, kicking up divots of sand with each step.

At two o' clock Hubert is nearing heat exhaustion, and worse yet, hasn't seen a hint of the quarry. Sweat streams down his face and drips onto his burlap sack, which has become a shade darker from the sweat emanating from his torso. His vision is marred by sweat running into his eyes, causing him to blink at an accelerated rate and rub his eyes repeatedly with the backs of his thumbs. The temperature is above the average 120° F Satan fastidiously maintains. Hubert sees dense, wavy refraction lines above the surface of the sand, and at times, the heat shimmers appear to rise up infinitely into the sky.

With the refraction effect growing more intense by the moment, Hubert hauls up another dune and stops on its peak, disbelieving what he sees a few hundred yards yonder – the pyramid site, 558D – it must be a mirage, Hubert repeatedly tells himself in a panic, waving his hands in front of his eyes, expecting the image to be wiped away. It remains, clearer than before, while the heat lines thicken around it in three-hundred-sixty degrees, creating the impression of a tunnel. Hubert yowls and tries to exit the tunnel by taking a step back. The illusion follows, Hubert retreats another step, loses his footing, and tumbles to the bottom of the dune. He lies on his back looking at the clear blue sky. The swirling tunnel is no more, but that trip is immediately replaced by a true mirage as the sky transforms into a pool of water filled with floating, bobbing hieroglyphs.

Hubert rebounds from the mirage in the early evening, and lying on his back looking at the darkening sky, replaying the experience in his head, qualifies it as an affirmative and final case of dejá vu. He was an archaeologist in his mortal life who specialized in Ancient Egypt, thus the latent familiarity with the hieroglyphs, and maybe even his precociousness as a chiseler. The iconography that kept repeating itself depicted redemption and resurrection. This is it, Hubert realizes, the last piece of the puzzle. He is now convinced he was wrongfully sent to Hell, and is determined to plead his case to Satan as soon as it can be arranged.

Chapter 8

"That's malarkey, Huey."

James is having a hard time believing Hubert's account of his whereabouts and doings over the last three-plus weeks. He had no problem with the jail part, for he has been to Hell's prison, but the outer space aliens, and the hieroglyphs, and the vultures, and now the mirage and its implications. Not likely.

"Let me spell it out for you, buddy. I-KNOW-I-AM-NOT-SUP-POSED-TO-BE-HERE," Hubert continues.

"Man, if I had a dollar for every time ya said that," James replies, practically to himself.

"Except this time I *know*."

"Sure ya do. So what happened after this mirage? Ya ever find the quarry?"

"Yeah, but first I went back to the pyramid and found Mr. Foreman..."

"Don't all them space men look the same? How'd ya single him out?"

"...Because they're not all Greys, for starters. Some were Reptilians, basically big, green lizards, others were Nordics, tall, pale, human-looking folks, and then there were some wild ones I thought existed only in the imaginations of Hollywood screenwriters and sci-fi authors. I could pick out Mr. Foreman from the other Greys because he was the only one, so far as I could tell, who carried a ball-peen hammer. Union rules I guess."

"Wow, them union cats don't mess around, even on other planets."

"Apparently not. When I found Mr. Foreman I told him I couldn't find the quarry. He was disappointed, but true to his character, willing to help. I showed him the map and explained my course. Turns out, I misread the scale and the quarry was farther than I thought. I had the direction right, but like I said, obviously I veered off at some point on the second day and circled around the pyramid. Mr. Foreman gave me a compass and an odometer and sent me on my way. It took three days to get there and I could only carry back one chunk of slate. It was heavy and I ended up dragging it most of the way. When I got back, the foreman must have figured it was in the best interest of the project to expedite the process, so he gave me a camel and a sled. 'Now we're in business,' he told me."

"You ain't ever ridden a *horse* before, Huey, let alone a camel. How'd ya manage that?"

"I don't know, it comes natural. The foreman gave me a quick tutorial and it caught on. They say camels are stubborn, which is true if the camel I had is any indication, but you have to counter that by being even more stubborn."

"Fight fire with fire, huh."

"Right. There were a few hiccups here and there, like the camel would stop every so often and root around in the sand, probably looking for bugs to eat, but we got along OK. In one trip we carried enough slate to replace the deficit at a surplus. Then I did the four days of work I owed and they sent for a carriage to take me, uh, home."

"And now here ya are, master chiseler and former archaeologist."

"It would appear so."

"Well, I'll grant ya most of the story, but it's gonna take more than a mirage and some mummy epitaphs to convince me of what you've convinced yaself."

Hubert glimpses over James' shoulder and sees Lawrence and Claudia standing by one of the biker gang tables, trays in hand, looking about their surroundings. They must be looking for me, Hubert thinks, and he waves once, twice, and the third time draws their attention. They smile, tilt their trays up in lieu of a wave, and walk over to Hubert and James.

"Hi, Huey. What a relief, this is the fourth meal where we've gone looking for you. We were afraid we'd never find you," Claudia explains. She sits down next to Hubert, patting him on the shoulder, and Lawrence sits down next to James, who leers disapprovingly at the older white man.

"That's because this is my first time here since returning from the desert. I was sentenced to two hundred hours of manual labor there. How convenient of you guys to show up, by the way, I was just telling James here about my adventures over the last few weeks, and now, James, here are two vital components of those adventures in the flesh. Claudia, this is James. James, this is Claudia."

"Nice to finally meet you, James. I've heard you're a wonderful man and a loyal friend," Claudia says, daintily extending her hand to shake James'.

"And I've heard you like to party; my kinda lady. Good to meet you," James responds with a wink. He goes to kiss Claudia on the hand, but she pulls her hand away before recognizing his intentions.

"You'll get used to him," claims Hubert, "Lawrence, that there is James. James, Lawrence."

"Great to make your acquaintance, James," says Lawrence. He shakes James' hand with enthusiasm, but is met with dispassion.

"Yeah, sure is. How much ya think it's worth, my acquaintance?" James drolly asks.

"I beg your pardon?"

"What's the market value of a brother like myself's acquaintance? Adjusted for inflation."

"I don't think I follow you, James."

"Uh-huh. Yer a real slickster, Lawrence. I'm on to ya." James wags his finger at Lawrence and returns to eating his lunch, french fries, of course. Lawrence shifts around in his seat, not sure how to take James' unfriendly reaction to him.

"Forgive him, Lawrence. He's grown a little paranoid over the years. Why don't you guys tell James about our time in jail? It appears my word alone isn't credible enough," says Hubert.

"Sure," Claudia volunteers, "there are eight cells down there all lined up in a row, and the three of us were in the eighth cell for miscellaneous offenses. The first seven are for each of the deadly sins..."

"I know what it's like," James interrupts, raising his left hand, palm out, while continuing to work on the plate of fries with his right hand, "I've been there, probably more than the three of ya combined. What I wanna know is if any of these shenanigans about the desert are true, but ya'll can't answer that 'cause ya'll weren't there."

"On the contrary, James, I've been there, done manual labor there," Lawrence declares. "You were at one of the pyramids, Huey, is that right?"

"Yes."

"And there were extraterrestrial beings overseeing the construction, Greys, Nordics, Reptilians, and some insect-like ones who seemed less advanced, but not to be meddled with..."

"Correct." Hubert raises his eyebrows at James.

"And there were elaborate pulley systems and giant derricks to move the stone blocks into place, and big holes in the ground where sediment had been removed..."

"That's right."

"And there were Hellions running around with wheelbarrows, and ten-foot high mixing barrels for mortar, and camels hauling one thing or another, and a blast horn..."

"Exactly. You convinced yet, old buddy?" Hubert asks James, who chews and swallows another mouthful of fries.

"It seems to check out," James replies. He turns to Lawrence, narrowing his eyes again. "What was your work assignment there?"

"I was one of the mortar runners; the ones responsible for wheelbarrowing mortar from the mixing barrels to the base of the pyramid. It was the toughest job on site, a lot of backache and anaerobic burn. I must have sweated off fifteen pounds in the ten days I was there," proclaims Lawrence.

"Karma, that's what that was. Ya got a little taste of yer own," says James, nodding his head several times.

"Oh, now I understand your cryptic allusions. Huey must have told you about my former life. Well, sir, judge not lest you be judged first. What did you do to end up here? Lie? Murder? Rape? Steal? The Dark Lord regards all sins as equal. Am I not equal to you?"

James humphs and looks down at his plate. The man is right, he admits to himself. He uses a fry to smear the dollop of ketchup left on the plate in a sinusoid from edge to edge. The essence of nature. Beautiful. Simple. Not like me, the funnyman drug addict with spousal issues, James reminisces. Always out for attention and approval. Always out to prove them wrong, to stick it to the man. But man, when I got on that stage I killed 'em. Had 'em in stitches. God needs to get a sense of humor. He send everybody to Hell for tellin' jokes? Humor is a virtue and laughter is a cure-all. Heaven should welcome me with open arms, at least let me moonlight with a clean act for all the straights. Naw, forget it, not worth compromising my artistic integrity, even for the Almighty. James sighs and peels away from the ketchup cosine wave and his daydream.

"Yeah, Lawrence. Ya got a good point. It was profanity and blasphemy that did me in though. Along with some hedonism and infidelity. A lot of drugs and prostitutes.

One time I got so high I saw God, he said, 'My son, what are you doing in this dirty hotel room with all these lowly women? You're rich, my son. If you're going to violate all that's right and holy, at least go to the Four Seasons and hire some classy broads. This is no way to live...'"

"Alright, old buddy. We get the picture," Hubert interjects. Facing Claudia, he says, "Party animal, this guy was. But he has a penchant for embellishing his stories. Either that or his memory is fuzzy from the drugs."

"Not true. I'm sharp as a tack," James disputes. He leans over the table toward Claudia. "You see, the embellishment, that's part of my craft. I was a stand-up comedian in the time before, and a very successful one at that. Used to fill three thousand seat theaters, even did a couple arenas. Whole arenas, howling at my jokes and chanting my name." He rocks back and addresses Lawrence, nudging him in the ribs, "And the ladies, they *really* chanted my name, ya know what I mean?"

"Yes, you mean while in the act of coitus, I presume?" Lawrence replies, trying not for Claudia to hear.

"Ya got that right, brotha." They high-five and chuckle.

"I had a few damsels chanting my name in the time before. They used to call me 'Mighty Hickory.' Some of them could have been your great-great-grandmother." James scowls at Lawrence, then bursts out laughing.

"Man, I misjudged ya, Lawrence. Yer alright."

"You guys find some common ground over there? Mind filling us in on all the excitement?" Claudia asks, suspending her conversation with Hubert.

"Oh, it's nothing worth mentioning. We were just talking about old friends," says Lawrence.

"That's right, no one you guys would know," James adds, winking at Lawrence. "Hey Huey, how about ya tell Lawrence and Claudia about yer latest epiphany? Maybe they can convince ya to give up these fantasies about not belonging, 'cause I sure never have any luck."

"OK, remember I told you guys about dejá vu and how each episode is like a piece to the puzzle of my mortal life?" Lawrence and Claudia nod and lean toward Hubert, intrigued. "I saw the final piece: a mirage out in the desert. I was an archaeologist who specialized in Ancient Egypt. A plain, wholesome, dutiful scientist. I *know* I was wrongfully sent here, and I'm going to set things straight."

"What do you mean 'set things straight'?" Lawrence inquires.

"I'm going to present my case to Satan and demand a transfer to Heaven," Hubert asserts, dignified. James slaps his hands on the table and cries out in disbelief.

"Ya lost yer marbles, Huey. A *transfer* to Heaven? That's lunacy," James exclaims. "It's that desert heat talking, residual effects from that desert heat."

"Thanks for the vote of confidence, pal." Hubert presents James an obscene hand gesture. "Lawrence, Claudia, do I have any support here?" Lawrence and Claudia look at each other, searching for the right words.

"I don't know, Huey. I think you're wasting your time," Claudia submits. "I thought there was some truth to your claims when you first told us about them, and I still do, but maybe James is right and it's best you give it up."

"Hellion Survival Rule Number One," says James.

"Right, whatever that means. You might have been wrongfully sent here, Huey, and that's awful, but I've never heard of anyone getting a personal meeting with Satan. And a transfer to Heaven? Come on, even if there *was* an administrative mistake or something and you belong in

Heaven, you have to admit that sounds a little batty," Claudia continues. Hubert frowns.

"No, I have to admit I'm a little disappointed, Claudia. I thought you would be in my corner on this one, but I guess I misread your pity for genuine sympathy back in the jail cell," Hubert professes.

"Now hold your horses, folks. Claudia, what you've heard about the implausibility of meeting with Satan isn't entirely true. Yes, Satan has never scheduled personal meetings with Hellions, but I have heard of Hellions committing offenses so vile they were sent to Satan's office to be punished by The Dark Lord personally," says Lawrence. Hubert and Claudia's eyes widen, while James knits his eyebrows. "Huey, if you are willing to risk it, then you could at least be granted Satan's presence. Then, who knows, he might hear you out."

"This sounds apocryphal, but I'll entertain it fer my good friend's sake. What kinda dastardly deeds would Hubert need to engage in ta earn a trip ta the principal's office?" James asks.

"Yeah, I'm willing to do anything, but if assaulting a professor only warranted a handful of community service, then I can only begin to imagine how far I would have to go to wind up in the Devil's lair," observes Hubert.

"And that is precisely the challenge we face, for I've never heard what any of these alleged offenses were, only that they were bawdy enough to achieve the end you're seeking. We must use our imaginations," Lawrence avouches.

"I imagine this going terribly wrong for Huey, but since this is important to him, I'll join James in entertaining the notion. We know streaking won't make the cut, so we can file that under 'insufficient' along with assaulting a minion," says Claudia.

Nudity and violence, not thorough, Hubert notes. The four friends sit in silence for a few minutes to have individual brainstorming sessions. Hubert taps his fingers on the table and stares absentmindedly at the fake wood surface. Claudia twirls her hair. Lawrence crosses his arms and closes his eyes meditatively for ten second intervals, with five seconds of open eyes spaced between. James plants his chin on the palm of his right hand and yawns several times. He's gonna end up with a 'corporeal regeneration' for this, James thinks, won't look like Huey no more, prob'ly a Frank, or a Joe, or an Al. For some reason, picturing Hubert as Frank, Joe, and Al sparks a creative flare in James' funnyman right hemisphere. He lifts his chin from his hand and snaps his fingers.

"I got it! What does Satan hate more than anything?"

Chapter 9

The four friends depart from the cafeteria following a lengthy discussion about Satan's peeves. With James' initial suggestions in mind, Hubert sets out to do something so heinous he will be sent to Satan's office, where he will attempt to delay what would inevitably be the harshest punishment of his Hellion career by trying to convince Satan he deserves a clean slate and admittance to Heaven. Bonkers. Completely bonkers, but Hubert has nothing to lose and all the time to not lose it. He figures he might as well spend part of that time doing something crazy which, if successful, will leave a mark on the place.

(The indelible mark of the Beast).

Hubert's first stop is Professor Gramble's classroom. He arrives punctually, about which the professor is visibly disappointed, and sits in the front row, directly in the middle. Today is a special day, even more special than the day of the black squirrel, and Hubert wants to be front and center to optimize the view for his audience. It's "Monday," and on this "Monday" the class will be studying the Koran instead of the Bible.

For the majority of Hell's existence, only the Bible, Old and New Testaments, was studied in Satan's classrooms. But with the rise of Islamic fundamentalism in the second half of the twentieth century, Satan had to introduce the Koran to the religious curriculum to accommodate the explosion of the Muslim Hellion population. The texts of the Eastern Religions have not yet been implemented, not because there are no Buddhists, Taoists, Hindus, etc. in Hell, but because the Devil doesn't find these religions punitive enough to suit his purposes. No fire and brimstone. It confounds him that Eastern Religion produces so many ascetics.

Professor Gramble distributes Korans to his pupils, then goes to the chalkboard, places his copy on the chalk holder, open to about one-third of the way through, and begins writing notes under the heading, "Muhammad's Moral Conscience." Hubert leans from one side to the other, trying to see around Mr. Gramble, a broad-shouldered being, even for a minotaur, to get a clearer view of the content of the ensuing lecture. Best to get a head start on the class, impress old bull face there, get his guard down, then spring my distasteful prank on the lot of them, Hubert thinks. His chair creaks as he leans a little too far, straining the rickety legs and rusty screws, the class murmurs as Hubert checks his balance with his hand, and the minotaur professor turns to inspect the noise, but is too late, finding Hubert sitting straight up, eyes ahead and hands folded on his desk. Real smart alack, that one, not the ripest potato in the sack, the professor tells himself, masking a scoff with a cough while returning to his notes.

After lecturing for most of the class period, pushing his students to the brink of catatonia, the blowhard minotaur professor finally opens a discourse by asking, "Is there a moral conflict between Muhammad, the prophet, and Muhammad, the warrior?" An uncomfortable silence follows, as per usual, and as per usual, Professor Gramble does his signature toe tap. Hubert carefully constructs a response in his head, rehearses it once, word for word, and raises his hand.

"Yes, Mr. Raymer, what light can you shed on this dilemma?"

"As I see it, there is no moral conflict between being both a religious prophet, a disseminator of the word of God, and a warrior, an enforcer of the word of God. Muhammad was compelled by messages from God to engage in armed conflict, and he often consulted the Koran in justifying military expeditions, particularly with his raids of Mecca. Just because Jesus was a pacifist doesn't mean all prophets need to 'turn the other cheek.' Muhammad was more 'an eye for an eye,' and I don't think there's a dilemma with that."

"Mmm, good reasoning, Mr. Raymer. Apparently, you've been paying closer attention than I thought. Do we agree with Mr. Raymer's assertion or does someone hold a different view?"

Another awkward silence. Hubert's classmates shrug their shoulders and tilt their heads. Some turn the pages in their Korans and run their index fingers through the text. Most look down at their laps or at the floor on either side of their desks. Hubert wishes someone would say something, anything, even if it trumps his response. Bunch of nimrods, Hubert thinks, can't they see I'm trying to run a gag here? He unconsciously begins tapping his toes along with Professor Gramble. Finally, a young man near the back speaks up.

"'An eye for an eye leaves the whole world blind.' Isn't that right?" Inane drivel is not what Hubert was wishing for. He sighs.

"It is, Mr. Olivier. I'm sure many of you can relate to that social code and its repercussions. Your rebuttal, Mr. Raymer?" asks the minotaur professor.

"Oh, well, uh, I don't think that really warrants a rebuttal. It does nothing to detract from my argument. I never defended Muhammad's violent inclinations, I just said they don't conflict with his status as a prophet. God is heavy-handed, why shouldn't his prophets be? Seems congruent to me," Hubert posits.

"And perhaps it is, Mr. Raymer. What do you think, Mr. Olivier? Does God's contempt merit a similar temperament in his prophets? Or is the path Jesus walked the right and only way?" Professor Gramble, professional moderator, inquires.

"'I am the way, and the truth, and the life. No one comes to the Father except through me.' John 14:6," Olivier recites.

"'I am the Light of the world; he who follows me will not walk in the darkness, but will have the Light of life.' John 8:12," says another of Hubert's classmates.

"'With whom did He consult and who gave Him understanding? And who taught Him in the path of justice and taught Him knowledge and informed Him of the way of understanding?' Isaiah 40:14," quotes another. Hubert throws his hands into the air and turns around to face the entire class.

"I'm sorry, am I supposed to answer that? What is wrong with you people? Are you not capable of producing independent thoughts? All you can do is sit there and proselytize?" Hubert waits for a response, but is met with sullen expressions. "I meant for you to answer that!" He turns back around to direct his indignation at the professor. "And *you*, I can't believe you condone this vapid twaddle, even encourage it!"

"You better choose your words very wisely, Mr. Raymer," warns Professor Gramble.

"Oh, phooey. It's miraculous they allow you to teach here, let alone give you tenure. It's supposed to be Koran day, we're supposed to be discussing the moral conscience of Muhammad, and they're quoting the Bible and touting Jesus. Chri-...I mean, golly, let Jesus alone for one lecture!" Hubert has worked himself into a frenzy; not part of his original plan, but an improvement anyhow. He stands up on his chair. Ranting from a soapbox.

"Crap! It's crap I tell ya, an insult to Islam. You might as well go ahead and do this..."

Every jaw in the classroom drops as Hubert squats over the Koran on his desk, hikes up his burlap sack, and defecates on the sacred text. The gentleman sitting next to

Hubert turns away in disgust, dry heaving and gagging. Someone in the back cackles and a small contingent, led by Olivier and the two other evangelists, applaud Hubert's symbolic anti-Muslim bowel movement. They have either missed the point of it being an indictment on them, or they simply don't care and enjoy the sight of a soiled Koran. Professor Gramble moves swiftly to his desk, procures the whip, and shuffles back to the front of the class, positioning himself at optimal striking range for Hubert's exposed derriere. The minotaur professor allows Hubert to finish his business, not wanting to generate an unnecessary mess, and lets it rip, catching Hubert on his bare rump with the first lash before he covers up in burlap. Nine more lashes follow and no further punishment ensues.

Satan doesn't hate human bodily functions nearly as much as James theorized.

Disappointed, Hubert moves on to the next idea. Needs more shock value, more obscenity, more *sinfulness*, Hubert thinks. First, he rendezvouses with James, Claudia, and Lawrence in the cafeteria for a recap of the "Koran scatological experiment," as James dubbed it at their previous meal. Hubert's dejection is apparent as he sits down at the table.

"Based on the look on your face and your mere presence, I gather the plan didn't go too well," Lawrence deduces.

"Darn skippy it didn't. Ten lashes of the whip. A lousy ten lashes," says Hubert. He faces James, who sits next to him munching on yet another plate of fries. "Despite your unshakable confidence in it, your plan was a complete dud. Care to offer an explanation?" James continues chewing the fries, swallows, and clears his throat.

"Maybe yer doo-doos aren't repulsive enough; not sufficient for tha call of duty. Or maybe yer professor doesn't care for Islam as much as some of tha others," James responds.

"Yeah Huey, ever since the 'kufi riots' I've noticed a considerable upturn in Islamaphobia among the minions," asserts Claudia.

"As have I," Lawrence concurs.

"OK, regardless of the reason – excuses really – I sure hope the next plan is more fruitful," says Hubert, rubbing his temples. "Old buddy, how about you enlighten us with the details again, I could use a refresher."

"And so could yer classroom," James quips, causing Lawrence and Claudia to chuckle against their will. Hubert is unimpressed. "Oh come on, Huey. Ya catch my pun about the 'call of duty'? Ya know, like *dootie*." James runs his hand under his nose to indicate something foul-smelling. Hubert fights off a smile, but breaks after a few seconds.

"Alright, that was a pretty good one. Now get serious and recount your next brilliant experiment."

After listening to James outline the plan and trace it out with his fingers on the table, Hubert says goodbye to his friends and sets out to shock another room full of Hellions, and hopefully arouse the fury of the Prince of Darkness. Hubert walks out of the cafeteria into the tumult of the hub and goes right. He hurries along the expansive hallway for a few minutes doing his usual bob and weave and enters a radial corridor with pacifying, light blue lighting. The pleasant effects of the lighting, however, are offset by the unbearable humidity of the corridor, which intensifies as Hubert travels farther down the passageway and makes the itch of his burlap clothes maddening instead of merely bothersome. Eventually the hike brings Hubert to one of several doors which read "Bathhouse." Steam pours out from the sliver of space underneath the door, thickening and dampening the already soupy air. Hubert turns the dewy, glistening doorknob and ventures into the warm, foggy white yonder.

The bathhouse resembles the archetypical Roman bathhouse of the ancient empire, albeit with modern amenities. There are a number of pillars delineating an ovular central space, the atrium, where several Hellions socialize with towels around their waists. The atrium is surrounded by a rectangular portico covered in porcelain tiles. The side opposite the main entrance is where the communal shower is located, the side to the left is the hot bath, and the side to the right is the cold bath. Hubert walks across the moist tiled floor to the communal shower with small, gingerly steps to avoid a humiliating slip and fall. A werewolf guard greets him at the open doorway with a gruff, "Welcome, sinner," and hands him a towel.

The communal shower is squarish and large; much larger than any shower Hubert had ever seen in his mortal life, but about average for Hell's many communal showers. According to various Hellions, the huge showers in American prisons are not nearly as spacious as Hell's smallest ones. Reflecting on that alleged fact makes Hubert uneasy. He stands in the threshold of the muggy room, thinking of Hell as the biggest, baddest prison imaginable with showers that could accommodate a Roman legion. And what happens in prison showers? Or Roman showers for that matter? The guard might not even hear Hubert scream, maybe just hear the echo bouncing off the ceramic walls from a hundred yards away. Hubert tries to imagine something else as he sizes up the other bathers, all men. Better at least make it someone decent-looking, he thinks. There's a relatively handsome 20-something with an open shower head next to him, and Hubert sashays over to claim the spot, doing his best alpha male impression on the way. No one pays particular attention to him and Hubert doesn't know whether to be relieved or disappointed.

A shower in Hell is an exceedingly rare treat and a privilege, one Hubert has never taken for granted. As he turns the lever past the 'H' on the dial until it stops, and hot water rushes out of the shower head in a glorious, conical cascade, he quietly thanks an anonymous, unseen force for the occasion. Hubert steps into the spray for a second until his nervous system recognizes it as too hot; he yelps and jumps back from the water, drawing the attention of a few bathers in his immediate area, including the young man next to him, whom he accidentally brushes against in his instinctive jolt.

"Pardon me, hotter than I expected," Hubert remarks with a sheepish grin. The young man shrugs it off, barely interrupting the process of shampooing his hair.

Hubert moves back to the perimeter of the scorching spray and turns the lever about an inch back toward 'C.' After a few seconds, he can feel the water cooling in the air around him and he double checks with an outreached palm. Better, he decides, and tentatively steps under the shower head. As the water drenches his uniquely-thinning hair, Hubert squeezes a dollop of shampoo into his hand from the dispenser above the temperature dial. He lathers and rinses his head, then begins washing his body with handful after handful from the soap dispenser. Hubert whistles a popular soul song James has recited many times.

Although he told himself he would waste little time in accomplishing what he came for, Hubert cannot squander the opportunity to indulge in a full-blown shower experience. More precisely, his nerves are getting the best of him and he's looking for an outlet through the reassuring bathing routine. However, the lengthy shower only creates a catch-22: the longer Hubert waits the more concerned he becomes that the young man will leave before he takes action. The young man has finished washing and has been standing under the shower for several minutes, simply procrastinating. Hubert knows he could turn off the water and depart any second now. Time to move, Hubert thinks, *get moving jello legs!* He takes a deep breath and taps the gentleman on the shoulder.

"Geeeeaaahhhkk!"

The stranger lets out a repulsed squeal as Hubert grabs him by the shoulders and tries to kiss him on the lips. He cranes his neck and reels his torso back and forth, reflexively countering each of Hubert's movements.

Every action creates an equal and opposite reaction.

To the other Hellions in the communal shower, they appear to be engaged in an unusual dance. If Hubert's intentions were more clear, they'd see it as a mating ritual. A few onlookers step away from their stalls to get a closer look. The wet porcelain tiles soon prove an ill-suited surface for the shuffle and scuffle, and Hubert and the young man tumble to the floor, eliciting enraptured gasps from the other bathers. Fortunately for Hubert, he ends up on top of his resistant make-out target. With a resolute thrust of the neck and shoulders, he at last plants a slobbery kiss on the young man's lips. More gasps, but this time with a palpable note of disgust.

"Hey, what's all the fuss about down there?" shouts the werewolf guard from the entryway. He is only a dark silhouette behind a curtain of steam. The silhouette gradually enlarges as the werewolf lumbers toward the gathered Hellions.

The young man squirms under Hubert's weight, and Hubert, awaiting the arrival of the werewolf, relinquishes for a moment. His victim spits and splutters, propelling barely distinguishable bursts of saliva into the dank air. He wipes his mouth multiple times with the back of his hand.

"What the heck, man! You perv, you freak, what do you think this is?!" the young man cows. Hubert rears back, peeps the werewolf nearby and lances forward one last time. He lands a culminating smooch just in time for the minion to witness.

All Hell breaks loose.

Hubert pushes the young man into the floor with domineering delight. The poor sap's sturdy, fleshy lats squish into the floor, sending a sheen of hot shower water out in a heart-shaped mass, like fluid butterfly wings. The young man kicks viciously. Hubert presses his hand into the stranger's face and twists with equal viciousness. Two onlookers spring onto the fray and try to separate the two combatants. Bodies collide, limbs sprawl out in jerky spasms, better consciences do not prevail.

"Halt, fiends, stop this right now!" the werewolf guard commands.

In an instant, Hubert ceases all movement. He raises his hands in a sign of surrender and spreads himself out over the slick ceramic floor. Exhaustion surrounds and besieges Hubert. He pants triumphantly.

"OK, you got me Mr. Werewolf," Hubert confesses.

"Pissant, sinner, imp, what took place here? Stand and face me," charges the hairy sentry.

Hubert clambers to his feet and assumes a proud, contumacious stance. The werewolf guard is on him in a flash, forfeiting no reaction time. They skid across the wet floor like two pucks on a shuffle board court. Much rowdier and consequential than your everyday shuffle board match, of course; a grown human man and a grown, hirsute, half-man, half-canine leviathan. They bounce off one of the walls, deadening their momentum, and come to a stop. The werewolf hops up and pins Hubert to the floor with a clawed foot. Hubert grabs the werewolf by the ankle and tries to uproot the foot, but finds it's like trying to remove a stop sign from its cement base. He pants defeatedly. The werewolf howls and globs of hot drool fall onto Hubert's chest and neck.

"I'm...done...spent...finished. You can take your clodhopper off me now," says Hubert, struggling for oxygen. The guard disregards him and howls again. "Hey, beast! Did you hear me? Stop howling, you're drooling all over me!"

"Tough luck, fiend. Now you know how it feels to be on the receiving end of that sexual assault you just committed," the werewolf coldly replies.

Hubert is glad to hear the guard saw enough to deem it 'sexual assault,' harsh as it sounds for a messy kiss or two. 'Public display of affection' was all Hubert was going for, and he would protest the misapplication of 'sexual assault' had it not played in his favor on this particular occasion. The werewolf guard howls once more and shortly thereafter two demons arrive at the scene to assist him.

"Werewolf brother, how can we be of service to you?" asks one of the demons.

"Demon brothers, thank you for your prompt response. This Hellion kissed another bather on the lips. I will not tolerate this kind of behavior in my bathhouse. Get him out of my sight," requests the werewolf.

"Will do, brother. What should we do with him? What is his punishment?" the second demon inquires.

"I don't care. Take him to the jail and let the officers sort it out."

And sort it out they did, but not to Hubert's liking: six weeks' banishment from all the bathhouses and permanent banishment from the bathhouse where the incident took place.

Satan doesn't hate human displays of affection nearly as much as James theorized. Not even those of the homosexual variety. Disappointed once more, Hubert moves on to the third idea. This one takes place in the cafeteria, which encourages Hubert because he will have the moral support of his friends. Hopefully they will offer their tactical support as well. The four Hellion compatriots gather at their usual table. James, Lawrence, and Claudia forgo the formality of asking Hubert about the "Bathhouse PDA experiment"; his presence alone says enough. James delves right into the logistics of the current task, drawing things out with his fingers on the tabletop.

"...And with the biker gang tables right over there, we have a distinct strategic advantage. We hit them first, covertly, they react with indiscriminate outrage, targeting everyone in sight, and it snowballs from there. Before you know it, we're responsible for a full-scale riot and Hubert gets his long-awaited and well-earned trip to the principal's office," James explicates.

"Sounds great, but I think I'm gonna have to end it with flair. The first two plans failed because they lacked punctuation. This plan needs a finishing touch, something extreme the minions won't forget," says Hubert.

"Like what, Huey?" asks Claudia. Hubert pauses to think it over. His eyes widen with self-satisfaction.

"Let's just say I'm gonna stick it to the man."

After finalizing the arrangements, Hubert, James, Claudia, and Lawrence fan out around the biker gang tables, lunch trays in hand. There is enough commotion around them to camouflage their movements into position. One of them stands on each side of the three-table rectangular area which forms the biker gang domain; Hubert across from James, and Claudia across from Lawrence. James snags a handful of fries off his plate, wags his head twice, and on the third wag a synchronized attack commences. James launches his fries at the middle table, Hubert throws a half-eaten ham and cheese sandwich at the same spot, Claudia hurls an unpeeled orange at the near end table, and Lawrence lobs a bowl of oatmeal – grenade style – at the end table on his side.

The attack results in numerous casualties, particularly due to Claudia and Lawrence's munitions. Claudia's orange bursts upon contact with a biker's chest, spraying citric acid into his eyes and those of the men sitting on each side of him. Lawrence's bowl of oatmeal indeed has the effects of a grenade, projecting bits of oatmeal shrapnel in a semi-circle which lodge themselves in several beards, speckling bristly black masses with gooey beige dots.

As James predicted, the bikers begin lashing out at everyone remotely close to ground zero, while the instigating foursome slinks back to their table. Once there, they proceed to empty their trays, flinging food in every direction, but primarily toward the bikers. Hubert cannot believe the density of airborne edibles whizzing around them, like a swarm of locusts overtaking a savannah, blotting out the sun. The cafeteria does, in fact, appear to be darker. A wad of rice pudding hits Hubert in the forehead and trickles down his face. He catches some of it with his tongue before it reaches his chin and drops to the floor. Tasty armament, Hubert thinks.

It isn't long before James, Hubert, Lawrence, and Claudia clear their trays. Gluttony is the reason many Hellions are Hellions to begin with, and Satan puts a weight limit on the cafeteria fare: one pound per tray per Hellion per meal. With their one pound of firepower expended, the four friends are left vulnerable and begin searching for reserves. Hubert salvages items from the floor, only to find them ineffectual due to the damage incurred from their first use.

"Push left, folks! There are some abandoned trays a few tables over," James hollers, signaling for them to move left. "Stay low! Use the tables fer cover." At this moment, Hubert imagines James as a soldier in the time before, an inspiring and adept military leader.

The foursome pushes left, staying low and threading between Hellions who are variously standing, crouching, kneeling, and prone, like actual soldiers assuming ideal firing positions. James is doing a military crawl. Lieutenant, Hubert decides. Lieutenant James Jenkins, decorated combat veteran. They reach the designated table and the food cache, but not before Lawrence is doused with hot chicken noodle soup. Fortunately, most of it hits his burlap coverall. The rest splashes his arms, hands, and neck, causing him to call out in pain. Bright red spots crop up on the exposed skin and Lawrence wets his fingers with saliva and massages them. Claudia soothingly blows on the afflicted areas.

No ice packs in Hell.

SCRAAAAAAAAAWWW! While the four companions go to work at their new station, a Hellbird sounds the alarm. This screech, however, doesn't signal the end of the meal period. It has a slightly different tone – more bass – a distress call. Streams of demon guards file into the cafeteria from the multiple entrances. They are dressed in riot gear similar to that worn by human police. Some of the guards have megaphones.

"Hellion scum, disperse or prepare for defensive measures."

"Drop the food and return to your seats."

Hubert and his friends have no intention of cooperating, and instead hurl their next deployment at the nearest cluster of guards. The guards block most of it with their shields, but a branch of grapes eludes their cover and bashes one of the guards in the face. James, responsible for the direct hit, pumps his fists and lets out a celebratory yell. Hubert, Lawrence, and Claudia give him high-fives. The guards pick out the festive attackers from the surrounding riff-raff and close in on them in seconds.

"Here we go fellas, death before dishonor," says James as the guards descend on them, raising their billy clubs.

The other three want to tell James they're already dead, but decide it's a moot point. Claudia and Lawrence assume boxing stances, holding their lead hands out in anticipation of parrying the billy clubs. Hubert grabs a plastic fork and knife from the table. He holds the knife with a reverse grip and slashes at the air. The demon guards bull rush them. Bones crack and bodies crumple to the ground as the guards lash out with their billy clubs. The four felled friends lie on the floor clutching various body parts and moaning in pain.

"Resisting was a mistake," grumbles Lawrence, holding his knee, "I think my kneecap is fractured."

"That's right, sinner. Resistance is futile. Now get up, all of you! You're under arrest for disorderly conduct and assaulting a minion," shouts one of the demon guards. Hubert hides the fork and knife in the cups of his hands.

They do as they're told and stand tall before their captors, except Lawrence who stands cockeyed, favoring his inflamed right knee, which has already swollen to the size of a grapefruit. He places a hand on Hubert's shoulder to further relieve the discomfort. The guard who was struck by the grapes sees Lawrence's mangled knee, and with a demented grin, reaches out with his billy club and applies a moderately forceful, but pernicious tap to the feeble area. Lawrence folds over like a lawn chair, screaming and cursing whilst clasping his knee with both hands. He falls on his back with his leg bent over his torso, and holds his knee to his chest as if he's stretching his glutes.

Hubert turns to help his friend, but quickly redirects his attention to his first priority. *Panache, something they won't forget.* He wields the fork and knife and lunges at the guard who salted Lawrence's wound. He pokes and slashes with reckless abandon, but the plastic utensils inflict little damage. The serrated knife actually leaves marks, although it cannot break the demon's skin, while the fork pitifully bends back with each impact. The minion seems to be enjoying the transaction. He allows Hubert to carry on with his quaint roguery until it becomes boring.

"OK, pagan. Give up the cutlery before you poke an eye out," the demon insists. "One of *your* eyes, that is."

The request may as well have never been posed. Hubert knows compliance is no way to land yourself in Satan's office; insubordination is the name of the game. He continues poking and slashing, determined to make the guard, ideally guards, physically restrain him.

"Look, brothers, this little bugger is hellbent on skewering me," the demon announces to his partners. "I'm not gonna ask you again, knave, give me the cutlery."

"When you pry it from my cold, dead fingers, you sadistic thug!" shouts Hubert.

"That's how it's gonna be, huh?" asks the demon, turning to the other minions. "You hear that, brothers? Let's pry away."

It only takes two of them to extract the fork and knife, although Hubert achieves a significant consolation in poking each of them in the eye with the fork before they are able to confiscate it. That suffices for panache, Hubert tells himself as he's being dragged out of the cafeteria, a demon hoisting him under each armpit, like bouncers do with a disruptive drunk. James, Lawrence, and Claudia cheer, whistle, and clap for him, as do many other Hellions. The last thing Hubert sees as he's pulled through the obsidian doorway is a wave of demon guards and a crest of raised billy clubs converging on his exultant contingent of admirers, including his best friends.

Heroism comes at a high price.

This act of heroism isn't heroic enough to earn an appointment with Satan. Instead, Hubert has to eat glass at every meal for two weeks, a cruel and unusual punishment, but one he supposes fits the crime.

"What does a man have to do around here to get sent to the Devil's office?" Hubert wonders aloud at the cafeteria table one day, conservatively chewing several shards of glass. In a sense, it's a rhetorical question.

"Plan X, Huey. Time to implement Plan X, bust out the big guns," says James with a gleam in his eye.

"Yeah, I was afraid it would come to this. Desperate times call for desperate measures."

"Darn skippy, but this measure ain't desperate, it's foolproof and downright cold-blooded."

"That's what I'm afraid of, chief. I might get a whole lot more than I bargained for. Isn't that why we reserved Plan X as the last possible resort?"

"Naw, Huey. We just saved the best for last. It don't get worse than a trip to the boss' office. That's why ya never hear about it happenin'."

"He's right, Huey. The worst you're up against is the preferred outcome," Claudia assures.

"I concur. Our combined experiences have likely covered the spectrum of corporeal and psychological punishment. Take a look at yourself, Huey, you're eating glass for supper for goodness sake. You can withstand a meeting with Satan, and whatever comes along with it,"

Lawrence proclaims. Hubert swallows a parcel of glass, rocks back in his seat, and leans back into the table.

"Alright, thanks for the vote of confidence, folks. James, hit me with the rundown," says Hubert.

With high hopes, Hubert sets out with James to do the most dastardly deed they and their friends can imagine. They go to the most isolated and secluded bathhouse they know of – one that is typically scarcely occupied – and James enters the communal shower while Hubert waits by the utility closet. James heads to the last shower head, turns it on, waits for the water to get hot, then does a pratfall and wails in pretend pain. The werewolf guard pokes his head around the open entryway, and unable to see the origin of the bawls through the steam, begins walking down the row of shower heads to investigate.

Hubert opens the utility closet, takes out a bucket, and closes the door. He hustles to the entryway of the shower room, checks to make sure the werewolf is out of sight, and tiptoes to the first shower head. He turns the dial about halfway and lays the bucket on the floor under the spray. James' cries grow louder just in time to cover up the drumming of water on plastic. For someone who has been here for so long, James has a good sense of time, Hubert thinks as the water rises to the brim. He shuts off the shower, picks up the bucket, and shuffles out of the bathhouse into the radial corridor on the outside.

After walking a few hundred feet of empty corridor, Hubert approaches his unsuspecting victim. The Helldog sits on its haunches with its back turned to Hubert, who sidesteps against the wall to remain as stealthy as possible. He creeps up behind the Helldog undetected and raises the bucket to his hip with both hands, one gripping the brim and the other on the bottom edge. He can feel his heartbeat in his throat as he rocks the bucket back and swings it forward, dispelling the contents in a continuous, globular body.

KSSSSSSTTTT.

The water drenches the Helldog from head to tail and splashes outward onto the floor, extinguishing the mutt's carapace of fire as it goes. The hound yelps, shrieks, and howls, and takes off down the corridor, a trail of smoke swelling up from its hindquarters. Hubert races to catch up. Eventually, he finds the Helldog curled up on the floor with a demon guard stooped over it attempting to comfort the canine. The Helldog is hairless and Hubert covers his mouth to muffle laughter. The once intimidating beast now looks small, pitiful, and ugly, lying on the floor shivering and whining.

"Fiend, are you responsible for this despicable act of animal cruelty?" the demon bellows, accusing more than asking.

"Yes I was," Hubert responds emphatically. "What are you gonna do, report my offense to PETA?"

"Silence! This is no time for sass and sarcasm." The demon grabs Hubert by the arm and pulls him forward. "You're coming with me, straight to Satan's office. He's gonna make you wish you had to deal with PETA."

The guard pats his thigh and whistles for the Helldog to follow. It grunts and tentatively joins them, cantering delicately at their heels. Hubert expects the dog to bark, growl, or snarl – hassle him in some way – but it carries along with its head down looking sorry for itself. Hubert begins to feel bad about what he has done, but then the palatial doors of Satan's office appear ahead and Hubert decides it doesn't matter how he feels about it. Time to face the music and find a way to work the instruments.

Chapter 10

They stand at the massive double doors of Satan's office. The doors rise at least twenty feet above the floor and are made of thick, knotless oak. The doorknobs are shaped like goat feet and made of solid gold with obsidian for the hooves. There is a torch on each side of the gold door frame about halfway up, ostensibly the source of the muted smell of oil in the air. At the top of the door frame is an orange neon sign reading "The Management." Hubert finds this tacky, but not unexpected enough to raise eyebrows. The demon guard presses a buzzer on the right door frame.

"Hello, this is the Devil Himself, state your business," replies Satan through the small speaker above the buzzer.

"My Lord, my Dark Lord the Vile, I have a dissenting Hellion here who just drenched one of your beloved Helldogs with a bucket of water. Hydrated him so bad he lost his hair," the demon explains.

"One of my Helldogs?! Bald you say?! At the hands of one of my residents?! By all means, enter," says Satan, peeved.

The demon pushes open the doors with ease, but Hubert believes there's some sort of automatic mechanism aiding him, hydraulic perhaps, to explain for the absence of noise. The room inside is magnificent, unlike anything Hubert has ever seen in Hell, not that he was expecting anything less. The floors are parquet, cherry and mahogany in a herringbone pattern, and a long, narrow Navajo rug runs through the center of the room. The ceiling is slightly higher than the doors and bowed and has three thick oak beams running across in either direction at equal intervals, creating sixteen perfectly square sections of cream sand plaster.

On the left side of the room is a large brick fireplace with a portrait of Satan above the mantel. There are two gargoyles on the mantel, one on each end. On the right side of the room is an identical brick fireplace, but it has a portrait of Satan in the form of Lucifer above the mantel. It too has two gargoyles on the mantel. A Hellcat naps on the granite outer hearth in the warmth of a crackling, heaving fire. Hubert thinks the image is rather comforting and out of place.

The walls of the office are adorned with many family portraits, and photographs of Satan in the company of various infamous celebrities: Ty Cobb, Genghis Khan, Mae West, Karl Marx, and other notable individuals who strayed from the righteous path. The family portraits, like the portraits above the fireplaces, are done in oil and impart a grace and elegance in the subject that reminds Hubert of Renaissance portraits of European royalty. There is a portrait of a Hellcat, presumably the one lying by the fireplace.

Satan loves his Hellpets like they are his children.

The Dark Lord sits at the back-center of the room behind a finely lacquered oak desk with gold inlay around the edges. A consigliere stands next to him and there's a Helldog on each side of the desk. In front of the desk is a red and gold Persian rug. Beyond the desk, composing most of the back wall of the room, is a large, multi-paned window. As Hubert approaches he can see the window overlooks the cafeteria. He cannot believe he'd never noticed it before. Perhaps the window is in an unfamiliar section of the canteen, somewhere far away from his usual table and territory.

"Loyal minion brother, please take the Helldog to the infirmary. I'll handle the Hellion cretin from here," says Satan to the demon.

"Yes master, as you wish," the demon answers, bowing his head. He and the Helldog leave the room. Hubert doesn't turn to watch them go. He's fixated on the window and the scene below.

"It uses a holographic camouflage to blend in with the surrounding rock. That's why you've never noticed it before," Satan assesses, turning ninety degrees in his swivel chair to look out the window with Hubert.

"Oh, that's crafty," Hubert blandly responds. Maybe my table *is* down there somewhere, he supposes. He conceives Satan spying on him at every meal with the telescope in the corner of the room.

"Yes, I like to think it is. I invented it myself. One of my many patents."

"I didn't know you were an inventor."

"There are a lot of things you don't know about me, sinner. Before you arrived here, you probably didn't even believe I exist."

"No, I suppose I didn't."

"Alright then, well I guess I did my job." The Devil turns the chair back to face Hubert directly. "And now you've made my job harder by making a pest of yourself," he says in a tone more of annoyance than anger.

"I would say I'm sorry, but..."

"But nothing, fiend." He raises a scaly, clawed maroon hand to silence Hubert. "You've gone and committed a crime that has never been committed before. With the Helldog that is. Now I'm faced with a conundrum because there's no precedent on which to base your punishment."

"That must be a terrible inconvenience."

"Imp, dare not patronize my master. When you speak, speak plainly and with the utmost respect or I'll cut out that sharp tongue of yours," hisses the consigliere, leaning across the desk in a threatening manner. Satan puts his hand on the underling's forearm to calm him.

"Easy Ginvoo. Let's not get overzealous." Ginvoo moves back to his master's side and gives Hubert an icy stare. "Yes, Mr. Raymer, it is a terrible inconvenience. I'll need some time to think of an appropriate punishment."

"Sir, before you do that I need to confess something I hope will redirect your course of action," Hubert exclaims. Satan raises his eyebrows and his triangular ears twitch. Ginvoo's stare becomes more condemning.

"An unusual request, but OK, what is your confession?" asks the Devil.

"I didn't throw water on that Helldog out of sheer malice. I did it in a calculated, premeditated attempt to be sent to your office, so I could stand here before you and make this confession." Hubert pauses and tries to read the expression on Satan's face. He appears interested, but as yet unmoved. "For the longest time, I had no recollection of my mortal life. I couldn't remember the person I was and what I had done to end up here."

"That doesn't make you special, Mr. Raymer. I call it 'heathen amnesia' – the selective overlooking of one's sinful ways – and it's quite common. Please, cut to the chase."

"You see, sir, I've recently been experiencing recurring epiphanies, dejá vu if you will, and I've come to remember the time before. I was a good man. A diligent archaeologist and an upstanding citizen. I believe I should be reevaluated for admittance to Heaven." Satan snorts.

"Mr. Raymer, I don't know how you think we do things around here, but that is completely out of the question. Never been done before. What do you expect me to do, try you before a jury of your peers? Once you're here, you're here." The Devil intertwines his fingers and props his goateed chin on his hands, waiting for a response.

"I understand, but I think you're overlooking the big picture here." Hubert takes a step closer and bends slightly over Satan's desk. "This has serious marketing and PR potential, sir. If you reconsider my status – not a jury, but you personally – and perhaps consult with God, it will make you seem merciful and Hell progressive." Satan takes his chin off his hands, shuffles his fingers, and wags his jaw.

"Hmm, merciful and progressive. I like that. It's a little soon for another renovation though."

"Not a renovation then, just a minor upgrade, a rejuvenation if you will. Think about it, 'Dark Lord the Merciful' and 'Hell Deux'." Hubert makes a scrolling motion with his hand above his head, indicating the heading on a billboard or digital sign.

"I'm not sure about 'Hell Deux,' but 'Dark Lord the Merciful' is good. Try it on me, Ginvoo."

"My Lord, my Dark Lord the Merciful," hisses the consigliere, bowing to his master.

"Tremendous!" cries Satan with a clap of the hands. "It suits me well and Jehovah will appreciate it, given His sensibilities."

"Exactly, sir. It will put the two of you on common ground, make it easier to work together," assures Hubert. "After all, it's a codependent relationship."

"Alright, sinner, I'll take you up on your offer," Satan pinches his chin between his thumb and forefinger, "but I can't guarantee your wish will be fulfilled. If what you say is true, it means God made a mistake, and he's stubborn as a mule in admitting to one, let alone reconciling the difference." He smiles, a wistful, almost regretful smile, and looks over at the Lucifer portrait. "We're very much alike in that regard, Jehovah and I."

"I believe it, sir, and I believe a reevaluation of my status will benefit both parties." Hubert takes a step back from the desk to his original spot. "Thank you, Dark Lord the Merciful, and good luck."

"You're welcome, Hellion. Don't get too giddy though. You have a comeuppance to face, remember? I'll go and talk to God, see if something can be done about your little situation. In the meantime, prepare for the worst punishment imaginable. Whatever becomes of this debacle, my Helldog's baldness will not be in vain."

"Yes, sir. I haven't forgotten."

"Good. You're dismissed."

Satan bids Hubert adieu with a flick of the wrist, and Ginvoo hisses at the sinner as he walks down the Navajo rug and out the doors. When the doors close behind him, Hubert pumps his fists and jumps and clicks his heels. This could be the beginning of something wonderful, Hubert thinks.

A small step for Hellion, a giant leap for Hellionkind.

Chapter 11

Once Hubert has left the office, Satan pushes himself away from his desk on the rolling swivel chair, rotates, dismounts, and strolls to the panoramic window. He puts his hands on his hips, purses his lips, and sighs. He looks down upon the cafeteria, which is empty aside from the cooks in the kitchen. Ginvoo appears at his side and appraises the scene below before addressing his master.

"What is on your mind, my Lord? This Raymer business is uncharted territory," says the ogreish confidante without shifting his eyes away from the window.

"Indeed it is, Ginvoo. You didn't protest during our conversation. I'm assuming you support my decision?" Satan queries, while also continuing to gander down yonder.

"Yes, master. I have my doubts, but I believe solidarity is important in the executive duties of your office, this case notwithstanding. I wouldn't allow the Hellion to impress dissent upon me and therefore doubt your authority." Ginvoo opens his head and shoulders to the Devil, who makes eye contact.

"Methodical as always, my loyal friend. Pray tell, what are your doubts?" The consigliere looks back out the window with a pensive expression.

"This is a Pandora's box situation, Lucifer. Once an exception is made for this Raymer fool, then a litany of similar plea bargains will come out of the woodwork." Ginvoo scratches his pale, scaly temple with the sharp fingernail of a pale, scaly forefinger. "I support your conferring with God on this, but if you move forward with the Hellion's requital it must remain a secret."

"Absolutely. If Jehovah and I decide to transfer Mr. Raymer, he will be a ghost. The other Hellions will forget he existed. Now, if you'll excuse me I'm going to attend to my affairs in the attic."

Satan leaves the window and pushes his chair back into the alcove of the desk. He opens one of the desk drawers and takes out a silver pocket watch. He holds the watch in the palm of his hand, checks the time, then removes a small, black, moleskin notebook from the drawer and records the time. He closes the drawer and walks across half the width of the room to the Lucifer fireplace and stands on the outer hearth, relishing the warmth on the soles of his hooves. The Hellcat mews, rises from its resting place, and winds between Satan's ankles, intermittently rubbing its head against his hooves and kneading its claws on his scaly maroon skin. The Devil doesn't seem to mind.

Satan the scratching post.

He bends down and scratches the Hellcat behind the ears and pats it on the top of the head. The blazing beast purrs, rolls on its side, and bats at Satan's hooves with its forepaws, trying to coax its master into a play session.

"Not now, Thermopylae. Time for a business trip. When I get back, though," Satan promises. He gives Thermopylae a reassuring pat on the belly and slides open the gold coal gate. Ginvoo approaches.

"Let me get your coat, master," utters the consigliere. He waddles to the coat rack next to the fireplace and removes a lone pea coat. "We don't want you catching a cold." Satan holds out his arms and Ginvoo pulls the coat sleeves over them.

"Excellent, Ginvoo. Thank you," says Satan as he buttons up the coat, "wish me luck." Ginvoo bows his head.

The Dark Lord steps through the gap in the gold coal gate and into the flames. He pulls a chain resembling a flue opener and his body begins to emit a bright white light. His effulgent figure slowly ascends the firebox into the flue and out of Ginvoo's sight.

Satan reappears in his stock form at the Pearly Gates, which rise up from the clouds and glisten in the sun in their gold and silver splendor. He sneezes and wipes the ash and soot from his coat. He shivers uncontrollably under the thick wool.

"I can't believe these saintly schmucks can spend eternity in this blistering cold," he mumbles through chattering teeth.

He scuffs along the clouds to the jamb at the center of the gates, takes hold of the door knocker, a white marble, silver-cased dove, and raps three times. A soft thunder resounds across the sky. Satan knocks again a little louder. God soon appears, walking out of the clouds on the other side of the gates. He undoes the latch and opens the gates for Satan, who steps into Heaven on uneasy, tremulous legs.

The eternal forces of good and evil greet each other, but there's no animosity. They're like former business partners who found greater success in their own endeavors. They walk side by side and engage in congenial conversation: health, family, work, earthbound news, things along those lines. There's a palpable skepticism underlying mutual respect. After about twenty minutes the conversation turns to locker room banter.

"Finally, I get her into bed and we're going at it rough. The headboard's banging against the wall and all that. She starts screaming, 'Oh God, oh Jesus, yes!' and I say, 'Honey, they don't have anything to do with this. It's just the worm and worm junior here,'" Satan exclaims. God chuckles.

"You call your package 'worm junior'? And I'm the source of its frustrations? You shouldn't be telling me this,

Lucifer. Tally up another point for the good guys," God responds.

"Since the dawn of man, countless women have said your name while reaching sexual climax. That's a compliment to their male partners; a comparison to divinity. You're the greatest whore in the history of time. Mere men are glad to be mentioned in the same class, but it digs at me."

"You'd prefer women to cry, 'Oh Satan' or 'Oh Lucifer'?"

"Absolutely."

"What about, 'Oh Worm' or 'Oh Horny Goat'?" Satan frowns.

"Now you're just being vulgar and cruel. That's not like you, Jehovah."

"You're right. I'm sorry, I got carried away." God extends His hand to Satan and seals the apology with a hearty handshake. "Now, to what do I owe the pleasure of your company? I can tell there's business on your mind, Lucifer. You didn't just come here to shoot the breeze."

"No, I didn't. Although that wouldn't be too bad of a way to spend the time. The breeze up here today is invigorating." Satan removes the top button on his pea coat, exposing a tuft of chest hair. "Ah, that's nice. I came to discuss the peculiar circumstances of one of my residents and propose a revolutionary change."

"Go on, you have my full attention."

"His name is Hubert Raymer. He was sent to me recently after having dumped a bucket of water on one of my Helldogs, permanently disfiguring the poor soul."

"Jiminy crickets, that's awful," God submits, holding His hand up to His mouth.

"Yes, quite possibly the worst offense ever committed by a Hellion. You know how I feel about my pets." God nods.

"It's never been done before and so when Hubert was sent to me for punishment, I found myself in a bind. I have no frame of reference, no standard operating procedure to determine his consequences."

"Perhaps Mr. Raymer understood the uniqueness of his crime and knew it would put you at odds."

"Without a doubt, because this resolute rapscallion took the opportunity of our meeting to eschew the topic of his punishment and tell me about a revelation of his. For the longest time, he couldn't remember much about the time before. He tells me repeated episodes of dejá vu have revealed to him that he lived a clean, honorable mortal life."

God narrows His eyes and draws His lips back on one side. "He was an archaeologist, something like that. He's positive he doesn't deserve to be in Hell and he wants us to reconsider his status. He thinks he should be transferred to Heaven."

God is silent and gazes off into the distant sky. His Almighty vision is acute enough for Him to see beyond Earth's atmosphere into outer space, where He beholds the stars and Venus despite it being the middle of the day. He thinks through all the residual effects of permitting a Hellion to join the ranks of Heavenites.

A Hellion in Paradise.

That sounds like a sitcom, God thinks. Not exactly the tone I want to set around here. The name 'Hubert Raymer' recalls a harmless man with a bizarre form of male pattern baldness. Despite His incertitude, He cannot refrain from sympathizing with Satan's subject. Compassion is a part of God's nature. He stops walking and looks down at the sandals on His feet. Satan stops next to Him and decides he might as well look down at his hooves until God shares His thoughts about the ordeal. The Dark Lord begins wishing he could wear sandals, and that maybe a pair could be customized to fit his hooves, when God finally speaks.

"You know, Lucifer, this is uncharted territory we're talking about."

"You're the second person who's said that today," says Satan, somewhat vexed.

"Good, I'm glad the magnitude of what we're dealing with is obvious." God resumes their stroll and Satan matches Him after taking another look at his hooves. On second thought, sandals aren't for me, he concludes. "Say, how did Mr. Raymer slip through the cracks?"

"I don't know, Jehovah. Our hands are full. He thinks there was an administrative mistake."

"Poppycock, that's never happened on my watch and never will."

"OK, well how else do you explain it?"

"I suppose it doesn't matter. I'm vaguely familiar with Hubert Raymer, unassuming fellow with weird eyebrows, and I second your impulse about him. You believe this man is earnest, and regardless of how a good man ended up where bad men burn for eternity, it would be a sin not to rectify the situation. Pardon my choice of words." Satan shrugs and makes a short, horizontal gesture with his hand.

"No offense taken. I'm happy to see you understand our moral obligation. I think this will be beneficial to both sides. You will be viewed as more liberal and Heaven more inclusive, and I will be viewed as more merciful and Hell more progressive."

God furrows His brow and considers Satan's words. He knew there would inevitably be a sales pitch attached to the proposal. As compassion is a part of His nature, self-aggrandizement is a part of the Devil's. He would be more skeptical about the transaction if Satan hadn't included a marketing angle. 'What's in it for me?' is probably the first question he asked Mr. Raymer, the Lord speculates. Moral obligation my left foot.

"I don't think bending the rules will benefit either side, Lucifer, only Mr. Raymer, which is how it should be. We want the impact of his reassessment to be as minimal as possible. A ripple in an ocean. Practically nonexistent. You understand?" God looks sternly at His counterpart.

"Yes, Jehovah. Prudence is a must. Ginvoo and I were having that very discussion before I came to see you."

"Well then lay those fantasies of reinventing ourselves and our kingdoms over this to rest. You can't have it both ways."

"I reckon you're right. What can I say, I got caught up in the moment." Satan grins a court jester's grin.

"That's alright. Send Mr. Raymer to me when you get back. I'd like to form my own opinion of him and then we'll see what can be done. Is there anything else?"

"No, not presently. I think your thermostat is broken though."

"I'll look into it."

God and Satan shake hands and Satan leaves in the direction of the Pearly Gates. God watches him, tail swaying on a four-'o-clock to eight-o'-clock path, until he vanishes over the top of a big cumulonimbus cloud. The sun appears from behind a smattering of gray clouds and live classical music plays somewhere in the background. God moves His hands to the tempo of the music like a conductor and heads toward the ruckus.

Chapter 12

Hubert lies on an orange sleeping pad in a gray tent. It is hot and humid, and the sun beats furiously on the nylon shell of the tent, giving the material an incandescent quality. The synthetic is translucent enough for Hubert to see flies fluttering about on the outside. He wishes he would've bought a black tent and dealt with the additional heat conduction; anything to not be rudely awakened by the intrusion of the morning sun, and then kept awake by the shadows and silhouettes of insects parading around the exterior of his sleeping quarters.

A loud yawn splits Hubert from his grumpy early morning thoughts. His wife, Janice, stirs next to him. She rubs her eyes, turns on her side, looks at Hubert, and smiles. He smiles back, but with less sincerity.

"Light wake you up again?" Janice asks.

"Yeah, I knew we should've bought a black tent."

"And then you would be woken up by a puddle of sweat. Come on, Huey, we agreed gray was the ideal compromise." Janice sits up and leans over and kisses Hubert on the cheek.

"Maybe I should go to bed earlier so I get a solid eight in before the sun rises." Hubert crawls to the door of the tent and unzips the flap. He squints as the tent fills with sunlight and looks back at Janice.

"Another ideal compromise," she says, turning away from the door and lying back down, "you're more adaptable than you give yourself credit for, honey."

"I'm going out to make coffee, you coming?"

"In a few minutes. Make two cups for me, please."

Hubert exits the tent and zips up the door flap from the outside. The tent is at the edge of a triangular glade surrounded by jungle. Before Hubert in the clearing is an ancient building complex, the Mayan city of Tikal in Guatemala. Three other tents and a portable canvas gazebo complete the rest of the campsite. Hubert, Janice, and their six colleagues obtained a permit from the Guatemalan government to work at the ruins for four weeks. Hubert is beginning to worry four weeks will not be enough. There is plenty of work yet to be done, and plenty of discoveries yet to be made. The team has had one breakthrough though, which they've been laboring over exclusively for the past two days: the remains of what they believe is one of Tikal's rulers. There are only fragments of the skull and an intact femur, but it appears the king was injured or killed by a jaguar based on puncture wounds seen on two of the skull fragments. Hubert is confident they'll find more of the body, as well as some related artifacts, given they abandon their other interests and focus on the doomed king for the remainder of the dig. Now is the time to convince the team, he thinks, as he pushes through the door flaps of the gazebo and greets three colleagues sitting at a foldout table.

"Good morning, fellas."

"Morning, Huey," they respond synchronously. Hubert goes straight to the coffee maker and dumps out the negligible amount of coffee left from the day's first pot.

"Hope no one wanted that," he snickers.

"No, but I'll have some of the pot you're about to make. Extra strong, please," says one of the archaeologists. "We all know Huey likes that wimpy brew. 'Extra strong' to him is 'regular' to us," the man whispers to his colleagues.

"I heard that, Jared. 'Extra strong' it is my friends."

Hubert starts the coffee maker and turns on the hot plate next to it. There is a miniature refrigerator and a plastic bin containing various kitchen wares under the table, from which he produces a carton of eggs and a small pan. He sets the eggs on the table and places the pan on the burner.

"Eggs anyone?"

"No thanks, I already ate," says one of them. A second shakes his head.

"I'll have three, please. Over-easy," requests Jared. He's the largest of the bunch – the largest of the entire team for what it's worth – built more like a rugby player than a scientist.

"Hollow-legged Jared over there. You've never missed a meal before, have you?" Hubert jokes. Jared smirks and the others chuckle.

"Heck, I've never missed seconds, nor an appetizer, nor a dessert, nor a snack. If ever I was presented with food, it's safe to assume I didn't miss the opportunity to consume it," Jared proudly avouches. Everyone chuckles.

"You sure you don't want four, then?" Hubert questions.

"Don't tempt me, Huey."

Hubert finishes the eggs, puts his scrambled ones in a bowl and Jared's over-easys on a plate, turns off the hot plate, and goes to sit at the table. He slides Jared's plate across the table to him and hands over a plastic fork. Jared takes a small bite as if testing them. He nods approvingly.

"Pretty good, thanks. Hot sauce?" he asks with his mouth full. Hubert slumps his shoulders, tilts his head, and glowers at him. "Just kidding, I'll get it myself." Jared gets up from the table, lumbers to the makeshift kitchen counter, and returns with a bottle of hot sauce.

"Better now?" asks Hubert.

Jared nods and smiles, his teeth littered with yellow and red wads. The rest of the table shake their heads in disgust. There is silence for a while as Hubert and Jared eat their breakfast and the other two scientists return to reading; one a scientific journal and the other *Hombres de Maíz* by local hero Miguel Ángel Asturias. Hubert eats slowly in order to buy time to figure out how to broach the subject of committing to the skeletal remains. No piece of cake here, he thinks nervously. Jared is about as enthusiastic about the bones as he is, but the other two are decidedly unmoved and have other projects to attend to, namely a hidden compartment in a burial chamber and a cache of spearheads. Hubert polishes off his eggs and goes to pour himself more coffee.

"Any more coffee, guys? Alex, Dan, time for another round?"

"No thanks," says Alex.

"Sure, just a small cup though," says Dan.

Hubert tops off his mug and fills a styrofoam cup for Dan. He serves Dan the coffee and sits back down, blowing loudly on his steaming cup of brew so as to distract Dan and Alex from their morning reading. His prodigious puffs send ripples across the surface of the coffee. Dan and Alex look up from their reading material at Hubert and frown. Jared winks at no one in particular, leans back in his seat, and crosses his arms.

"You could try putting an ice cube in there," Dan glibly suggests, rubbing his temples.

"Oh, I'm sorry, I didn't mean to create a stir. Ice is no good, it waters down the coffee," Hubert replies. Dan lays the scientific journal on his lap and Alex puts the novel on the table. Hubert eyeballs them and devises to introduce his resolution. "Now that I've got your attention, I was hoping we could discuss a work-related concern of mine."

"What is your concern, Huey?" Alex inquires.

"It's about the skeletal remains. The ruler. I'm afraid we're not going to have enough time to uncover whatever else might be accompanying him."

"There's not much we can do about that, aside from ask the government for an extension, and I don't particularly want to do the paperwork," Dan submits. "How about you guys?" He looks to Alex, who shakes his head and mouths 'No,' then to Jared who shrugs and points with his thumb to Hubert.

"I think there's an alternative. My suggestion is to withdraw from the other jobs and consolidate our energy and expertise on the ruler dig. We're literally scratching the surface of something big here, and I don't want to miss out on it because of time constraints."

Dan and Alex aren't in the least bit receptive to Hubert's design, considering it an affront to their findings, which to them are equally impressive and worthy of the team's devotion. Jared disagrees, siding with Hubert on account of the predation implications. Dan and Alex are pretty sure Jared is simply attracted to the blood and gore, or the irony of a Mesoamerican leader dying at the paws of his culture's most sacred and venerated animal.

The four men retrieve the rest of the team to help settle the gridlock at the breakfast table. Everyone decides to settle the issue by vote – majority rules. Hubert wins five votes to three. The individual who sides with Dan and Alex is the expedition's second woman, a doctoral student of Alex's who everyone suspects is bedding him, which not only makes Alex an adulterer to his wife of seventeen years, but a cradle robber as well: the student-lover is twenty-two years his junior.

Highly unprofessional.

They decide to spend one final day working on the multiple assignments before incorporating. Hubert, satisfied with the compromise, thanks his opposition for their good sportsmanship, and moves to a collection of suitcases at the back of the gazebo. He unlatches his suitcase, opens it, sifts through the contents, and removes an orange and green plaid shirt and a pair of worn blue jeans. He closes the suitcase, wishes his colleagues a good workday, and returns to his tent to change into his work clothes. While Hubert is hunched over and standing on one foot trying to slip into the second leg of the blue jeans, Janice flicks the door of the tent with her fingernails. Hubert starts and falls over. Slim chance he was a flamingo in a former life.

"Huey, I'm heading over to the site, you want me to wait up?"

"No, I'll be right behind you."

"OK, I have the tools."

Hubert watches Janice's shadow quickly shrink away as she leaves the tent. He grunts and wriggles into the jeans. He figures it's probably best to remain on his butt to put on his boots. He crab walks a few feet to the door of the tent and reaches out to grab the boots from beside the entryway. He shakes them out to make sure there aren't any scorpions or other creepy-crawlers napping inside. There are not, and Hubert throws on the boots, slinks out of the tent, zips up the door flap, and begins walking to the dig.

The remains are at the base of one of Tikal's several pyramids, originally buried under a foot of dirt. The location has mystified the archaeologists and inspired much conjectural discourse; usually Mayan rulers are buried in tombs inside pyramids or other monumental buildings. The reigning theory is tomb raiders sometime in the last couple hundred years removed the entire skeleton from its tomb under the temple, the escapade went awry, and the parts Hubert and the team have uncovered were left behind and subsequently interred by rain wash sediment.

When Hubert gets to the site Janice is carefully brushing the right orbital cavity, one of five skull fragments found so far. There's also the majority of the mandible, the right nasal bone, the right temporal bone, and the left half of the parietal bone. The latter two have the bite marks, one on the temporal and two on the parietal. The team, Hubert in particular, is languishing over not having found any teeth – of the human or cat variety. Hubert hopes to do so in the ensuing days with the entire team on the case. He stands next to Janice, on her knees and elbows in the dirt, and adoringly watches her doctor the orbit. Janice is much better at precision tasks than Hubert, who is encumbered by his large, clumsy, calloused man hands. He often tells himself he'd be a superior archaeologist if he had dainty lady hands. Then, of course, he wouldn't be able to do man things as well, like chop wood and repair cars. Hubert rubs the callouses on his right hand with his thumb and clears his throat.

"That might be the cleanest orbit of any man in Guatemala – living or dead," he chides. Janice brushes on.

"Oh, bug off. You know I'm meticulous about this stuff. Just wanna make sure we didn't miss any tiny nicks or scratches. Eyeballs could be a delicacy for jaguars," Janice remarks.

Hubert smiles and kneels down in the dirt beside his wife. He looks on in silence for many minutes, perhaps even an hour, and basks in the mid-morning sun. He remembers the sunscreen in his pants pocket, takes it out, and applies some to the back of his neck and his face. Then he rolls up the sleeves of his shirt and puts a thin coating on his forearms. He holds the bottle out to Janice, who peeks out of the corner of her eye and declines with a shake of the head.

After returning the sunscreen to his pocket, Hubert rises to his feet and circles around to the other side of the excavation, opposite Janice, who is now removing soil and rock aggregate from around the femur with her fingers. In sections of one-half square foot, Hubert examines the dig area looking for indications of where more material might lie, especially decorative accessories. Where are your flashy things? Hubert asks, staring interrogatively at the orbital cavity as if to siphon information from the spirit of the ancient ruler. He does a second sweep of the site, and finding nothing suggestive, rejoins Janice and helps her pick away the sediment enclosing the femur.

By lunchtime Hubert and Janice have successfully withdrawn the femur, fully intact and undamaged, and noted a puncture wound on the underside of the bone. They contentedly walk hand-in-hand to the gazebo to make some sandwiches and report the latest. The other team members are already grubbing away at peanut butter and jelly and cold cuts. Jared is double-fisting, a PB&J in one hand and a salami and cheese in the other. Hubert passes Jared on the way to the kitchen table and pounds his ravenous friend on the back, causing him to choke and spit out a hunk of partially chewed PB&J.

"Hey!" cries Jared.

"That should teach you not to eat like a slob," Hubert remarks.

"It won't."

Jared picks up the hunk, now with a few blades of grass added to the mix, and places it back in his mouth. Everyone either laughs, gags, or does both. Dan throws an apple at Jared which hits him in the shoulder and falls to the ground. Jared picks it up and puts it in his pocket.

"An apple a day..." he says, winking at Dan.

Hubert finishes preparing sandwiches for himself and Janice and sits with the team around the two folding tables. He eats about half the sandwich and then briefs his colleagues on the fourth bite mark. They agree with Hubert about the auspiciousness of the find, and he and Janice leave lunch feeling they've allayed the resistors and boosted team morale.

"Did you hear Alex? He said he was 'looking forward to checking it out,'" Janice exclaims as they amble along one of Tikal's causeways toward the excavation.

"Yeah, I think we're winning hearts and minds. We're like the U.S. military," Hubert quips. Janice soughs and nudges Hubert in the side with a fist.

They turn off the causeway and begin crossing the main plaza. There are several dozen tourists spread out on the grounds, gawking and taking photographs. Most are gathered around Tikal Temple I, the largest temple in Tikal and its main attraction. Hubert and Janice walk by the tourists to the side of the temple, where the ruler's remains lie in the shade of the rainforest about twenty feet from the base of the structure.

The husband-and-wife archaeological team get back to work as before, Janice brushing off the femur and Hubert scouring the dig looking for clues to the next find. He eventually starts digging three-inch deep holes with a spade, spaced six inches apart in a grid. When he finishes the site looks like it's been aerated, or prepped for spring gardening.

"Oh, I forgot the tulips and buttercups back at the campsite. Do you mind?" mocks Janice.

"Hilarious. This method works, you know. Mary Leakey used to do it. This is how they found Lucy."

"I thought it was an Indiana Jones technique."

"Don't make this any harder than it is. Mesoamerica is not my specialty, it's yours. It was your turn to pick the destination, so here we are. I could go back to the tent and take a nap, or spend the afternoon in the gazebo reading magazines, or go for a damned nature walk, but I'd rather be here helping you."

Janice glances up at Hubert with a petulant expression and quickly goes back to tending to the femur. Hubert shakes his head, sighs, and peers off into the jungle. Maybe a nature walk isn't such a bad idea, he thinks. Then he imagines all the nasty insects and snakes out there waiting for him. Hubert settles on a walk around the ruins.

"I'm going to check on the others," he tells his wife, and sets sail across the main plaza.

Hubert makes it back to the ruler dig shortly before quitting time, which was a predetermined decision. Janice is on one knee comparing the puncture wounds. She holds two skeletal fragments at a time, one in each hand, manipulates the bones to bring the puncture wounds close together, examines, sets the fossils down, writes a note on her yellow pad, and rotates the bones counterclockwise, swapping the one that had been on the ground for the one that had been in her left hand, and moving the one that had been in her right hand to her left hand. An entire rotation only takes her eight seconds on average. Hubert has tracked this over the many hours they've worked together. If museums had live performers, Janice would be the headliner.

'Janice the Amazing Fossil Juggler.'

"And you have the audacity to poke fun at my grid tactic when this is your shtick," says Hubert, assuming his spot standing next to Janice.

"We could join the traveling circus. Get one of those mobile labs." She puts down the skeletal remains, stands up, pats the dirt off her knees with her hands, and leans into Hubert to kiss him. He reciprocates. "I suppose it's time to close up shop." Hubert looks at the dwindling sun.

"Yep. Tomorrow we begin anew."

The couple gathers a tarp from beside the excavation and begins unraveling it over the area. They manage to cover most of the dig before Hubert has to maneuver to another corner of the tarp to pull on the slack. He ends up straddling the imprint of the femur and impulsively takes several looks at it. On the fourth glimpse he notices something shiny in the head of the femur relief, no more than a centimeter in diameter. He flings the tarp away from him and bends over to run his right index finger over the shiny thing. It's metallic, probably silver.

"Huey, what are you doing?" Janice asks from the far corner of the tarp.

Hubert holds up the same finger he used to touch the mystery metal and calls Janice over with a 'come hither' motion. She walks around the tarp and without saying anything sees what Hubert has been eyeballing and diddling.

"My goodness, how did we miss that?"

"I don't know, but let's see what it is."

Hubert scrapes the sediment away from the object with his fingers and in a few minutes its identity is revealed: a silver necklace pendant with none other than a jaguar tooth. Hubert and Janice slap five and giggle like schoolchildren. They take a good, long look at the charm, then Janice places it with the skeletal remains, covers them all with a cloth, and lends Hubert a hand in stretching the tarp over the remainder of the site.

That evening at dinner they tell their fellow scientists about the pendant. Jared proposes an interesting theory: the ruler was not attacked by a jaguar, but rather assaulted by another human, perhaps an aspiring usurper, with the jaguar tooth pendant. Alex and his doctoral student-lover bust out laughing and pound their fists on the table.

"What?! I'm serious. Either the antagonist used a loose jaguar tooth and the ruler survived the attack, and had the tooth made into a necklace charm as a reminder and symbol of his sovereignty. Or the ruler already wore the pendant and the mutineer snatched it from his neck, fatally wounded him with it, and buried him with the very item that killed him, cursing the fallen king eternally," Jared elucidates.

"That's an absurd and unscientific deduction," Alex charges.

"I didn't claim it's reasonable, or scientific. I simply recognize the importance of an alternative view for the purpose of maintaining objectivity."

"Well, in this case the alternative view is counteractive to the objective of objectivity."

"Whatever, man. You're just mad because you didn't come up with it." Satisfied with his petty rebuttal, Jared rolls his shoulders, tilts his head, and engulfs the beans and weenies on his fork.

"You're a dolt. A genuine, muscle-bound schmohawk." Alex expects a quick comeback, but Jared concedes the point, nodding his head, pursing his lips, and forking up more beans and weenies.

Janice changes the subject and the eight archaeologists eat and talk, mostly about international affairs; the Berlin Wall had fallen only a few months ago. Did this signify the end of the Cold War? Following dinner and a nightcap of red wine, half of the party hits the hay, while Hubert, Jared, Alex, and Dan get a game of gin rummy going. Hubert wins the first game and Jared the second. Hubert insists on a third game to break the tie, and Alex and Dan, offended by Hubert's implication, bow out of the showdown. Jared, despite having imbibed seven glasses of wine, wins the tiebreaker by a small margin.

"OK, best of five," Hubert protests.

"Not a chance, Huey. Big day tomorrow and I wanna be well rested."

"Alright, alright. To be continued."

Hubert picks up the cards and puts them back in the box. Jared corks the wine, returns it to the mini fridge, and turns off the electric lantern on the kitchen table. The two friends say 'goodnight' to each other and head to their tents in the moonless night.

With the new moon comes a new chapter in the expedition. The full team eats breakfast together in the gazebo that morning. Hubert is in a jolly mood, but he and Jared need three cups of coffee to regain their footing after a late night. At the two folding tables, Janice gives an overview of the ruler excavation and her expectations of each of her peers, including her husband. Hubert smirks at this, while Jared makes a whipping gesture at him.

The dig goes well that day. Everyone performs their duties to the best of their ability and is cordial to their colleagues. They expand the site by ten square feet, and most importantly, find more bones: three metacarpals and four distal phalanges of the right hand. Hubert thinks there's a chance of finding a nearly complete skeleton. How exciting! His colleagues agree. One by one the crew begins calling it quits around four-o'-clock. By five it's down to Hubert and Janice.

"Come on, Huey. Let's punch our time cards, we've made plenty of headway today. Help me with the tarp," says Janice.

"I'm gonna stay awhile. You go ahead, I can manage the tarp myself."

Janice realizes this is not negotiable. Though annoyed, she finds an underlying gratification in seeing her husband take such interest in a non-Egyptian assignment. Maybe he's not a one trick pony after all, she thinks.

Hubert spends another hour scrutinizing and brushing down the hand bones. He holds them against the corresponding bones in his own hand for comparison. Not much of a difference; the same large, clumsy, calloused man hands, but presumably more tan. Once satisfied with the cleanliness of the bones, Hubert sets them in their original positions and covers them with a cloth. He unrolls the tarp and drags it by one corner across the side of the dig nearest the jungle. He positions the corner of the tarp and squats down to press the anchoring stake into the eyelet when he sees something move in the undergrowth.

When Hubert stands up to investigate the movement, a black jaguar is staring at him with a stoic expression. Only its head and forequarters protrude from the thick foliage, which makes Hubert, already terrified beyond belief, even more frightened because he can't see what the predator's hind legs are doing. It could be preparing to pounce, Hubert considers. A robust bead of sweat falls from his jaw onto the toe of his nubuck work boots. He quickly looks down at the dark spot on the beige leather, then back up at the feline. It hasn't moved. The standoff between the archaeologist and the big cat lasts around a minute, but to Hubert it seems like a lifetime. After the minute, the jaguar unceremoniously backs into the rainforest. It never growls, roars, grunts, bears its teeth, or licks its muzzle. It shows no aggressive behavior; no emotions of any kind for that matter. Hubert finds this awfully peculiar.

It's no easy task for Hubert to finish covering the excavation with the tarp, partly because he's shaking from head to toe, but primarily because his mind is preoccupied with the close encounter of the four-legged kind. Is it an omen of some sort? he wonders. Is a black jaguar the same as a black cat? Was it summoned by the spirit of the ruler and his pendant, or is it coincidence? Could it be the ruler reincarnated? Despite their superstitious nature, all of these questions seem pertinent in Hubert's rational and scientific mind. He leaves the tarp shabbily draped over the dig and runs back to the campsite to tell the team about the jaguar.

"It was the darnedest thing guys, it just stood there, impassively gazing at me. Its eyes barely moved, like it was trying to hypnotize me," exclaims Hubert to his colleagues around a bonfire. "It didn't make a noise and didn't move its body until it retreated into the jungle." Hubert guzzles some of the canned beer in his hand.

"You're a lucky son of a gun, Huey. That thing could've sliced and diced you. I knew a guy once, he was working up in Teotihuacan, and a jaguar came into their camp one night, snatched him out of his tent. They found some of his organs on a riverbank two miles away," says Jared.

"Bullcrap," Dan contends. Jared deliberately shakes his head and chucks a branch into the fire.

"Is not. Dr. Lester Gunterson was his name. I'm surprised none of you know about it."

The team spends the evening telling stories around the bonfire. A considerable pile of empty beer cans accumulates in the recycling bin, many of which were discarded by Hubert and Jared. The drunker Hubert gets, the more he thinks about the jaguar. At one point, he reenacts both ends of the standoff by the dig. When he first crouches onto all fours like the cat, he tumbles headlong into the grass. Janice, half-embarrassed and half-infatuated, allows her husband to finish the performance, then announces their retirement for the night. She takes a bow for Hubert and guides him to their tent.

Nobody sleeps well that night. They are awakened periodically by the mews and rumbles of the jaguar, whose reverberations seem loud enough for it to be right at the doors of their tents. With each haunting sound, Hubert waits for the moonlight to cast a lurking shadow on the side of the tent, but it never does. The episode gives everybody the heebie jeebies and they arrive at breakfast with ruffled hair and bloodshot eyes.

"It's pretty clear you weren't lying about that jaguar, Huey," Alex observes, eliciting knowing looks from the rest of the group.

"Yeah, what was that thing in heat? It wouldn't shut up the whole night. Looks like between the eight of us we might've gotten a full eight hours' rest," Dan laments.

Hubert stands by the coffee maker waiting for it to fill the last quarter of the pot. Janice is next to him cracking eggs and dropping them into a pan atop the hot plate. They look at each other through bleary eyes and smile.

"You think my reenactment would've been better if I included some of those sounds? Pretended to be in heat?" Hubert asks Janice. She looks down at the pan and laughs.

That afternoon at the excavation the jaguar appears again, and this time behaves more boldly. It lingers for a few minutes in full view of the archaeologists, but never strays from the safety of the tree line. Jared startles it by slamming a shovel against a rock, after which it scampers behind the temple, appears on the other side, surveys the area on its haunches, and proceeds to prowl around the periphery of the city in a ninety-degree arc. The jaguar's patrol forces the tourists to concentrate near the center of the complex and their collective frame of mind shifts from the jovial spirit of human sightseers to the nervous energy of an antelope herd in fight-or-flight mode. The tourists are relieved in a little over an hour when the jaguar quietly slips back into the jungle. They wait a few minutes before daring to move about freely, monitoring the boundary of the rainforest – some with their binoculars – and when the coast seems clear their jovial spirit is restored and they continue with their sightseeing duties. Hubert and the team watch the entire phenomenon, and return to the campsite that evening feeling the big cat has spoiled the Tikal experience for everyone.

A bad juju jaguar.

"I'm going to kill that thing if we see it again," Jared declares, puffing his chest.

"No, no. That's not our responsibility. Besides, we'd probably be breaking the law. Jaguars are protected in most of their range," say Hubert. "If we see it again, we'll contact the park rangers."

Which they did, because the next day at dusk the jaguar ambushes a tourist, a retired American man, and drags him into the jungle, never to be seen again, at least not in a recognizable condition.

Chapter 13

Hubert and James are on all fours, scrubbing the floor of one of the huge communal showers with toothbrushes. Satan chose this as a preliminary punition while he continues to exact an appropriately scaled retribution for Hubert's act of animal cruelty. He included James in this janitorial task because he was an accomplice to the lesser offenses. James has seen a lot worse, and hasn't failed to remind Hubert every time his friend complains about their tedious chore.

"These chemicals are giving me a hellacious headache. We're gonna get cancer from this," Hubert gripes, putting down his toothbrush and rubbing his forehead.

"Ya gonna get more than a headache if ya don't keep scrubbing," says James. Hubert picks up the toothbrush and lethargically carries on. "Use some elbow grease, Huey. We're never gonna get done with ya acting like yer gonna hurt the tiles. Ya ain't giving it a massage."

"I can't concentrate. It feels like there's a percussion section where my brain used to be."

"Man, let me tell ya about headaches. One time I used hypnosis to train a Hellbird to talk, ya know mimic words like a parrot. The minions found out about it and locked me in this little room with another Hellbird, and the thing screeched as loud as it could, non-stop for who knows how long. My ears literally bled. I thought I was gonna go deaf, dumb, and blind my head hurt so bad." James squeezes his eyes shut for a moment as if trying to block out the memory.

"Sounds traumatic. My nostril hairs feel like they've been singed off. Are you getting that sensation?"

"Yeah. Tell me more about the Devil's office, that'll get ya mind off this chemical and migraine business. What other kinda wild stuff does he have in there beside the portraits?"

"Some ostentatious rugs. An immense Navajo runner, at least thirty feet long, and a red and gold Persian in front of his desk. Expensive stuff, I wonder if he has an interior decorator?"

"Naw, he picks that crap out himself, I know his taste. He's a new money type-a-dude," James claims, nodding his head, "prefers the outlandish and pricey to try to forget his origins."

"Is that so?"

"I've been here a long time, Huey. How many times ya seen me stand corrected about something concerning this place?"

"Well, not too long ago you had some ideas you were sure would get me sent to the very office which happens to be the subject of this conversation." James looks up at Hubert and rubs his nose with his thumb. "You stand corrected. Three times by my count. Three dud plans."

Before James can summon a response, he and Hubert are forced to bite their tongues when Ginvoo appears in the entryway of the shower. They lean closer to the floor and pretend to be caught up in their work. The trollish hunchback walks up to them with his hands behind his back.

"Hello, sinners. How is the cleaning coming along?" he hisses. Hubert and James act surprised by his presence.

"Oh, good to see you Ginvoo. Nice of you to stop by. It's good, I think we're both getting the hang of this. James has a technique, actually, it really blasts away the grime. Tell him, James," says Hubert with a beguiling smile.

"Yeah, so the key is to work in figure eights. It's that simple really. Ya want them to be..."

HHSSSSSS!

"Fiends, I didn't come here to seek advice on how to clean linoleum tiles," Ginvoo objects.

"But you asked how it was going..." Hubert murmurs.

"Shut up!" Ginvoo mumbles something to himself in Latin. Hubert and James exchange frightened looks. We're about to see something straight outta *The Exorcist*, James thinks. "Raymer, The Dark Lord seeks your company. Come with me. You – keep on scrubbing."

The ogre looks at James and makes a figure eight motion. Hubert hands his toothbrush to James and walks out of the shower with Ginvoo. James begins working double time, a toothbrush in each hand, and hums "Roll, Jordan, Roll."

Hubert and Ginvoo arrive at the door to Satan's office. Instead of pressing the buzzer, Ginvoo removes a key from his pocket, turns it in the keyhole, producing a resonant 'click', and pushes the door open by a margin just wide enough for an adult human to fit through. He stands against the door and holds his hands out toward the opening, welcoming Hubert in.

"Sinners first, I insist," he hisses.

Hubert holds his hands against his chest to feign humility and slips past Ginvoo into the room. The interior is as extravagant as Hubert remembers it. However, as Hubert follows Satan's consigliere down the lengthy Navajo rug, he notices two differences. The photographs of the Devil with famous Hellions have been switched out for new ones featuring more palatable subjects: Babe Ruth, Alexander the Great, Lauren Bacall, and Lucretius. Also, the lighting has changed. Whereas before the room had a reddish ambiance, it now has a whitish-yellow glow. It seems as if Satan exchanged the candles and torches for incandescent light bulbs, but that is not the case. Hubert figures he used his sorcery to alter the type of light emitted by the flames. Maybe the firewood is different, too. Whatever the case, the lair of the Prince of Darkness is lighter and more inviting, less befitting of his name.

The beginnings of 'Dark Lord the Merciful' and 'Hell Deux'?

Satan sits in his high-backed swivel chair facing the panoramic windows at the back of the room. When Hubert and Ginvoo reach his desk, he holds up the index finger on his left hand and asks Hubert to sit down. Ginvoo walks around the desk and stands at his master's side. Satan continues to face the window. From Hubert's perspective, only his elbows are visible on the armrests of his chair. It reminds Hubert of a James Bond villain.

"Welcome back, Mr. Raymer. I've heard the showers have a nice spit shine to them," says Satan.

"Yes, James and I have been working hard," Hubert responds. He leans a few inches to the right to try to get a better look at Satan, but Satan, not a second behind, counters by turning his chair a few inches to the left.

"I'm not going to waste time with small talk and congenialities. God can do that for me today, because you two have a meeting shortly." Satan slowly turns around in the swivel chair.

The Hellcat is in his lap, and he pets its head and neck, coaxing deep, rumbling purrs from the exotic pet. It sounds like an idling car engine. "Isn't that wonderful, Mr. Raymer?!" The Devil grins and pats Thermopylae on the back of the head.

"Why yes, that's fantastic," Hubert dumbly agrees, not knowing what else to say. He's not at all prepared for a meeting with the Almighty. He wishes there was a mirror available, but doesn't dare ask Satan, more for fear of Ginvoo's reaction.

"OK then, let's get you on your way. Come with me."

Satan gets out of the chair and struts toward the Lucifer fireplace, cradling the Hellcat in his arms, who stares at Hubert through narrowed eyes. This makes Hubert uneasy, although the irony comforts him in some way: of the three personages in the room, the Devil has been the most hospitable. They stop on the apron of the fireplace and Satan pushes the gate aside.

"Get in," directs Satan. Hubert hesitates and looks askance at Satan, begging further explanation. "You'll be fine. This fireplace doubles as a teleport to the Pearly Gates. Stand in the flames, pull the flue opener, and off you go."

"Um, alright." As Hubert steps past Satan, the Hellcat hisses at him. His whole body flinches.

"Silence, Thermopylae! Bad kitty!" Satan yells. "Sorry, Mr. Raymer, go ahead."

Hubert takes his place amongst the flames. He closes his eyes, crosses his fingers, and pulls on the chain. As he rises up into the chimney, his material frame morphing into a chrysalis of sparkling white light, he waves to Satan. Satan waves back.

"Bon voyage, Hellion. God speed," he says.

The soul of Hubert Raymer hurtles unimpeded through the cosmic soup at light speed, compliments of a private wormhole, "The Business Expressway," a direct link between Heaven and Hell accessible only to God, Satan, and their authorized guests. This is great, Hubert's consciousness jabbers, another item off the bucket list! Plunging down a wormhole was one of many thrills on his bucket list, along with skydiving, climbing Mount Washington, and deep sea fishing, none of which have been checked off.

After an untold time and distance, crossing several dimensions and conceivably the entire multiverse, the metamorphosis reverses itself and flesh-and-bone Hubert emerges before the Pearly Gates. He looks at the backs of his hands, his palms, and down at his feet, wiggling his toes. Apart from a fomenting nausea, everything is on the level.

"What a trip," Hubert whispers.

He tests his footing on the clouds, which have the consistency of marshmallows, and approaches the gates. He marvels at the luster of the gold and silver and runs his hand over one of the posts. The pleasant coolness of the metal reminds him of the doors to the circle of sloth. He puts his forehead against the post and enjoys the therapeutic rush, wishing he could stay there forever, but upon noticing the door knocker is reminded he has somewhere to be, and someone important to meet.

KNOCK!

The pound of the door knocker is followed by a low thunder burst, which echoes across the sky and causes the Pearly Gates to vibrate. No one answers. Hubert counts to ten and raps again. God appears from a bulge in the clouds on the other side of the gates and waves to Hubert. Hubert bashfully returns the gesture. The gates open on their own and God meets Hubert at the outset.

"Welcome to my Kingdom, my son," He bellows.

God holds out His hand for Hubert to shake, and Hubert obliges, his tiny human-Hellion hand engulfed by the gigantic, alabaster mitt of the Almighty. At the conclusion of the handshake, Hubert is unsure what to say or do. He feels insignificant and unworthy of his host, and avoids eye contact, choosing instead to look at the fine linen of God's robe, which ruffles in the crisp breeze, adhering tightly to God's statuesque figure, a geometric wonder of sharp lines, precise angles, and perfect proportions and symmetry, attributable to the hands of Michelangelo or, well, the Creator Himself.

Hubert considers getting on his knees and worshiping the clouds He walks on. Too desperate and fanatical, maybe even patronizing, he decides. After staring myopically at the robe and the contours of the washboard abs and lumberjack chest underneath, Hubert finally lifts his eyes and takes his first good look at God's face. Square-jawed, blue-eyed, avuncular, and luminously pallid, it's everything Hubert imagined, except one feature which causes him to furrow his brow. Realizing the conspiratorial implications of his gesticulation, Hubert raises his hand in front of his face and pretends the sun is in his eyes. The Lord, of course, is not fooled by such diversions.

"What's the trouble, my son," He says in a mildly saturnine tone, "not what you expected?"

"No, well um, I mean yes...your facial hair is surprisingly modern," Hubert explains, reviewing the closely trimmed chinstrap beard to see if there's anything he missed.

"Sometimes you have to reinvent yourself, Hubert. I kept the long hair, though, hope that validates whatever image you had in your mind." God runs a hand through His long white hair, which falls to the point of His shoulder blades.

"It looks spectacular. I wish I still had all of mine." Hubert tilts his head down and points to the unique bald spot. God leans over to inspect it.

"Resembles a storm system."

"Yeah, I know, my friends used to call it 'Hurricane Huey'." Hubert chuckles and God joins him.

"That's rich. Please, walk with me, my son."

God puts His arm around Hubert's shoulder and leads him across Heaven's grounds. They walk two or three hundred yards of nothing but bare clouds until a set of tennis courts appears. There are two pairs playing singles and one quartet playing doubles. God and Hubert watch for a few minutes, clapping deferentially after each point like the crowds at professional tournaments.

"These are some of my residents. Heavenites as I like to call them," the Lord pronounces. He points to one of the players, a middle-aged man wearing a visor and bearing a strong resemblance to Pierce Brosnan, and says, "Archibald over there is our finest player. He's a great technician and plays with a fire in his belly, kind of like John McEnroe."

They watch Archibald and his partner break deuce, an exhilarating battle which eventually turns into a war of attrition, requiring fourteen points for Archibald to claim victory. Owing to several instances of Archibald beginning to hammer his racket into the ground in frustration, then restraining himself at the last moment, arresting the racket's kamikaze descent an inch above the grass court surface, Hubert determines the man has more than a fire in his belly, but a volatile disposition tempered only by the holy surroundings, and in this case, God's watchful eyes. He is sure the man will be cursing, throwing his racket, stomping the ground, and generally throwing a tantrum as soon as he and God leave.

The next attraction on their afternoon walk is a colossal white and gold church. It's an all-encompassing place of worship, featuring architectural calling cards of many religions, Western and Eastern: the spire and flying buttress of the Catholic cathedral, the pinnacle and lancet window of the Protestant church, the tiered roof of the wooden Jewish synagogue, the hemispheric dome and minaret of the Islamic mosque, the onion dome of Russian Orthodoxy, the pagoda of Buddhism, the shikhara of Hinduism, and the sweeping roof of Taoism. Hubert finds the building rather disorienting, and wants to tell God he didn't know Dr. Frankenstein had an architectural firm, although he knows he isn't nearly familiar enough with His sense of humor to attempt the joke.

"What a sight to behold," Hubert exclaims, looking up one of the spires.

"It was a labor of love," replies God, "and a labor of labor, too. It took my angels two years and twenty-nine days to build this church. Over sixty thousand man hours." Hubert whistles at the magnitude of the undertaking.

"I'll bet it was worth it. It's like the Swiss army knife of churches; fits every worshiper's needs. The Heavenites must love this place."

"Why don't we go in and you can see for yourself. We're just in time for the ten-o'-clock service."

God leads Hubert up the stairs of the church and through the front doors, where a Heavenite usher hands each of them a program. The vestibule, with its creaky, lacquered wood floor and mantled candles, is a flashback to the church houses of old and enchanting in its simplicity. The nave, on the other hand, is an august Romanesque-style room, one hundred and sixty feet high and two hundred and forty feet long, with gorgeous fan vaulting and stained-glass windows. At the center of the ceiling is the underside of the hemispheric dome, which is covered by religious frescoes rivaling those of the Sistine Chapel.

Hubert pads alongside God down the middle aisle, staring open-mouthed at the upper reaches of the church, and consequently bumps into one of the pews. 'Charlie horse!' Hubert yells inwardly as he reaches for his left quadriceps. He massages the contused area and hobbles past a few more pews to where God has taken a seat near the front of the assembly. All the Heavenites in the row lean forward to look at the Lord and the intruder; a friendly, servile glance for their Savior and a rude, accusatory glance at Hubert. They look at Hubert as if he's on fire, and given where he came from, he's surprised he hasn't yet gone up in flames, sitting in a church in Heaven, his blindness, poorness, pitifulness, and wretchedness stinking up the joint. He feels leprous and unwanted. God, ostensibly hearing His guest's thoughts and sensing his anxiety, pats Hubert on the knee, leans forward to look at the faces in the pew, which instantly turn shameful upon meeting God's eyes, and clears His throat loudly and suggestively. The Heavenites keep their eyes forward on the altar for the rest of the service.

The service is unlike any Hubert has ever seen. There is no particular order to the proceedings and no identifiable leader or clergyman. Hubert refers to the program to try to make sense of things, but it appears the program is only a schematic for all the services the church offers. It provides no date, time, or title for today's service. The front cover reads "Worship with Us at the Temple," and the inside reads like a menu of suggestions: "Take Communion," "Shema Yisrael," "Wudu and Salat," "Meditate in the Rock Garden," and so forth.

Hubert looks around the nave and finds all these rituals taking place. There are Heavenites up front by the altar singing the "Lord's Prayer" and breaking up communion wafers and dipping them in a chalice filled with the host wine. To the left of the altar is a group reading aloud from a Torah. As the Torah is passed from one reader to the next, so is a seven-branched menorah with the middle branch lit. The Muslims convene underneath the dome, set their prayer rugs on the floor, bow and kneel, and begin their recitations facing the front right corner of the nave. How do they know that's the direction of Mecca? Hubert asks himself. He doubts they can see the surface of the Earth through the thickness of Heaven's clouds. "East" seems to have as little meaning in Paradise as it does in Hades. A group of hippie-types sit in half-lotus in the right aisle repeating a mantra that sounds like it's in German – an amusing juxtaposition – while a few others of their ilk walk up and down the aisle with their eyes closed and their hands woven together against their chests.

"Where is the rock garden?" Hubert asks God in a whisper, cupping his mouth confidentially with one hand and pointing in short, piston-like jabs at the Heavenite monks with the index finger of the other hand.

"It's in another part of the building. There's a vihara near where the pagoda is seen from the outside. Our Buddhists generally use it on their own time throughout the day. The Temple never closes. During service hours, everyone likes to stay together in the main nave here," God explicates.

God's response causes Hubert to further question the usefulness of the services. Before beginning a new line of questioning, he is distracted by some activity not mentioned in the program.

In one corner of the room, a contingent of Heavenites is huddled together and partaking in a ceremonial dance. One of them, an elderly black woman and the apparent leader, holds a cowrie shell in one hand and an exotic plant leaf in the other. A girl, no older than ten, is kneeling in the center of the gathering in a trance, periodically speaking in tongues while the others dance around her, stamping their feet up and down to the rhythm of a drum. The old lady stands over the girl and blesses her with the cowrie shell by pressing it lightly against her forehead and each of her shoulders. This increases the severity of the girl's possession and Hubert nervously shifts in his seat as her eyes roll back completely and her utterances become louder and more frequent. Nothing about this ritual seems kosher to Hubert. The old lady crushes the leaf in her hands and helps the girl chew and swallow some of the pieces. At this point, the drumming slows down and the dancing arrests proportionally. A minute passes and the girl snaps out of the trance. Her eyes open fully and she gets to her feet, standing flimsily before the old lady, who circles around the girl and examines her patient with oblique glances. The medicine woman stops in front of the girl, stands on her toes, pries open the girl's eyelids, and takes a good look at her pupils. Rocking back onto her heels with a torpid smile, the old lady pats the girl on the head one time and the ceremony is over. The girl has been cured.

"Is that what I think it is?" Hubert asks God, who turns to him with a blank expression, pretending not to know what is going on. "Those people were doing Santería." Hubert points to the corner where the group now stands about in casual conversation.

"Looks to me like they're talking," God postulates.

"Yes, but not a minute ago they were doing a type of cleansing ritual. That old woman there, she was blessing that little girl in the spring dress with the cowrie shell. See the cowrie shell in her hand?"

"Ah, I see now. Her name is Lucia de la Paz. She's a priestess."

"Of Santería."

"If that's what you want to call it. They prefer 'Regla de Ochá'."

"Right. And no one else is bothered by this? The primal dancing and the speaking in tongues? I assume there's some animal sacrifice from time to time as well."

"It's funny you mention those things, my son."

"Why is that?"

"You'll see. Come with me to my throne and we can discuss your proposition."

God wraps His arm around Hubert's shoulder and walks him out of the Temple. They walk atop the clouds awhile in silence and Hubert uses the occasion to tune in to the many wonderful sounds of Heaven: the chirps and whoops of songbirds, the splashes and gurgles of fountains and streams, the low buzz of a distant lawn mower, a wind chime, a bullfrog, and church bells. Hubert closes his eyes and immerses himself in the atmosphere. After several minutes a harp joins the auditory sampling, and Hubert opens his eyes to find the Lord's throne on the peak of the next cloud, sitting vaingloriously on a gold pedestal in the company of an angel strumming a gold harp.

"Welcome to my sanctum," says God.

He steps onto the pedestal and holds out His hand to help Hubert up, but instead of simply checking Hubert's balance and providing some forward momentum, He lifts His guest into the air and drops him on the sheeny surface of the platform with the nonchalance of a fisherman pulling the day's catch out of the water and tossing it on deck. Hubert takes a false step upon landing and laughs at the absurdity of the situation. He isn't sure if this is deliberate rough play or if the Almighty doesn't know the limits of His might.

"Thanks for the lift."

"My pleasure. Please, have a seat."

An angel pulls up a chair for Hubert which looks like it belongs in a dollhouse compared to the immensity of God's throne, and further looks like it belongs in a flea market or garage sale compared to the grandeur of the Creator's blessed seat. However, in relative terms it's a nice chair – an ergonomic oak rocker with a white leather seat fastened by silver snaps – and Hubert is exceedingly grateful for the pleasure to sit in it. He thanks the angel for bringing the chair and tests its rocking ability. The smoothness of the rocker is peerless and its rhythm hypnotic. The curved bands are silent and effortless, wasting no energy as they appear to float on air rather than ride across solid ground. Hubert closes his eyes and imagines he has saddled the cushy bob of a perfectly calibrated pendulum that has been swinging for centuries, its perfect trajectory uninterrupted over incalculable oscillations. Hubert places himself on a porch in a bucolic setting, a cold beer in his hand and a baseball game broadcasting from a radio on a stand next to the armrest, rocking, sipping, and listening from afternoon to evening, from early April to late October, year after year after year. That's Heaven.

"What was that, my son?" asks God, jarring Hubert from his daydream.

"Hmm? Oh, I'm not sure. I must have been murmuring. Was I murmuring?"

"Yes, but that's OK. How is the rocking chair? Smooth as butter, isn't it?" God nods His head assuredly with a touch of pride as if He built it Himself, which Hubert suspects He did.

"Incredible. It feels frictionless, like it's not even touching the ground."

"That's because it's not, my son. The bands have a special invisible buffer. Of course, technically no two solid objects actually ever touch on an atomic level. The rapid vibration of the atoms creates an infinitesimal space of resistance between the two objects. Friction and the illusion of touch is caused by the combating energies in that space. Anyway, the buffer extends the space and eliminates friction."

"A novel invention."

And one of God's many patents.

The butler angel reappears with a bottle of white wine and a tray with cheese and crackers and two glasses. The cherub presents the bottle to God, who inspects the label and subtly nods His approval, and His winged servant draws a corkscrew from behind his back with the sleight of hand of an expert magician, uncorks the top until it sits just below the opening, then grabs the neck of the bottle with both hands and pops the cork with a flick of the thumb, sending the woody cylinder sailing through the air where it eventually falls back to the marshmallowy clouds and bounces out of sight. The popping sound provokes peals of thunder in the background. These folks take their wine seriously, Hubert muses. The angel pours a sampling into one of the glasses and God takes it, swirling the wine around and sniffing it in the traditional manner of an oenophile before raising the glass to His lips and taking a sip. He nods again in the same way He approved the selection pre-testing.

"Wine, my son?" God asks.

The inevitable offer puts Hubert in a predicament. He planned on asking for water to keep up appearances, but after the lofty theatrics of the wine presentation he feels he no longer has that option; it would put him in better standing to oblige. Hubert dawdles for a moment, pretending to admire the wine bottle and the golden-yellow magnificence of its contents, then capitulates.

"Certainly, please," he says.

The angel pours an ample amount in each of the glasses and hands them to his master and the guest of honor. Hubert waits for God to take the first sip and follows after a brief delay. They take the second sip in unison and the Lord raises His glass for a toast.

"Here is to second chances, my son." The sunlight twinkles on His glass and a burning hopefulness emerges in Hubert's loins at the implications of the statement.

"Amen," Hubert confirms. They tap glasses and the resulting clinking sound is the purest and most harmonic Hubert has ever heard produced from a glass-on-glass toast. Instead of ringing and cutting sharply through the air, startling the ear drums, it hums and fades gracefully into nothing. Hubert looks closely at his glass and slowly turns it in an attempt to discover the secret to its wondrous acoustics.

Tonal Glass™, another of God's many patents.

"Now, let's talk about what brought you here. First, I must reveal to you why you ended up *there*."

God points downward with a peevish expression as if pointing out a stain on the floor. He tells Hubert his son is the leader of a violent, depraved cult which has been responsible for several abhorrent crimes, including annual attacks on New Year's Eve characteristic of an Islamic terrorist group. According to reconnaissance intel His angels have collected, the cult is called 'The Brotherhood of the Black Squirrel,' prospective members must endure an intensely painful initiation ceremony, members are known as 'Brave Minions,' the leader is affectionately referred to as 'Virtuous Leader,' and the organization has international chapters, including in the Middle East, which acutely concerns the United States government. Also, in keeping with one of the honored traditions of genocidal cults, the leader is engaging in sexual acts with many of the female members. Hubert thumbs through his memory banks and recalls the daydream about his pregnant, dying wife, followed by the appearance of a burning black squirrel in his theology classroom.

"Well I'll be darned," Hubert says, "I had a dream not too long ago about my wife. At the end of the dream, she was on the verge of death and almost nine months pregnant. When I woke up, there was a black squirrel in Bible study and it was on fire." Hubert wishes he hadn't told God he was sleeping in Bible study, but he figures concealing the context of the story would be pointless since God likely already knows.

"What happened to the squirrel?" God inquires.

"Is that a rhetorical question?"

"Don't be so paranoid, my son. I may be omniscient, but contrary to popular belief, I don't have a hand in everything. I have minimal clout in Hades and Lucifer keeps me in the dark about some of what goes on there, if you'll excuse the expression. The same goes for him and my Kingdom."

"Oh, I guess I never thought of that, sorry. My professor killed the squirrel and I saw it as a tragedy.

Anyway, what does any of this cult stuff have to do with me? I can't account for my son and his choices, especially not from the grave."

"As the inequity of the fathers is visited upon the children, so shall the inequity of the children be visited upon the fathers," God mechanically explains.

"Where is that in the literature?" Hubert pouts, subduing his indignation.

"It's not. Sometimes Satan and I have to ad lib, in this case to help balance the Hellion and Heavenite populations."

"But that's ludicrous! You're cooking the books! That's what sheisty businessmen and common gangsters do, not all-powerful deities!"

"Relax, my son. We're willing to make exceptions and that's where you come in."

Hubert perks up, straightening his posture and making direct eye contact with his maker. He rubs his hands together and waits for the good news, the magic words he has been expecting to hear ever since he set foot on the marshmallowy clouds of Paradise, and which he has dreamed of hearing long before then: "Welcome to Heaven, my son Huey." God measures Hubert's countenance and pauses for several seconds to allow him to settle down.

"I'm afraid I cannot reverse my judgment of you, but Satan and I have made a compromise I think you'll find fair and satisfactory."

All Hubert hears is he will not be admitted to Heaven. He feels like a child on the school playground waiting to be picked for a basketball game, but instead of being picked last, he is left on the sideline to watch a game of five-on-four. God might as well have reached out with a giant stamp, "Rejected," and pressed it onto his forehead. He feels an acrid sickness roiling in his stomach and chest. His eyes well up with tears and he tries to hold them back, but the wind exacerbates the problem and a rogue bead trickles down his cheek. He blinks several times in succession to squelch the reserves lapping at the precipices of his eyelids, then wipes his dampened eyelashes, pretending the wind has blown something into his eyes. God pardons him and gives him another several seconds to regain his composure, and pride, before continuing.

"We have decided to create a sanctuary in Hell, a place for people like you who are wholesome, but have been sentenced to damnation due to external or unforeseen forces. Extenuating circumstances, shall we say."

Despite the encouraging news, Hubert hasn't moved past the rejection. Instead of feeling bitter, he feels stupid and naïve for getting his hopes up, but realizes the compromise, this so-called sanctuary, is better than the alternative.

"A sanctuary in Hell," he says, stroking his chin, "now that I can live with."

"Excellent, my son. I know it's not what you were hoping for, but rest assured you'll enjoy its friendly confines, and you'll be in good company as well; Satan and I have granted membership to your friends James, Lawrence, and Claudia."

"Really?! You know, I kind of overlooked that aspect of my proposition. No offense, but what good would it be to make it to Heaven and leave your friends behind in the process?"

"A tough dilemma, my son. You may be loyal to a fault." God guffaws at what He sees as Hubert's misplaced priorities. Hubert doesn't seem to notice.

"I've been accused of worse. This sanctuary thing might actually be what I've been seeking all along." Hubert grabs his wine glass from the loo table between his rocker and God's throne and raises it for a toast. "Here is to second chances, and, uh, what will this sanctuary be called?"

"'Hell's Paradise,'" God proclaims with emphasis on 'paradise'.

"Yes, here is to 'Hell's Paradise.'"

Chapter 14

Hubert, James, Lawrence, and Claudia wait in a long line with other minor sinners. The line twists and turns and runs up and down several radial corridors, finally ending in a remote part of the hub where an area has been partitioned by a tall concrete wall to make room for Hell's Paradise. The four friends have been inching along the line at a disabled snail's pace for many, many hours without food or water. They're weary and their feet are sore, but they've made it to the hub and the gates of their new residence are visible, which has raised their spirits and inspired a festive mood in the occupants of the last leg of the line to the good life. Those at the front of the line jump up and down, thrusting applications marked "APPROVED" above their heads for all to see, like a wide receiver would a football after scoring a touchdown, while those farther back high-five and hug. Hubert, remembering the disappointment he felt back in Heaven after counting his chickens, finds the celebratory atmosphere presumptuous. Nobody knows precisely what lies within the concrete walls, yet they carry on like Deadheads about to enter an acid rock festival.

Not wanting to spoil the moment, Hubert keeps his thoughts to himself and chats enthusiastically with his friends, who are trying their best not to let the moment get spoiled by the riff-raff: the word has gotten out about Hell's Paradise and several Hellions who were rejected, the major sinners, are heckling the line with screams of "goodie-goodies," "scabs," and "Benedict Arnolds." The occasional rock is thrown, causing a minor sinner to drop to the ground, his head submerging in a sea of bobbing heads and surfacing a moment later.

Hellion Whack-A-Mole.

Lawrence, the accident-prone of the bunch, is hit on two separate occasions. He curses and reels around to try to identify the culprit, but the heckling assailants are swift and elusive. James says they remind him of the Vietcong. As much as the gang would like to retaliate and relive the food fight operation, Hubert reminds them of the sacrifices he made to get them into the line.

"We're residents of Hell's Paradise now and should act accordingly."

"At least until we get through those doors," Claudia quips.

When they reach the front of the line, there is a commotion at the gates. A man is kicking and screaming while two demon guards strain to drag him away from the entrance. The man's face is bruised and bloody, and one of the guards has blood trickling down his leg. At least he went down with a fight, Hubert notes, before taking a closer look at the man's swollen face. Recognizing that the distorted features cast a degree of uncertainty, he is nearly positive he knows the man from school.

"Damned scum! Hypocrites! You'll get your comeuppance," the man yells.

Hubert feels compelled to speak out and help the desperate man and searches frantically through his memory banks for the man's name before he is taken away. However, after retrieving the name he clams up, his inner conscience tugging at the impulsive R-complex, trying to talk sense into him before he blurts out something regrettable for the sake of a man he barely knows.

Hellion Survival Rule #1: Don't draw attention to yourself.

"George," calls Hubert.

The man looks at him and opens his mouth to reply, but is preemptively bashed in the jaw by one of the guards.

The guard glares at Hubert in a way that suggests it is incumbent upon his health to stand down.

"I thought you were better than this," is all he can muster.

"Guy musta faked his application or posed as someone else," says James. Lawrence and Claudia nod in agreement.

They are called forward one at a time to be examined by a demon posing as a doctor. The minion asks them to strip down and they happily remove their burlap sacks. Another demon covers them in a delousing agent, tossing the powder in generous handfuls onto every inch of their bare bodies from a plastic bucket, and a third sprays them down with a hose. The water is only lukewarm, cool in comparison to what Hellions are accustomed to, and Hubert gyrates and uses his arms to shield the powder on his sides from the spray in an artful attempt to extend the wash as long as he can. After about thirty seconds the minion catches on to his tomfoolery.

"Cretin, stop moving around and raise your arms," commands the demon.

Hubert does as he is told and the demon rinses off the powder on his sides and under his armpits. The doctor hands him cotton pants and a cotton shirt and his legs almost give out when he feels their softness. It's low quality cotton, perhaps made in one of the sweat shops Satan is rumored to operate in the circles of gluttony and sloth, where he employs violators of the respective sins and chronic troublemakers of the worst kind, but Hubert cannot recognize the difference. He looks dumbly at the doctor, expecting the clothes to be some sort of gag gift, and the doctor grunts and crosses his arms.

"Put those on and scurry over to the door, you imbecile. You're holding up the line," the MD says caustically.

A demon guard holding a torch and donning the standard-issue bottle of vodka on his utility belt waits for Hubert at the gate. The demon tilts the flame of his torch in front of Hubert's face and examines his features in the light. Hubert avoids eye contact by fixing his eyes on the flame and his pupils rapidly dilate to pinholes. The demon notices this.

"Fiend, are you on drugs? Your pupils are dilated, have you been rubbing?" the guard accuses, grabbing Hubert by the collar and pulling him so they stand nose to nose.

"You mean with SensoRize™? People still do that? No, of course not, I was staring at the torch – that probably explains it," Hubert contends. The guard softens his grip, moves back a few inches and looks at Hubert's eyes once more, then lets off his collar.

"OK, sinner, I believe you. But I'm gonna be watching you." The demon makes his index and middle fingers into a fork and points from his eyes over to Hubert's, and when Hubert passes by to enter the gates of Hell's Paradise the guard leans toward him and whispers, "You're no saint, Hubert Raymer. Don't let all this go to your head."

Hubert ignores the barb and takes hold of the vertical brass door handle, composed of two thick coils with ornate geometric patterns etched into the metal, and pauses to take in the moment before entering a new chapter of the afterlife. The feeling of the brass on his palm soothes him and he looks up to the top of the tall mahogany door where a white banner with red print says, "Welcome Minor Sinners." He turns ninety degrees and surveys this derelict part of the hub, which he has never seen before and hopes will never see again. He pulls the door open and a rush of cool air sprouts out and tantalizes his body, inviting him to step into the new environs.

James, Lawrence, and Claudia are awaiting Hubert on the other side of the doors. When he appears, they joyously greet him the way families receive their loved ones at an airport baggage claim. They embrace him, pat him on the back, and nudge him on the shoulder, and not knowing what to do with themselves from there, for no protocol or agenda had been prescribed for the opening of Hell's Paradise, stand in a semi-circle and gawk at the unfamiliar surroundings like children lost in a theme park.

"The temperature sure is mild in here," Lawrence observes, breaking the ice.

"Compared to regular Hell it's chilly, marvelous indeed," Claudia seconds.

"A brotha could get used to this," says James.

"I'm not even sweating," Hubert announces. He holds out his arms for the others to see. They note the dryness of his skin and check out their own arms, which are also anhydrous.

"What do we do now, companions?" asks Lawrence.

Hubert, James, and Claudia are taken off guard by the question. They raise their eyebrows, crinkle their foreheads, and scratch their chins. After a lengthy brainstorming session, Hubert looks at James and Claudia and shrugs his shoulders.

"Beats me. What do you think, Lawrence?" he answers.

"I suppose we give ourselves a tour. Everyone else seems to be doing it," Lawrence replies. The other Hellions are moving past them and scattering along various walkways at the far end of the entrance area.

"Seems logical," agrees Claudia. "Most blokes are going down that path." She points to the widest of the walkways where most of the foot traffic is heading.

"I can dig it. Let's go make ourselves at home," says James.

With James' affirmation, the gang strolls toward the walkway and joins the confluence.

The rocky path is divided from the others by a river, and unlike every other river in Hell, this one is composed of water instead of magma – boiling water, albeit – but water nonetheless. A handful of Hellions have already tried going for a swim, and quickly regretting their impulsive decision, are seen clambering up the steep bank with welts and burns all over their bodies. One Hellion claws at the top edge of the bank, struggling to make the final push up the near-vertical grade as the loose sediment crumbles under his weight and prevents him from establishing a reliable foothold, while his peers topside walk past time and again, choosing to either ignore his calls for help or stop momentarily to look at him with pretentious scorn and shake their heads.

As Hubert approaches the man, he decides he will be the good samaritan and tells the rest of the gang to wait up. He holds out his right hand and the man, realizing a stranger with common decency has finally arrived to help, exchanges his pitiful, scared, and entreating disposition for one of gaiety and gratefulness. The man takes Hubert's hand and Hubert grabs the man by the wrist with his other hand and yanks the poor sap up onto the walkway in one herky-jerk motion. Steadying himself against Hubert with his left arm, the man shrugs and rolls his right shoulder before shaking his right arm and wincing in pain.

"Ahh, ouch," he moans. "I appreciate the help, but did you have to pull my arm out of its socket, Hercules?" Hubert drops his jaw, astounded by the man's stipulated appreciation.

"Man, is this cat serious, Huey?" James interjects, overhearing the complaint. Hubert holds up the palm of his hand, signaling for James to leave out. "Listen, lobster man, we coulda left ya rosy butt hanging on tha side of tha river like everybody else did, but it so happens my friend Huey here is tha minor-est of tha minor sinners, and ya should be thankful he came along and dragged ya outta that mess even if he pulled ya arm straight off." The man apologizes to Hubert and heads off along the walkway, clutching and massaging his shoulder. "Unbelievable."

The group continues their self-guided tour and notices several more improvements in addition to the water-filled river. First, it is lighter than in regular Hell. Second, there are few minions around, suggesting residents are free to behave more like the sinners they are, instead of the saints they're pretending to be. Third, residents are not relegated to rugged, unforgiving environments. There's not a desert, jungle, volcanic expanse, tiny island, or frozen tundra to be found. The whole of Hell's Paradise is a collection of open areas in enormous chambers strung together by pathways, and bodies of boiling water fill the space in between the parcels of solid ground. Lawrence estimates Hell's Paradise is eighty percent water, similar to the composition of Earth. They come across a fountain in one of the open areas, a granite spray fountain with a hexagonal pool featuring a sculpture of Satan and an anonymous Hellion, the Hellion kneeling before Satan, who is touching his subject on the shoulder with a quill pen in an implied act of forgiveness. The inanimate interaction reminds Hubert of a knighting, and he becomes unsettled by the idea of the Hellion representing him, although this concern is pacified by the fact he and the statue look nothing alike.

"Anyone up for a swim?" Claudia asks, not hesitating to strip off her cotton pants and shirt.

Hubert hasn't seen a nude female body since the time before and is stricken with feelings he had long forgotten upon seeing Claudia in her birthday suit. Her small, tender breasts jiggle as she prances up to the fountain and jumps atop the rim of the pool. Hubert, almost forgetting himself in schoolboy fantasies, averts his eyes from the mammarian intrigues, erotic relics from his mortal life, and holds up a hand to protest the bathing idea and the nudity, seeking to remind Claudia of the cause of their meeting in the first place, and of the burnt flesh and agonized screams of the last Hellions who went for a swim. However, before he can utter a peep, Claudia plunges into the fountain, followed in such rapid succession by an equally nude Lawrence that they look like a pair of synchronized divers. Hubert cringes and covers his eyes in anticipation of hearing the telltale signs of excruciating pain, but instead hears splashing and playful snickering. He opens his eyes and Lawrence and Claudia are frolicking in the milky, waist deep water, batting handfuls of water at each other while bobbing and weaving to avoid the incoming fire.

"How's the water?" James asks, walking up to the fountain with caution, trying not to get wet until he knows the water is amenable to his strict standards.

"Fantastic," Claudia calls after spitting out a mouthful of water.

James leans over the wall of the fountain and puts an index finger in the water, followed by his entire hand, then his arm up to the elbow.

"Say, Huey, it's like a hot tub," he says. He steps up onto the rim of the fountain and cannonballs into the water. "Bonzai!" James' entry displaces a substantial amount of water which crashes down on Lawrence and Claudia.

"Impeccable form, James," Lawrence compliments. "What do you call that?"

"That's a cannonball, jack. They didn't have those back in yer day?"

"Well, there was such a knees-to-chest technique so as to maximize water displacement. I don't remember it having a name, though in hindsight 'cannonball' is the obvious choice."

"Hey Huey, get in here. We need one more to play chicken fight," shouts Claudia.

Hubert appeases them by running up to the fountain wall, and using it like a springboard, launches himself into a devastating jackknife. The impact disrupts the entire pool and sends small waves over the edges where they splash out onto the ground, their pitter-patter echoing across the chamber. Once the water settles, James comes out from the safety of the pool bottom, wipes his eyes, and gives Hubert a hearty high-five. The fleshy slap causes another echo, this one more piercing than the first, and a penny-sized piece of stalactite falls into the fountain at Hubert's side.

"Oops," says Hubert, watching the light brown chunk sink and disappear in the translucence, its stony essence disintegrating and mixing into swirly trails with the water, "maybe chicken fight isn't the best idea."

"Yeah," murmurs Claudia, looking up at the sandstone ceiling with a mix of resentment and reverence, "it's probably better we take it easy."

The four friends quiet down and spend a long time relaxing and enjoying the nourishing warmth of the fountain pool. They joke about the unlikelihood and irony of a spa day in Hell. However, as much as they love the perks of their new digs – the cotton clothes, the mild temperature, the water, the increased light, the reduced minion presence, the tolerable landscape – they can't ignore that the anguished moans and wails of their peers in regular Hell still permeate the air.

Chapter 15

The residents of Hell's Paradise prepare for a ceremonial ball in honor of Hubert. A contingent of minions, mostly ogres, minotaurs, and werewolves owing to their strength, move the heavy equipment into the main chamber where the party is being held, while several Hellions – a self-elected ceremony committee – work around them carrying the lighter items and ironing out the details of the set up. Four minions are cutting an amphitheater into the rock with jackhammers, and two others lift ten-foot-high concert speakers onto the sides of the stage. Two Hellions stand on metal ladders and pin a banner, "Hell's Paradise Inaugural Ball," on the corners of the stage scaffold, directed by a third who stands at the top of the amphitheater and helps square and center the headline.

Meanwhile, back in regular Hell, Hubert is in Satan's office expressing his reluctance to be considered a hero and an icon. He sits in the visitor's chair across the desk from Satan and taps nervously on the armrest. Ginvoo glares at Hubert's fingers bipping and bapping at the leather and grinds his teeth, trying his best to contain his agitation and not interrupt his master as he works his rhetorical magic on their prized Hellion.

"Believe me, Mr. Raymer, this is not just about you. This is about the rejuvenation of my kingdom, remember? The movement toward a more progressive Hell. I'm 'Dark Lord the Merciful' now and I want to make that clear to my residents. It's a team effort, Mr. Raymer, aren't you a team player?" the Devil expounds. Hubert opens his mouth to respond, but Satan holds up a finger to stop him and continues his argument. "Of course you are, that goes without saying. This ceremony goes beyond you or me or my minions, or even Hell itself. It marks a new era in our relationship with the folks upstairs. It took no small effort to build the trust needed to make Hell's Paradise happen, and this ceremony is necessary to assuage God's apprehension about granting us a favor." Satan folds his hands on the desk and waits for a response.

"OK, when you put it that way it clears my conscience a little. I don't want to be a distraction is all," says Hubert.

"You won't be, Mr. Raymer. I give you my word. There will be a brief acknowledgment of your contributions at the ball, after which you can be as anonymous and ordinary as you wish."

"Fair deal. Anonymous and ordinary is my wheelhouse."

"That's good, though you've certainly made an interesting existence for yourself outside of your comfort zone. I'm glad we straightened things out, and now if you'll excuse me I have a poker game to attend and you have a ceremony to prepare for."

Satan leads Hubert to a bookshelf next to the Lucifer fireplace which doubles as a hidden door leading to a passageway to Hell's Paradise. The passageway was completed only a few days ago, and Hubert is the first Hellion to have used it and the only Hellion who knows about it, a secret he has promised to keep until further notice. Satan yanks on the spine of a leather-bound copy of Tolstoy's *War and Peace* and the bookshelf turns ninety degrees. Hubert steps into the opening, says goodbye, and walks into the torch-lit hallway, the hidden door closing behind him.

Back in Hell's Paradise, he meets up with James, Lawrence, and Claudia, who are lending a hand in the ball preparations by assembling a cloud machine – basically a smoke machine designed to produce tiny clouds to imitate Heaven's grounds. The three can barely contain their excitement about the party and their new home and elevated status, forgetting to ask where Hubert has been and what he's been doing.

"Check this out, Huey," says James. He gesticulates with the nozzle of the cloud machine in his hand, then puts the plastic component to his mouth and makes something like a moose call. "It's a minotaur mating call."

The rest of the gang busts out laughing, including Hubert, and their cackles draw aggravated stares from several of the minions, who continue to work on the amphitheater and stage. James, Lawrence, and Claudia give Hubert the rundown on the progress of the preparations and explain the functions of the cloud machine, which can be adjusted to produce any cloud that exists in nature, from the dispersive cirrocumulus, or "mackerel sky," to the dense cumulonimbus, or "thunder cloud."

Yet another of Satan's many patents.

"Wow, I wonder how it does it," Hubert muses as he turns the dial from the leftmost setting to the rightmost and then to the middle, labeled "Altostratus." "Put the nozzle back on and power it up. I wanna see what 'altostratus' looks like."

James snaps the nozzle into the opening in the front of the machine and presses the power button. The machine makes a dull humming noise and after a few seconds ejects puffs of aerosol into the air in rapid succession, about three per second, which gradually arrange into a featureless sheet of clouds halfway between the cavern floor and ceiling. The formation reminds Hubert of the dreary skies above major cities which seem to be a reflection of the stolid grayness of the concrete and steel jungle below. The constant clattering of the minions' jackhammers adds to the mood, and Hubert, despite feeling partially transported to the realm of mortality

by the sights and sounds of the metropolitan bustle, finds the
atmosphere he has created scabrous and disconcerting.
"That one's no good. The occasion calls for something
fluffy and jocular."
"I agree," says Claudia. Lawrence, looking up at the
cloud with a disapproving grimace, points at Claudia and
nods his head. "Yeah, Huey. I can't get my groove on with *that*
hovering over me. Looks like the haze above the L.A.
skyline. Try 'altocumulus,'" James suggests, poking his head
into the instruction manual. "I like the way it looks in the
picture." He hands the booklet to Hubert and taps the
illustration.
"Ooh, that's nice," Hubert croons. He gives the
manual back to James and sets the dial on "altocumulus,"
then steps back to admire the machine assemble a fluffy and
jocular cloud formation deserving of a place in the "Hell's
Paradise Inaugural Ball."
That evening the residents gather under the
altocumulus clouds in the main chamber wearing the finest
formal attire the Devil could afford, mostly outdated cocktail
dresses and sports coats Hellions were wearing when their
numbers were punched, which have since been stockpiled in
linen closets in the bathhouses, or in a few cases, homemade
outfits the party-goers believe were derived from loose pieces
of fabric sourced from the linen closet stockpile and stitched
together in one of Hell's sweat shops. In fact, several
residents recognize some of the patchwork articles as part of
their personal production line, although the effects of space
and time betray their full confidence, and the elusive nature
of the sweatshops – namely that no Hellion, even supposed
former seamstresses, knows the location of a single one –
further discredits their claims. Other residents make similarly
dubious claims about recognizing an original item as the

clothes they died in. Hubert is approached by a Latino man who believes the zoot suit he is wearing is the one the man had on when he was crushed to death in the infamous Zoot Suit Riots of 1943. Hubert asks the man if he would like to swap outfits, thinking it a nice gesture since the zoot suit might have sentimental value, but the man declines, insisting the suit is cursed and suggesting Hubert had better put on something else.

"Man, that's just some old Mexican mumbo-jumbo, Huey, don't mind him," James assures when the Hispanic stranger walks away. "I remember some of them riots. Ain't nothin' cursed about gettin' killed by racially-fueled violence. That's America." Hubert looks down at his wide-legged pants and pointy French dress shoes and contemplatively twirls his gold watch chain around his index finger. For someone with an affinity for blue humor, he sure went dark there, Hubert thinks.

A line has formed on each side of the room for the evening's main attraction, two massive punch bowls filled with a sugary alcoholic concoction, green in one and red in the other, which Hellions are ladling out into clear plastic cups, pausing to slurp the overflow, and refilling the cup to the edges, often resulting in more overflow and a revision of the process, much to the dismay of the rest of the line, who find themselves justified in mimicking the ravenous behavior when it's their turn to wield the ladle. Hubert can clearly make out the recovering, and soon-to-be relapsing, alcoholics in the room based on the way they unsteadily handle the ladle, their hands shaking uncontrollably, barely capable of bringing the ladle to the cup without spilling most of the contents back into the punch bowl. Many of these forsaken sons and daughters of God, penniless winos in the time before with a bottle-a-day habit, abandon the ladle and dunk their cups into the bowl, fingers and all, in a most unsanitary act of desperation. Even worse, some lean down and drink directly from the bowl, lapping at the green or red spirit like a wild animal at a watering hole. Hubert puts his palm to his face when he finds, not to his surprise, that Claudia is one of the Hellions submerging her cup in the red cocktail reserves, tainting the supply. Lawrence stands beside her as she does this, laughing instead of commiserating.

"You see this?" Hubert asks James, nudging him on the shoulder and pointing at Claudia and Lawrence across the way.

"Oh, dang, she must be sauced already," James remarks.

"Yeah, maybe. This is the first I've seen them at the punch bowl, though."

"Well let's not let 'em get too far ahead of us, come on Huey." James places his hand on Hubert's back and leads him to the back of the line for the red beverage. Hubert turns them around and takes them to the back of the other line.

"Better go with the green," he says, "who knows where that woman's hands have been." James laughs and snorts.

"I can think of one place, and I wouldn't mind tastin' *that*." Hubert chuckles guiltily with a sour expression on his face as James licks his lips in an exaggerated fashion.

"Then I guess you also wouldn't mind a sore or rash of some kind," Hubert rebuffs.

"As long as it ain't chronic. Ain't no shame in my game, jack."

The two friends, after occupying themselves with a debate over what kind of boundaries a man should set with a strumpet like Claudia, eventually reach the punch bowl. They each ladle a cup full without spilling and exit the line promptly. James looks at the Hellions behind them with a suggestive smirk and a slight raise of his cup.

"I hope they know the drill," says James, turning back to Hubert. "I don't wanna be spendin' the whole evening waitin' for refills."

"I'll toast to that," Hubert agrees.

They tap their cups together, producing a dull, low-pitched, and abrupt clank, which becomes exceedingly disappointing when Hubert recalls the pure, harmonic clink and subsequent projecting hum of the wine glasses he and God toasted with in Heaven. He flicks his cup with the fingernail of his left index finger and groans at the unsatisfactory sound. James furrows his brow and looks at Hubert with concern.

"Ya alright there, Huey? It's a plastic cup with green booze in it. I don't think it's gonna respond to Morse code."

"Cheap plastic. You would think Satan could get something better for the occasion. Maybe even splurge on some actual glassware."

"Yeah, Huey. He should just break out the fine crystal for all us moderate sinners. Ya know, 'cause we earned it."

Hubert frowns at James' sarcasm. James takes a sip of his cocktail and nudges Hubert on the shoulder with the cup. "Man, be happy ya got a drink in yer hand and enjoy yerself. I ain't gonna let ya spoil my good time, no sir."

James takes another sip, smiles, places his hand under Hubert's cup, and insistently guides the cup to his friend's mouth. Hubert reciprocates and relaxes a little as the alcohol works its way through his system. They stand around for several minutes observing the room, occasionally tilting their drinks and nodding their heads at people they recognize from the cafeteria, until the room gradually becomes quiet and they can hear the clinking of glass from a distant corner of the cavern. Satan's voice suddenly slices through the silence and caroms off the rock walls.

"Welcome, Hellions, to Hell's Paradise and the Hell's Paradise Inaugural Ball. I'm your host for this evening, Dark Lord the Merciful." James looks at Hubert with a smirk and Hubert rolls his eyes and shrugs his shoulders. Satan continues. "Tonight is dedicated to the fabulous ladies and gentlemen I see before me, and the examples you all have set for sinners everywhere. I want to take a moment to recognize the special Hellion who helped make this dream come true. Hubert Raymer, raise your hand and let us all know where you are." Hubert blushes and ducks his head, then reticently raises his hand. Satan frames his field of vision with both hands and looks around the room like a sailor scanning the horizon. Someone near the front of the audience muffles their laughter with a snort. Satan pretends not to hear and continues looking, but fails to identify Hubert, even after James shoves him in the elbow, sending his hand flying up well above the heads of their peers. "Forgive Mr. Raymer folks, he must be feeling shy. We have entertainment for you tonight in the form of Hell's very own house band, The Infernal Rackets, who are warming up right now in the amphitheater. Please, give them a round of applause, folks." A polite golf clap ensues, over which someone can be heard yelling, 'How come Hell's Paradise doesn't have its own house band?' The Devil signals for one of his minions to accost the individual, then resumes his speech. "Please, enjoy the music, cocktails, and food, and most importantly, the company of your fellow residents." Satan pauses and raises his glass, which appears to be filled with the red punch. Hopefully Claudia got to that punch bowl before he did, Hubert thinks, imagining Satan with a libelous sore on the corner of his mouth the next time he is called to his office. 'Oh, this? It's only a cold sore,' he'll say, knowing darn well no one ever got a cold sore in Hell. "If you'll all raise your cups, I'd like to propose a toast. To Hell's Paradise and many wonderful evenings like this in the years to come." A chorus of the unsatisfactory plastic *clunk* fills the room as the Hellions turn to their neighbors and touch cups. Some choose to throw their empty cups into the air afterward, like graduates do their caps at a commencement ceremony.

"This group is awfully presumptuous," Hubert remarks, almost unconsciously, remembering the scene at the front gates. He catches one of the discarded cups in his free hand.

"Lemme have that, Huey," James urges, holding out his hand. Hubert passes the cup over. "Thanks, I've been meaning to double-fist these suckers. Punch ain't strong enough."

From his corner of the room, Satan tries to regain the attention of his subjects, but it's too late. The Infernal Rackets begin to play and the crowd shifts toward the amphitheater. A significant proportion of the gatherers lag behind and attend to the punch bowls, while an exclusive club, eight Hellions to be exact, mingles in the center of the cavern, engaging in a drunken interpretation of a square dance. Hubert and James scan the room looking for the other half of the gang and find them paired together in the square dance. Intrigued, they walk over to the octet of dancers, bobbing their heads to the rhythm of the music, James in an exaggerated and mocking fashion.

"Howdy, ya'll," says James in a Southern twang, tipping an imaginary hat to the group as he two-steps along the outside of the square, stopping beside Lawrence and Claudia. "Looks like ya'll are havin' a serious *hoe*down." James eyes Claudia when he says this, and Claudia, recognizing the pun and not in the least amused, stares daggers back at him. "Mind if I cut in, pahtna?" Lawrence complies and takes James' drinks off his hands.

For the next two songs, James shucks, jives, shuffles, and jigs in a dazzling performance, which he hams up with an occasional whoop, whistle, or "yeehaw" accompanied with a clap and stomp. Hubert and Lawrence stand aside and cheer him on, taking sips of their punch each time James calls, claps, and stomps. They tap each other on the shoulder and comment about James' showmanship, but most of their conversation is about how impressive it is that Claudia is doing a fine job of keeping up with him. She is usually a fraction of a beat behind her partner and her movements are not as natural, forfeiting energy and suggesting calculation, whereas James' seem to flow from some otherworldly dance spring, as natural as the grass is green and the sky is blue; however, despite Claudia's deficiencies in innate talent, her industriousness serves as the perfect contrast to James' panache, making them a captivating duo.

The gang and the rest of the minor sinners dance and drink the night away, cajoling the band into one encore after another until they run out of songs to play. The spiked punch has been imbibed with such voraciousness that most of the Hellions' lips have been dyed green, red, or some repellent shade of brown. Having gorged themselves with liquor, the residents of Hell's Paradise rove around the room in a sort of waking coma, spending the waning moments of the first ceremonial ball bumping into each other and proposing toasts with empty cups, the punch bowls having been refilled and exhausted for the final time. Dozens of pieces of formal attire have been shed and discarded on the ground, left behind by their owners for the purpose of ducking into the dark corners of the cavern to partake in raunchy sexual acts. Hubert, perhaps the soberest of the bunch in both the literal and figurative sense, looks upon his peers with an ineluctable sense of disappointment and regret. The scene is nothing short of a hedonistic orgy, and Hubert couldn't have expected any better from the experiment. He comes across a blue evening gown which he recognizes as Claudia's and picks it up. He thumbs the frills on the single shoulder strap, sighs, and ruminates about the present condition of his wild child friend. He hopes she isn't somewhere in the shadows doing the hanky panky, but if she is, he hopes it's with Lawrence. It would be reassuring to think, alternatively, she was with James, but Hubert knows it's out of the question. James and Claudia are fire and ice. While every other woman would be sent into passionate spasms at the sight of James' dancing, especially if they were his dance partner, Claudia dismissed it as another chauvinistic display of black male bravado.

A dejected Hubert slowly exits the cavern with the blue evening gown dragging behind him. He decides to go for a long walk – a search for greener pastures – and starts by heading toward the jacuzzi fountain he and the gang discovered on their first day in Hell's Paradise. Meanwhile, in the shadows of the cavern, perched atop a limestone crag that two Hellions below are using as a prop in a dithyrambic dry humping session sure to go the distance, is Rubio, God's personal harpist and trusted spy, sent from Heaven to do reconnaissance on the ceremonial ball. Rubio doesn't like what he sees, although he has seen worse out of Hellion society, most notably the looting and brawling that transpired in reaction to the rumor of Satan's affair with a transvestite hydra. He takes a mental note of Hubert's solemnity, spreads his wings, and takes flight back to Heaven carrying perturbing news.

Chapter 16

With a hop, skip, jump, and a few flaps of his wings, Rubio voyages back to Heaven at breakneck speed to report to God. At the Pearly Gates he is accosted by several of his angel companions, who demand an account of his mission before he forwards the news to their master. Rubio is reluctant to be delayed in fulfilling his duties, but his peers remind him of an obligation to uphold the angel code, which dictates that any angel privy to classified information or breaking or sensational news must, if possible, share said knowledge with fellow angels before conveying it to the Almighty. Admitting they are right, Rubio begins with a description of Hell's Paradise, emphasizing its contrast with regular Hell, specifically the difference between minor and major sinners. His audience, which began with four angels, soon grows to seven, then ten, then thirteen, each succession of newcomers drawn by the 'oohs and aahs' of the present crowd. Once Rubio finishes describing Hell's Paradise, he segues into the tale of the ceremonial ball with a suspenseful preface.

"Now, the scene I'm about to recount is like something straight out of a smut magazine. The Hellions called it the "Hell's Paradise Inaugural Ball," and it was held in honor of the subject of my assignment, a minor sinner named Hubert Raymer." Rubio withholds Hubert's special correspondence with God to avoid causing panic. The other angels, arranged in a semi-circle around Rubio, inch closer to their orator and those in the front can now feel his chilly breath on their rosy, sun-kissed cheeks. Rubio, in exquisite detail, goes on to narrate the debauchery he witnessed at the party.

"...And when the night started winding down, and the booze had been consumed down to the last drop, and the

Hellions had sore feet and aching joints, and the band had played its last deranged tune, a great orgy ensued, consisting of tremendously vulgar acts not meant for virgin eyes. Oh, the horror!" Rubio dramatically places the back of his hand against his forehead and closes his eyes, signifying a faint.

"What kind of vulgar acts, Rubio? Tells us, tells us," one of the younger angels urges.

"I wouldn't dare speak such slander on this holy turf and in front of this wholesome audience. Some things are better left to the imagination."

With that the angels disperse and return to their various posts, many rubbing their chins and scratching their heads while churning through their minds trying to attach images to the vulgar acts Rubio alluded to, only to find little to nothing of a pornographic nature in their sanitary cerebrums. Meanwhile, Rubio flies on the double to God's throne to complete his assignment. He arrives to find his master combing His beard and cringing as the comb continually gets snagged in knots of thick, bristly white hair.

"Good afternoon, sir. I have returned from my espionage in Hades," Rubio announces. God forces the comb through an unusually stubborn knot, pulls out a lump of hair, and grunts as He glares at the comb in disgust.

"I saw you near the gates with the others, Rubio," God arraigns. Rubio opens his mouth to retort, but knows better than to interrupt. "I know you and your brethren have an unwritten rule about these things, but in this case, as monumental as recent events have been in the battle between good and evil, with this Hellion Hubert Raymer presenting himself as an ideal mediator between myself and Lucifer, you should know to come directly to me." An embarrassed Rubio looks down at his feet and shuffles his heels from side to side.

"You're right, sir, my cohorts could have waited until later. I'm sorry." Rubio looks up and sees God fussing with another tangle. "Here, sir, let me help you with that." As if He had been anticipating His servant's offer from the start, the Lord relinquishes the comb to Rubio with a grateful smile.

Rubio works through the beard, then expertly plaits God's hair and inspects His scalp, picking occasional dead ends out of the otherwise flourishing mane. He shares his observations of the inaugural ball in Hell's Paradise and offers his advice for troubleshooting the problems presented by the freedoms recently bestowed upon the minor sinners of the underworld. God listens with open ears and allows His magnanimous servant to complete his monologue without interruption. Rubio works all the kinks out of the Lord's hair and reaches under His throne for a shaving kit, from which he produces a bottle of shampoo and a bottle of conditioner. He proceeds to lather and rinse God's hair, but is stopped partway through the deed. God holds up a hand. Indignant voices can be heard far off across the expanse of the Kingdom.

"Do you hear that, Rubio?" God asks. As yet, Rubio has heard nothing.

"No, Jehovah. What is it?" Rubio inquires. While God can hear almost anything that takes place within His realm, Rubio and the other angels merely have the hearing sense of a dog or bat, phenomenal compared to a human, but marginal compared to the Creator.

The source of the banter is a mob of disgruntled Heavenites, recently introduced to the notion of a diluted version of Hell approved by their Savior in collaboration with their eternal inveigle and nemesis, Beelzebub, the worm, the antichrist, Mephistopheles, or otherwise known as Satan. The mob consists of two divergent schools of thought:

one, the majority, which is led by no one in particular, seeks to dismantle Hell's Paradise and return things to normal, while the second, a small group led by Archibald – the tennis playing Pierce Brosnan doppelganger – is determined to create a "Heaven's Sanctuary" to maintain the balance. Marching their way toward God's throne, the divisions of the mob recite their respective slogans, "No Normalcy, No Dormancy," and "If Heathens Deserve Better, We Deserve Better."

God sends Rubio to intercept the rioters and buy Him time to think of how to handle their protestations. He wishes He had trained one of His angels to specialize in public relations, but for the time being Rubio is the best asset He has for such matters. Rubio heads off the contumacious crowd a few hundred yards from God's throne and tries to quiet them by motioning up and down with his hands. The Heavenites attempt to push by Rubio, who realizes he cannot contain them on his own and whistles for help. Within seconds a quartet of angels arrives and spreads out in front of the advancing mob, batting their wings in the faces of the dissenters and tossing handfuls of angel dust into the air, anything to distract, disorient, and frustrate the Heavenites. After a minute or two, the angels' efforts have proven effective and the fomenters are sedated, except for a few pugnacious souls on the front line.

"Ladies and gentlemen, there is no reason to fret, please be calm. Your concerns will be heard by your Lord and Savior in due time, but you must be civil and dignified," Rubio announces.

"Oh, baloney! Tell that to the degenerates running amok in Hell's Paradise," shouts an older woman up front.

"No Normalcy, No Dormancy!" the majority chants in muted tones.

"If Heathens Deserve Better, We Deserve Better!" the minority attempts to yell, but instead projects in hoarse bellows. The Heavenites waggle their heads and shoulders as the spell of the angel dust gradually wears off.

"Alright everybody, that is enough. Until you demonstrate a sense of order and respect, we will not allow you to go forward to share your thoughts with God," says Rubio. A middle-aged man in the front row steps forward. It's Archibald. Say, this man looks like that one actor who played James Bond for several film installments, what was his name? Rubio thinks.

"Dear cherub, I apologize on behalf of my fellow Heavenites," Archibald submits. Although he shares the facial features of Pierce Brosnan, Archibald is a paunchy man, a little on the short side, with cropped brown hair and designer eyeglasses. He looks like he could have been a computer technician or mechanical engineer in his former life. "Our behavior has been uncharacteristically reactionary and I hope you understand our displeasure. Very few of us have heard news as jarring as that of Hell's Paradise. It's a shock to our systems."

"I appreciate your explanation and accept your apology. What is your name, sir?" Rubio asks.

"Archibald. Archibald the Egret." Heavenites don't retain their last names. Instead they are given titles by their guardian angels.

"Ah, Archibald the Egret. Thelonious is your protector, correct?"

"Yes."

"Thelonious always had a fetish for unusual titles. Archibald, do you consider yourself the spokesperson or leader of this group?"

"I'm the de facto leader, yes. However, we are divided into two factions. I represent the minority which desires to create a "Heaven's Sanctuary." Fair is fair."

"And the majority?" Members of the majority look at one another with uncertainty in their eyes.

"I don't believe they have a leader," says Archibald the Elder. "But they want Hell's Paradise destroyed and things returned to normal."

"Well, I guess they don't need a leader as long as their message is clear. And why aren't you and your constituents satisfied with the opinion of the majority, Archibald?" Rubio inquires.

"I, er, *we* have our reasons, but we're inclined to withhold our case until it stands directly before our Lord." Archibald crosses his arms and a smug grin traces itself across his face. Rubio doesn't like the man's hubris, but is willing to appease him. Jehovah will put this self-assured pinhead in his place, the angel thinks.

"Very well," says Rubio, confident he has delayed the mob's progress long enough, "you and your comrades may go forth to speak with God. Remember: civility reigns supreme."

Archibald half-bows in front of Rubio and he and the crowd march onward. Rubio takes flight and reaches his master's side while the Heavenites are still about one hundred paces from the throne. He updates God on the situation and profiles Archibald the Egret. Underneath a veil of imperturbability, God finds Himself anxious and unassertive for the first time in millennia, and before He can rehearse an amenable discourse for the rioters, they are at the foot of His gold pedestal.

"Almighty Lord and Savior," Archibald announces, "your disciples come to you in droves with deep-seated concerns about the business of Hell's Paradise." God steps down from the pedestal to be at the level of the Heavenites.

"My children, I am aware many rumors have been spread throughout the Kingdom about the cooperative between myself and Satan. I cannot deny the existence of Hell's Paradise, and my involvement in its creation, but I am here to dispel whatever false rumors you have heard and am open to your contentions and suggestions," God proclaims.

A long and impassioned discussion ensues with both sides of the Heavenite assembly arguing their stances, more often with each other than with God, who assumes the role of moderator and frequently has to redirect the debate, or instead asks Rubio to toss angel dust on the group until they have been drugged into a suggestible state, at which point the Lord reminds them of the purpose of their visit. Eventually, the discussion retreads the same points and topics so many times God has to suspend the affair. The blowhard and incorrigible Heavenites have left Him with no other option than to consult with Satan. Archibald is insulted by this decision.

"That's your solution! To speak with Satan! Hypocrite!"

The Almighty would ordinarily smite thee for such blasphemy, but His enthusiasm for dolling out punishment has been drained, and He signals for Rubio to escort the Heavenites back to their quarters. He tugs at His beard as they walk away and disappear over the peak of a cloud, and thinks about the dilemma He and Lucifer have brought about. I hope Hubert Raymer proves himself worthy, God thinks, returning to His throne and resuming the combing of His beard.

Chapter 17

After combing His beard into a tame and presentable condition, God reaches for a walkie-talkie on the end table next to His throne and turns the power on. The radio emits a flurry of static and God presses the 'up' channel button four times, changing from channel two to channel six, which is clear of static and silent. He thumbs the transmission button and holds the device up to His mouth.

"Lima Six, come in Lima Six, do you read me? Over," He says. Several seconds pass and then someone can be heard fumbling with the walkie-talkie on the receiving end. A loud thud is heard through the speaker followed by some explicit language. Finally, there is a response.

"10-4, Juliett Six, I read you. Over," Satan broadcasts.

"We need to talk, Lima Six. Something has come up, over."

"Is it urgent, Juliett Six? Over."

"Yes, over."

"OK, well come over to my office and we'll hash it out. Over." The line is silent for a moment.

"It would be better to talk in my domain. Over." The line is again silent for a moment.

"No go. We had our previous meeting there and my fingers and toes have yet to fully recover from the frostbite. This time we meet here, over." Another pause.

"I guess it would only be fair. I'll go get my water canteen and miniature fan. See you momentarily. Over and out."

"10-4, JS. Over and out."

God switches back to channel two, pushes the transmission button, and asks for Rubio to bring Him His water canteen and miniature fan. Rubio arrives promptly with the vital items wearing a familiar look on his ruddy face, a mixture of compassion and repressed sanguinity, a reflexive response to the pathos of fetching the "slumming supplies," a pejorative term Rubio has adopted for the canteen and fan.

"Here you are, sir, as requested. I filled the canteen with fresh water from the Fountain of Youth and put new batteries in the fan. Safe travels," says Rubio, handing God His survival tools.

"Thank you, gallant Rubio. Wish me luck."

"God speed." Rubio stands at attention and gives his master a military salute, all the while struggling to keep a straight face. The Lord rolls His eyes and smiles. Although He's seen this act many, many times over, He never grows tired of the tacky attempt at ironic humor.

Rubio leaves Him to His business with a genuine, sprightly wave, and God takes a seat in His throne with the water canteen slung over His shoulder by its leather strap and the miniature fan in the breast pocket of His robe. He mutters something in Hebrew, crosses Himself, then reaches under the left armrest and presses a red button. An unseen force, possibly an agent of the mystical gold throne, or simply God's own power, launches Him up into the overhead clouds, from which He is shot downward in a violent and blinding lightning bolt.

The lightning bolt consumes the Lord's physical form, transforming Him into the Holy Ghost, and His spirit rides the lightning bolt into the time-space continuum, where He is deposited onto "The Business Expressway." He catapults through the vastness of space between Heaven and Hell in what to Him is a blink of an eye; to Hubert Raymer the same commute had no relative meaning and could have covered the gamut, taking seconds, minutes, hours, days, weeks, months, years, decades, centuries, millennia, eons, or gigaannums. As God approaches the exiting end of the wormhole, His physical form gradually reassembles until He finds Himself in a fully corporeal state, sitting in His robe in a smoldering pile of ash in the firebox of Satan's fireplace. Thermopylae hisses at Him from the opposite side of the gold coal gate.

"No! Bad kitty," Satan hollers, snapping his fingers at the Hellcat, "leave our guest alone." Thermopylae wheels around, bolts into the middle of the room, and settles underneath one of the couches. His crimson eyes pierce through the darkness like the moon of a lunar eclipse. Satan approaches the fireplace and opens the coal gate for the Lord. "Sorry about that, Jehovah, he is very suspicious of strangers, although by now he should recognize you. After all, you don't look like any old rake who comes in here." Satan offers a hand to God and helps Him out of the firebox.

"Thanks, Lucifer," God says as He pats the soot out of His robe.

"You're welcome. Say, you look parched, let me get you a glass of water." God holds up a hand in protest and shakes His head.

"No, no, I brought my own," He says, tapping the water canteen hanging around His shoulders. "I appreciate the offer though."

"Oh nonsense, Jehovah. My water is as good as any from Heaven. Think, who knows how that water of yours was affected by its trip through the great unknown. There could be Martian bacteria in there, now we don't want that." God, a veteran of this routine, figures He better appease His host.

"Very well, you win Lucifer. Bring me some of that famous Hades water."

Satan, grinning from ear to ear, goes to a cabinet against the same wall as the fireplace. He takes a small key out of his goatee, unlocks the cabinet doors, and removes a glass and a pitcher of water from inside the cabinet. He fills the glass and puts the pitcher back in the cabinet, then turns the key and places it back in the bristly hair of his goatee.

"You don't have a better place for that key than your beard?" God asks.

"What better place than that? It's always on my person and I don't have any pockets." Satan passes the glass of water to God. With this comment, God notices, as if for the first time, that Satan only wears a loin cloth. Of course, the loin cloth is fastened by an alligator skin belt with a bombastic gold buckle. Savage, but balanced with a helping of Western vanity, God thinks. "And please, it's a goatee, Jehovah."

"A goatee, right I forgot." God gulps down half of the glass of water. "An appropriate name. Came up with it yourself, no doubt." Satan nods while God finishes off the bottom half of the glass of water.

"All the young men are wearing goatees these days. I do believe I'm a trendsetter."

God gives the glass to the Devil and asks for a refill. Satan walks back to the cabinet, retrieves the pitcher, fills the glass to the brim, returns the pitcher to the interior shelf, and closes and locks the door. Thermopylae's luminous crimson eyes follow his every move. He carries the water over to God, careful not to trip on any of the space rugs, and hands God the glass with a disingenuous bow.

"Try not to drink it so quickly. It's best to rehydrate at a moderate pace," says Satan. God furrows His brow and turns His chin upward a few degrees.

"Is that right, Lucifer? And when was the last time you drank water?" Satan looks down at his clawed fingers and begins counting off units of time on each scaly digit, surpassing ten and starting anew, eventually stopping at fourteen.

"That would be about 1,400 years ago...yep, fourteen centuries if I remember correctly. I haven't refilled that pitcher since then, so that water you're presently consuming is at least 1,400 years old." God peers into the glass and holds it under His nose to sniff the contents.

"Well, either you're pulling my leg or the water in these parts maintains its purity for a long time." Satan withholds a belly laugh.

"I'm sorry, you're right. I replenish that pitcher every week. Of course, you're about the only person who uses it. If I allowed my residents such indulgences, what kind of Dark Lord would that make me? Anyway, let's stop putzing around. Please, come sit at my desk and let us discuss business."

Satan ambles over to his desk and sits in the swivel chair, while God takes a seat on the other side of the desk, stopping first to glance at the Persian rug and thinking the room would be better off without it. Satan puts his hooved feet up on the desk, legs crossed, and grabs a fountain pen and a notepad from atop the desk. He twirls the fountain pen in his hand and appears to examine something on the front page of the notepad before turning it a few pages to a blank sheet.

"Maybe you should hire a stenographer, Lucifer," God chides. "Surely one of your followers was a stenographer in his or her past life. Perfect fit."

"I had one. She struggled with my coding system and her handwriting was at times illegible. I had to fire her," Satan explains. "Turns out she lied on her application. She was actually a doctor in the time before." Satan slaps his thigh and bleats. God smiles and shakes His head.

"I like that. Pretty clever."

"Thanks. Came up with it myself." Satan turns his head a little to the right and assumes an inconscient stare over God's left shoulder. After several seconds, he gets back on track. "Business, yes," he virtually whispers to himself. "What is the urgent matter you came here to tell me about, Jehovah?"

"I have a predicament in my Kingdom involving my pupils. Civil unrest might be the best way to describe it. The Heavenites have become privy to the existence of Hell's Paradise and a large group of them is decidedly upset about it." Satan etches on the notepad.

"OK. And what do they want?"

"Well, they are of two schools of thought. One, which appears to be the majority, wants Hell's Paradise to be demolished. The other, smaller faction, wants me to construct a "Heaven's Sanctuary."" Satan stops writing and taps the pen against the pad with one firm, punctuated strike.

"A "Heaven's Sanctuary," why that's ludicrous!" the Devil cackles. "Have your children no shame? They live in *paradise,* doggoned, what more could they ask for?" God covers His brow with His hand and rubs His temples.

"An exclusive country club, apparently."

"And who gets to live in this exclusive country club, this "Heaven's Sanctuary"?"

"The purest of the pure. The most pious of my adherents."

"I see. All the suck-ups and brownnosers in a special fraternity." The wheels begin turning in Satan's head as he thinks of how the situation could play to his advantage. *A house divided against itself will not stand,* Satan thinks, quoting the Bible and Abraham Lincoln. In his house, such division is the normal state of things. No one thinks any less of a disorderly and tumultuous Hell. But in Heaven, well, the reaction would be entirely different. The Heavenites would be disillusioned, and more importantly, once the Hellions caught wind of the conditions in Heaven, their condition would seem comparatively better. Morale would be at its highest in years. The minor sinners would no longer resent the major sinners. Dark Lord the Merciful would finally...

"Lucifer," God says, waving His hands in front of Satan's face and breaking him from his trance, "stay with it. Which group do you agree with? I'm in favor of dismantling Hell's Paradise, but if you can convince me otherwise I'm all ears."

"Don't be silly. We cannot do away with Hell's Paradise on the whim of some bellyachers in your midst. I initially laughed at the idea of a Heaven's Sanctuary. I mean, how sanctimonious can Heavenites get? However, while I was lost in deep thought a minute ago, I realized it's imperative to the PR of both of our kingdoms to go through with this." Knowing God's psychic abilities are significantly diminished by the unfriendly confines of Hades, Satan is able to deliver this lie with confidence.

"What makes Heaven's Sanctuary imperative to our PR?"

"Solidarity, Jehovah. We must remain consistent in our standards. If the Hellions are granted an exclusive club, then so too shall the Heavenites."

"I'm beginning to regret ever having endorsed this project." This is also a lie, for God too has ulterior motives, ones Satan cannot begin to fathom given the brevity of his foresight and hindsight. "But you're right, Lucifer, we cannot appear irresolute. Heaven's Sanctuary it is."

The all-powerful beings shake hands and the era of Heaven's Sanctuary begins.

Chapter 18

Hubert and James are on their hands and knees, again scrubbing the floor of one of the communal showers, only this time they've been granted the use of standard scrubbing brushes. Hell's Paradise has its perks, but chores are still a part of the everyday regimen of a minor sinner. Hubert and James expected nothing less and neither seems to mind his present bathroom duties. Hubert scrubs away at the grimy ceramic tiles at a high tempo, alternating between 120 bpm and 90 bpm, like a disc jockey mixing on a turn table. James, in rhythm with Hubert's scrubbing, whistles a scat jazz rendition in the style of Ella Fitzgerald. After jamming for several minutes, the two friends take a breather.

"That sounded real smooth, brotha," James pronounces.

"Thanks, buddy. I love that riff you did toward the middle, that '*do-do-dodo / do-do-dodo / DO-WOO*'," Hubert responds while rubbing and kneading his triceps. "My arms are really spent from that high tempo. Whaddya say we do something mid-tempo for the next round?"

"Fine by me. Yer the orchestrator. Man, they shoulda let *us* play at tha ceremonial ball. We woulda torn tha house down."

"Yeah, well maybe there will be more events to come. We should practice and prepare a whole set. You know, those Infernal Rackets played a tight set themselves. I think we should seek out advice from them." James retracts and grimaces.

"Shoot, those cats were hogwash. They didn't have style or stage presence." James rubs at a speck on the floor with his index finger. "On top of that, summa tha music they played was somethin' a brotha might hear in tha wrong neck of tha woods."

"What are you talking about? You enjoyed it by my account. I seem to recall a particular black man getting busy in a square dance." Hubert gets to his feet and does a quick imitation of James' moves.

"I was just ingratiating myself with them white folks. That wasn't genuine enjoyment ya witnessed, Huey."

"Right, well, you're a good sport then, James. You made Claudia's night." James waves a dismissive hand at his friend. They both know Claudia could never truly appreciate such a gesture – to her, chivalry is not only dead, it's burdensome to begin with – but Hubert appeases James nevertheless. "Boy, she could really move. I mean, not like you, but Lawrence and I were impressed."

"Yeah, she can move all right. Move right outta tha scene with Lawrence and some young jezebel. A *sister* jezebel." James spits on a stain on the floor and vigorously scrubs it.

"I guess that explains why we haven't seen them for so long. Where in the hell do you think they've been?" Hubert smiles at his pun.

"This ain't time for jokes, Huey. I'm worried, man." Hubert sets his brush down and sits straight up, hands on his knees.

"What for? Claudia can take care of herself."

"It ain't Claudia I'm worried about. I'm uncomfortable with the idea of a drunk Lawrence wandering off with a black woman."

"Oh, come off it, James."

"Naw, naw. That's nothing but a slave owner fantasy, some Thomas Jefferson fetish. I bet it wouldn't be tha first time he got some darkie love, no siree."

"Cripes, I should never have told you anything about his past."

"I woulda deduced it anyhow. I have cracker radar. It's tha sixth sense of the American negro, at least for those of us born within three generations of slavery. After that it tapers off with the memories." Hubert chuckles and slaps his thigh. James smiles back. "I'm serious. In my day we were vigilant. The Panthers never got hood winked by no cracker. These brothas nowadays lost their edge. Why ya think rappers and athletes keep getting duped by white record executives and white agents?"

"Weak cracker radar," says Hubert, happy to play along.

"Darn skippy."

SCRAAAAAAAAAAWWW!

A Hellbird signals the beginning of the lunch period and Hubert and James rise to their feet. They inspect their work, and after convincing themselves of a satisfactory job, leave the shower and walk through the atrium of the bathhouse to the exit. They proceed down the radial corridor along with a gaggle of other hungry Hellions heading the lunch rush. Once inside the cafeteria, they stand on opposite sides of the door and look around for Lawrence and Claudia. No sightings. They carry on to their signature table next to the biker gangs and are surprised to find it empty. Standing back to back, they survey the canteen again and again find no signs of their friends' presence. They shrug their shoulders and take seats across from each other.

"We need ta start a petition ta have a cafeteria built inside Hell's Paradise. I hate having ta come out here and botha with these libertines," James complains.

"Libertines, James? You know we fit right in with the status quo. The whole selection process was corrupt anyhow. Minor sinner, major sinner, I don't see the difference," Hubert replies.

"Yeah, yer right, 'separate but equal.' I know how that is. Lookin' like the Jim Crow South in this cafeteria."

They both chuckle. The cafeteria has, in fact, been segregated, although no official statute has been enacted. During the first few meals following the opening of Hell's Paradise, the minor and major sinners naturally bisected the room. Hubert and James' table is situated near the dividing line with the biker tables delineating the beginning of the major sinner area. Old friends, torn apart physically and socially by separate designations, no longer convene three times a day in the cafeteria. They make new friends within their population and move on. Occasionally they will bump into one another in the kitchen line, but words are rarely exchanged. Instead, a sentimental and sympathetic expression passes from one old friend to the other and they quickly return to staring at their trays or the backs of the heads of the Hellions waiting in front of them.

Nostalgia is taboo in Hell.

"Another one of Satan's games. He couldn't help but dangle the carrot in front of both the haves and the have-nots."

"Shoot, he's just cheap Hubert. That's all this is. He'll build us an upscale community, but he'll be damned ta put a cafeteria in it. He needs that money ta furnish his office and develop technology fer his next patent."

"I did notice a new antique lamp in his office the last time I was there."

From somewhere nearby, Hubert and James hear a familiar bout of the giggles. They turn their heads and find Lawrence and Claudia sitting a few tables away, partially hiding their faces behind lunch trays. The two mischief makers pretend they haven't been detected and resume a fabricated private conversation. James snaps his fingers at them.

"Hey, ya'll know we saw ya. Stop playing dumb," he shouts.

Hubert invites them to the traditional table with a wave and an inviting smile and Lawrence and Claudia wander over, snickering to each other about some inside joke. Claudia sits next to James and Lawrence passes around the end of the table and sits beside Hubert. No words are spoken for the first few seconds as the four friends exchange a flurry of intersecting glances.

"Where are your appetites?" asks Claudia, pointing to the empty table space in front of both Hubert and James. "How about some french fries?" She slides her tray gently in James' direction.

"Don't give me that funk, Ms. Claudia. Ya'll two got some explaining ta do before we can talk about french fries. Things ain't even soggy," James retorts. Claudia draws the tray back and picks up a fry. Lawrence looks at her, then James, and takes a bite out of his sloppy joe.

"What our friend James meant to say was, 'Nice to see you guys. It's been a blue moon. We'd love to hear what you've been up to,'" says Hubert.

"I mighta said that if she hadn't opened with a disingenuous french fry appeasement," James comments, reaching for a fry on Claudia's plate. She allows him the fry, but not without a slap on the back of the hand. "She-devil." Claudia sneers and sticks out her tongue.

"Alright, you two. James, you're right and I'd love to offer a brief narrative of our adventures since we last saw you," states Lawrence.

"And when was that? The last time we saw ya?" James inquires.

"Well, the ceremonial ball, of course."

"Right, but I mean the circumstances." James narrows his eyes and Lawrence puts his hand to his chin while attempting to measure the question.

"Oh, yes. Claudia and I left with a young lady. I imagine we all had a nice romp after that, but I'm not too sure. We were rather inebriated."

"A nice romp, ya say?"

"You heard him alright, James. We had a nice romp. What's it to you?" Claudia intervenes.

"I wonder whatever became of that young lady," Lawrence ponders aloud.

"I dunno, maybe she found her way ta the circle of sloth. I bet they would find good use fer her there, wouldn't they Lawrence?" asks James.

"How would I know? I'm not a minion. Personally, I don't think she'd be much good for hard physical labor. Her skin is too soft."

"Uh huh. So, she'd be more of a breeder than a laborer." Lawrence pounds his fist on the table.

"Enough! What do you think, I'm daft? You're ornery because of that girl's skin color. Tell me, Mr. Race Crusader, was I trying to act out some slave master sexual fantasy?" Hubert places a hand on Lawrence's forearm to keep him from shooting for James' neck.

"Fellas, fellas. Live and let live," says Hubert, but his plea falls on deaf ears.

"I'll bet that wasn't the first time ya been with a black woman. Ya got jungle fever, don't ya Lawrence?" James posits.

Lawrence thinks about his son, Harold, the one who was conceived with one of his slaves, Melinda, an ebony beauty with green eyes who was second-generation property of the Rutledge family. Her mother, Harold's grandmother, was from the Congo region of Africa and was bought at an auction on the island of St. Lucia by Lawrence's father. Her father, Harold's grandfather, was one of the Rutledge field hands, sold to another trader not long after Melinda's birth. Lawrence didn't mean for things to happen the way they did with Melinda, for he wasn't the aggressor in the relationship. Melinda inveigled him over a period of a few months, flirting and stealing kisses from time to time, and they eventually consummated the affair on top of a hay bale behind a barn in a secluded part of the Rutledge estate. When Melinda discovered she was pregnant, they were both overcome with anxiety and regret. Lawrence's wife, despite her progressive views on race and her abolitionist leanings, was a proud woman and a devout Christian, believing deeply in the sanctity of marriage, and would have a conniption if she found out about the affair. Even worse, Lawrence's father was still alive, and though a ripe eighty-eight years old, practically a relic by the standards of colonial America, he continued to rule the plantation with an iron fist. He despised miscegenation, or "mongrelization" as he preferred to call it, and would have disowned Lawrence, possibly even sold him into slavery, and subjected Melinda and her unborn baby, his grandson, to unspeakable cruelty. Lawrence and Melinda had decided to sneak away to Richmond to visit an abortionist Lawrence knew about, when miraculously, the old man died of internal bleeding when a mule kicked him in the gut. Six and a half months later, Harold Wilbur Rutledge was born. Lawrence's wife never confronted him about the suspiciously fair-skinned boy's paternity. She suffered the betrayal in silence, and Lawrence has forever felt indebted to her fortitude, resilience, and forgiveness.

Her gravestone reads "A loving mother and wife, and a world-class stoic."

No, the young damsel from the night of the ceremonial ball wasn't the first time Lawrence had been with a black woman. James' cracker radar hadn't failed him in that regard, but it failed to access the significance of Lawrence's perceived racist sexual behavior. Lawrence senses this and decides to enlighten James with an anecdote about his biracial son.

"Maybe I do, James. In fact, I have a mulatto son to prove it," says Lawrence. Hubert grimaces and palms his face at hearing the antiquated racial epithet.

"Yeah, and I bet he and his mother got the Sally Hemings treatment, didn't they?"

"No, as a matter of fact I freed his mother and got her a job as a nurse in a nearby hospital. That way, she was close enough to see our son on a regular basis, and far enough to avoid any confrontation with my wife." James raises his eyebrows. "As for my son, Harold, I'd say I did right by him. He and my other son, Terrance, inherited my estate and turned Rutledge Tobacco Company into a household name." James' eyebrows drop and he spits out a glob of mushed french fry.

"You?! *Your* family is the namesake of *the* Rutledge Tobacco Company?! Get outta here!"

"It's true."

"I'll be damned, Lawrence. I shoulda put two and two together. I used ta smoke those Rutledge Menthol 100s like crazy. Sometimes two packs a day." James pauses and looks up. "Eugene Rutledge, that was his name, the Rutledge President and CEO in my day, and this brother was dark as night. Must be like yer great-great-great-great-great grandson." Another pause and James looks back at Lawrence, smiling. "He was on the cover of Forbes magazine: 'Meet America's First Black Billionaire.' This cat had on a white seersucker and a fedora tilted to the side. Man, yer alright, Lawrence. Ya made that possible,

America's first black billionaire. Yer a part of black history."
Lawrence blushes.

God works in mysterious ways.

"Congratulations, honey, your one positive contribution to humanity was shagging a black woman," Claudia jokes. They have a good laugh at Lawrence's expense, Lawrence included.

"Well, shagging her and getting her pregnant, let's be specific," Hubert adds. Lawrence's complexion grows even redder. "Anyhow, glad you two have found some common ground."

"Speaking of common ground, I suppose you and James have heard the rumors," Claudia postulates.

"Hmm, I don't think so, have we old buddy?" Hubert asks, looking across at James, who picks up another fry from Claudia's plate and shrugs.

"I hear alotta rumors, ya'll know that," James replies. "I heard a wild one about a chimera and some disco biscuits recently."

"No, this one is of a serious nature," Lawrence proclaims.

"OK, out with it then."

"Since we last saw you two, Claudia and I have talked to several minor sinners who claim a "Heaven's Sanctuary" is being erected in Heaven in response to our new residence."

"That was only a matter of time," says James, shaking his head. Hubert mumbles something to himself. "What's up, Huey?"

""The road to Hell is paved with good intentions." I knew this was gonna open Pandora's box," Hubert replies with a detached tone.

Hubert reflects on the choices that eventually lead to this juncture. Instinct, intuition, and impulse. The three 'I's' of an inevitable predicament. Why did I have to be so self-righteous? he thinks. Hubert knew better than to trust the Devil, but hadn't expected God to allow the situation to transgress further than his initial request. There have to be more agents at work than meets the eye, Hubert concludes. He is no dilettante observer of the ways of the afterlife.

"Listen, Huey, what goes on up there is no skin off yer back," James asserts.

"Yeah, you can't feel directly responsible for this. Besides, a "Heaven's Sanctuary" can't be all that bad. Seems inconsequential to me," Claudia remarks. She is not nearly as sagacious as her friend Hubert.

Chapter 19

Heaven is buzzing with jubilant chatter and the popping of champagne bottles. Archibald and his followers are celebrating their successful bid to segregate Heaven, and it's an august affair. The inhabitants of Heaven's Sanctuary, who have come to call themselves the "majorly pious," are dressed in fine white linens and sip Moët and Chandon from crystal glasses. They toast to various self-serving causes, such as their health, their children, their futures, their standing with God, and of course, their new digs, which ironically exhibit no physical differences from regular Heaven other than the fancy wrought iron gates demarcating the bounds. The gateway has an ornamental design commemorating Heaven's Sanctuary with ecclesiastical motifs, including saints, crucifixes, angels, doves, ichthyses, and the like. Such imagery is plentiful in regular Heaven, and thus the only meaningful difference between Heaven's Sanctuary and regular Heaven is the inhabitants.

And what distinguished inhabitants they are, and indulgent in their triumph over the baseness of their counterparts, who they have come to call the "minorly pious." The scene in Heaven's Sanctuary is reminiscent of the "Hell's Paradise Inaugural Ball," and the general temperament of the revelers compares favorably, or more appropriately, disfavorably, to that of patrons at an invitation-only art exhibition or a $200-a-plate fundraising event. There is enough elbow-rubbing, back-patting, and adulation, of both the inward and outward variety, to put a political rally to shame. The minions in the circle of pride would have a field day with this crowd.

True to form, Archibald is the center of attention, the consummate people pleaser, working from one peer to another, kissing babies and old ladies on the cheek, shaking hands with the influential, tipping his hat to beautiful women; whatever is necessary to self-aggrandize. As always, he is one degree stuffier than the person he is engaging. The leader of the majorly pious is not to be outdone in the arena of stuffiness.

Born into privilege, Archibald Nathaniel Ingram III had opportunities most people can only dream of, and to his credit he made the best of his fortunate circumstances by dedicating his life to philanthropy and self-improvement. He founded a number of charitable organizations, including Literacy and Life Skills, Inc., which taught illiterate adults how to read and earn a decent living, Stand Down for Veterans, Inc., an anti-war cause which collaborated with veterans to promote isolationism and disarmament, and Rights for White Rhinos, Inc., a conservation group dedicated to saving the white rhino and its habitat (Archibald would find out the organization was doing more to hurt the white rhino than help it; in fact, the species went extinct not long after his death).

When Archibald wasn't operating his non-profits, he was embarking on one personal adventure or another in the constant pursuit of becoming a Renaissance man. He played piano and loved to sing, although no one other than one of his ex-girlfriends knew about the latter because he was embarrassed by his sopranist voice and only sang in private. Painting was his second artistic passion, and he spent thousands of hours in the studio in the basement of his house painting in the Post-Impressionist style of Vincent van Gogh. Most of his paintings ended up in the garbage, a tip of the hat to Pablo Picasso, but the good ones became birthday or Christmas gifts, or were simply given away. Of the hundreds of paintings Archibald produced, he only ever kept one for himself, a landscape of Crater Lake in Utah he entitled "Moated Mount," which he kept hanging above the headboard of his bed. In addition to his creative pursuits, Archibald was an avid outdoorsman and spent much of his free time on his treasured sailboat, a thirty-five-footer he named "Santa Margarita," which he captained on four circumnavigations of the world, two of which were solo. He went helicopter skiing in Alaska and the Swiss Alps, hunted and successfully killed the Big Five in Africa (ironic considering his rhino charity), hiked the entire Appalachian Trail barefoot, and at the age of fifty-five, summited K2 without oxygen. At the insistence of his friends and family, Archibald wrote an autobiography about his conquests of the natural world and donated the profits to Literacy and Life Skills, Inc.. The book sold over one million copies and was optioned to a film studio, but the project halted in "production hell" and never made it to the silver screen. Archibald was relieved by this.

The local Presbyterian church was another important part of Archibald's non-professional life. He was baptized twice, once as an infant, and once at the age of thirty-three because he felt he needed to reaffirm his commitment to Christ. The age was no coincidence. As a child, he attended Sunday school and participated in many of the church's volunteer events, a custom he continued until he became too old to lead an active life. Despite a longing to do so, he never joined the church choir for fear of humiliating himself with his high-pitched voice. Instead, he served as the regular pianist, and was lauded throughout the community for his enrapturing renditions of various Christian harmonies. Archibald was a close friend of the pastor, Pastor Simmons, and was often invited to speak at congregations, where he would impart wisdom he had learned from operating his charitable enterprises and lessons nature had taught him from his outdoor hobbies. He would accompany these reflections with scripture and was told time and time again by fellow church members what a great catechist he was, and that he should become ordained. When Pastor Simmons died, a semi-retired Archibald did exactly that, and served as the pastor during his twilight years.

Archibald's home life was equally fulfilling as his public life. He married his high school sweetheart, a leggy brunette named Pamela, and they exchanged vows in the very church Archibald would eventually preside over as its pastor. Pamela came from a secular family, and despite her reservations, Archibald convinced her to be baptized before the birth of their first child, a healthy nine-pound, six-ounce boy they christened Joshua. One year and a few weeks later Pamela gave birth to their second child, a girl they christened Hannah. Archibald was the proud patriarch of a rich man's family. He was an active and authoritative parent, frequently attending Joshua and Hannah's athletic events and piano recitals, overseeing their schoolwork, and disciplining them when necessary in an absolute, but fair manner. He and Pamela involved the kids in family decisions they deemed age-appropriate, and gradually granted them more autonomy commensurate with their age and maturity. One might say they were model parents, and in many ways they were model spouses. Of their fifty-six years of happy marriage, a period spanning over 20,000 days, Archibald can only recall two days of relative unhappiness: the day Pamela turned fifty and Archibald made a comment about her crow's feet, and the day the first family dog died and they argued about what to tell the children, each holding different opinions about whether dogs have souls and if there is a dog heaven. Pamela won the argument and they told Joshua and Hannah, then nine and eight, respectively, that their Yorkshire Terrier, Rufus, had a good and wholesome spirit and had risen to dog heaven, where he would spend eternity romping and pooping on endless fields of verdant grass with canine icons like

Lassie, Benji, Rin Tin Tin, and Old Yeller. Meanwhile, aberrant dogs like Cujo and Scoobie Doo had found themselves forever running from animal services, taking baths, and being besieged by vacuum cleaners in dog hell.

Though Archibald was an accomplished man, and an exemplary citizen, father, and husband, he wasn't free of fault. As a self-confessed adrenaline junkie, his thrill seeking wasn't limited to the aforementioned activities. He also got his fix by driving fast and recklessly in any of a number of sports cars he owned throughout his adult life, including his favorite, the Porsche 911, which he bought new with each model year. It was in this car that Archibald's habit went from dangerous to deadly when he hit a motorcyclist at ninety miles-per-hour, killing the man instantly. Fortunately for Archibald, the motorcyclist was involved in a street race and had blown through a red light, thus nullifying the possibility of vehicular manslaughter charges. Instead, he spent the night in jail and received a costly speeding ticket. Archibald became a cautious and tentative driver from that point on. The incident weighed on his conscience for years afterward, manifesting in recurring nightmares where the victim would appear in the form of the Ghost Rider and destroy Archibald's 911 with his hellfire chain.

Archibald's other flaw was the inflated sense of importance he acquired from a lifetime of achievement. His neighbors and extended family found him pretentious and incorrigible, and his wife was the only one capable of keeping his ego in check. He had difficulty making and keeping friends because of his boastful ways, and the few friends he did have were also blowhards, the kind of men who turn every social interaction into a pissing contest. Archibald was always happy to oblige them.

Yes, Archibald Nathaniel Ingram III is an ideal candidate to campaign for something like Heaven's

Sanctuary, and now that the objective has been reached, he wants to play the gracious host and make his constituents feel at home. He approaches an elderly woman with a pearl necklace, gently takes her hand, and kisses it.

"Good day, Mrs. Everson, how are you ma'am?" he opens.

"Why, I'm quite well, Archie. How about yourself?" Mrs. Everson asks with a Southern drawl.

"I couldn't be better. And I couldn't ask for a better day to celebrate a new beginning, and with the most wonderful of people at that."

"Oh, isn't that nice. I'm glad to be here with you, son. Say, would you be a dear and fetch me another one of these?"

Mrs. Everson holds out her glass of champagne and Archibald, not wanting to upset the Southern belle, does the gentlemanly thing and defers. God has enlisted a number of His angels as a waiting staff, but none appear to be in the vicinity. Drats, Archibald thinks, now I have to play butler for this onerous beldam. He looks around once more for a waiter, finds none, and submits to a trip to the bar.

"Yes, ma'am. Seems there are no waiters nearby, give me a minute to run to the bar." He half-bows and turns to pursue his task.

"Archie!?" Mrs. Everson calls.

"Yes, Mrs. Everson," replies Archibald, turning back around.

"Make sure it's chilled."

"As you wish."

Archibald wheels around and walks through the gauntlet of the majorly pious toward the bar, nodding and waving at friends and acquaintances as he moves along. When he reaches the bar, an oblong wood structure with a marble countertop, he whistles for the angel bartender and holds up the empty glass when the cherub looks in his direction. The angel finishes drying off the glass in his hand, wipes down the counter in front of him, drapes the white cloth over his shoulder, and strolls over to Archibald, who is tapping his fingers on the countertop.

"More champagne, sir?" the bartender asks. He is taller than usual for an angel, and is further distinguished by his dark hair and medium complexion. Archibald notices a birthmark on the side of his neck resembling a spade. Or is it a heart? he wonders.

"Yes, please," says Archibald, tilting his head to try to get a better look at the birthmark. The angel gives him a suspecting look and Archibald stops. "And please make sure it's chilled. It's for someone else and she's particular, to say the least."

"Thoroughly chilled, coming right up." The angel picks a champagne bottle out of an ice bucket, holds it up to his cheek, nods his head, and removes the cork. He expertly fills the glass nearly to the rim without spillage, stuffs the cork back into the bottle, and buries it up to the base of the neck in the ice bucket. "Here you are, sir." He sets the glass on the counter and hands Archibald a napkin,

"Much appreciated." Archibald places a piece of thread from his linen shirt on the counter and the angel smiles and takes it. There is no currency in Heaven. Instead, symbols of the simple life serve as tokens of appreciation, such as thread, buttons, seeds, and splinters of wood.

"Thanks." The angel looks up and down the empty bar and back at Archibald. "So you're the head honcho around here, huh?"

"Yes I am," Archibald says flatly. "How did you deduce that?"

"Oh, come on, mister. We angels have eyes and ears everywhere. We know everything." He pauses. "Except what only God knows."

"Right, how silly of me. I bet you know my date of birth, social security number, blood type and all." The angel clenches his jaw, draws the cloth from his shoulder, and begins wiping the counter.

"Me personally? No, I only know your blood type, O. If I pooled the resources of all my brethren, we could surely come up with the other two. Probably your former home address, too." Archibald guffaws.

"So much for privacy. I didn't know Heaven was teeming with G-men. We've been exhaustively screened by virtue of being here, minorly pious included, what's the purpose of keeping all this information?"

"Control? Beats me, I'm just following orders."

Truth is, God had never instituted any sort of protocol for collecting the Heavenite's personal information. The angels decided to do this without consulting Him, and justified it as falling under the realm of the executive functions of their order.

Checks and balances in the highest government.

Archibald is shaken by the implications of the angel's comments, especially his mention of control. He recalls the latter years of his mortal life when legislation like the Patriot Act, passed nearly fifty years before his birth, and resulting abuses of the privacy of law-abiding citizens in the early 21st century on the part of government intelligence agencies, eventually escalated to an outright surveillance state with a global reach. An Orwellian nightmare come true. Archibald always felt he had died at the right time, just before the situation reached catastrophic levels, only to find out the afterlife is infested with marplots as well, in the form of dusky cherubs.

"Just following orders, huh. What is your name, good servant?"

"Edward."

"Thanks for the champagne, Edward. Have a nice day."

Archibald returns to the spot where he left Mrs. Everson and finds her with her arms crossed and her toes tapping. He smiles, but the smile is returned with a hardened stare.

"About time, Archie. Were you smashing the grapes yourself?" Mrs. Everson rebukes. Archibald avoids eye contact and hands her the glass. She takes it, removes the white gloves she has on, and gauges the temperature with her bare hands. "Still cold. I guess I'll settle for bad service if it means a good product." She pulls the gloves back on her hands and sips the champagne.

"Sorry, ma'am. I was accosted by the bartender. He revealed some unsettling information about him and his fellow angels," Archibald explains.

"Is that so? Well, I think you ought to worry about your own backyard first." Mrs. Everson points to a group of Heavenites walking toward the perimeter fence.

"What is their deal?"

"I'm not sure, dear. It seems the folks back in regular Heaven have caught their attention though." Archibald excuses himself and follows the group up to the wrought iron fence.

Back in regular Heaven, not much of anything is taking place to draw the attention of the majorly pious. Business carries on as usual. The Heavenites worship their various divinities in the nonsectarian church, play tennis, take naps, attend food festivals, tend to their gardens and vineyards, organize book clubs, make love, and all the other things that fill the day in Paradise. They maintain their gentleness and humility as if the majorly pious had never left them. The consensus regarding the absence of a substantial proportion of their peers is indifference. Some express relief about the exodus, especially its wannabe Moses, Archibald.

"Good riddance," said one man at the produce market.

"That Archibald sure thinks his scat don't stink," a child observed to her playmates.

"Those poor souls would follow ole Archie into the abyss," a weathered old man commented.

Archibald reaches the fence, lined with the majorly pious, and pries his way between two people to get the best view possible. He clutches two parallel bars and leans his head and shoulders into the adjoining gap, like an inmate trying to scope out his cell block. Since there are no walls on his periphery, Archibald realizes this actually limits his field of vision and he pulls his head back onto the Heaven's Paradise side of the fence. He watches the scant scene for about a minute and wonders what the fuss is about. The only activity he sees is a pair of Heavenites passing along the clouds about eighty yards away, their presence marginalized by the red-and-white striped onion dome of the church towering in the distance and glistening in the sunlight.

"Hey!" Archibald shouts at the minorly pious passersby. They don't even look his way. "What's going on here?" he asks, turning to the man on his right. He is a tall, pale fellow with rosy cheeks and curly blonde hair. He could easily be an archangel.

"Shh," the man responds, pressing an extended index finger against his lips. He then whispers, "Listen, can't you hear them out there?" Archibald stands still and listens. Several seconds pass and he hears nothing but wind.

"No, am I missing something?" Archibald looks down one side of the fence and then the other, and realizes everyone gathered along the fence is doing the same thing – standing in silence and listening.

"Try again."

Archibald turns his head to the side and leans against the fence, placing his ear into the open space between the bars. He raises his hand to his ear, cups his earlobe with the crook of his thumb, and fans out his palm to funnel sound into his ear. He closes his eyes and focuses on nothing but his auditory functions. Still he hears nothing with a Heavenite source, only the faint croon of a songbird.

"Nothing. Complete, utter silence," he says to the man on his right. He narrows his eyes at the man and begins to think he is being pranked.

"Exactly, compadre. It's like we were never even there. No riots, no squabbling, no false rumors, not even a hiccup. Nothing."

"They aren't bitter or jealous or anything," says the man to Archibald's left. He looks at Archibald with a tristful face. "Our efforts were all for naught."

Archibald realizes the man might be right and waves of hot flashes pass from his chest to his head. He slams his fist against one of the wrought iron bars and the sound echoes across the clouds. A dole of white doves, startled by the reverberations, flees from the onion dome far off in the background as Archibald marches away from the fence in disgust.

As always, the ever-watchful Rubio sees the whole scene unfold from his perch in a nearby cloud, and noting the unsportsmanlike conduct of the majorly pious, takes flight to report the infractions to God.

Chapter 20

It's New Year's Eve in Times Square. Snow covers the ground and thousands upon thousands of people in knit caps and wool mittens fill the square in anticipation of the ball drop. Several news outlets have stages set up around the area, and the main stage, located in front of Times Tower, features a number of headlining performers. The power metal band, New York City's own The Junkyard Dogs, will have the honor of playing the midnight spot. Consequently, the festivities have attracted a particularly young and rowdy crowd, a menagerie of devoted fans known as Dingbat's Dogs, in honor of lead guitarist Darryl "Dingbat" Thompson, who wear masks of various dog breeds, each representing the type of fan who lies underneath. For instance, a Chihuahua or Corgi mask means the person is a relatively new fan, and a Rottweiler or Pitbull mask means the person is aggressive in the mosh pit.

Meanwhile, a few blocks away on the eleventh floor of the St. Regis, a different kind of costumed loon gathers in a luxury suite. Twelve members of The Brotherhood of the Black Squirrel stand in a circle wearing their formal garb; eleven with gray cloaks and one, Virtuous Leader, with a white cloak. They each hold tumblers containing whiskey and ice. Virtuous Leader asks them to kneel and hold hands. He steps out of the circle and removes a leather necklace with a bronze locket from beneath the collar of his cloak.

"This, Brave Minions," he announces, tapping on the locket, "represents an annual tradition. It will be a first and a rite of passage for some of you, and just another day on the job for others." He pauses and opens the locket, which contains a clear plastic vial holding a clear liquid. "For those of you who are new, welcome and fear not. I personally selected each of you at the conclusion of an intensive vetting process. I know you will prove yourselves worthy of our cause tonight."

Virtuous Leader walks around the circle of Brave Minions and adds a drop of the unnamed liquid into the glasses of whiskey and ice. He then adds one to his own drink and rejoins the circle, taking the open hand of the adherent on either side of him. The cult members proceed to recite a harmony in tongues. At the end of the outburst, they raise their tumblers to the ceiling, drop them to the floor, and say, "bona fortuna," before dispensing the contents down their gullets in one swig.

The circle rises to its feet and each member collects a black overcoat from one of the two coat racks in the room, puts it over his cloak, and follows Virtuous Leader out of the door and into the hallway. They walk to the nearest elevator in single file with a military cadence to their steps – left--left--left-right-left – and wait in line for the elevator as Virtuous Leader presses the 'down' button, their feet still marching in place. When the elevator doors open, a young couple dressed in pea coats stands before them, arm in arm, and steps to the back left corner of the car.

"That's OK, there's a bevy of us, we'll wait for the next one," Virtuous Leader tells them with a reserved smile.

"Are you sure?" asks the woman.

Virtuous Leader simply nods and the couple stares at the eccentric group for a few seconds. Why are they marching in place? the woman wonders. What's the story with the black overcoats? the man wonders. There are only four Brave Minions visible from their vantage point, and the woman moves to the front of the car to try to see around the corner of the elevator lobby, but her boyfriend grabs her by the back of her pea coat, offers Virtuous Leader a conciliatory smile, and presses '><' on the button pad.

"Have a happy New Year, mister," says the man through the gap of the closing doors.

"Sure will," Virtuous Leader responds, rising to the balls of his feet.

The next elevator car is vacant, and the dirty dozen pile in and arrange themselves in a four-by-three matrix. Virtuous Leader stands at the corner of the grid by the button pad and presses 'G' followed by '><'. The doors slide together and the car descends with a sedative hum. After the '4' button lights up, the car's descent slows and the hum becomes a faint creak as the elevator comes to a stop at the third floor. The doors part and a family of five stands in front of the open jamb.

"Oh goodness, what a party," the father exclaims. "I suppose it'd be too much trouble for us to cram in there."

"No trouble at all," Virtuous Leader replies. The father looks at the mother, who looks at their baby in a stroller, who looks at Virtuous Leader and begins crying.

"I think we can wait, honey," the woman says to her husband. She eyeballs the curious bunch in the elevator, narrows her eyes at Virtuous Leader, and reaches down to pat the baby on the head. "Besides, there's no room for the stroller."

"Nonsense," inserts Virtuous Leader, "if you carry the little one and fold up the stroller it will work." The woman flares her nostrils and transfers her attention from the baby back to Virtuous Leader, who can see the annoyance in her body language. He rubs his hands against the sides of his overcoat in delight.

A squirrely sadist.

"I'd rather not, sir, but I appreciate your willingness to accommodate us. Have a happy New Year."

"Sure will." He rises to the balls of his feet again and closes the elevator doors.

The elevator reaches the garage level and the twelve members of The Brotherhood of the Black Squirrel exit the car and walk out onto the pavement of the underground parking facility. Virtuous Leader leads them directly ahead past two rows of parking spaces to a fleet of six black, full-size vans abutting the wall of the garage. The crew boards the vans in pairs of two, the engines rumble, and the vans back out of the diagonal parking spaces and cruise toward the exit ramp in an evenly spaced convoy. Virtuous Leader, driver of the commanding van, stops at the toll booth and hands the tenant the parking slips for all six vans.

"How are you today, gentleman?" asks the toll collector. He is a middle-aged white man with a thick New York accent. Virtuous Leader finds the accent quaint and endearing. Poor sap probably hasn't left the five boroughs in his entire life, he thinks, what a shame.

"We're doing well, thank you," says Virtuous Leader with a nod and a smile. The passenger nods and smiles as well.

"You have six tickets here," the attendant huffs, clearing his throat. Virtuous Leader can't tell if it's a question or statement.

"Yes, I do. I will be paying for myself and these five vans behind me."

"So, you're the bankroll for this here black van affair, huh?" The man leans forward in his seat and looks at the other vans idling behind the first one. "Must be some kind of party you're all heading to, a real humdinger."

"Actually, it's a funeral party," Virtuous Leader asserts. The toll collector takes his comment literally, having no reason to believe he is talking to the founder of a pernicious cult with an annual tradition of committing terrorist acts on New Year's Eve.

"Oh, jeez, I'm sorry to hear that." He punches the tickets and taps some buttons on the cash register.

"Not a problem. It's only a distant cousin of mine."

"Well, either way, it's a bummer to be going to a funeral during the holidays." He places the tickets in the cash drawer. "It's gonna be fourteen ninety-two, sir."

"OK, here you are." Virtuous Leader hands the attendant a twenty-dollar bill. "Keep the change."

"I'm not allowed to take tips," says the man, reaching into the cash drawer for the change. "Sorry, here you are." He tries to hand the five dollars and eight cents to Virtuous Leader, but Virtuous Leader nudges the man on the forearm and winks.

"If you're supervisor gives you guff about it, tell him you dropped the money in a Salvation Army tin. Have a happy New Year, uh," Virtuous Leader squints at the name tag on the toll collector's lapel, "Victor."

Before Victor can protest, Virtuous Leader puts the van in drive and scoots off, waving the five other vans along with him. From his stool inside the toll booth, Victor tries to get a look inside the cockpit of each of the passing vans, but the windows are darkly tinted. After the last van turns out onto the street, he stares at the five-dollar bill in his hand and sighs.

"Screw it," he mumbles, and puts the bill in his pants pocket. He'll use the five dollars for a bottle of wine to toast to the New Year with his wife. The eight cents will go into a Salvation Army tin.

A fair compromise in the holiday spirit.

The six vans head west on 55th Street in heavy traffic. Virtuous Leader figured the streets would be mobbed and consequently allotted thirty minutes of travel time to the mere ten block drive, an excursion that could ordinarily be done in less than a third of that time. It would probably be quicker to go on foot, even with the congested New Year's Eve sidewalks, but the vans were made necessary by the manifest Virtuous Leader devised during the planning phase of the operation, which called for several hundred pounds of cargo. Given the delicate and dangerous aspect of the materials, Virtuous Leader preferred not to have it transported by human handlers.

The vans reach 7th Avenue and turn left. The traffic is even heavier on 7th Avenue, an essential yellow river of taxi cabs slowly transporting passengers downstream to Times Square, the bright lights of which can be seen eight blocks to the south. Virtuous Leader straightens up in his seat upon seeing the lights, and a narcotic-like injection of dopamine floods his body, filling his stomach with a tingling sensation. He drums his fingers on the steering wheel, leans toward the windshield, and squats a few inches off the seat to try to see above the long column of traffic. The incessant cry of car horns pierces the brisk night air, adding yet another element to the cacophony of festive and jarring sounds characteristic of a metropolis on New Year's Eve, another particulate joining the conglomerate of urban noise pollution.

It takes almost ten minutes for the caravan to reach the traffic light at 51st Street, the midway point in the southbound second leg of their trip, and the large dose of anticipation and excitement in Virtuous Leader's system becomes contaminated with shots of impatience and unease. He looks at his watch: 11:40pm. Still on schedule. The light turns green and the procession of vehicles begins to creep forward, and the six vans eventually enter and cross the intersection, however, the sixth van is halted upon reaching the far end of the intersection when a homeless man with a shopping cart unexpectedly darts into the crosswalk. The driver of the van slams on the brakes and skids into the paint of the crosswalk, stopping only a few inches away from the man and his rolling suitcase of worldly possessions. Without saying a word, the street urchin grabs a panel of cardboard from the bottom shelf of the cart and holds it up in front of the van. In black marker, the message "The End Is Nigh" is scrawled across the makeshift canvas in freakishly neat and mechanical print.

"Predictable, paranoid homeless guy raving," the driver comments to the passenger.

"Unoriginal, but tonight he's going to feel awful prescient," the passenger replies. "My, look at that handwriting. It looks like he used a stencil."

"Yeah, a prophet and a scribe, standing here before us in a ragged suit and burlap booties. Chalk it up to coincidence." The driver rolls down his window. "Hey! Nostradamus! Move it along!"

The homeless man, with an inviolable sort of dignity, as if his destitute circumstances had never once broken his spirit or sense of humanity, returns the sign to its holding place, tips his hat – an unusually mint ascot – grabs the handle of the shopping cart with both hands, and trudges across the intersection, his stride moderately retarded by the effects of cheap vodka.

Once clear of the homeless man's transitory embargo, the tail van rejoins the convoy and flashes its headlights at the preceding vehicle. That vehicle does the same and the message makes its way up the line to Virtuous Leader, who, looking in the rearview mirror, shakes his head and dabs sweat from his brow with a handkerchief. He looks at his watch: 11:43pm. Three and a half blocks to go, and then five minutes to set positions. Could be worse.

At the intersection at 47th Street, Virtuous Leader continues south on 7th Ave., while the second and third vans turn right. The fourth and fifth vans follow Virtuous Leader and the sixth van puts on its hazard lights and attempts to parallel park in a small space near the northwest corner of the intersection. It requires multiple turns and readjustments, but the van eventually squeezes into the space, attracting both the awe of local pedestrians and the ire of passing motorists. Virtuous Leader and the succeeding van go straight through the light at 46th Street, while the third van in their miniature convoy, the fifth van in the original group, slows and searches for a place to park. At 45th Street, Virtuous Leader turns right and the other van goes through the intersection, flips on its right turn signal, and proceeds to parallel park in a spot about one hundred feet south of the light.

Virtuous Leader drives west on 45th Street and stops in front of the Imperial Theatre. The façade reads, "Jubilee," in bright white lights, and hanging above the façade is a purple and yellow show board with an image of a bejeweled crown and staff. Virtuous Leader puts on his right turn signal, shifts the van into reverse, honks at the gatherers in front of the theatre until they make a clearing, and slowly backs into an alleyway on the side of the theatre. He stops about a quarter of the way down the alley, shifts the van into park, turns off the headlights, and shuts off the engine. He looks at his watch: 11:55pm. Showtime at the Imperial Theatre. His co-pilot hands him a walkie-talkie and he presses the transmission button.

"Positions, Brave Minions, positions, over," Virtuous Leader announces.

"Van two, 46th and Broadway, set, over," replies the driver of the second van.

"Van three, 47th and Broadway, set, over," proclaims the driver of the third van.

"Van four, 45th and 7th Ave., set, over."

"Van five, 46th and 7th Ave., set, over."

"Van six, 47th and 7th Ave., set, over."

"Affirmative. Van one, extraction point, set, over," says Virtuous Leader. He looks at his watch: 11:57pm. "Unleash the reckoning, over and out."

In the next thirty seconds to a minute, a succession of transmissions reading, "reckoning unleashed," come through on the radio. After the fifth transmission, Virtuous Leader and the passenger exit the van and trot around to the rear bumper. Virtuous Leader opens the back doors and dozens of black squirrels dash out of the cabin and scamper down the alley toward 46th Street. Each one has a timed bomb strapped to its back with a digital clock set to explode at midnight.

"Good luck my little martyrs," Virtuous Leader whispers as the last few stragglers hit the concrete running.

Chapter 21

A restless and impatient Hubert Raymer paces back and forth along an isolated portion of the outer gate of Hell's Paradise. With its dim lighting, low ceiling, cover provided by a series of sandstone outcroppings, and, most importantly, narrow moat, this small corner of Hell's Paradise has become Hubert's preferred point of communication with major sinners. However, his contact and confidante is running late. Very late by his account. He picks up a palm-sized rock and taps it against each gatepost he passes, not concerned about the sound attracting unwanted attention; in the many visits to this particular spot, Hubert hasn't once seen a minion guard on either side of the gate. Besides, he's bored.

"Raymer, cut the racket. You trying to get us flogged?"

Hubert turns to find his contact approaching the far bank of the fiery moat. He is in his sixties, wears glasses, and has unkempt, red-brown hair hanging nearly to his shoulders, and extending outward to the end of his collarbone. He has a longish, almost equine face, a nose with a crooked bridge due to time spent as an amateur boxer, and his sharp jawline is still perceptible despite the effects of aging. By no means is he a handsome man, but there is an astuteness in his features and an ageless wisdom in his bleary blue eyes, the beauty of which cannot be ignored. The man edges up to the moat and stands with his hands clasped together behind his back, awaiting a response. The heat from the lava draws large beads of sweat from his forehead, and a few beads drop in succession into the moat, which produces a short measure of sizzles and crackles, loud enough for Hubert to hear across the twenty-foot breach.

"Me? How about you? By now your sweat makes up about ten percent of that moat. It's gonna flood sometime."

The man, looking down into the lava, smiles and takes a step back.

"Sorry, Raymer, I was just admiring the terrific color of the magma. You're probably right, I shouldn't dilute its brilliance."

"Anyway, what have you been doing? It seems like I've been waiting here for, heck, days."

"You know, this, that, and the third. I've acquired a couple more pupils. The management doesn't seem to notice."

"Pupils, Doc Bischoff? You're still out there teaching lessons in Ancient Sumeria? What about the cause? Get some sympathizers, not pupils."

In the life before, Doctor Bischoff was Hubert's doctorate professor, a demanding, but fair pedagogue with a knack for extending lectures many minutes beyond their due length by accentuating points and facts with personal anecdotes. He often drew analogies to boxing, and believed his mastery of the pugilistic arts was second only to his mastery of archaeology and history. As a young man in Germany, he was a local amateur champion. Hubert had been one of his favorite pupils, a smart and assiduous understudy, whose obsession with Ancient Egypt, particularly hieroglyphics, seemed borderline unhealthy to Doc Bischoff, a proponent of academic versatility, even at the doctorate level, and a self-proclaimed polymath. Not wanting to discourage Hubert's immersion in one area of study, after all, it was rare Doc Bischoff found a doctorate student willing to commit to anything other than a grant or publication, the wily professor never once suggested Hubert focus his studies elsewhere. His motto was to never let his agenda conflict with that of his students, a rarity among educators in America's higher institutions.

A German-imported national treasure.

"Don't jump the gun, there, Raymer. I was going to get to that, too. I've attracted a few more sympathizers. In fact, my newest pupils are also sympathizers. It's a two-birds-with-one-stone operation. They think they're only getting arch and history lessons, and then I change gears and appeal to their political sensibilities." Doc Bischoff pauses and stares into the moat. "It's unbelievable how many are motivated by jealousy, as if they haven't learned a thing since coming here. Need to spend more time in *that* circle."

"I'm not sure I care what their motivation is, so long as they're aboard. When push comes to shove, I doubt Satan will care either. It's all about impetus. Have you given any thought to the petition?"

"Not much, but I will. You wouldn't believe how hard it is to find paper and pen in this place, or any sort of writing media for that matter. Maybe you should leave that responsibility to your friend James. He's resourceful."

"I have to lure him over to our side first, remember?"

"Right, right. Forgive me, my recall isn't what it was in the time before."

"No worries, Doc, you're still one of the sharpest tools in the shed."

"If you're talking about this shed," Doc Bischoff looks up at the ceiling and sweeps his hand in a large circle next to his obstreperous mane, "then yes, I would certainly hope so."

"Here, there, now, then, wherever and whenever, you'll always be one of the biggest eggheads in the room. I bet you'd be at the top of the class in purgatory as well."

"No, Raymer, you'd be at the top of the class in purgatory. I'd be teaching the class." Doc Bischoff kicks a pebble into the fiery moat for emphasis.

"Alright, alright. So long as you let me play devil's advocate." They both let out a hearty laugh.

"Boy, remember some of those classes and symposiums? Rooms full of hive-minded automatons, idiots some of them, really, and you and I would give them the old rhetorical run around." Doc Bischoff's eyes widen in anticipation of Hubert building on his wistful reminiscence.

"Yes, well, some of it at least. One thing I distinctly remember, just came back to me not long ago, is one of the faculty members blurting, "Here comes the riff-raff," when we entered an auditorium. I forget the occasion. She said it just loud enough for about half the room to hear. Some laughed, others threw balls of paper at the gal." Hubert picks up a clump of porous sandstone and lofts it into the moat to reenact the action.

"That was Doctor Moretti. She was a real krampus, that one. Her and her cohorts used to refer to us as 'the Sorcerer and the Apprentice.'" Doc Bischoff shakes his head and crinkles his bent nose. "You know she almost got me fired from the Academy?"

Hubert shrugs and shakes his head. His professor delves into the story about Doctor Moretti nearly causing his termination from the Academy, and like in the old days, Hubert takes a seat, only this time Indian-style on the ground instead of cross-legged in an ergonomic school chair, and listens intently with his chin propped on his palm. Doc Bischoff was framed, he insists, for writing sexist slander in the school bulletin board, specifically directed at women in academia, and precisely regarding the female faculty at the Academy. Doctor Moretti, new wave feminist that she is, according to Doc Bischoff, personally headed the campaign to defame his character, expulse him from his position, and consequently ruin his career.

"She really had it out for you, huh?" Hubert comments.

"Sure did." Doc Bischoff picks a loose fiber out of his burlap clothes. "Listen, I better be on my way. I have some time to put in in the circle of pride."

"OK, yeah, I'm sure my friends are wondering about me by now. Thanks for coming by, I'll see ya next time, Doc."

"Take care."

Doc Bischoff waves goodbye and walks into the shadows at the foot of the entrance to one of the radial corridors. Hubert watches him go, picks up another clump of sandstone, tosses it into the lava, and turns to leave as the lava sizzles and crackles from the intrusion of the sandstone. Despite what he told Doc Bischoff, he is in no hurry to get back to James, Lawrence, and Claudia. He walks slowly down a narrow pathway bounded by magma and stops to admire a pattern in the rocks on his left side. The pattern, which may be a water stain and not a natural anomaly in the coloration of the surface, Hubert realizes, resembles the profile of an elephant. The trunk and tusks are particularly well-defined. Hubert does a full pirouette and notes his surroundings in case he decides to return to the elephant, which he has decided to name Spiffy. He retrieves several pebbles and lays them on the edge of the path in the shape of an 'S' for insurance. Satisfied, he wipes his hands together to clear the dirt, takes a final look at the area, and heads farther along the path, this time at a swift pace since he is eager to tell the gang about the elephant in the rocks.

Hubert reaches the main cavern, the social nexus of Hell's Paradise, and the usual hangout spot for the gang, but his three friends are absent. There are several groups of Hellions spread out across the room. They are either sitting, kneeling, or crouched on their hands and knees. Hubert pads toward the nearest group, a trio, and realizes they are playing marbles with semi-spherical stones. He had heard marbles had become a popular pastime among minor sinners, however, he had yet to see the game in practice, perhaps because he had been spending so much time at the outer gate conducting business with Doc.

All work and no play makes Hubert a dull boy.

He stands over the three strangers, two men and one woman, and observes the action with his hands on his knees. The players don't seem to mind his being a spectator, in fact, they hardly seem to notice his presence. Hubert watches for several minutes in silence, transfixed by the irregular roll of the ovoid stones and the hollow pop of the colliding pieces in the vastness of the main cavern. It makes Hubert think of two asteroids smashing into each other in deep space. A colossal, violent event indeed, but fractional given the context. Hubert watches some more and tries to pick up on the rules of the game and the names of the players. They remind him of James, Lawrence, and Claudia; around the same ages, similar rapports with one another, although neither of the men are black. There is a pause in the game and Hubert decides it's as good a time as any to speak up.

"Excuse me." One of the men, the current shooter, shudders, apparently startled by the unexpected voice. He fumbles the bowling marble and looks up at Hubert with an annoyed expression. "Sorry, do you folks mind if I get in on the next game?" The three participants glance at one another, searching for an answer.

"Sure," says the man whom Hubert frightened. He picks up the bowling marble and hands it to the woman, who kneels to his left. "You know what you're doing?"

"Not really. It'll all come back to me as we go, though." The three players smile. They like the intruder's cavalier attitude.

"Alright, rookie," the woman submits. "First rule: don't talk while another player is bowling. Like in golf, you never talk during someone's swing." Hubert nods. "You ever play golf in the time before?" Hubert shakes his head. Truthfully, he isn't sure.

"Never played golf and is unfamiliar with marbles. Must be a true middle-classman, split right down the centerline," proclaims the second man to his companions. "Say, Rookie, what did you do in the time before?"

"He was a taxidermist," a fifth voice declares. Hubert and the marble players look up to find James approaching with Lawrence and Claudia a few steps behind. James carries a small burlap bag, which dangles from his right hand. The bag has a knot at the top and a bulbous figure with a nubby exterior.

"Well if it isn't ole dead-eye himself, James Jenkins," says the jittery man.

"Gentleman," James replies, casually saluting the two men. "Miss." He tilts his head and shoulders forward and winks at the woman.

"James, you know these friendly neighbors?" asks Hubert.

"Sure do, although I wouldn't call Freddy friendly." James makes eye contact with the jittery man. "He's been salty ever since I nearly wiped him clean. Got me his precious salt-and-pepper Apache tear. Ain't that right, Freddy?" Freddy grumbles and kneads the marbles in his hands.

"Yes, James. That's right. Problem is, you still owe me the redemption game you promised."

"And yer surely gonna get it. But until that day comes, I'm gonna enjoy tha spoils of war." James loosens the cinch on his bag, dips his index finger and thumb into the opening, and pulls out a miraculously spherical nodule of obsidian, about an inch in diameter, with checkers of white and black on the surface. "Behold, Osiris, destroyer of worlds."

"And egos," Claudia chides. Freddy glares at her. He is becoming tired of this harassment.

"Say, James, how about you take your taxidermist friend here and teach him the ropes," suggests Freddy. "I'd rather leave the apprenticing to a superior player. Then, when he has a feel for the game he can join the circuit, and I'd be honored to be his opponent in his first official game." James looks at Hubert and smiles.

"Ya hear that, Huey. Poor Freddy here wants ta sabotage his career." He turns his attention to Freddy. "Ya want me, tha only man with an undefeated record against ya, ta coach a novice, show him all tha angles on how ta beat ya, and then ya want ta play him in his first official game?"

"You have excellent hearing, James. If only your ears were as prolific as your mouth."

"Yer words cut ta my core." James presses his fists against his chest and apes swooning. Freddy wants him out of his sight.

"How about it then?"

"Sounds like a plan, Freddy," Hubert confirms. "I was looking to catch up on things with James and company anyway. Thanks for your hospitality, and we'll see you folks around."

"Take care, Rookie," says Freddy. The other man and the woman nod and wave. "Remember, I got dibs on your first game on the circuit."

"It'd only be right. Have a good one."

Hubert joins the gang and they walk to one edge of the cavern and settle in a private area next to a big limestone outcropping. It's hotter in this area of the main hall than in other parts, but Hubert doesn't mind because it's blissfully quiet. The four companions gather in a circle and kneel while

James opens the burlap bag, removes the Apache tear, and with a practiced, measured motion, dumps the rest of the marbles onto the ground, causing them to bounce, skip, ricochet, roll, and finally settle in a nearly symmetrical spread of about five feet. The look of contentment in James' face is the same one seen in a pool player after a good break. Hubert examines the spread with a boyish wonder, attributes images and patterns to the arrangement – a moon and star, a Celtic knot, a dog paw – and convinces himself for a second that James intentionally produced the motifs. He guesses how many times his friend has done this, begins to ask him, then decides it makes no difference. There are more important issues that need to be addressed. Issues far more important than marbles.

The gang shoots through one game, during which James, Lawrence, and Claudia provide pointers and explain rules to Hubert as they go. Despite Hubert's attempts to redirect the conversation to politics and morale in Hell's Paradise, his friends are focused on discussing the game, namely in the form of trash talking. Like in all things, James and Claudia have developed a heated rivalry and use psychological warfare to try to gain an advantage on the playing field. James mostly employs sexist remarks about the inferiority of women in recreational pursuits. Claudia, annoyed by James' meretricious bowling style, relies on racial stereotyping, implying black men are all style and no substance whenever James misses a shot. Lawrence, an experienced third wheel in such scenarios, stands by vigilantly in case things get physical and his bouncing skills are needed. Hubert, who realizes the best opportunity for a serious discussion will be between games, silently roots for whomever is leading and jinxes the second and third place players. Since he has been in last place since the first go-round, he does his part by keeping his turns as brief as possible; no calculating, minimal aiming, just grip it and rip it as they say. After a seesaw battle in which the lead changes about ten times, Lawrence clears the field in the fourteenth round, claiming three marbles, but it isn't enough. James wins with a count of sixteen to Lawrence's fifteen. Claudia scores thirteen and Hubert five. Not bad for a Rookie, he thinks, especially one whose main concern was expediting the game. While the gang stretches their legs in preparation for the next game, Hubert sees his opening and takes it.

"So, guys, what's the scuttlebutt these days? I've heard some of our peers have been yearning for the old days," he posits. James looks at him with an expression one-part puzzlement and two-parts revulsion, as if Hubert should be ashamed of his words.

"Whaddya, nuts? Nobody I know wanna go back to *that*," James replies with conviction, pointing at the far wall of the cavern, roughly the direction of the shortest route to the outer gate. "I think you've been spending too much time corresponding with yer professor friend."

"Maybe, but I didn't hear it from him. In my travels to and from those meetings I hear many things. You know, from fellow travelers. If you guys got away from the interior of this place more often it might open your eyes."

"Only time I wanna get away from the bosom of Hell's Paradise is ta go to the canteen. Even then I'm reluctant. Sometimes I'd rather go hungry in here than ta feel nourished out there."

"Oh, bollocks! Don't listen to him, Huey. He's just being a stubborn old mule," says Claudia. Hubert fights back a smile. He can always rely on Claudia as an ally when pitted against his best friend.

"Darn skippy, but that don't mean I'm wrong. If there was talk about wishing fer things ta be like they were, first place you'd hear it is here," James asserts, pointing at the soil at his feet. "Aside from tha cafeteria, this cavern is the epicenter fer gossip."

"He's right on that point," Lawrence says to Hubert.

"Except he's overlooking one very important factor. Spies," Hubert pronounces. The three others look at him with varied expressions and await further explanation. "You see, since the main cavern here attracts the highest concentration of minor sinners, it also attracts a large following of spies, from both inside the ranks and outside, and thus discourages conversations pertaining to sensitive matters."

"Is that right, Huey? Man, ya turned into a conspiracy yahoo," James contends. "Nobody thinks about spies around these parts. Look around ya." He does a half-turn with one arm held out to the side, drawing attention to the groups of marbles players spread out before him, then turns back to face Hubert and jiggles the burlap bag in his other hand. "See that? That's what freedom looks like, at least by Satan's standards. I can count on my ten fingers how many minions I've seen since coming here, and if I'd crossed paths with some sleeper cell or double agent, I'd have sniffed it out." Claudia blurts out a shrill cackle.

"Would you now, 007? Honey, you can be so far up your own arse sometimes I'm surprised you don't think Hell smells like methane instead of sulfur," she exclaims.

"Woman, I'll give ya a taste of brimstone." James holds up the back of his right hand to Claudia and shakes it in a mirthfully threatening way. Claudia takes a step toward him and cocks her foot back several inches as if to strike at his groin.

"I'll cook those eggs over easy."

"Not without me disfiguring that pretty face of yers."

"Alright, alright," Hubert interrupts. "Dolemite, femme fatale, simmer down." The combatants' limbs slacken and they trade impish smiles.

"You gather they remember what we were discussing?" Lawrence asks Hubert. Hubert shrugs.

"Listen, James, what I said about spies is a moot point. No need for you and Claudia to pummel each other back to the Stone Age. The fact is, our fellow minor sinners miss their major sinner friends and vice versa," Hubert reiterates. James rolls his eyes. "But why tell you when I can show you. Come on, let's go for a walk."

The quartet, led by Hubert, sets out from the main cavern to the meandering path Hubert had taken on his return from the rendezvous with Doc Bischoff. It isn't the most direct way to get to their destination, but Hubert wants to show them Spiffy, the elephant in the rocks. When they arrive at the spot, Lawrence actually notices the pebbles laid out in an 'S' before Hubert says anything.

"It appears someone has left a marker for something. I doubt these pebbles happened to congregate this way through natural occurrences," he observes.

"Look up to your right," says Hubert. Lawrence, Claudia, and James gawk at the pattern in the rocks, mouths agape.

"Ah, an elephant, interesting."

"Do you think it's the coloration of the rock or a water stain?" Before responding, Lawrence inches to the edge of the pathway, his toes hanging precariously above the bubbling lava. He stretches his neck forward, pinches his chin with his thumb and forefinger, and narrows his eyes.

"I can't say for sure, but I'd wager it's a water stain. The probability of such a specific and complex image arising through iron staining and oxidation must be very low."

"Ha! Whaddya a geologist now? We in Hell, Lawrence, ya dense honkey. There's no way that's a water stain," James declares.

"Why shouldn't it be? Sure, it's few and far between, but there's still water in this inferno. Maybe one of the communal showers is up yonder on the other side of the wall."

"You have to admit, that's a solid theory, James," offers Claudia. James dismissively waves his hand at her without taking his eyes off the elephant in the wall.

"Whatever tha cause, it is something ta feast yer eyes on. But tell me, what does this have ta do with what we were talking about after tha marbles game?" asks James, turning to Hubert.

"Oh, we didn't get there yet. This was just a side attraction. Let's go."

The gang continues along the path and soon reaches a fork. Hubert takes the opposite route of the one that leads to his and Doc's secret meeting place, and after a few hundred paces they reach an opening with an obsidian crag on each side of the walkway. The wall on the left continues for another fifty yards, and slightly beyond the end of the wall the outer gate can be seen extending perpendicularly from the wall, bounding the open space to the right. Hubert takes them around the right crag, and upon turning the corner into the flatlands they see at least a dozen minor sinners lined up on the near side of the gate. As they get closer to the group, James, Lawrence, and Claudia realize their fellow residents are gesturing and talking to an approximately equal number of major sinners on the far side of the gate, the intimacy of their conversations limited not only by the brass partition, but by the thirty feet of lava moat separating the two parties.

Hubert stands back and lets his friends take in the scene. After several minutes, he walks up to James and clutches his shoulder.

"What did I tell you, old pal?" He points from one Hellion to another on both sides of the barrier. "This separation is gonna doom us all. The more I think about it, the more disillusioned I become with this place, it's ideal. It only plays into Satan's hands and it's about time I try to make things rights again."

James thinks this over for a moment, then crosses his arms and slowly, repeatedly nods his head.

Chapter 22

Underneath a starry night sky with a waxing gibbous moon, God sits in His throne accompanied by His premier angel, Rubio, who dusts and buffs his master's grand saddle with a cloth. God stares up at the firmament above Heaven, and with His elbow propped on the armrest, raises His right forearm and wills a shooting star into existence, then guides it across the vault of the cosmos with His index finger. Rubio, fully engaged in his chore, doesn't notice the meteorite at first, but as the astral body dives out of sight beyond the horizon of Heaven's clouds, it passes into the angel's peripheral vision and he turns to admire it with a smile. When he was a newborn, his mother would refer to shooting stars as "angel tears," and claimed they were harbingers of a bittersweet event on Earth. Rubio carries this mythology with him in adulthood, although not one of his peers has corroborated the theory.

"Did someone special die tonight, sir?" he asks.

"Not that I know of," the Almighty responds. His confidante is aware of His ability to create meteorites and every other order of cosmic phenomena, but He tends to do it when no one is looking. It maintains the illusion that the universe is entirely spontaneous and phantasmagorical.

"Oh, well that shooting star was something else. The tail could have stretched across a solar system."

"Maybe across a sun, I don't know about a whole solar system. Unless it was a tiny solar system."

"How small do you think a solar system can get?" God plucks at His beard.

"The smallest I've ever seen was about 3,000 miles in diameter. It consisted of one miniature sun and one miniature planet with no moons. But, I created that one. There could be a smaller one out there that developed through its own mechanisms." Rubio spits on his cloth and pauses before continuing to work on the legs of the throne.

"You think nature would try to trump you like that, Jehovah?"

"Try? Don't be silly, Rubio, nature can't *try* to do anything. I like to work on a grand scale, it makes my job manageable. Nature doesn't operate that way. In theory, there could be a solar system the size of your fingertip. There could be a solar system the size of a single skin cell in your fingertip if you care to imagine it." The cherub examines the end of his plump left pinky, turns it over and flicks at the fingernail with his right thumb, then shakes his cloth and returns to polishing.

"Seems far-fetched to me. Forgive me sir, but I think you've been spending too much time talking to that theoretical physicist guy."

"Dr. Eliades? He's an astrophysicist, actually. Now that you mention it, I haven't seen him since his admission to the Sanctuary. Speaking of which, how are things over there? I heard a bit of a rabble a few evenings back."

"I'm glad you asked because I'm becoming worried about the state of affairs in the Sanctuary." Rubio stops working and stands to address his master. "The behavior of the inhabitants, at least in some cases, is not consistent with that of a Heavenite self-described as 'majorly pious'." The Lord raises His eyebrows, leans forward in His throne, props His elbows on the armrests, and folds His hands in His lap. Rubio knows he has His undivided attention. "I'm especially disappointed in Archibald the Egret."

"He is their leader, is he not?"

"Yes, but he has increasingly become more of an agitator than a leader. A divisive figure is an apt way to describe him at this point. Now, I told you recently about his petulant reaction to the perceived lack of dolor and jealously within the ranks of the regular Heavenites." God nods. "Mind you, he wasn't the only one. Well, things have escalated since then."

"How so?"

"Basically, there are two parts divided against Archibald. One group sees the indifference of the 'minorly pious,' a term the residents of the Sanctuary have adopted for the regular Heavenites, as a failure on Archibald's part." God closes His eyes and slowly, gravely shakes His head, once to the right and once back to the left. Rubio, perpetual bearer of news both good and bad, has seen this gesture many, many times, but nevertheless nervously bites his lower lip and waits for God to refocus His attention. "The other group feels intimidated by Archibald's increasingly despotic behavior, which has been spurred by the distrust expressed by the first group. They are generally disappointed with the motives and attitudes of their peers."

"At least someone has tentatively earned the designation of majorly pious." The Almighty pauses and pats His thumbs together. "How do the two groups compare in terms of numbers?"

"I'd say about even. The latter group might be slightly larger."

"I see. And how about in terms of vehemence?"

"Oh, the former group is qualitatively stronger without a doubt. The second group is timid. They're scared of Archibald. Frankly, Jehovah, it doesn't matter. A mutiny is imminent one way or the other if we don't intervene."

"Mutiny, Rubio? You're quite the sensationalist." The angel blushes and looks down at his feet.

"Sorry. It was for lack of a better term. A figurative mutiny."

"Very well. Figurative or not we cannot let things get out of hand. If you'll pardon me, I ought to confer with Lucifer."

"As you wish, sir."

Rubio bows to the Lord and flies off into the moonlit sky, leaving his rag draped on the edge of the gold pedestal of the throne. God gets off His hindquarters, picks up the rag, and places it on the end table beside the throne. He takes the walkie-talkie from atop the table, cradles it in the palm of His hand as if testing its weight, and sets the channel to six. He presses the transmission button and raises the device to His jawline.

"Lima Six, come in Lima Six, do you read me? Over." Half a minute of silence passes. "Lima Six, this is Juliett Six with an urgent matter, do you copy? Over."

"I read you, Juliett Six...Urgent matter you say?...How do I fit in?...Over," Satan responds, short of breath.

"It's about Heaven's Sanctuary. I need you to come to my Kingdom and see for yourself. Over." On the other end, Satan mutters profanities before thumbing the transmission button.

"OK, but this time have a hot cup of tea ready when I arrive. Over."

"Sure. How many sugars? Over."

"Just one. And use two bags. I want it strong. I'll be there momentarily. Over and out."

"10-4. Over and out." God sits back down in His throne, switches the channel to one, and pushes the transmission button. "Romeo One, come in Romeo One, do you read me? Over."

"Juliett One, this is Romeo One, I read you loud and clear. Over," Rubio announces over the airwaves.

"Romeo One, sorry to be a bother after I just dismissed you, but I need a hot cup of tea on the double. It's for Lucifer, he's on his way. Over."

"10-4, sir. How many sugars? Over."

"One. Oh, and use two bags. See if you can dig up that expensive Earl Grey, I want our guest to be satisfied. Over."

"One sugar, two bags, expensive Earl Grey. Copy, over."

"Thank you, Romeo One. Over and out."

God settles into the velvet upholstery of the throne and closes His eyes for some much needed rest. After only a few minutes, He is out cold and snoring loud enough for all of Paradise to hear, a calamitous din that sounds like a pig combined with a jet engine. He dreams of the Seven Days of Creation, simpler times when the universe was a blank canvas and He was free of the burdens of His creations, particularly those of the sixth day, Man, His finest and culminating invention. Floating before Him on the silver screen of dreamtime is a mosaic of human activity – the good, the bad, and the ugly – a detailed, chronological account of prominent events in the history of the species *Homo sapiens*, from Adam and Eve, to the invention of the wheel, to 17th century witch hunts, to the moon landings, to the creation of the neutron bomb, and finally, to the colonization of Mars. An accomplished, yet fallible species, prone to both moments of triumphant love and unspeakable hatred, some Great Emancipators and others Grand Inquisitors, all created in His image. Perhaps I should have created something else on the sixth day, something not in my image, God thinks, His voice emanating across the dreamscape.

Before the Almighty can dream any further and reexamine the opportunity cost of creating humans, instead of, say, tyrant lizards on the sixth day, His eyelids are coaxed open by the rising sun. He massages the fuzziness out of His eyesight and finds a figure approaching from the horizon, its silhouette boldly set against the yellow disk of daybreak. As the figure enlarges with each passing second, God notices the unmistakable form of goat horns protruding from the top of the animation. Lucifer has arrived for their meeting. God wets His fingers and strokes His hair a few times to smooth out the bedhead, claws at His beard to straighten the tangles, and hand irons His robe before retying the gold cincture to give the robe a more svelte fit. With these cosmetic preparations complete, the Lord begins to panic at the realization that Rubio never came with the cup of tea, but He turns to find a chinaware mug of steaming amber brew set on a hotplate on the end table. He relaxes and steps down from the pedestal to greet His guest.

"Morning Lucifer, pleasant travels?"

"They were until I rematerialized here on this glacial plane," the Devil responds through chattering teeth. "I wish the fireplace would malfunction from time to time and send me to Venus."

"Oh, come on now Lucifer, you don't mean that. A little clean, cool air should be a welcomed change every now and then. How about a blanket?"

"Certainly." God takes a wool blanket off the backrest of His throne and grabs the teacup from the end table. He drapes the blanket over Satan's shoulders and hands him the beverage. Satan holds the two ends of the blanket together with one hand and the teacup with the other. "Much better, thank you Jehovah."

"You're welcome. Now that you're comfortable, let's go for a walk. I want to show you the recent disturbances in Heaven's Sanctuary."

"You don't have a coach that can take us there?" God shakes His head. "A rickshaw?" God ignores the question and begins walking. "What about a hot air balloon? We could use my breath as the heat source, you wouldn't even have to waste fuel."

"We're walking. Now get your rear in gear." Satan takes a few sips of the tea to help prevent spillage, then scurries up alongside his host.

"My Jehovah, this tea is delectable," Satan opines while raising the cup for another taste.

"Glad you like it. I requested a special blend of Earl Grey for you. It's rare and expensive."

"Well, I only drink the best back in Hades, so I know good tea when I taste it." Satan takes another sip, swirls it in his mouth for a second, and sets his nose up to the rim of the mug before swallowing. "Is that ginger I taste? An Earl Grey with ginger, how inventive."

"I doubt it. We don't have an Earl Grey with ginger that I know of, and I've never known the angels to add ginger unless it's requested." Satan glances at God, then looks into the teacup and tilts his head. "I believe that's the inherent taste of the water you're detecting. We've been getting a lot of acid rain lately. Emissions are up with the addition of the Sanctuary."

In a relatively short period of time, the material excesses of Heaven's Sanctuary, including high-wattage sound systems, coal-burning chimeneas (nearly one for every four residents), amusement rides, a monorail, and as Satan noticed on his walk from the Pearly Gates to God's throne, hot air balloons, have had a palpable impact on the environment, resulting in anomalies like smog, sky glow, and acid rain. Although this is cause for concern, God is chiefly occupied with addressing the behavioral issues observed in His children in the Sanctuary. The environmental degradation is only symptomatic of the ethical infirmity of the majorly pious, however, He is prepared to cite the ecological changes in order to strengthen His case for reform, whether it be to Satan, His adherents, or the angels. Or Hubert Raymer.

"Acid rain, you don't say. I don't think I would have guessed that. It's an excellent touch either way." God looks into the middle distance at an inchoate formation of cumulonimbus clouds. "Do you think I could take a jug-full with me when I leave? Ginvoo would rave about this."

"Sure," God responds absentmindedly, still gazing at the developing rain clouds.

They come to a gradual upgrade in the clouds and Satan realizes there is solid ground underneath them. Less than one hundred yards ahead, a grassy hill breaks through the surface of the clouds and rises another thirty feet above the fluffy white cover. The Devil has never been to this place before, and he feels slighted because it's obviously an important destination for the Almighty. They reach the peak of the hill and God stops.

"Welcome to Heaven's observation deck," God pronounces. "On a clear day, the visibility up here is twenty-five miles with the naked eye, assuming 20/20 vision. You can see around half of the total area of my Kingdom, and with *this* you can see it all." He removes a spyglass from His robe and extends the contraption to its full length. It's made of a beautiful mahogany with no detectable blemishes in the grain, and has pure silver rings affixed to each of the three folding points. Satan thinks of the bland, stock-made telescope in his office and, once again, feels inadequate. "You turn the eyepiece to adjust the magnification. Clockwise to increase, counterclockwise to decrease, like so." God twists the eyepiece back and forth. "This spyglass also has a special feature. If you press in on the bottom brace here, the silver ring, it picks up the audio of whatever you're viewing." The Lord produces a pair of circumaural headphones from His robe and plugs them into the audio jack on the bottom piece of the monocular. "Here, take a look around."

Satan dons the headphones and holds the spyglass up to his right eye. He does a sweep of the clouded valley below and pauses momentarily to watch a few points in a game of badminton in the foreground. He activates the audio receptor and listens to the Heavenites as they whip the birdie from one side of the net to the other, and is surprised to hear an inordinate amount of trash talking taking place. Out of the corner of his left eye, Satan peeks at an unwitting God and smirks.

"What?" God asks.

"I doubt you'd approve of the language being used down there on the badminton courts."

"Oh, I know all about it. Since they're in the heat of competition, we agreed they'd only be reprimanded for using my name in vain."

"All else is fair game?" Jehovah nods. Lucifer snorts and puts the spyglass back up to his right eye.

After concluding his eavesdropping on the badminton players, Lucifer turns to his four-o'-clock to admire the predominant feature of the panorama, the illustrious, egalitarian Temple. Satan turns the eyepiece clockwise, increasing the magnification, and narrows in on the flying buttresses, followed by the pagoda. While perusing the pagoda, his eye is drawn to a brightly painted, red and greed dragon motif embedded in the dugong eave of the top tier of the structure. The image is reassuring to the Devil and his black heart fills with joy. Symbols of the macabre are omnipresent, even in Paradise, he muses, and his infatuation with the Chinese dragon is so strong he decides Ginvoo will set to creating such a beast to add to the Dark Army. Satan lowers the monocular and turns to God.

"That's some pagoda you have incorporated into the church, Jehovah. I didn't know there was a place for Eastern religion here."

"There's a place for all forms of worship here, Lucifer. We're well past the restrictive, puritan ways of the early Kingdom, you know that. You're in what, your Great Third Renovation, well we're in something like our 102nd Reclamation. You'd have to ask Rubio what the exact number is and what changes have been made in the last three or four iterations. That's innovation for you."

"Something we in Hell have no intention of promoting. Anachronism is the name of the game. In fact, I think The Great Fourth Renovation will be retrogressive. I'm worried the sinners are getting comfortable with our relative modernity."

"Whatever suits your purposes. I'm not going to tell you how to captain your ship."

"Nor will I yours, but I must say," Satan begins, twirling the spyglass in his hand, "the level of surveillance made possible by this monocular is decidedly *not* in the spirit of the progressive Heaven you speak of." God claps Satan on the shoulder and turns him several degrees to the right.

"See that wrought iron fence over yonder, beginning about a mile out? That bounds the Sanctuary. Take a look inside and tell me what you see."

Satan positions the spyglass and zooms in on the fence, which he follows out toward the horizon until he reaches the main gateway. The ecclesiastical ornamentation proves insipid to him, and after a quick once-over, he tilts up to the insignia and increases the magnification. It reads "Heaven's Sanctuary" in the likeness of secretary script, the wrought iron letters painted a matte silver to stand out from the rest of the gateway. Nice touch, Satan considers as he moves his sights from the gateway into the grounds of the Sanctuary. He pans left for a moment until the first Heavenite subjects enter his field of vision, a group of seven, three men, two women, and two children, one a boy and one a girl, gathered around what appears to be a brick oven. One of the men reaches into the oven with a pizza peel, while the rest of the adults dillydally, the children running about at their feet and occasionally making laps around the oven. Unimpressed with the pedestrian activity, Satan continues panning left only to find one group of Heavenites after another, with the occasional loner thrown into the mix, engaging in unassuming undertakings.

"What exactly am I supposed to be looking for? Hordes of restless conspirers? Evidence of weapons of mass destruction?" Satan asks in frustration.

"Keep looking. There's more going on down there than meets the eye. And don't just look, listen," God responds.

The Devil resumes his search and begins to think the Almighty is wasting his time when he finds a crew of the majorly pious sitting on the steps of a lodge, a rectangular stone building with a peaked, wooden slat roof, and the letters "AA" affixed to the face of the building in an arrangement of two-by-fours painted red. How delightful, Satan thinks, an Alcoholics Anonymous meeting in Heaven's Sanctuary. He activates the audio function on the spyglass.

(*I'm afraid our pact is in its death throes, gentlemen. The meeting was practically empty today other than us.*)

(*Sure is a shame. Our dear Archie didn't even stay around afterward, just bailed out the side door with a worn look on his face.*)

One of the men passes another a sheet of paper and a fountain pen.

(*Never thought I'd be signing off on this.*)
The man signs the paper and stares at the contents.
(*Don't lose sleep over it, brother. Archie has to have
seen this coming for a while.*)
(*Now that we have that monkey off our backs, let's
say we go to the tavern and have a spirit or two, fellas.*)
The men stand, descend the steps, and carry on to the
tavern. Satan lowers the monocular and pinches his goatee.

"Well, I don't know if it qualifies as a threat to state
security, but I did just find some suspicious activity."

"Which was?"

"A group of men appear to have broken a pledge to
themselves and one of their companions. The poor soul is
going to have to fight the good fight without them." Satan
stifles a laugh.

"That is precisely the kind of fractious activity we
have had our eyes on. My angels have pinpointed two
distinct groups leveraged against one man and perhaps a few
of his straggling followers. This man is the original de facto
leader of the majorly pious. Tell me, what did this individual
look like, the man who was betrayed by the others?"

"Can't say, he wasn't there. Name's Archie, though."
God snaps His fingers.

"Ah-hah. That's the one, Lucifer. Archie is the
catalyst for all of this conspiring." Satan resists another
chuckle.

"I'd say there's a conspiracy going on, all right.
Archie is some kind of fascist teetotaler and his so-called
allegiants want off the wagon."

"What are you talking about?"

"I saw nothing but a bunch of boozehounds relapsing
after an Alcoholics Anonymous meeting." Satan offers the
spyglass to God. "Here, I can point out their meeting hall to
you." God erupts in a torrent of laughter, which shakes the

ground beneath them and affrights a colony of seagulls, who set flight from the clouds at the foot of the hill.

"Lucifer, the 'AA' lodge you speak of belongs to a group called The Archibald Alliance, not Alcoholics Anonymous." Satan's black heart reels. He feels foolish and sophomoric, ineffectual and small, but luckily his embarrassment will not show outwardly. Blushing only mimics his skin's natural state.

"Is that right? Looked like friends of Bill to me, Jehovah. One guy had a styrofoam cup of coffee and another had a cigarette."

"An honest mistake."

"Well, now that we've cleared that up, I must admit your grievances are well-founded. This goes without saying, given the symbiosis between our two kingdoms and your penchant for espionage, but the situation in Hell's Paradise is not much different." God rubs His nose and looks down at the valley. The late-afternoon sun casts a long shadow of the Temple across the valley floor.

"I figured as much, although I'll have you know my spies haven't been infiltrating your territory much lately. Intuition alone can be a tremendous resource."

"In case you need me to fill in the blanks, I've been sensing an uprising or a petition to return Hell to its former state."

"Hmm. I guess we're both up the creek without a paddle. Let's come to terms, then, shall we?" Satan nods. "If one of us is forced, compelled, or otherwise resigned to restore his kingdom to its former state, the other shall be informed immediately and shall do the same. Deal?"

"Deal."

They extend hands and shake on it, but behind the small of his back where God cannot see it, Satan ties the end of his tail in a knot.

"Oh, before I leave Jehovah, how about some of that acidic water?"

Chapter 23

Since exposing the gang to the widespread separation anxiety disorder taking place across both Hellion populations, Hubert Raymer has been spending most of his time at his and Doc's secret meeting place, only it's not usually for the purpose of conversing with his old friend, but rather to pace along the outer gate or sit cross-legged against a wall, alternately mulling over existentialist questions about his place in the ongoing predicament, and making amateurish attempts at transcendental meditation. When he is MIA, Hubert's friends have grown to assume he went to his "thinking place." They already know, James especially, what he's thinking about, and wait with bated breath for him to get on with it, their support and participation a foregone conclusion.

Hubert weighs the pros and cons of returning to regular Hell, then meditates, stretches, and reassesses the issue with a clear head. He thinks about the ethics of a Hell divided, and though it's a secondary discourse, he considers the same for Heaven, lamenting the "trickle up effect" of his selfish actions, then meditates, stretches, and reassesses the issue without assuming responsibility for what's going on in Paradise. Out of sight, out of mind, he says to himself. He debates the justifiability of God's reason for sending him to Hell. The crux of the issue. The million-dollar question. He settles on one of several viable arguments, then meditates, stretches, and resumes pacing, this time viewing things from God's perspective.

All of this inner dialogue is nothing more than a mental exercise, however, since Hubert has had his mind made up for a fortnight or two. The pacing and questioning and meditating, if anything more than a mental exercise, serves to gather the fortitude needed to go through with his decision. Things must return to the way they were, or at the very least, Hubert must return to regular Hell. The segregation of Hell, in his eyes, is as unfair as God's reason for sentencing him to eternal damnation, and he cannot prolong this hypocrisy at the expense of others and the exclusion of friends like Doc. Money cannot but happiness in mortal life, and status and privilege cannot achieve that end in the afterlife. In Hell, happiness is a relative term, virtually nonexistent in its traditional sense, and friends are about the only constant worthy of a smile, a laugh, or an increase in morale. Without friends, a Hellion would experience an average total forque level closer to the maximum of one hundred than the mean of ninety. These days Hubert has been bearing the burden of a near-100-forque existence, and he needs to take the load off.

His biggest fear has been that he won't be able to convince James, Lawrence, and Claudia to leave Hell's Paradise with him. Despite James' gestural agreement with his expressed disillusionment while taking in the scene at the outer gate recently, Hubert is afraid the gang has developed a strong attachment to their improved surroundings. His dread is only reaffirmed when, upon seeking out his friends to inform them of his final decision, he finds them goofing around in the same fountain they patronized their first day as residents of Hell's Paradise. Hoping to break the ice with frivolity, Hubert sneaks up on them using a military crawl, then lunges over the wall of the fountain, lets out a hysterical growl, and crashes into the pool with outstretched arms, reaching toward a screaming Claudia with one hand and a dazed James with the other. Lawrence, more composed than his companions, mimics Hubert's attempt at a scary monster growl, which Hubert can hear above the surface as he rolls over on the bottom of the pool and briefly admires the reticulated, crystalline tableau of the limestone cavern enveloping the water.

"Gotcha!" Hubert cries as he breaks the surface. Claudia takes a step toward him and shovels water up into his face. Some of it gets in Hubert's mouth, and he immediately spits it at Claudia in a wide stream.

"Ugh! Gross, Huey," she shrieks. Some of the backwash makes it into her mouth and she spits over the rim of the pool while trying not to gag. "That's a violation of the rules of engagement. War criminal!"

"War criminal! War criminal!" James and Lawrence chant together. They stomp through the water toward Hubert and wrangle him, one man under each armpit.

"Sorry, pal. Ya been convicted of a war crime. Time ta face tha firing squad," James informs him. They drag a nonresistant Hubert to the middle of the fountain and set him against the base of the statue. "Lawrence is gonna read yer last rites."

"O holy hosts above, I call upon thee as a servant of Jesus Christ, to sanctify our actions this day in preparation for the fulfillment of the will of God," Lawrence exclaims. Hubert smiles, enjoying this elaborate game his friends must have developed in his absence.

"Ya think this is funny, prisoner? It won't be so funny in a minute when ya get blasted into oblivion," James declares.

"This is marvelous, fellas," says Hubert. He looks at Claudia, who stands in the middle of the pool watching the proceeding. "You must be the executioner, then, Claudia."

"Shh!" she responds, pressing an index finger to her parted lips.

"I call upon the great archangel Raphael, master of air," Lawrence continues, placing his right palm against Hubert's forehead, "to open the way for this to be done. Let the fire of the Holy Spirit now descend that this being might be awakened to the world beyond and the life of Earth, and infused with the power of the Holy Spirit."

"Do you remember this from the time before?" Hubert inquires, facing Lawrence. No response. He turns to James. "Or did you pull a few strings to get your hands on a Bible?"

"Shh!" asserts Claudia.

"O Lord Jesus Christ, most merciful, Lord of Earth we ask that you receive this child into your arms, that he might pass in safety from this crisis. As thou hast told us with infinite compassion: "In my Father's house are many mansions: if it were not so, I would have told you. I go prepare a place for you." So let it be done."

"So let it be a nice mansion, Lord, if it's not too much to ask," Hubert interjects.

"Any last confessions you'd like to make, prisoner?" asks Lawrence. "Speak now or forever hold your peace."

"Yes, uh, in the seventh grade I plagiarized an essay in history class. Also, I once fed the family dog chocolate. He almost died, had to have his stomach pumped."

"You are forgiven, child." Lawrence dips his right thumb in the water and rubs a cross on Hubert's forehead, top to bottom, then left to right. "By this sign thou art anointed with the grace of the atonement of Jesus Christ and thou art absolved of all past error and freed to take your place in the world He has prepared for us."

"That all? You gonna blast me now?" Hubert is growing tired of the shtick.

"Shh! You'll get yours in due time, criminal," Claudia remarks, swiftly passing her open palm above the water in a threatening manner.

"And thus do I commend thee into the arms of our Lord of Earth, our Lord Jesus Christ, preserver of all mercy and reality, and the Father Creator. We give Him glory as we give you into His arms in everlasting peace, to be prepared to return into the denser reality of God the Father, Creator of all. Amen, amen, amen."

"Amen, amen, amen," James and Claudia echo.

James and Lawrence lift Hubert and sit him on the base of the fountain. They prop one of his arms on each of the statue figures, exposing his torso to the imminent barrage of water, a metaphorical baptism. Hubert looks down at his dangling lower legs, the water up to mid-ankle, and stirs his feet in wide arcs, creating a milky broth of the area within his reach. While in the midst of this, he realizes his friends have left him a mode of defense. Not the most formidable defense, but a defense nonetheless. Once they unload on me, he thinks, I will let them have it with a flurry of kicking feet. James and Lawrence stand back with Claudia and Lawrence raises his arm.

"Ready, aim, fire!"

Lawrence drops his arm and the three executioners go ballistic, slapping fans of water at Hubert with both hands and churning the pool into a small typhoon. Hubert is overwhelmed by the hostile deluge, which stings and reddens his skin, and sneaks into his mouth and eyes, simultaneously choking and blinding him. He is too busy spitting out hot, alkaline water and wiping it from his eyes to return fire. For a second he begins to hate the gang, then the fury subsides. He clears his eyes to find them with their hands on their knees and their chests heaving.

"Is it over?" Hubert asks, worried that if they continue this mild form of torture it will put a serious dent in their friendship, and at the most inopportune of times.

"Yes," Lawrence pants, "I think we've exhausted ourselves."

Hubert hops down from the fountain and Claudia lashes him with a final, exclamatory spray. She disarms him with a demure smile and approaches with an extended hand.

"Truce," she says.

"Truce," Hubert replies as he takes her hand and shakes it.

James, overheated by the feverish activity, walks to the edge of the pool and sits on the rim of the basin. The rest of the group, likewise feeling on the verge of fainting, join him. They sit in silence awhile and enjoy the open air, occasionally turning their hands over to check the de-pruning process on the tips of their fingers. They idly kick at the water and James eventually begins to whistle to break the silence.

"Man, I was roasting like a lobster in there," James comments.

"Yeah, you'd have to be careful coming here alone. One could fall unconscious in the pool and drown," Lawrence hypothesizes. James and Hubert nod.

"You chaps mean to tell me you've never bathed in here alone?" asks Claudia.

"Never thought to. I was merely making an observation. This place could benefit from a lifeguard," Lawrence responds.

"Sure could, but ain't nobody, Hellion or minion, gonna volunteer fer that," says James. "I'm guessing from tha way ya phrased that question ya been in here by yer lonesome, huh Miss Claudia?"

"From time to time." She slips back into the water and turns on her back, arms stretched above her head, chin tilted upward, palms facing the ceiling, and floats with impressive buoyancy and balance. "I like to come here and float like this in silence. You know, clear out the cobwebs in my head." This comment catches Hubert's attention, which had previously been more reserved for the motion of the water at his feet than the conversation.

"No kidding. I've been doing a form of solitary meditation myself recently," Hubert submits. Claudia lowers her chin and meets his eyes.

"Is that so, Huey? Pray tell."

"Well, I've been making an effort to practice mindfulness in the Buddhist tradition. I sit in a modified lotus position, since I can't achieve full lotus without cramping up or pulling a muscle, and basically contemplate questions relevant to the here-and-now. It's more about self-analysis than clearing out the cobwebs, as you say, so it diverges from true Buddhist meditation a bit, but the foundation is there."

"I see. And what kind of questions have you been attempting to answer? What ancient wisdoms have you learned thus far?" Unlike the previous question, a sincere inquiry, this one is rhetorical. Hubert, sensing the foreknowledge of the gang in Claudia's tone and James and Lawrence's body language, is relieved to have been provided with a segue, one he assumed would require labor and tact.

"I'm glad you asked, Claudia," Hubert glances at James and Lawrence, who sit on either side of him, to inform them of their inclusion in the subsequent exchange, "because I came to see you guys to tell you I've made up my mind about this Hell's Paradise dilemma." Hubert looks at each of his companions and probes their faces for indications of surprise. As expected, he finds none. "I've decided to request a return to regular Hell." James and Lawrence place a hand on each of his shoulders and Claudia abandons her floating position and kneels in the pool, the waterline gently undulating at the cup of her breasts.

"That's a bold decision, old pal, but no worries – we've been anticipating this fer many a moon," James assures.

"So how about it? You guys gonna attempt this transfer with me or what? Regular Hell wouldn't be quite the same without you." James flashes a pensive look at Lawrence and Claudia, then pats Hubert on the knee.

"Of course we will, Huey. We love it here, but this place was yer brainchild, and yer vacancy will strip it of its appeal, like Mötley Crüe without Vince Neal, or Microsoft without Bill Gates."

Some shoes are impossible to fill.

Hubert is smitten. Despite his willingness to embark on this mission solo, it would have been a tough pill to swallow, a zero-sum game, to sacrifice the friendship of the gang for peace of mind. Lacking an intelligible way to express his gratitude verbally, Hubert instead bounds from his seat and claps each of his friends on the back of the hand while looking them intently in the eye. He thanks them individually and receives a nonchalant smile or nod of the head in return.

"I won't leave you all hanging in the balance any longer. I'll take my, *our*, entreaty to Satan straight away. I shall return," Hubert announces.

He exits the fountain and heads down one of the pathways at a modest pace, waves to the gang without looking back as he disappears behind the first bend, and picks up the pace once he is out of sight, not wanting to betray his adolescent urgency in view of his friends, who have graciously entrusted him with their fates. The path continues uninterrupted for a few hundred yards before Hubert makes a left at a fork, followed by a series of turns in either direction, some sharp and some oblique, and finally a switchback, which opens up to the promenade of the main gate of Hell's Paradise.

A quintet of minor sinners loiters at the foot of the gate, yelling sarcastic pleasantries at the major sinners passing by on the opposite side, and asking passersby on their side for directions to places that, to the best of Hubert's knowledge, only exist in their imaginations. One of the two demon guards minding the gate walks over and prods the vagabonds with a staff, imploring them to move on less they want to be impounded, but his halfhearted attempt makes little impression on the group of lawless carousers. With the one guard occupied with the vagrants, Hubert approaches the other and smiles.

"Hello, good sir, my name is Hubert Raymer."

"I know who you are, sinner. You're the reason I have to be standing by this eyesore of a gate. State your business," the demon gruffly replies. Hubert takes the cue from the demon's cold reception and opts to streamline his spiel.

"I need to see Satan about an urgent matter. Can you get in touch with him, please?"

"Sure thing, cretin. It might take him a day or two to get back to you, depending on his schedule."

"Not a problem. Thanks for your help." Hubert reaches out to shake the demon's hand. The demon snorts and spits, covering Hubert's hand and forearm in a thick mucus. Hubert looks at his hand and his stomach wrenches. "It's service with a smile, not service with a snot."

"Carry on, Hellion."

Hubert walks off, rubbing the saliva off on his cotton shirt as he goes.

Chapter 24

Several days, maybe weeks, pass without a word from Satan and Hubert begins to lose faith until one day, while enjoying dinner in the canteen with James, Lawrence, and Claudia, The Dark Lord appears. In a comical attempt to blend in with the natives, he's dressed in the standard-issue burlap sack of the major sinners, but unaware of the segregated seating arrangement, immediately blows his otherwise tenuous cover as soon as he sits down with the gang. Minions on both sides of the dividing line whisper to each other and ogle their master out of the corners of their eyes. Satan hunches over, elbows on the table, and addresses Hubert in a huggermugger tone, like an agent would one of his field contacts in a public place in a spy thriller.

"Mr. Raymer, I've been informed there's something important you'd like to speak about," he says, speaking into his shoulder and not making eye contact.

James, Lawrence, and Claudia shift in their seats, gooseflesh raising on their exposed skin. They've all seen the Devil in person, only not this close, and this is the first they've heard his voice other than in PSAs. James feels compelled to reach out and touch him. Lawrence, perhaps reverting to 18th century superstitions about witches and demons and other things that go 'bump' in the night, turns his eyes away, thinking eye contact will turn him to stone or capture his soul. Claudia stares at his long, curved fingernails, sharply edged and charred black by soot and smoke, and feeling a mixture of disgust and envy looks at her own fingernails, bland except for faint lines of dirt under the tips and cuticles, and wishes they could attract attention of any kind. Hubert casually looks up from his saucer of beef stew and lays down his spoon.

"Yes, there is, sir. I've been anticipating a visit from you for a while. I was beginning to think the guard I trusted to forward the message was only blowing smoke," Hubert explains.

"Oh no, Mr. Raymer, I received the message promptly. I've been busy lately is all." Satan speaks into the collar of the burlap sack this time, pulling it up to his nose ski mask-style.

"Did ya forget the flimsy baseball cap?" James asks. It takes a second for Satan to realize he's the subject of the question.

"Excuse me, minion. I'm not sure I understand your question."

"Ya came in here with yer spy outfit on, trying ta look indiscrete, only ya forgot tha flimsy baseball cap ta shroud yer face, like in tha movies."

"Didn't you see me do that with the burlap, minion? I can pull it up over my mouth, thereby hiding my face and thwarting any potential lip readers. Two birds, one stone." Satan demonstrates again.

"Very well, sir, but those horns are still tha most conspicuous thing in tha room." Satan gropes the keratinous appendages atop his maroon scalp and frowns, as if suddenly aware of their potential to draw stares. "Also, ya overlooked a critical detail about this here environment. Since tha inception of Hell's Paradise, tha cafeteria has been divided in two, one side fer minor sinners and one side fer major sinners. Ya should have worn one of our cotton get-ups if ya wanted to blend in. Ya also woulda been a lot more comfortable."

The touch, the feel, of cotton. The fabric of minor sinners' lives.

Satan looks about and realizes the minion is right: he's a blotch of brown in an otherwise immaculate tapestry of white, a steaming brown feculence in a fresh snowfield. He imagines walking into a fresh snowfield in the arctic landscape outside the circle of pride and soiling it with his excrement. What an embarrassment, what a disgrace, he cries to himself. He pounds his fists on the table.

"That worthless Ginvoo, how was he not aware of this?!" the Devil wails.

The gang looks from one member to the other, knowing someone has to defuse the hissy fit unfolding before them, but unsure who's the right one to do it. If Satan loses his cool, it could very well sabotage their agenda. It could also mean every warm Hellion body in the cafeteria will be smote or banished to one of the six deadly habitats, all because of Ginvoo's ignorance. Several seconds pass, and James, Lawrence, and Claudia's eyes settle on Hubert. Satan curses to himself under his breath in Latin.

"You're the reason he's here, Huey," Claudia whispers, nudging him in the ribs. "Go ahead and say something." Hubert looks across the table at Satan, rehearses what seems like an appropriate comment, then dismisses it for a better one.

"Ah, dictum factum," says Hubert. Satan stops talking to himself and straightens up in his seat.

"Verum," he replies.

"Sic vita est."

"Etiam, discendo discimus." The Devil nods his head and scratches his left wrist with his right forefinger.

"Aqua sub pontes, rectus?"

"Profecto. Non vetera et vetera."

Hubert, who studied Latin in grammar school, searches his word bank in hopes of continuing the exchange, but all he seems to remember learning was proverbs. Given the content of the dialogue so far, he's not convinced Satan knows any more conversational Latin than he does. The gang looks at him with raised eyebrows and he begins to blush. Feeling the pressure to break the silence, Hubert decides to smooth things over in English.

"Forgive me, sir, but my Latin is very limited."

"Oh, that's OK, Mr. Raymer. I appreciate the effort. It's rare I have the opportunity to speak it with others. It's farcical, really, a Hell without Latin. I've been thinking of enforcing it as the first language in the next Great Renovation. In fact, I was just talking to Jehovah the other day about making The Great Fourth Renovation retrogressive, and what better way to set a precedent than by instituting an obsolete language."

A dead language for dead people.

"Well, sir, you're the boss. I have no opinion on the matter. I'd have a leg up on the rest of the Hellions, though."

"You certainly would. Now, before we discuss your reason for my being here, let's go somewhere private. I've arranged a gondola for us. Please, follow me." Hubert looks at each member of the gang and shrugs.

"Sir, I'm hoping that means all of us? You see, my three friends here are my cohorts in the matter. It's kind of a package deal." Satan, already stepping away from the table, stares down James, Lawrence, and Claudia with a steely reserve. James worries his flippancy has jeopardized the group aspect of the mission. He folds his hands on the table in front of him and tries to appear contrite.

"OK, Mr. Raymer, if you insist," the Devil replies. He taps a finger on the table and sways his head toward the nearest exit. "Let's go."

They walk across several rows of dining tables to the obsidian archway of the exit and out into the main corridor of the hub. Satan directs them to the left and they walk past one doorway to the radial corridor, followed by another, and another, and another, until Hubert feels they've done an entire lap around the hub. Not the case. They keep walking and all four friends, like children on a long road trip, are tempted to ask, "Are we there yet?", but their adult loci of control prevent the question from slipping their tongues. Hubert begins counting doors and when he reaches thirty-four, Satan breaks the silence.

"The passageway is right around the bend, only six more doors."

For the first time, Hubert notices the click-clack of Satan's hooves on the rocky ground. Something about his voice injecting the stagnant air with life drew Hubert's attention to what had been the only consistent sound in the corridor, apart from the footfalls of the occasional Hellion pedestrian or the distant cry of a Hellion in distress.

Desensitization in an infernal nation.

They come to a radial corridor with an unusually triangular doorway and Satan leads them into it. The tunnel is devoid of light sources and once the light from the hub extinguishes they walk in complete darkness. Hubert puts his hands out in front of his face and tries to follow the sound of Satan's hooves, but he continually trips on the ground, which has an unpredictably transmutable grade and slick texture. He curses at low volume each time he stubs a toe and hears his comrades doing the same every few seconds. The sound of the Devil's footsteps stops, and the gang stops and peers into the darkness ahead of them.

"From the looks of it, you all could use some light," Satan's voice emanates.

"Boy, whatever gave ya that idea," James replies, immediately wishing he had kept silent.

Three snaps of the fingers echo off the walls of the corridor and in an instant a set of five lights appear about fifteen yards in front of the gang, illuminating Satan's figure from shoulder height. Initially, Hubert believes the yellow-orange lights are lanterns, before realizing they have no frame or base. He attributes this to Satan's black magic, perhaps another of his many patents, say, Float-O-Lanterns™, until four of the lights begin to move toward him and his friends and he sees they're not lights at all, at least not in the traditional sense, but rather lightning bug-like creatures. Despite being about the size of a robin, their flight produces nothing more than a barely perceptible drum, and Hubert finds them as beautiful as any one human can find an insect, a feeling he shares with earthly lightning bugs. The four flying fluorescents settle one after the other next to each of the four Hellions at head level. The fireflies create a 3D radius of ten feet of clear lighting. Enough to light the way, but not too much to spoil the suspense and solitude of parts unknown.

"How's that for service? A personal visibility escort," says Satan with a trace of pride. "Ginvoo and I bioengineered them ourselves. We combined the genes of a firefly with certain bioluminescent jellyfish to make their lights constant. We also altered some of the proteins to make them larger. Impressive, huh?"

"Are they docile?" Claudia asks as she stares at her lightning bug's intimidating and grotesque mandibles.

"Of course, dear, not all of my minions are malevolent. Some serve a benevolent purpose, though the average Hellion will never enjoy its services. You sinners happen to be exceptions."

"Um, thanks?" says James.

They continue along the corridor for another one hundred or two paces and a triangular doorway at the other end opens up into the bank of a wide fiery river. There's a gondola docked a few yards downriver and Satan leads them to it. The gondolier, a hobgoblin with dark green skin and long, floppy ears partially covered by a straw boater, greets

Satan in Latin, shakes his hand with a leathery, four-fingered claw, and helps the Hellions board the craft one at a time.

"Welcome aboard Lady Herodias, fiends," says the oarsman after all four of the gang are safely aboard. They sit side by side near the stern of the vessel, facing the bow, and nod at their strange green host.

"Glad to be here, mister," Hubert replies flatly, hoping to dissuade the hobgoblin from further engagement.

Fortunately, Satan safeguards Hubert as he climbs onto the gondola unassisted, pats the hobgoblin on the shoulder, and hands him a gold coin, cuing him to take his place at the helm. The hobgoblin abides, picks up his oar, and starts the gondola down the lava flow. The Devil takes a seat facing his guests, stomps his heel on the hull, and smiles.

"I don't think we'll be needing these anymore," he declares, petting the lightning bug perched on his shoulder. He snaps his fingers three times and the creatures fly away in a V-formation. Hubert watches their yellow-orange abdomens fade in the distance and it reminds him of airplanes in the night sky from the time before. "Beautiful, aren't they?"

"By bug standards, absolutely. As beautiful as can be," Hubert proclaims.

"Beauty is in tha eye of tha beholder, old buddy, and I think they're woefully ugly. Remind me of these diving beetles at tha pond behind my grandmother's house down Alabama. Nasty suckers," says James.

"Just like you to try to spoil a wonderful thing, James. I was skittish at first, but I agree with Huey. Gorgeous little buggers, they are," Claudia adds.

"I think 'gorgeous' is a bit excessive. They are fascinating specimens, though. I bet they could be trained to do all sorts of things aside from what they're naturally designed for," Lawrence observes. James eyes him and purses his lips.

"Ya would think some exploitative bull like that, wouldn't ya, Lawrence. Man, if ya were running this place ya'd clip their wings and brand them, have some pouring ya lemonade and others polishing yer shoes. Ya know, sir," James continues, addressing Satan, "ya should strongly consider hiring this man as a consultant." Satan chuckles and snorts.

"My cretins, what delightful banter you have," he says with widening eyes. "Pardon my poor manners, but I forgot to get your names."

"I'm Claudia."

"Lawrence Rutledge. Senior member of the group."

"James Jenkins. Token negro of the group." Satan nods and looks at Claudia.

"And I guess you're the token woman of the group, Miss Claudia?" he asks.

"I suppose, but that's a dreary title. I think of myself as the brains," she replies.

"Think on sister, 'cause that sure ain't tha case," James reproofs. Satan ignores the slight.

"Is that so? I pegged Mr. Raymer as the brains of the operation."

"No, sir, I believe my role is undefined. I'm somewhat of a generalist," Hubert expresses.

"Jack of all trades, master of none. Well, what you lack in mastery you make up for in ambition and initiative."

Hubert blushes. The idea of being flattered by the Prince of Darkness makes him want to jump out of his skin. He suddenly realizes how hot it is on the fiery river, and that he can feel the magma boiling on the other side of the hull. It prickles at the soles of his bare feet and draws up sweat from his ankles. He tugs on the collar of his shirt to try to facilitate airflow to his neck and chest. Satan detects his discomfort and allows him to wallow in it for a moment. He has given this man preferential treatment and the illusion he's important, or at least not as bad as the others, and he must remind him from time to time who's who and what's what. As an extension of Hubert's irritation, James, Lawrence, and Claudia wriggle in their seats and stare aimlessly into the sluggish stream. Satan relishes the metronomic sound of the gondolier's paddle splashing in and out of the lava, and checks the banks for outside observers. He sees none. Satisfied with his brief reassertion of power, and the solitude of their present geographic position, he resumes the discussion.

"Please, loyal servants, now that we have some privacy, tell me why I've been asked to pay a visit. What's the agenda?" Hubert clears his throat and stops playing with his collar.

"To be succinct, sir, we've had a change of heart. We would like to return to ordinary Hell." Satan knits his brow and leans closer to the gang.

"A transfer. Yes, indeed. You wouldn't be the first," Satan lies, "but unlike the others, this is sure to make waves."

"You mean there have already been minor sinners who have made this request?"

"Oh, sure. Within days of the Inaugural Ball the first transfers showed up at my office. There haven't been many, but they trickle in here and there."

James finds these claims apocryphal. Something about the Devil's tone isn't right, and the absence of rumors about said transfers is highly suspicious. Private deals like that don't remain confidential for long. Instead of disputing the claims, James decides to play along, hoping to punch the gang's ticket back to regular Hell by demonstrating an aloofness to the situation, an indication that with or without its founding members, Hell's Paradise will move forward uninterrupted and its folklore will be shaped by the whims of its residents.

"I heard a whisper or two about folks leaving. Didn't necessarily believe it at first, but then I hadn't seen this friend 'a mine, Walter Lewis, fer the longest time. And it wasn't like Walt ta go AWOL like that. Ya could find him at marbles like clockwork. Anyway, word got around he requested a transfer and I haven't seen 'em since," says James, a practiced fibber.

Satan is surprised by the anecdote, but lacks the proper context to call James' bluff. In a kingdom replete with liars and charlatans, derelicts of every sort, fact and fiction exist in a Venn diagram, where the universal set, which Satan has come to call "fabricated truths," is disproportionately large. James was relying on this quandary when he decided to corroborate Satan's lie.

"Walter Lewis, huh, can't say I remember him. You could be right, though, he might be toiling in the circle of envy as we speak. And I must say it perplexes me why you folks would envy *his* position, and I'm somewhat disappointed, Hubert, after all we've been through, but who am I to deny you what I've already given others. Congratulations sinners, transfer approved."

The four companions thank Satan and shake his hand. He tells them he'll set an appointment and have one of his minions send for them to sign the necessary paperwork in his office. The hobgoblin stops the gondola and helps the gang find their footing on the bank, while Satan remains aboard the barge.

"Farewell, my devious children, I'll see you soon," Satan calls as the gondolier pushes off the bank.

"Bon voyage, sir," Hubert replies. When Satan is out of earshot, Hubert looks at his friends with discerning eyes. "That seemed too easy."

"Yeah, and I don't believe his story about tha other transfers. Not one bit," James avows. Lawrence and Claudia shrug, and the group sets foot upriver back toward the hub.

Satan returns to his office after a leisurely boat ride where he had time to think over his decision. He sits at his desk, props his hooves on an open drawer, and stares at the walkie-talkie lying under the lamp in the far corner of the desk. Thermopylae appears from beneath the desk, mews, and begins rubbing himself against the undersides of Satan's legs. The Devil pats his lap and the Hellcat pounces into his master's awaiting embrace.

"I guess I should inform Jehovah, isn't that right, Thermopylae?" he asks the feline. He pinches its cheeks and looks it in the eyes. "Sure, sure, that's all he needs to know. Anything further he'll have to find out through his spies."

Satan picks up the radio and switches to channel six. He tells God he's allowed Hubert Raymer and three of his friends to rejoin the general population, and that he expects others to follow. God expresses an interest in arranging another meeting with Hubert, whom he calls "a bright prospect."

From disenfranchised sinner, to minor sinner, to major sinner, to bright prospect. The many faces of Hubert Raymer.

Chapter 25

It's only a matter of hours before Hubert and the gang are called into Satan's office to complete the transfer paperwork. James blows a kiss to the main gate of Hell's Paradise as they exit the premises of their posh home for the final time. No more hot tub fountains, no more marbles, no more song and dance. On occasion, James, Lawrence, and Claudia will regret leaving a life of relative comfort, but in the end the sacrifice for their friend will be worth it, because for Hubert there are no regrets. Their regrets will pass with the hands of time and one day Hell's Paradise will be remembered like a foggy dream, some too-good-to-be-true reminiscence in a neglected crevice of the mind.

"The right way is rarely the easy way," James says to himself on the drawbridge spanning the river of fire that separates Hell's Paradise from regular Hell.

The four friends, escorted by a demon guard, make their way to the hub and hike up a gradually ascending radial corridor to the executive wing above the cafeteria. James, Lawrence, and Claudia are ravished with anticipation. This will be their first visit to the Devil's suite. The demon guard leads them into a hallway where the herculean double doors of the infamous office mark the end of the road.

"Does anyone else smell oil?" Claudia asks. James and Lawrence lift their noses and sample the air. After several more paces, Hubert points to the torches mounted on the door frame. "Ah, oil-burning torches, how quaint."

"Yeah, but that sign...not so quaint," James opines, pointing at the neon, "The Management," sign at the top of the door. The sign has been changed from orange to green, something Hubert fails to notice.

"More of a red light district, strip club vibe," Claudia confers. The demon guard looks at Claudia and grunts. She decides to be quiet until he leaves them.

The five travelers approach the egress and James, Lawrence, and Claudia stand with their necks craned, admiring the opulence of the door, while simultaneously scratching their heads at the jarring juxtaposition created by the seediness of the neon sign. Claudia reaches for the door, hoping to gauge the quality of the oak, only to have her hand swatted down by the demon guard. He grunts at her with the same tone as before and presses the buzzer.

"Hello, this is the Devil Himself, state your business," Satan announces through the speaker. James, Lawrence, and Claudia hadn't noticed the red buzzer and its accompanying black speaker in their initial inspection of the door, and decide it further contributes to the unseemly side of the visual dissimilitude.

"Good afternoon, master. The four sinners you requested to sign transfer agreements are here," states the minion.

"Excellent, bring them in."

The guard pushes open the doors and holds the right door for the gang. Claudia thinks of thanking him, but instead nods her head and offers a toothless smile. Rather than grunting, the demon communicates his disapproval by flaring his nostrils. A little etiquette wouldn't undermine your purpose, Claudia muses. They stand in the entryway and James, Lawrence, and Claudia take in the expansive and lavish quarters, while Hubert puts his hands on his hips and looks around for Satan, who isn't in his usual spot at his desk. The demon guard closes the doors behind them and urges them forward with a gentle shove to the backs of James and Lawrence.

"Go," the beast commands. He points toward Satan's empty desk at the opposite end of the room. They walk down the oversized Navajo runner and Hubert continues to search for their host.

"Welcome, dearest cretins. Wait by my desk, I'll be right over," Satan hails from somewhere to the right of the visitors.

They turn to the right wall to find Satan on the top rung of a wood ladder attempting to center his Lucifer self-portrait. The top corners of the frame are beyond an arm's length, and he uses a meter ruler to push the painting into position. It looks as if he could easily lose his balance and fall onto the stone apron of the fireplace, potentially breaking his hip and any number of crooked bones in his limbs. This image gives Hubert pause for thought, and a mischievous smile traces his face as he stops himself short of wishing the accident would happen.

"Need a hand, my Lord?" the demon inquires.

"No, no, thank you though," Satan responds, making a final adjustment to the picture. "There. Perfect." He climbs down, lays the ladder on the floor, and stands back from the fireplace to check his handiwork. Satisfied, he wipes his maroon mitts together like a carpenter ridding himself of sawdust, and joins his servant and the Hellions at his desk. "How have my favorite Hellions been?" he asks, plopping into his chair.

"No complaints," says Hubert. His compadres nod in agreement.

"Good, and who's going to listen anyway, right." Satan chuckles and slaps his hand on the desktop. His guests, including the minion, force a smile. "I would ask you to sit, but this will only take a minute." He removes a folder from a filing rack on the desktop, opens it, thumbs through the contents, takes out a few papers, and slides them across the desk to Hubert and company. "Those are the transfer documents. There is one for each of you with your name in the heading. Please read it and sign at the bottom, and voila, you're back to being residents of the Hell we all know and love."

The Hellions step forward to the edge of the desk and pick up their respective paper. They read the agreement: *I, the Hellion signed below, voluntarily and willingly agree to reenter the major sinner community in what is colloquially known as "regular Hell." I do this with the full knowledge of the consequences of my decision and a thorough understanding of the lifestyle to which I am ascribing. I also am aware of the benefits I am forfeiting by choosing to leave Hell's Paradise. If, at any time, I decide I would like to return to Hell's Paradise, I may do so at the discretion of Satan, Dark Lord the Merciful, and a committee of elder minions. However, if such a return is approved, it will be my last change of address. I will remain in Hell's Paradise for eternity or, given unforeseen circumstances, until the colony is dismantled, whichever occurs last.* Beneath the statement are lines for the signature and date, and in the bottom right corner of the document, a note in fine print: *Satan, as ruler of all in the infernal kingdom, maintains the right to revoke the residential status of any Hellion at any time, whether they are members of regular Hell or Hell's Paradise.* The gang thinks little of the disclaimer and they each sign and date their document and pass it across the desk to the Devil.

"Excellent," says Satan, picking up the papers and examining the signatures, "and that's it. Painless, wasn't it? You can immediately rejoin the major sinners as soon as you leave this office."

"Thank you, Dark Lord the Merciful," Hubert obliges.

"Yes, thank you, sir," says James.

"It's greatly appreciated," Claudia proclaims.

"A fine gesture, sir, thank you," Lawrence submits.

"You're all welcome, and you're dismissed." Satan gestures toward the door with a raised hand. "Hold on, Mr. Raymer, I'd like you to stay to discuss something particular to you."

"I'll catch up with you guys in the canteen," Hubert tells his departing friends. They nod and walk down the Navajo runner, and along with the demon guard, exit the room. The dense oak doors close with a forceful thud and the walls shudder.

"Those door hinges really need some tuning," Satan notes. "Sorry about the racket." Hubert shrugs it off. "Listen, Mr. Raymer, God has summoned you to Heaven again. He said 'immediately,' and this was days ago, so let's not waste any more time." Satan gets up from behind his desk and motions to the Lucifer fireplace.

"Uh, sir, did He happen to tell you what this is about?" Hubert inquires. The Devil shakes his head and puts his hands on his hips.

"Hellion, when the Almighty says 'jump,' you say 'how high?'. If it were regarding something pedestrian, what, you'd respectfully decline? Come on, giddy up cowboy."

Satan snaps his clawed fingers and points to the fireplace as if commanding a dog. Hubert concedes the irrelevance of his question, but doesn't appreciate the patronizing. He follows Satan to the outer hearth of the fireplace and Satan opens the gold coal gate for him. Remembering the routine, Hubert steps through the gate and ducks into the firebox. He turns to The Dark Lord and pulls the ignition chain.

"Have a good trip, Mr. Raymer. Represent us with dignity," says Satan.

Hubert arrives on the other end of "The Business Expressway" in one piece. Two-for-two in interdimensional, light speed travel, not bad, he tells himself. He takes a few trial steps toward the Pearly Gates to remind himself of the consistency of the clouded terrain. Marshmallows. Taxing on the calves. He trudges up to the Gates, lifts the door knocker, and lets it fall against the jamb under its own weight.

CLACK!

To Hubert's dismay, the sound is as loud as those produced by the full-blown knocks of his first visit, only with a lower pitch. The thunder rolls and the Gates vibrate. Wind chimes rustle somewhere nearby. Hubert counts to ten and reaches to knock again, but is stopped by the sonorous voice of the Lord.

"Hello, my son. Welcome back." God emerges from the clouds to Hubert's right and swiftly paces to the Gates and parts the doors. He smiles and steps aside to allow Hubert to enter. "How was your trip this time?" Instead of a handshake, He proposes a fist bump with an extended right fist. Hubert flounders over the imprudence of the invitation, then meets His stout knuckles with a light jab.

"Better than the first I guess. Can't say it's something I'd ever get used to," Hubert answers. God places a hand on the back of Hubert's shoulder and they begin walking across the clouds in the direction of the magnanimous Temple.

"It's an unforgiving journey, believe me. I must have made that commute tens of thousands of times, and I still wind up queasy when I arrive at one end or the other. Lucifer and I call it DOA: dizzy on arrival." Hubert fakes a smile. "I know, I know, it's trite. The Devil and I have little use for good humor. That's one of the things I admire about Man."

"What, that we have a use for humor?"

"Yes."

"Is laughter not a sufficient purpose? Surely you can put that to use."

God doesn't respond. He runs His hands down the sides of His robe, adjusts His gold cincture, and looks out to the horizon. Hubert does the same and commits to memory the blueness of the sky and the brightness of the late-morning sun. He gazes a few degrees below the disk of the sun and contemplates its yellow-orange glow. Funny how something can be the source of both tremendous joy and overwhelming suffering, he muses.

Fire. Helios and Hades. The paradoxes of nature.

"Sometimes, Hubert. But laughter has had no place around here lately."

"No?"

"You've probably heard by now that I have approved and created a "Heaven's Sanctuary" to counterbalance Hell's Paradise…"

"Yes, through the grapevine. I was compelled to believe it."

"Good, at least there are no surprises in that regard. However, you may be, as I've been, unpleasantly surprised by the outcome. Please, come this way."

The Lord nudges His guest in the direction of the sentry hill where He had taken Lucifer not so many days before. Hubert marvels at the emerald bluff as it appears in the distance and he cranes his neck as it gets closer and closer and rises higher and higher, eventually becoming engulfed in the overlying clouds. They reach the foot of the hill and begin the climb, and Hubert gasps at the exhilarating feel of the meticulously manicured grass on the soles of his feet. The sensation and the aesthetics of the turf conjure up memories from his mortal life. A long fairway. The dimples of a golf ball. The metallic thwack of a club face.

FORE!

"Kentucky bluegrass," Hubert asserts.

"It sure is. We use it on most of the golf courses in the Kingdom, except for the sub-tropical and desert courses. For those we use Bermuda grass."

"Do you play?"

"No, I'll caddy for my angels from time to time though."

They arrive on the peak of the hill and Hubert is stunned by the view. The visibility is several miles, twenty to twenty-five in Hubert's estimation. He can't recall anything like it from the time before, other than the view from the window of a commercial airplane. He caps his brow with his right hand and surveys the valley below, straining his eyes to make out details in the shadows cast by the aloft clouds.

"What is the elevation here, relative to the valley floor?"

"2,720 feet. Slightly taller than the tallest building on Earth."

"They make buildings that tall nowadays?"

"Sure do. If they make them any taller, I'll have to terraform this hill to retain its superlative status." Apples to oranges, Hubert thinks.

"How tall is the Temple?"

"Oh, the tip of the spire, its highest point, is about 1,500 feet." Hubert wonders why God didn't build the spire, or any other part of the structure, to be taller than the tallest building, but he doesn't bother to ask. "But enough about golf and heights, my son. I brought you here, and to this lookout point specifically, to show you the precarious condition of the Heaven's Sanctuary experiment. The petulant behavior of its residents has sealed its impending dissolution."

"You don't say. Coincidentally, Hell's Paradise is in a comparable state." God crosses His arms and looks out at the valley. "But you already know that, don't you. Which means you must also know I left." God nods and looks at Hubert with gentle eyes.

"Yes, Hubert, I know practically all there is to know. Please, take a look at Heaven's Sanctuary. Even at this distance, its madness is evident." The Lord points out the gates and Hubert immediately notices several buildings in disrepair and trash drifting in the breeze. However, after searching for another half minute, he can't discern much else in the way of chaos.

"I see some buildings that have fallen victim to negligence and a considerable amount of trash. Is there more?"

God unsheathes His spyglass and hands it to Hubert, who props it against his eye, adjusts the magnification, and discovers a verifiable shanty town. Mangy, ostensibly feral cats and dogs roaming about and nipping at trash. Children left to their own devices. Unattended fires. Lots of overgrown grass and shrubbery and battalions of slipshod trees.

Third-world conditions in a first-class zip code.

"I dunno. It looks like the neighborhood my friend Carl Eaton grew up in. Carl was from the other side of the tracks, as they say. Maybe the residents of Heaven's Sanctuary have limited economic opportunities or they've succumbed to chemical dependencies. Those were the major problems in Carl's neighborhood," Hubert comments.

"Well, my son, you're only seeing what's on the surface. As with many things, there's more than what meets the eye, as they say," God replies, parroting Hubert's tone.

"OK, then tell me what I'm missing. I didn't come up here to the roof of Heaven to play *Where's Waldo?* with MacGyver's monocular." God chews at the corner of His mouth and Hubert relents. "Forgive my impudence. Please, fill me in."

The Almighty explains the gradual moral degradation of the majorly pious, beginning with their efforts to incite envy from the minorly pious, followed by the internal strife, conspiring, and coup against Archibald the Egret, and ending with the present state of anarchy and defection. Thus far, thirty percent of the population of Heaven's Sanctuary has opted to return to regular Heaven. They were greeted with open arms, but that didn't erase their tarnished images from the memories of the minorly pious.

Forgive, but don't forget, as they say.

"I can't believe it," says Hubert with a shake of his head, "although my gut told me it might end up this way. The parallels between this fellow Archibald and myself are uncanny. The selfishness and the egocentrism. The delusions of being special. The latent need to be in a position of influence." Hubert looks at God and pauses. "I guess the only difference is he started here," he puts his hand at chin level, "and wanted to be here," he moves his hand above his head, "while I started here," he puts his hand at knee level, "and wanted to be here," he moves his hand up to his waist. "That doesn't make me better than him, though."

Hubert gazes out at the valley and strains to keep tears from falling from his dampened eyes. The contrast between the beauty and purity of the landscape below and the vanity and fallibility of the human spirit, embodied by the example set by himself, the sinner, and Archibald, the saint, bears down on him. How can anyone be worthy of this impeccable promised land when, as a whole, we're prone to fault and folly? he wonders. God places a hand on Hubert's shoulder and he flinches, which forces a tear down his cheek. He wipes the stain off and looks into the eyes of his Creator.

"You've made an excellent analysis, Hubert. I've always been impressed by your moral conscience," the Lord proclaims.

"You have?" Hubert asks.

"Absolutely. The true test of a man's moral backbone is not whether he makes mistakes, but whether he is able to recognize those mistakes and grow from them." A short pause to clear His throat. "My son, it's time you heard the truth about your mortal life."

"What truth? I've been able to reclaim memories of the time before over the last several, I don't know, months. That's the reason I came to you, or Satan rather, then you, in the first place. What am I missing?" The stony expression on God's face makes Hubert nervous. He balls his hands into fists and squeezes his fingertips into his palms.

"Hubert, it is not your son who is the leader of a violent religious cult. It was you."

"But, you said…why did you lie to me?" Anger creeps into Hubert's voice. God reaches out to touch him, but he sidesteps the advance.

"I work in mysterious ways, Hubert."

"I didn't ask to be condescended to with proverbs. I want a legitimate explanation."

"I was getting there," God grumbles. "I implemented the lie to see if your better conscience would prevail despite the fact you were under the impression of being a minor sinner, whatever that means. Major sinner, minor sinner, majorly pious, minorly pious, it's all semantic nonsense. Anyway, I would never sentence anyone to damnation solely on the basis of the actions of his kin. I knew the injustice you would feel from this would set you on a path of self-discovery and redemption. I chose you from birth, Hubert, as an experiment to prove to Satan that, despite their sins and setbacks, humans are inherently good."

"A rat in a maze." Hubert chuckles and rolls his eyes.

"You're a lot more than that, my son. You prevailed, didn't you?"

"I guess, but so what? My story doesn't prove humans are inherently good. Heck, the similarities I pointed out between Archibald and myself suggests the opposite. A minor sinner and a majorly pious man with equally fragile spirits. Look around you, Lord, no one is good enough for this place."

"More semantic nonsense. Plenty are good enough for my Kingdom because I have judged them so, and you, Hubert Raymer, are one of the worthy ones."

"Huh?"

"As a reward for substantiating my theory, I invite you to spend the rest of eternity here in Paradise."

Hubert is flabbergasted and thinks the Lord must be playing a cruel prank on him. He soon dismisses the notion, knowing God wouldn't joke about a matter as serious as this. Nevertheless, he feels something is awry. Is he really worthy of this? An admission ticket to Heaven, relatively free of charge, only requiring a one-word response. He thinks about James, Lawrence, and Claudia, and how disappointed they would be with him if he carpetbagged his way out of Hell. A man with a hardy moral backbone doesn't abandon his friends, nor does he accept undue gifts. Besides, accepting the offer would contradict his assertion that Heaven is too good to be true. This must be another test, Hubert decides.

"I'm sorry, sir, I have to decline. I don't belong here, and more importantly, all my friends are in Hell." God smiles and the sun twinkles on His pearly whites.

"A wise choice, Hubert. You truly are one of my children."

Chapter 26

Inside the ramshackle barn in the middle of nowhere there is an onerous moaning. The Brotherhood of the Black Squirrel gathers again and this time it's for a birthing ritual. Much like during the initiation ceremony, a bed of burning coals formed in the shape of a crucifix is the centerpiece of the barn floor, and now a pregnant woman lies on a wood gurney about three feet above the coals. She's in labor; the source of the moaning that can be heard through the sibilating spectators. The woman wears a red cloak with the emblem of the black squirrel on its left breast. The spectating cult members, the Brave Minions, are dressed in their traditional gray cloaks. A voice rises above the groaning woman and the murmuring from the crowd ceases.

"Good evening, Brave Minions. We are gathered here tonight to celebrate an awakening," Virtuous Leader proclaims. He's wearing his traditional white cloak and he pulls back the hood to reveal the face of our beloved subject, Hubert Raymer. "Tonight we welcome the birth of my son, my successor, and the ascension of a brave new era."

Hubert, Virtuous Leader of the Brotherhood of the Black Squirrel, circles the cross while the pregnant woman, his wife Janice, continues to emote suffering. He stops and stands beside her protruding stomach, removes a candle and matches from an inner pocket of his cloak, and lights the candle. He holds the candle steadily above his wife's belly until the wax begins to run down the stick. With the candle tilted at roughly thirty degrees, Hubert allows three drops of hot wax to fall onto his wife's bare midriff. Janice screams and kicks, then looks at her husband with the eyes of the demonically possessed and curses his name.

"This is supposed to induce labor? You nimrod! You're going to scare him into staying in there for another nine months!" she seethes. Hubert hushes her, puts his index finger to her lips, and caresses her stomach, tracing a pentagram with his fingertips.

"Dis, filius, dis. Venit ad lucem," says Virtuous Leader, staring at his wife's belly button.

"Venit ad lucem," the Brave Minions repeat as one.

"Venit ad lucem, dammit. Mommy's getting delirious here," Janice exclaims. Hubert hushes her again, traces another pentagram on her stomach, and gives her a hefty pat on the belly button.

"Easy, my dear. Any minute now," he assures.

In less than two minutes, the cries of a newborn boy supplant Janice's groans as the foremost sound inside the barn. Hubert cuts the umbilical cord and holds his son above his head for his subordinates to see. The cult members jockey for position to get a good look at their future leader. Some of them clap, while others coo at the precious little one.

"My Brave Minions, I give you your future Virtuous Leader, Irving!" Hubert announces.

The Brave Minions salute Irving and cross themselves. One of the gray cloaks passes a goblet to Hubert, and with the knife he used to cut the umbilical cord, Hubert gently cuts Irving on the palm of his right hand and lets the blood drip into the goblet. The boy barely bats an eyelash. Hubert gives the stoic child to his mother, helps her to her feet, and raises the goblet to offer a silent toast to his followers. He takes a sip of the blood and passes the goblet to Janice, who sucks the contents dry.

Chapter 27

Satan's office is empty when Hubert materializes in the fireplace upon his arrival from the return trip on "The Business Expressway." He shakes the soot out of his burlap sack and canters over to the panoramic window overlooking the canteen. He double checks the quarters to be sure he's truly alone, confirms his belief, turns his back to the window, lifts his burlap sack above his waistline, and presses his bare butt cheeks against the glass.

A full moon in Hell.

Hubert wiggles his rear until a steady beat of squeaks is produced from the friction between his skin and the glass. He laughs, covers himself up, and turns to face his audience only to realize there are fewer Hellions in the cafeteria than he can ever remember. Must be Chinese take-out day, Hubert thinks. After such days, an arresting paucity of Hellcats and Helldogs can be noted, and Hellions who've been around long enough have learned to avoid Satan's mythicized version of Chinese cuisine.

Hubert leaves the suite with the intent of going to the cafeteria and checking the menu, but instead his attention is caught by a faint din somewhere in the chambers below. He walks the path down to the main hub and hones in on the sound again, which is now a distinct mixture of drills, collisions, and explosions. It seems a demolition is taking place, and without taking the time to locate the origin of the sound, Hubert veers left and whisks away down the main hub with a specific radial corridor in mind.

Once in the radial corridor, the racket becomes increasingly louder, and Hubert reflexively picks up the pace. He walks into a cobweb and fans away the silky strands without breaking stride. He slips on a wet spot, regains his balance, curses into the darkness, and carries on. Light begins to creep into the hallway and Hubert upshifts to a light jog. The sounds become deafening and when Hubert breaches the opening of the corridor his suspicions are confirmed: Hell's Paradise is being reduced to a cloud of dust.

"No good Indian-giving bastards," a woman screams.

"Burn it to the ground, then piss on the ashes," someone yells.

"I hope someone displaces you one day, jerk offs," another shouts.

"You call that an explosion!? I survived Hiroshima, now that was an explosion!" a gruff voice roars.

A large gathering of Hellions, easily in the thousands, has come to witness the demolition of Hell's Paradise. The crowd is ostensibly split in their support of the project. Many cheer, whistle, and applaud, while others boo, hiss, and jeer. Hubert has never seen a spectacle of this magnitude in all his years in the inferno, and he feels validated to have been directly involved in something he knows is good. The dissenting voices in the crowd will come around sooner or later, he asserts. He puts his hands on his hips and admires the scene like a proud foreman.

"Raymer," a grisly voice bellows from nearby. Hubert half-turns to try to identify the speaker. "Yeah, you, Hubert Raymer, rabble-rousing Hellion scum!" the voice shouts, cutting through the worksite commotion.

A demon guard approaches Hubert with a disgruntled expression on his angular, flame-red face, one which could be considered handsome if it weren't for the scar tissue lining his brow and the transient blue flickers of light which appear at random at various points on his cheeks, muting his dashing features and giving him the aspect of a teenager with an otherworldly pubescent skin condition. Hubert follows the lights from one spawning point to another and thinks, perhaps, a Bic lighter animated by either a mischievous fairy

or an impersonal supernatural force happens to be igniting
repeatedly inside the demon's mouth.

"Yes, that's me," Hubert tells the demon, who now
stands in front of him.

"I know it is, fiend. Satan wants you in his office."

"Really? Because I just came from there..."

"I don't care if you just came from Buckingham
Palace. Satan wants to see you, and see him you will. Get
moving!" The demon clutches Hubert by the wrist and pulls
him along.

"Alright, alright, get your claws off me you damn,
dirty demon." Hubert pushes the demon's arm. "I'll be happy
to cooperate, no coercion needed."

The guard looks Hubert in the eyes, decides his
captive is sincere, and releases his grip. Hubert smiles and
walks stride for stride with the demon into the nearest radial
corridor. When they arrive at the main hub, a group of
Hellions pass, two of whom seem distinctly out of place.

"One minute, Mr. Demon Guard," Hubert tells the
minion. He begins to follow the group.

"Hey! Where do you think you're going?"

Hubert ignores the guard's call and catches up to the
group. He walks alongside them and tries to remember the
two foreign faces in the group. Some of the others look at
him with perturbed expressions. Hubert disregards their
judgement and continues to sneak glances at the two
intriguing figures. Several seconds pass and his memory
prevails: he saw the two individuals through God's
monocular while surveying Heaven's Sanctuary from atop
the hill in the clouds. Hubert halts and puts his hand to his
chin.

"What the heck is going on here?" he mumbles to
himself.

"You're pressing your luck, heathen, that's what's going on here," says the demon over Hubert's shoulder, his hot breath flushing the skin on Hubert's neck.

The demon grabs Hubert by the shoulder and turns him around. They travel smoothly and silently through the main hub, however, Hubert breaks stride on multiple occasions as he notices more alien faces he swears he saw among the rubble and desolation of Heaven's Sanctuary. They hike up the inclined pathway to Satan's suite and stop in front of the doors. Hubert smiles and points at the door knocker.

"Were you aware of this?" he asks the demon guard.

"Of course I am, I installed it myself," the guard replies with a touch of pride.

"OK, should I use it or should I use the buzzer? Or perhaps you have a key? See, there are too many options now. Hellions are dismayed enough as it is when they have to come here, and this will only add to their consternation."

"Is that right, Mr. Raymer? Wait, I forgot, you are the official spokesperson for Hellions everywhere, and for an alarming number of Heavenites too, it seems."

"I appreciate the sarcasm. Is it alright if I try the door knocker?" The demon nods.

Rap-rap. Tap-tap-tap.

The door opens and Satan extends his clawed hand to Hubert. They shake and Satan motions for the demon guard to leave them in privacy. Hubert steps inside the office and Satan closes the door behind them. A jet of hot air, with a forque level noticeably higher than the atmospheric forque level in the room, scoots from the undercut of the door and strikes Hubert in the heels and ankles. He yelps and does a brief tap dance in place. The Devil smiles, pats Hubert on the head, and leads his prized possession along the Navajo runner to his desk. Hubert sits in the guest chair and Satan walks around to his office throne, pivoting around the corner of the desk with a firmly placed hand atop the finely lacquered oak surface.

"Is there an elaborate prank going on here?" Hubert asks.

"What do you mean, Mr. Raymer?" The Dark Lord responds, pressing his right index finger to his right temple.

"On my way here, I saw several individuals I swear I saw in Heaven's Sanctuary the last time I met with God."

"Well, you probably did." Satan pauses and leans forward, folding his arms on top of the desk. "Hubert, the wistful desire of you and your friends to return to the original territory of my kingdom was widely shared within Hell's Paradise. I decided the best resolution was to dissolve Hell's Paradise completely. In addition," the Devil smiles and taps a talon-like fingernail on the desk, "all the members of Heaven's Sanctuary have been inducted into Hell." Hubert is left wide-eyed and slack-jawed.

"God approved of this? The Heavenites being sent here, I mean."

"Approve it? Ha! It was His idea." He waits for a reply from Hubert, but there is none. "Listen, Hubert, my dear, as you can see I'm quite satisfied with the return to normalcy, and especially satisfied with the procurement of new devotees from that wretched experiment in Paradise. However, I have no intention of being merciful in this new age. I may have undergone a subtle makeover at your behest, but I cannot afford to appear soft around the edges with these Heavenites gone awry. I'm sure you understand."

"I do, sir."

"Good, you may leave. I saw your friends James, Lawrence, and Claudia in the canteen not long ago. If you hurry you can grab a bite with them before they've cleared their plates."

Hubert power walks to the cafeteria and finds his companions at their traditional table, although it is crowded with strangers, presumably transfers from Heaven's Sanctuary. He sits down next to James, who faces Lawrence and Claudia. They give him the silent treatment for nearly a minute and he plays along contentedly.

"You really rocked the boat this time, ole buddy," says James with a mouthful of half-chewed fries.

"Yeah, I know."

"Check it out."

James points at a man in white cotton underwear who glides toward them on roller skates. The man skids to a stop in front of Hubert and adjusts the bulge in his underwear mere inches in front of Hubert's face. Hubert looks the man in the eye. The man smirks.

"Can I take your order, Mr. Raymer?" the man asks.

"See how famous you've become around here, Huey," Claudia comments. Hubert turns to her and rolls his eyes. He turns back to the waiter.

"Say, did anyone ever tell you you look like Pierce Brosnan?"

"All the time."

Although Hubert doesn't remember from the tennis match he watched during his first visit to Paradise, the man is the infamous Archibald, leader of the Heavenite rebellion which led to the construction of Heaven's Sanctuary, Hubert Raymer's analogue.

Poetic justice.

Chapter 28

Plunk!

A cork ejects from a bottle of champagne at high velocity and sails into the clear blue sky. It whistles as it elevates and emits what nearly constitutes a sonic boom as it reaches the peak of its flight and begins to fall, eventually disappearing over the horizon of the distant clouds. God holds the champagne bottle in His immense right hand, purposely covering the label to keep His expensive taste a secret from His adherents, what few are left. The Heavenites who remain with God in His Kingdom after The Great Purge, as it has come to be known, represent about one-quarter of the population before the historic exodus. The Heavenites and all of the angels have gathered around God's throne to celebrate The Great Purge, specifically the triumph of Hubert Raymer, who is now regarded as a folk hero. A quartet of angels plays trumpets and the Heavenites dance and cheer and carouse and make toasts to a new, improved Heaven and to Hubert Raymer. After a while, God rises from His throne and taps His glass with a silver fork.

Clink!

The Heavenites quiet down and God addresses them.

"My children, my dear, wholesome, loyal children. I am exceedingly grateful to be in your company on this beautiful and important day. I propose a toast to a Heaven free of sanctimony, and to Hubert Raymer, a Hellion we can practically call kin."

The Heavenities raise and tap glasses. They swig the champagne and return to dancing. While they dance, many of them share stories, mostly spurious, about Hubert's adventures and accomplishments. Even the angels indulge in some of the tales.

"I saw him in the temple one time. He was on his knees on a prayer rug and he was praising Allah. He must be Muslim, although he didn't have a beard. He was clean-shaven, and a handsome gentleman as well. Not just handsome, I would say he was gorgeous. He had an aura about him, a visible glow, as if he had been blessed by angels," says one woman.

"He once battled one of Satan's minotaurs with nothing more than a rock the size of a tennis ball. The minotaur dominated him for most of the fight, but Hubert was relentless and unafraid. He scratched the minotaur and bit him and poked at his eyes, then eventually knocked the creature unconscious with a strike to the head with the stone, which he threw at the minotaur from a distance of eighty feet. What an arm that Hubert must have. Talk about David and Goliath," tells a young man.

"There was a time I overheard him and God talking about his mortal life. From what I gathered, Hubert was a scientist. I believe he said his wife was too. They worked in a laboratory together and their focus was recovering DNA from human remains. It sounded like they were trying to create a database for early human DNA, for what purpose I'm not sure. I guess they wanted to trace human ancestry back as far as possible in a tangible form. Seems like a waste of time though, seeing as we already know it began with Adam and Eve," explains a cherub.

"He once played the Devil in a game of chess. The Devil was ahead early, taking one of Hubert's knights, one of his bishops, and two pawns, while only losing one pawn. After a few neutral moves, Hubert strung together five consecutive moves in which he took both of Satan's rooks, a knight, a bishop, and a pawn. Satan responded a couple moves later by taking Hubert's second bishop, but then Hubert took the Devil's queen with his remaining knight. The Devil was furious. Three moves later, Hubert checkmated him. I bet he could give the old Russian grandmasters a run for their money," claims an angel trumpeter.

"Ladies and gentlemen, quiet down please, I need your undivided attention for one minute," God bellows. The Heavenites and angels conclude their stories and turn to their master. "Thank you. I would like to announce that this day, March 12th, will henceforth be known as "Hubert Raymer Day." Aside from Christmas, Yom Kippur, and Eid Al-Fitr, it will be our most important holiday."

"So, it's the fourth most important holiday?" asks a Heavenite in a facetious tone. The Almighty frowns and furrows his brow.

"Yes, to be clear it will be the fourth most important holiday. Angels, if you'll please proceed with the memorial."

A group of angels produces a massive object covered in a canvas tarp from beneath the clouds. Using a comically large utility dolly, they pull the object to a spot about sixty feet from the foot of the Lord's pedestal, directly in line with the center of His throne, and set the object down. The angel trumpeters play a brief, intense tune to build the anticipation of the moment. God nods to the angels surrounding the memorial object and they remove the canvas, unveiling a ten-foot tall gold and marble statue of Hubert, a masterpiece that could have been sculpted by the hands of Michelangelo himself. The Heavenites gawk at the beautiful creation. Some blow kisses to it, while others bow or fall to their knees and pray. God steps down from His pedestal and rubs at His temples. Rubio, His personal harpist and trusted spy, sits down next to the Lord and slowly inhales and exhales. Two tears fall from his left eye and run down his rubicund cheek.

Epilogue

In less than a month since the erection of Hubert's gold and marble likeness, every single Heavenite is sent to Hell for idolatry. Satan and his minions rejoice, and Hubert feels more conflicted than ever. He finds solace in his friendships with James, Lawrence, and Claudia. The four are inseparable and simultaneously loved and hated by their peers. Petty, fickle folks Hellions are. In Heaven, the only residents are those who have arrived since the last Heavenite was banished for worshipping the statue of Hubert. The freshly minted Heavenites, not knowing the significance of the figure, pay little attention to it. God is pleased by this. The innocence of His new generation of devotees paves the way for a bright future. All is well that ends well.

43100738R00170

Made in the USA
Middletown, DE
30 April 2017